FOREVER MINE

SINNERS SERIES - BOOK 3

SUSAN LIBERTY

DIVA MOUNTAIN BOOKS

First edition August 2021

ISBN: 978-1-7371421-3-3

eISBN: 978-1-7371421-2-6

Book cover designer: Valory Waligoski

Published by Diva Mountain Books

www.susanliberty.com

For Kathleen. You be you, sister. Love and gratitude, alway and forever!

PROLOGUE

ULTIMATE BOOGIEMAN – JEWEL

A cold chill runs up my spine. I shiver, staring out the windshield of my Land Rover. Thanks to the clouds drifting slowly over the full moon, Sinners Biker Babe Boutique has shadows dancing across its clapboard walls. Dante would love it for his next slice-'em-and-dice-'em movie. The perfect setting—spooky as hell.

I want Beau—my protector from all things evil. Beau usually drives me here after dark. He's off hunting for the weekend with a few of the Sinners' brothers. I told him to go, knowing he won't leave me once I move up the mountain to my country home.

I blow out a breath and laugh at myself. *You've been watching too many horror films with the kids. You need to put on your big girl panties and be Reagan Sawyer: the brave young woman who took the world by storm.*

I sigh. After three long years, I'm transforming back to Reagan and leaving the sweet butt, Jewel, in my rearview mirror. It's frightening, but it's time. I've disrupted Joker's life long enough. An idiom pops into my mind: *if you love someone, set them free; if they come back to you, it's meant to be.*

Joker won't come back to me. He's a badass biker. Having his nightly threesomes with Honeypot and Marshmallow is his way of hanging on to the life he built for himself. *Ride free, die free, in brotherhood*—Joker needs his freedom.

Still, it confused me when he asked to feel my pregnant belly and then offered to give me a ride to the boutique. After all, Joker didn't break out the cigars and shout to the world he was going to be a daddy. No, for the past three months, Joker denied Finlan was his. He has let the world and me know: Reagan and Finlan Sawyer are an unwanted anchor. Letting him touch my baby bump is one thing; taking a ride with the three bed-buddies is a whole different story. Honeypot would chatter incessantly about something stupid. Marshmallow would hang all over Joker, marking her territory like a dog. I don't need that crap in my life. If Joker doesn't want Finlan, it's his loss. I run a hand affectionately over my tummy. Finlan is loved beyond measure by me.

Light rain patters against the driver's side window. I trace a droplet with my fingertip. It's late spring. Montana's weather is unpredictable —forty degrees tonight, low seventies tomorrow. Finlan will be born in sixty days. By then, the mountain will have fully awakened from its long winter's sleep: the wildflowers will be in bloom. The woodland creatures will be chittering, squawking, mewling, and frolicking. The Rocky Mountain maples will be covered in leaves. Like Mother Earth, I will bear a new life to nurture.

Joker won't be with me to welcome our son into the world. Love is a poison pill he vows never to swallow. I don't know if he still believes relationships and babies are endless money pits that drain a man's wallet dry. Frankly, I don't care. Three months ago, Joker found out my real identity via an event I find challenging to forgive and forget. He's aware I won't be "draining his wallet dry." Money isn't a problem—I have more than a hundred people could spend in a lifetime.

I glance back at the building and sigh. I should turn around and ditch the idea of working tonight, but Maggie is hoping to open the boutique by the Fourth of July. Right now, it's just a shell. I need to plan out the first and second floors—staging is everything. It sets the mood for people to shop.

"I freakin' hate the dark," I mumble and quickly exit my SUV. I run for the door, desperately wanting to be inside. A black shadow moves at the right of the building. Fear darts up my spine. I jump, squealing at the crunching sound. A raccoon scurries out into the parking lot. He looks at me, his beady little eyes glowing, and then runs in the direction of the diner. I blow out a breath, putting my right eye to the retinal scanner. The deadbolt makes a loud click. I flinch, quickly push open the door and slam it shut. I put my eye to the scanner—the deadbolt slides home.

Three years ago, I went head-to-head with the ultimate boogieman and lost. Now every shadow and every sound makes me edgy when I'm alone.

Geez, get it together and calm down. Just turn on the freakin' lights. I run my hand along the wall and find the light switch, flicking it on. Inhaling deeply, the scent of leather and sewing machine oil fills my nose. It's weirdly comforting.

I shrug out of my coat and toss it onto a sawhorse. Then I pull out my iPhone and scroll through my playlist. *What am I in the mood for?* Kelly Clarkson, "Invincible"—fitting, but not tonight. Nickelback, "Trying Not to Love You"—yup, that about sums up how I feel about Joker. I hit play and slide my phone back into my pocket. Then I pull out my sketchpad and get down to work. When the song ends, I don't choose another one; I'm in my groove.

Click. I look toward the back of the room. Maybe High let himself in to check on me.

High is a Sinners' brother and my best friend Cookie's husband. I love him as I would a blood brother.

"High? Is that you?"

I get a whiff of an all-too-familiar cologne. Terror infuses me. I tremble, scrambling to get to my feet. I stumble. My butt bounces on the hardwood floor. A sinister laugh comes from down the hall. The devil strolls in. "Honey, I'm home!" Ricky looks down at me. "Did you really think you could run from me, Reagan? You're my cheating whore."

I hold up my trembling hands in submission. "Ricky, I'll go with you." I pronounce in a shaky voice, "I'll do whatever you want."

He glares at my belly. "You've been busy, whoring yourself out to the bikers." Quick as lightning, he pulls back his leg and gives me a sharp kick to my stomach.

I scream out, retch, and try to roll away. Tears are streaming down my cheeks, blurring my vision. *Oh, God, please help me save my baby!* My phone, I need help. I slither my hand down and rip it from my pocket. I jab a button, not knowing if I've hit the number for Beau, High, Cookie, Maggie, Maria, or Joker. I can only pray one of them will pick up and send me help.

Ricky yanks the cell from my hand and whips it across the room. It hits the wall and clatters to the floor. He grabs my hair, jerking my head back. He punches me one…two…three times in my left temple. Like a speed bag, my head snaps from side to side with each powerful blow.

"YOU NEED TO LEARN, REAGAN! I'M YOUR MAN, I'M IN CHARGE!"

Pain rockets through my skull. White light and dark spots dance behind my eyelids. My bottom lip splits—blood streams down my chin. The metallic taste of iron fills my mouth. I can't move fast enough; his steel fists pummel my belly in rapid succession. I hang my head and vomit green bile, choking out, "Finlan! Oh…God…Finlan!"

"There is no help for Finlan," he sneers. "His father doesn't even want him. He's a waste product of his mother's whoring!"

I scream, biting, kicking, digging at any part of Ricky I can reach. I manage to weakly kick his balls before my belly ripples in crippling pain.

Ricky is shouting at me, punching me. I'm dizzy, my head is whirling, I can't make out what he is saying. I don't feel his iron fists striking me.

Joker's face comes into my fuzzy brain. "Will you let me feel my baby?" He grinned when Finlan's foot kicked his palm. I saw love in his blue eyes, or maybe it's just a mother's wishful thinking. It doesn't matter now. The boogieman has won again. I can't hold on, so I let go and slip into oblivion.

CHAPTER 1

The warm, salty air feels like a wispy kiss against my skin. The scent of brininess with a slight hint of fishiness tingles my nose. Closing my eyes, I tip my face up to the sun and inhale deeply. I have a million memories of growing up here: My dad teaching me to surf. My mom building sandcastles with me while explaining all the mysteries of life.

My childhood was straight out of a storybook—two loving parents who built their lives and careers around me. Jackson Finlan Sawyer was one of the most sought-after movie producers in the world. Jenna Reagan Jewel Sawyer was a famous nonfiction author.

Mom and Dad were not mainstream parents. My father was of the mind that mainstream culture consisted of conformists—mindless people with blinders on who followed the herd. Uptight social norms didn't allow people to think for themselves—they didn't permit creativity to bloom. While my friends were being raised by nannies or shipped off to boarding schools, I traveled the world, homeschooled by my parents—where they went, I went.

Pony, Montana, has a population of five hundred. It was my

father's sanctuary away from what he referred to as "the jungle"—big cities; movie sets; pompous, self-absorbed people; and gold-digging bureaucrats. Three months per year, June through August, our family moved into our secret country home, high and deep within the woods of Diva Mountain.

My father had built us an open concept two-story log cabin home. The top level has four bedrooms with en suite bathrooms, a laundry room, and two offices—one for Mom, the other for Dad. The lower level has a country kitchen and a vast living room with a massive stone fireplace. The game room was my father's playroom, complete with a billiards table, an enormous gun case, and a well-stocked bar. Dad built Mom and me a four-seasons room with a smaller stone fireplace and built-in pool.

The four-seasons room was my mom's favorite room in the house —the three glass walls allowed her to view the Rocky Mountains and wildlife. The walls are on sliders. Weather permitting, like clockwork, at noon, my mom would slide them back—the indoor space became an outdoor oasis.

Dad was afraid the paparazzi would get wind of our hideaway; he put the deed in my mother's maiden name, Jenna Reagan Jewel. No one ever knew about it except for a few Sinners, a one percent motor-cycle club with a clubhouse fifteen minutes down the mountain.

The Sinners own most of Pony: Callaghan's Bar, the Pony Motel, and Sinners Bike Shop.

Dad dropped by Callaghan's Bar, looking for a fishing and hunting guide. Beau, a Sinners' brother, took the job. Dad and Beau quickly became friends, and soon he was at our cabin, sharing meals with us.

I grin, remembering how my mother called him a hunky French-man. I guess it's true. Beau is tall: six-foot-one with longish black hair, piercing blue eyes, and a muscled body. But I never looked at him in that way. He was Beau, my dad's friend. I smile. Now he's Daddy Beau, my second father.

Beau, General, Pick, and Coin were the only Sinners Mom and I met in all the years we'd spent on Diva Mountain. I had seen the Sinners and Native American children. Like all kids, I wanted to play with them. But Mom explained that the Sinners were a subculture and kept to themselves. The Native Americans were afraid of white people because of all the injustices done to them by our government and prejudiced persons.

While my dad spent his time fishing and hunting, my mom got busy building Pony Library. She had great respect for the Native Americans and their culture. "Rea, it's important to share what the universe has gifted us. Books are powerful—they educate us, enlighten us, and preserve our individual cultures."

My mother filled the library with fiction and nonfiction books of famous Native American authors—James Welch, Joy Harjo, Joseph Bruchac, Zitkala-Sa, Charles Eastman, and Paula Gunn Allen, among others. Mom added the classic authors—Twain, Hemingway, Morrison, Steinbeck, Fitzgerald, Melville, Hawthorne, Faulkner, and Poe. My mother laughed when my father insisted she add her books to the group. Then Mom decided books weren't enough; she included Native American artifacts, transforming the library into a museum.

My time on Diva Mountain ended when I turned sixteen. I was accepted into the Parsons School of Design in NYC. It is one of the top schools with a long list of famous alumni—Donna Karan, Marc Jacobs, and Tom Ford. My dream was to become an urban fashionista. My parents were all in—they purchased an apartment in Manhattan overlooking Central Park. Dad asked Beau to move into our country home, seeing's how they wouldn't be coming to the mountain as often. Beau acquiesced to living in our house but refused payment.

After that, Mom and Dad would go to Diva Mountain a few times a year. I was far too busy. I had my sights on a master's degree in fashion management and making my mark as a leading urban fashion designer by the age of twenty-one.

I'd get a short text from Beau on birthdays and holidays. He'd get a massive text from me with pictures of everything happening in my world.

Jean Clemet was a leader in the fashion industry, and I caught his eye with my mixed mediums of leather, lace, and silk. I added vintage buttons, beads, and chains—bohemian meets biker babe designs. From afar, the Sinners drew me in and inspired my collection. I made my creations and paired them with outlandish hair and makeup. By nineteen, my image was splattered on billboards, buses, train stations, and subway terminals.

When I objected to modeling my clothing line, Jean said, "Darling, they're you. With that body and hair, we're going to make a splash in the Big Apple. Now go practice your catwalk for me."

Jean Clemet was correct; we succeeded in conquering NYC. I turned twenty-one and received an invitation to model my designs in Milan, Italy. My parents were over-the-moon happy for me. Dad was in the middle of shooting a movie in Brig, Switzerland, so they would meet me in Milan.

Kaboom! My life blew up and I swirled into the dark abyss. My father and mother's plane crashed into the Swiss Alps—no survivors.

My mom and dad were my only family, and without them, life seemed senseless. I didn't get out of bed for weeks. My career evaporated, and my friends disappeared. My dad's lawyer and accountant told me that I had money: my parents left me seven hundred mil. That amount didn't include my mother's jewelry, my parents' real estate, or any royalties. Wealth had never been a factor in my life; Dad took care of the money. He made sure my mother's and my needs were met.

I'd lost everything. I didn't care about money, stock portfolios, or real estate. None of those things could give me back my parents. I went back to Malibu and lived a solitary life.

But, for whatever reason, Beau stuck. He'd text once a week and always demanded I text back.

Eight months into my solitude, I met Richard Colin Briggs. I was running on the beach when he jogged up to me and introduced himself as Ricky. Ricky was hot—a Val Kilmer in *Top Gun* look-alike. He was a smooth talker with all the right moves. Ricky asked me out on a date. I refused. I wasn't interested in dating, and he gave me a weird vibe. Being young, I hadn't learned to listen to my gut.

Ricky smiled and said, "It's my lucky day. I just made a new friend." Six months into our "friendship," we became infrequent bed buddies. Ten months into our "friendship," his explosive temper started to emerge: I refused to let him move in with me. Bumping uglies every couple of weeks was good enough for me. A year into our "friendship," he was possessive and delusional. "Reagan, you're my woman. You'll do as I say." I was never Ricky's woman. I wasn't about to do as he said. I told him to get out of my house; our friendship had come to an end. I texted Beau: *I'm coming to Pony.*

I woke up in the hospital with a metal halo bolted to my head, a titanium left hip, a plaster cast on my right arm, and six fractured ribs. Beau was sitting beside the bed.

In the middle of the night, Ricky had broken into my house and beaten me to near death. I was told I called 911—I haven't a memory of it. I was also told Richard Colin Briggs had disappeared into thin air.

Six months later, at the age of twenty-three, the sweet butt, Jewel, was born. Ricky was on the loose, and I was terrified. I wanted anonymity and a safe place to hide. Beau fought against it. I told him, after everything I'd been through, having sex with handsome, badass bikers who didn't care to know me was just what I needed. I didn't tell him that the eight-foot-high chain-link fence topped with barbwire and the two brothers standing guard at the gate twenty-four seven made me feel safe.

I soon learned I liked being a sweet butt. I was numb, and there wasn't any pressure at the club. I didn't need to talk to anyone, think about my future, or dwell on fashion. I cleaned the brothers' rooms, helped the cook, Merrill, in the kitchen, and had uncomplicated sex.

I didn't befriend the other sweet butts. Josie was a witch. Marshmallow was a lazy loafer. Honeypot was a ditz. But Cookie was different: she was young, quiet, and sweet. Cookie somehow permeated the wall I'd built around myself.

Mama Cass was our house mama. She was great as long as you did your work and didn't make waves. Sadly, she was murdered by Jerome Reed's men. It's a long, screwed up, ugly story. General is the president of Sinners. As a child, I had met him, but I didn't know him. General was unexpected: a badass biker with a soft spot for his wife, her father, and the Native Americans. His wife, Raven, is the teacher at the Reservation's school, and she is a hoot. She always gets into trouble for interfering in club business.

Maggie MacCarthy Kincaid entered my life at age twenty-four. I had been a sweet butt for a year. Maggie is an intelligent, eccentric whirlwind of a woman with a pipeline to the afterlife. Maggie made me feel again. She had a boatload of bad experiences: her mother died of cancer when she was twelve, she lost Devilan to a devious woman before they were supposed to get married, her first husband was murdered, Josie tried to kill her, and the Italian Mafia and the South American Cartel wanted to kidnap her. The woman was amazing; she just plowed ahead. Maggie married her true love, Devilan—Mafia Man, to the club. Through it all, she helped the Native Americans start their businesses, adopted seven kids, and had three biological children.

I remember the day she walked into the club with a box full of burlap feedbags and a bunch of multicolored glass beads. "Jewel, you're going to design us hipster bags. They're going to fly off the shelves." I laughed. I knew Mafia Man had figured out I was Reagan Sawyer, and it didn't take a genius to figure out Maggie was trying to straighten out my head. That was the beginning of the end of the sweet butts.

Flame, Sinners' Sergeant of Arms, and his wife, Princess, the vice president's daughter, sealed our fate. I was put at the security monitor in the Sinners' war room because all the brothers were fighting a battle, trying to free Princess from Heaven's Portal—a cult in Utah. It's a crazy story that the best novelists couldn't write. The bottom line is Princess endured insurmountable heartache and physical pain, yet she persevered. Now Flame and Princess have five beautiful children.

I suppose knowing Maggie and Princess made it through horrible things and found happiness contributed to me letting my guard down. Joker was my Achilles' heel. He's off-the-charts handsome—a blond-haired, blue-eyed, tall, muscled hunk of a man with tatts and jewelry. The sweet butts and townies loved him. In bed, to put it simply, he was a god. Out of bed, he was funny.

To this day, I don't know how it happened, but we started hooking up in my room on a nightly basis. It wasn't intentional or something we talked about; it just happened. Then he started calling me from the garage, just for small talk, as friends do. We never discussed anything personal—our real names, birth dates, educational backgrounds, where we grew up, and biological parents were off-limits. Joker would tell me funny things about his hunting or fishing trips with his best friend, High. He'd ask me to wait and eat dinner with him.

My first mistake was thinking Joker and I had become friends with benefits. My second was changing my birth control: I got migraines and vomited two days per month. Polly is married to Lee, one of the brothers. She's my girlfriend and a nurse practitioner at Sinners Urgent Care. She prescribed me a lower-dose birth control pill, and I became pregnant with Finlan.

I found out very quickly that Joker still thought of me as gash. He discovered the pregnancy stick on the sink in my bathroom. How it got there, I haven't a clue. I hid it in my nightstand and didn't tell a soul. I needed to figure out what I was going to do: go back to Malibu or my country home on Diva Mountain. Neither option was great; I'd turned twenty-five and was putting my life back together. I felt as if I had family and friends again. I'd just started designing biker babe outfits. Maggie had talked me into creating the clothing line for Sinners Biker Babe Boutique, a store she wanted to open in Pony. I finally felt safe enough to venture out of the compound. It had been three years since my attack. No one had seen hide nor hair of Ricky. I was hoping he'd been killed and tossed into an unmarked grave. But hope isn't reality.

I knew when I left the Sinners I'd need to hire security. I couldn't take the chance Ricky would find me.

When Joker found the stick, he became someone I didn't recognize: an out-of-control badass biker with the ability to kill. All his rage was aimed at me. To say I was afraid would be like calling a tornado a little wind—I was terrified. He shouted obscenities at me and accused me of all sorts of crap. It cost me four stitches in the corner of my left eye. Joker whipped the pregnancy stick at the wall by my head. The momentum caused it to bounce off. The sharp edge hit me just right and split my skin wide open.

I recall the fear leaving my body as I cupped my eye. Blood filled my palm and seeped through my fingers. Once again, I was numb and done with the Sinners. Joker came to his senses and pleaded with me to let him examine my eye. I told him to get out, and he left.

Beau took me to Sinners Urgent Care; that's where I found out I was four months pregnant. I remember thinking there must have been something in Montana's water that prevented typical symptoms of pregnancy. Princess was also four months along when she found out she was pregnant with JJ.

Patriot sent me to Butte Hospital to have a plastic surgeon stitch my eye. I also needed to see an ophthalmologist for a corneal abrasion.

The shoulda-woulda-couldas will drive a person insane. Joker made the decision for me. I had planned to leave Pony that night and go back to Malibu. But Cookie said if I left, she was going with me. I said she was ridiculous; she had married High. They had a baby boy, CJ. That said, Cookie is my best friend: she would have come with me at the expense of her own happiness.

High came to me all freaked out. He promised to keep Joker away from me if I stayed in Pony. I agreed. Joker didn't think the baby was his—he wouldn't be an issue. I decided to keep to myself and go about my business: Sinners Biker Babe Boutique and the peanut growing inside me. I planned on moving to my country home as soon as I could get things in order.

Unbeknownst to me, Butte Hospital put me in their database as Reagan Sawyer. It was naïve on my part; I'd signed my real name on the admission form. I was in shock with a thousand messed up thoughts in my head. That's how Ricky found me. Three months later, he beat me and murdered my baby.

Knock knock knock.

I sigh. Letting go of the balcony's rail, I pull my robe tightly around me and stroll back into my bedroom. "Come in, Beau."

He struts in and looks over at my bed. "Jackie's still sleeping. The kids must have worn him out this morning."

I nod and smile at my twelve-month-old baby boy. He's the precious miracle I received after God had taken Finlan from me.

Beau walks over to the bed and drops down onto it. Then he pats the mattress. "Come and sit with me for a sec. We need to talk."

I grin at him. "Is Daddy Beau coming out to play?"

"Maybe," he smirks. Then he picks up the book on my nightstand —*Fifty is the Magic Number*. He tilts his head, staring at me. "Why are you reading your mother's book about domestic violence? Richard Colin Briggs is incarcerated. He got two life sentences, Jewel. He's never getting out."

I look down at my folded hands, nodding. "I know." I look up at him and shrug my shoulders. "I don't know why I was reading it. I'm good."

Beau runs his hand down his face, exhaling. "Maybe it's too soon to go back to Pony."

"Why? Because Joker lives in Pony, or because Finlan died in the building I'm planning to start...or, rather, restart Sinners Biker Babe Boutique in?" I don't add that this month is the second anniversary of Finlan's death. I take Beau's hand and give it a squeeze. "There are good and bad memories in Malibu and in Pony, Beau." I look into his worried blues, trying to reassure him. "Joker won't bother us. He signed the custody papers the day he received them. He wants nothing to do with Jackie or me. I'm sad for Jackie. But I'm okay with it."

Beau narrows his eyes at me. "You don't have any feelings for Joker?"

"Nope." I shake my head, lying through my teeth. Even after all the things Joker has put me through, I love him. He's my one and only; that will never change. I plaster a fake smile onto my face. "He was just a sperm donor." I put my arm around Beau's waist, hugging him. "It's my turn to ask you a question."

"Hm," he chuckles.

"Why are you going back to Pony? The Kincaids, Gallaghers, Callaghans, and Hunters are staying here for two more weeks. You love to deep-sea fish with the brothers. You should stay. Jackie and I will be fine driving the Cayenne. We'll stay behind Buck all the way."

Beau snorts. "It's too damn hot. We'll be back in October."

"Hm." I stand and toss the book into the box with the others. "I call bullshit. And I love you for it. I'll be ready in an hour."

Beau stands, hefts up the box, and kisses me on my crown. "Love you, daughter."

I giggle. "Love you back, Daddy Beau."

CHAPTER 2

WE'RE THE CLOWNS – JOKER

Beep…beep…beep! "Keep her coming, Buck!"

I moan, "What the fuck," and pull the pillow over my head. It feels like a thousand knives are stabbing my brain.

Honeypot leaps out of bed and runs over to the window of my Pony Motel room. "Oh my god, it's Jewel," she squeals.

I quickly roll out of bed and snatch up my boxers. I grab my head. Christ, it's spinning like a goddamn top. My stomach churns; acidic bile rises in the back of my throat. *Fuck, I need to puke.* Tripping over the empty bottle of Jack, I catch myself on the nightstand. The lamp goes crashing to the floor.

"Jesus, Joker! White Dove is going to make you pay for that." Marshmallow turns over, taking the comforter with her. "So the bitch is back in town. It would have been nice if she invited us to her *Ma-li-bu* beach house. Daddy Warbucks left Ms. Uppity Pants tons of dough." She grunts, getting to her feet, and waddles over to the window.

The name Marshmallow fits. She should lay off the doughnuts.

I get to the window and peer out. Jewel is holding a baby…*my baby*. Once again, bile rises in the back of my throat. I drop to my

15

knees, retching into the trash can. Bitterness mixed with old JD fills my mouth. I puke and spit.

"Joker," whines Honeypot. Gagging, hand-to-mouth, she runs for the bathroom.

I put my sweaty forehead to the floor. Rocking on my knees, I fight for breath. Memories of what I said to Jewel canter through my brain: *Did you think getting pregnant would get you the big house with the white picket fence?!* I moan and lift my head, puking again. *Do you think you're getting from me what Cookie got from High?!* I groan. In my mind's eye, I recall whipping the pregnancy stick at the wall. Like a goddamn bullet, the damn thing ricocheted off, hitting Jewel. The fucking blood, the two-inch gash, and the fear in her violet eyes will forever be embedded in my brain.

Jewel refused to let me see what I had done to her. She told me to get out of her room in the coldest tone of voice I've ever heard. I ran for Beau. I waited outside Sinners Urgent Care for him to come outside and give me some news. And he did. Jewel needed to be taken to Butte Hospital. A plastic surgeon needed to stitch her up, and an ophthalmologist examined her eyeball. Blurred vision—something was lacerated. My mind turns off. I can't go into the worst night of my life.

I wipe my tears away with my forearm. I want...no, I *need* to see Jewel and my baby. Crawling over to the door on my hands and knees, I reach for the knob and pull myself up. Blowing out a breath, I open the door. My heart is pounding; my legs are shaky. A sheen of cold sweat is covering my body. I tremble and lean heavily against the jamb for support.

Jewel is so beautiful. She's standing beside the eighteen-wheeler in a short denim skirt with pink fringe hitting four inches above her knees. Her top is made out of a thousand silver-balled chains falling just above her navel. I chuckle. The sun has kissed her skin—she's tan. And she's fit: every muscle in her arms, abs, and thighs is defined. The natural purple streaks within her ebony hair are shimmering in the sunlight. I look at her feet and smirk—chunky-high-heeled, open-toed biker boots. Sexy as hell.

My gut tightens as I look at my child. The baby has its mother's hair, longish and shimmering with the same purple strands. How can a man not know the sex of his baby? I run a hand down my face and blink away my tears. I don't know my baby's name, his or her birthday, or how much he or she weighed at birth. I was drunk when Pick gave me the custody papers. He told me to sober up and read them before I signed over custody of my flesh and blood.

I didn't listen to Pick. I don't deserve a child. I killed Finlan. No, I didn't physically murder my son; that was Richard Briggs. But I did nothing to protect Jewel when she was pregnant with Finlan. In fact, it was my actions that tipped off Briggs that Jewel was in Pony. She needed to sign the consent form with her real name at Butte Hospital. Richard Colin Briggs was a private in the Army. After he was discharged, he became a private eye in the civilian world. The fucker knew how to find Jewel. The asshole was a cat stalking its prey. Within three months, the opportunity arose, and Briggs pounced, beating Jewel senseless and killing my son in Sinners Biker Babe Boutique. I was less than five hundred yards away, getting shitfaced in Callaghan's Bar.

Richard Briggs was apprehended in Oakland, California, three months and two weeks after he killed my son. He'd been hiding out in a crack house.

Jewel doesn't know it, but I was in the back of the courtroom, listening to all the testimony. I had planned to kill Briggs outside the Los Angeles courthouse, but the police took the fucker in through a tunnel. I would have put the asshole to ground right in the goddamn courtroom if I could've gotten my weapon past security.

Corinne Hunter, Pick's daughter and Flame's wife, finagled her way into becoming the special prosecutor. She buried the bastard—two life sentences in a California state penitentiary.

I came home and moved into the Pony Motel. The club is too painful...the brothers are too painful...life is too painful. But death is too good for me. So, when I received the custody papers, I asked Rex to point out the line. I signed my name, giving Jewel all rights to our second child. Rex just shook his head, rolled his eyes in disgust, and moved down the bar.

"Jewel! Hey, Jewel! Welcome back!" shrills Honeypot. Excitedly, she waves her right hand. Her left is keeping the white bedsheet in place. "Stop by the salon. I'll give you a free deep condition. Saltwater and sun can damage your hair."

Jewel turns. My baby is on her hip. She pulls her shades down to the tip of her pretty, petite nose and stares at us as if we're some kind of circus act gone wrong.

I moan. I'm in my boxers, Honeypot is wrapped in a sheet, and Marshmallow is swaddled in the comforter—we're the clowns.

"Christ! Get back into the motel. We don't need to see that shit," barks Beau. He quickly ushers Jewel and my baby inside Sinners Biker Babe Boutique.

I back up into the room. "Fucking get out!"

"Get out?" repeats Marshmallow. "We haven't had breakfast. I brought Raine's doughnuts."

"Oh my god," hisses Honeypot. "You took Raine's doughnuts from the club? They were for Horse. He's going to kill you."

"GET THE FUCK OUT!" I roar at the top of my lungs, "OR I'LL THROW YOUR MOTHERFUCKING ASSES OUT!"

Honeypot is scooping her clothes off the pile that carpets the floor. "I need to get to the club and shower. My first appointment is in an hour." She shimmies into her psychedelic, multicolored spandex dress. "We'll see you after work."

I avoid looking at her; the goddamn circular pattern on the dress gives me the head spins. "No!"

"No," echoes Marshmallow. "What the hell do you mean, Joker?"

I glare at her. "No, don't come back here. Ever!"

"Don't come back here. Ever," she repeats. Then she snorts, staring back at me. "Do you think Jewel is going to give you a second shot? Clue in: she thinks you're the scum of the earth. Shit, she scraped off. You sealed that deal over two years ago. Four stitches, an eye abrasion, and a dead baby."

"Marshmallow! Stop!" shouts Honeypot, glaring at her.

"Look at him!" yells Marshmallow. She swings her fat ass around to look at Honeypot. "He hasn't been sober for more than an hour in a year and a half. And he thinks we're trash now that he found out Jewel is some rich bitch from *Ma-li-bu*." She tosses a hand toward me. "When Jewel was a sweet butt, he didn't give two shits about her or the baby he put in her belly."

"You fucking bitch," I snarl. I snatch her hair and drag her to the door.

"Ouch! Joker, let go," shrieks Marshmallow, slapping my hand.

I open the door and toss her fat ass into the dirt. "Don't fucking come back, or I'll put a goddamn bullet through your skull." I slam the door closed.

Honeypot skitters around me. "I just want to say, I totally get why you did that. And—"

I roar, "Leave!" and slam my fist into the wall.

"Okay," she says in double time. "If you need anything, call. Bye."

I exhale and put the heels of my palms into my eye sockets. I feel like roadkill. I get a whiff of my pits. Christ, I smell like it, too. Shower, and then see Jewel.

CHAPTER 3

JACKIE'S MINE – JEWEL

My body trembles as I look around Sinners Biker Babe Boutique. It wasn't from seeing Joker with Honeypot and Marshmallow. Lord knows, I endured seeing them together throughout my pregnancy with Finlan.

I've become an expert at hiding my feelings, especially where Joker is concerned. I don't blame him for not loving me. I don't hold any malice toward him for not wanting children. My heart hurts for Jackie. I run my hand up and down my son's tiny back. Jackie will never know a father's love, but he does know his papas', aunts', uncles', and cousins' love. The Sinners made him theirs before he was even born, and I'm grateful for it.

Beau stands behind me, running his hands up and down my arms. "You're shaking. Is it from being back here or from seeing Joker?"

I look up at him, not wanting to lie. "Joker…um…looked unwell." I set Jackie onto his feet, giving him my two pinkies to hold. "He's lost weight."

"Drinking nonstop will do that to a person." Beau gives my biceps a gentle squeeze. "General, Godfather, Pick, and High have tried to help him. He's lost in the dark."

Cookie told me Joker was going through a rough time. I know what it's like to be lost in an abyss of misery. The only thing I can do for him is stay out of his way and say a prayer he makes it to the other side.

Cole, Rascal, and Cue Ball are bringing in the boxes filled with the clothing line I designed for Sinners Biker Babe Boutique. It was part of my self-help therapy: I surfed, ran the shore, created a clothing line, and took care of my son. It helped me rid myself of all the demons that plagued me.

Voices come from the doorway. I turn my head; High has his hand in the middle of Joker's chest. "Joke, you can't be here. Now isn't the time, brother."

"Jewel, I just want to talk to you," says Joker. He's staring at my son with the saddest eyes.

Is he sad because he has a son? Or is he sad because he doesn't know his son? I can't tell. It doesn't make a difference—Jackie is breathing, and he's mine.

Beau starts to move in the direction of the doorway. I put a hand on his bicep, stopping him. "Wait."

Jackie decides to let loose, "Heee." His word for High. "Meee."

High looks over his shoulder and smiles at Jackie. "I'll be back for you."

Pain crosses Joker's face. His sapphire blues brim with tears. Joker drags his forearm across his eyes and clears his throat.

"Come with me, brother. I'll get you something to eat. We'll talk," murmurs High. He backs Joker out of the doorway.

Beau exhales a long breath and lifts Jackie into his arms.

I blank my face from the overwhelming emotions clouding my brain. *God up in Heaven, help me. Lock it down, Jewel. You can't help him. Getting involved in Joker's problems might hurt Jackie, and he's your priority.*

CHAPTER 4

HE'S A BOY – JOKER

High has his arm thrown over my shoulder, guiding us toward Pony Diner. I stumble on the first step.

High catches me before I do a face-plant. "Careful," he warns and opens the door. "Hey, Becca, we need a booth for two in the back. Bring us a couple of black coffees. Joke will have eggs, bacon, home fries, and rye toast. And bring him a couple of Motrin."

Becca glances at me and then at High. "Sure thing. Head back and pick your spot. Do you want anything to eat, High?"

"Nope, just the coffee. Thanks."

I follow High back to the booth and slide in. Setting my elbows on the table, I scrub my face and push my fingers into my burning eyes. My mouth is dry as a desert. And my head feels like ten drums are banging away in it.

Becca comes over with the Motrin, tomato juice, and coffees. "Grand Slam will be up in a few minutes." Then she slides the glass of juice in front of me. "It's my daddy's recipe for a hangover. The hair of the dog: tomato juice, two raw eggs, a shot of Southern Comfort, and a splash of hot sauce."

22

"Thanks," I mumble and rip the packets of pills open with my teeth. I pop all four into my mouth and down the tomato juice in three swallows—my stomach revolts, threatening to spill its contents all over the table. I squeeze my eyes shut.

"You gonna puke?"

I shake my head no. Deep breathing, I beat back the nausea.

High takes a sip of his beverage, waiting me out.

I exhale and stare down at my mug. "I don't know if my baby is a boy or girl."

High slowly lowers his cup. His eyes are glued to my face. What-ever he sees reassures him I'm ready for the intel on my child, because his lips curve into a bright smile. "Jackson Finlan Sawyer is a twelve-month-old baby boy. We call him Jackie."

Becca comes over and slides the plate in front of me. "Can I get you two anything else?"

"No, Becca, thanks." High nudges the plate toward me. "Eat. It'll make you feel better."

I take a few shallow breaths; the smell of the bacon and eggs is fueling my need to hurl.

High tips his chin to my plate. "Start with the toast."

I nod, pick up the dry toast, and take a bite. Chewing slowly, my mind starts to clear. The pounding in my head is going away. I take a sip of coffee. "Will you tell me more about Jackie?"

High nods and takes a gulp of his drink. "He looks just like his mama." He chuckles. "But he got your smile and personality. He's demanding as shit when he wants something."

I grin and take another bite of my toast. "That isn't a good thing. I'm weak. His mother is strong."

High shakes his head. "No, brother. Grief and guilt have kicked your ass. They take down the strongest of men."

High knows a thing or two about that. He was caught up in a web of deceit due to an affair he had with his high school girlfriend. His first wife grabbed his daughter and skipped town with her lover. His second wife, Cookie, saved him.

"Jackie has another thing you used to have, brother."

I snort. "Oh, yeah? What?"

"An appetite. Your son can pack it away. He used to be a little doughboy until he learned to crawl. A few weeks ago, Jackie learned to walk." High takes a slurp of his coffee. "He keeps Jewel on her toes."

I chuckle and take a swallow of my dark roast.

High tips his head back, thinking for a beat. "Jackie loves the ocean. Jewel takes him surfing."

"No way," I laugh.

"Yeah." High smiles, nodding. "Jackie screams and giggles the whole time. He likes to play in the sand." He snickers. "Jackie loves to build and smash sandcastles." High snorts. His grin widens. "He loves the kids, but he doesn't like to share his mother."

I laugh and look down at my mug. "Beau?"

"Beau is Jackie's grandfather. He lives with Jewel and helps her take care of him."

CJ comes running over and leaps up beside me. He'll turn four in a few months—High's eldest son.

He puckers his lips for a kiss and then wrinkles his nose. "Uncle Joke, you stink."

Cookie strolls up to the booth with Pete on her hip. She launches into a tirade of French. I catch my name; that's how I know she's talking about me. It's confirmed when CJ's eyes move to me, and he giggles.

High is about to translate. Cookie holds up her hand, palm out.

"I haven't said a word out of respect for you and the brothers. I thought in time, High could help you heal. Time's up, Joker. My sister and my nephew are back in town, and they will see you. I don't want my nephew to know his father has become the town's man whore and drunk."

"Cook," sighs High.

She gives her husband big eyes, effectively shutting him up.

"You smell like the *merde* pumped out of our septic tank."

"Shit," translates CJ, giggling.

"Yeah, I got that. Thanks, nephew."

Cookie hands Pete to High with two pill bottles. "Take the kids and

Joker home. Set Joker up in the guest room. Give him an Ambien; he needs to sleep. When he wakes up, we'll give him the Valium, so he doesn't go into the DTs."

"I'm not going into the fucking DTs," I grumble.

"Oh, really? For the last year, you've been sucking down JD like it's your life's sustenance. You've lost twenty-five pounds, or more, and you look as if you've aged ten years."

"Thanks for the assessment, Chéri," I hiss, adjusting my cock.

Cookie narrows her eyes at me. "What's wrong with your penis? Do you have an STD?"

"Cook, Jesus," bites out High.

"No." I rub my forehead and glance at her. "I forgot to take off a condom. My piercing is inflamed."

Cookie looks at the ceiling and then at High. She launches into another tirade of French.

High barks, "No!" shaking his head.

"*Oui*, Christian!"

I want to chuckle; Cookie has transformed into Chéri. Chéri has lady balls the size of boulders. I've known the woman for six years. Cookie, the biker babe, is quiet, meek, and nonaggressive. Chéri, the wife, is a Frenchwoman on steroids.

"Christ, Cookie, I'll look after he takes a shower."

"Mommy wants Daddy to look at your cock," giggles CJ.

Fuck! I lay my forehead down on the table. This shit can't be happening. Wake me up from this goddamn nightmare.

"I'm going to clean out Joker's motel room. Everything is going to need to be burned and the room fumigated. Get him to eat more than two bites of toast. Love you." She kisses High, CJ, and Pete. "I'll call Doc for the STD tests and a shot of penicillin." *Zoom*, and she's out the door.

High chuckles, shaking his head. He tilts his chin to my plate. "Eat, so we can get the hell out of here." He glances at me. "It's your lucky day. You're gonna get a Q-tip shoved up your piss hole."

CJ makes a yikes face and grabs his jean-clad privates.

I moan, "Fuck me," and fork a piece of egg. "I need a favor, High."

"Name it."

I slide my phone out of my pocket and set it on the table with a surprisingly steady hand. I can't remember the last time my hand didn't have a tremor. "I need a picture of Jackie and a piece of his hair."

He nods. His eyes go to my necklace. The silver cylinder charm holds a lock of Finlan's blond hair—he had my hair. Jewel has a cylinder just like it. Doc gave them to Jewel and me so that we'd have a part of our son with us. I don't know whether it helps or hurts. It serves as a reminder of what happened to him. But I'd kill anyone who tried to take it away from me.

"Yeah, brother, I'll get them for you."

CHAPTER 5

I LOVE JEWEL – JOKER

Inhaling deeply, my nose fills with the clean scent of lemons. I crack one eye open and wait for the dizziness to hit. But my mind is clear. I move my head gingerly to the side, ready for the daggers of pain to stab my brain. *Huh, none.* I rake a hand over my face and look out the window. The sun's bright rays are beaming into the room. I snort. The sun used to make my eyes burn and my head pound in agony.

What time is it? I swipe my cell off the nightstand and stare at the wallpaper. My eyes tear up instantly—it's Jackie giggling. High is right; my son has my smile. I have one message. Exhaling a breath, I jab the icon.

High: *Look in the Google Photos app, bro.*

I hit the app and entirely lose it. I'm laughing and crying like a lunatic as I start swiping through the photos. Tears stream down my cheeks and drip off my chin. I don't care; I keep swiping. There are hundreds of pictures: Jackie with Jewel, Beau, and our Sinners family.

I sniff, knowing I need to get Jewel back. *Get her back?* How the hell can you get back someone you never had in the first place? Fuck, I just need to show Jewel I've changed. I can be a good father and husband. *Husband?* Do I want to be a husband? Do I want to be like High, Mafia Man, Tank, Horse, Buck, General, Pick, and Flame? All married—catering to one woman.

Yeah, I do. I've loved Jewel for years, but I was too messed up to go there.

Afghanistan screwed with my mind: the endless poverty and children with AK-47s. And parents fucking like rabbits, making more mouths to feed when they couldn't provide for the ones they already had. After seeing that shit, I decided: no relationships, and no babies.

I do love Jewel. These last two years have been hell without her. At night, I want to drift, feeling her soft rhythmic breaths flutter across my chest. I want to love her awake in the morning like I used to do—soft and slow. She'd moan my name. I'd come deep and keep us coupled until nature called.

My cock stiffens. *Shit!* My goddamn tip is on fire. I squish up my face and pull my boxers out. Christ, the head is swollen and red. Thank god there's no pus. Goodbye, Prince Albert. I groan. Jewel loved Prince Albert. *She'll love you more with a functioning, non-gangrenous cock.*

Exhaling, I push myself up and look at the time—eight o'clock. I chuckle. When is the last time I've been awake at 8:00 a.m.? Then my eyes hit the date—no way. I have no memory of the last five days. *Bullshit!* I squint my eyes and pinch my forehead. *Think, goddamnit.* I blow out a breath. I recall Doc coming on the first day. He drew my blood—I roll my eyes—and Q-tipped my piss hole. I snort. *Extreme pain is always a treat.* Then he hooked me up to an IV...something about me being dehydrated and needing antibiotics. I remember vaguely High helping me shower. *Cookie? Fuck me, Cookie fed me.* That's it, nothing else. I'm blank.

Here goes nothing; I throw my legs off the edge of the bed. I'm just about euphoric over not needing to puke. I'm as weak as a newborn babe. But I'm not nauseous, and my head isn't spinning. It's a win. Now all I need to do is find a pair of sweats and take a piss.

I get to my feet and shuffle over to the dresser, finding a note.

Amour,

I grin. "Amour" means love. The note is for High.

*There are new boxers, socks, tees, and sweats for Joker in the
drawers. His new jeans, running shoes, and biker boots are in the
closet. His toiletries are in the bathroom. Don't forget to wash his
cock with antibacterial soap and apply the Neosporin beneath his
foreskin.*
Je t'aime,
Cookie

I groan, "Jesus," and pull out a pair of sweats and a tee. I amble
into the bathroom. Tossing my clothes onto the vanity, I look into the
mirror. I haven't a clue who is staring back at me. "You look like shit,"
I murmur to my reflection. My blond wavy hair is dull and hangs
limply to my shoulder blades. I run my hand over my stubbly cheeks
—they're sunken. There are dark circles under my eyes. I run my
hands down my abs. *What fucking abs?* They're gone, and they took
my man V with them. I close my eyes, hang my head, and exhale a
breath. Jewel saw me. There's no way she'll want this pathetic fucking
mess.

I turn on the tap and splash cold water onto my face and neck.
Reaching for the towel, I clock all my jewelry in a bowl on the shelf. I
take my necklace out and finger the silver cylinders. One has the
initials FJS and the other JFS. I smile. High got me Jackie's hair. I kiss
the cylinders and toss the chain over my head. Then I brush my teeth—
at least I have teeth. I take a piss without looking at my cock. I can't
even deal with that right now.

Sighing, I dress and head for the stairs. When I get to the bottom
step, I do a slow blink. General, Godfather, and Pick are sitting at the
table, sipping coffee with their noses in newspapers. They shouldn't be
here. They're supposed to be in Malibu with their families.

General lowers his paper. He grins. "You're awake. I was just about to head up and toss your ass in the shower."

Cookie comes running over to me. "I'll help you to the table."

It's ridiculous that tears are pricking the backs of my eyes. *No goddamn way!* I lock it down.

"I'm good, Cook. Thanks." I make my way over to the table and drop down in a chair. "Why are the three of you in Pony?"

General snorts and gets up. He goes to the monstrosity of a coffee maker: latte, cappuccino, espresso or a plain old pot; you need to be a barista just to work the damn thing. He pours a mug and returns to the table, sliding it in front of me. "Malibu isn't going anywhere."

That's all he says, but I know they came back for me.

I inhale the rich aroma of the dark roast—espresso. Cookie and her father-in-law, Rene, Dad to Cookie, are French-Canadian. They're particular when it comes to their brew. Folgers and Maxwell House are piss water to them.

I take a sip and savor the flavor. "Cookie, where is High? I need to thank him for the hair and pictures."

"High needed to go to Sinners Biker Babe Boutique. The furniture Jewel and Mika designed arrived today. I'll head over there as soon as I get everyone fed. Mom and Dad are at the Reservation, helping Awenasa. Mom said Awenasa is half crazy trying to keep up with the businesses while the family is out of town. CJ!" she calls. "Hit the table. Breakfast is almost ready."

I run my fingers around my mouth; my eyes are pinned on the brothers. "That's why you three are here. You're my babysitters."

Pick smirks. "We're your support, brother."

CJ comes running to the table. He climbs up onto the chair next to me and reaches for a granola bar. He holds it to my mouth. "Bite and chew," he orders in his badass-three-year-old way. When I don't act quickly enough for him, he wiggles it against my lips. "They're peanut butter protein bars. Aunt Jewel makes them. They're yummy for your tummy."

Godfather tips his chin toward my necklace. "She sent the bars,

Jackie's hair, and shared her Google Photos with you." He takes a sip of coffee. "She's a good woman with a heart of gold."

The goddamn prickling behind my eyelids is back, and my nose is tingling. *Christ.* I sniff and pinch my nostrils to make it stop. *Fucking get it under control.*

CJ shakes the bar in front of my lips. I laugh and take a bite.

He nods, grinning. "Good. Right?"

"Delicious." I smile, kiss his forehead, and take the bar from him.

He pushes his OJ in front of me. It isn't lost on me that he's taking care of me. I'm his uncle—family takes care of family. It's the way of the Sinners.

Cookie slides a plate of crêpes, eggs, and bacon in front of CJ and me. CJ is getting ready to fix my crêpes as Pick douses his with blueberry syrup.

I chuckle. "I have it, CJ. Eat."

Cookie glides a plate in front of General, Godfather, and Pick.

General takes a bite of his eggs. He looks over at me. "We need to know your feelings regarding Marshmallow."

I furrow my brow. My feelings? "Loathing" is the first word that comes to mind.

Cookie is at the sink, letting loose a tirade of French.

I smirk. "Do you have something to say, Chéri?"

She shakes her head, continuing to do the dishes.

"Mommy said the wickedy witches poured JD down your throat and used you as their pogo stick. They didn't even have the decency to remove your condom and wash your cock," translates CJ.

I choke, coughing, my eyes watering.

"Arms up," shouts CJ. Leaping to his little feet, he pounds on my back.

The brothers are roaring in laughter.

"CJ, please stop translating for Uncle Joker. He doesn't need to know everything Mommy says," chastises Cookie.

I stop coughing and run my forearm over my eyes. "I need to know everything your mother says."

CJ firms his little lips again, nodding.

"I need to go up and get ready. Leave the dishes," says Cookie, taking Pete from his highchair. She beats feet up the stairs.

General sighs. "Marshmallow hasn't paid rent in a year. She's lazy, with a big fucking mouth. The brothers want to cut her loose."

After the sweet butts ended, Marshmallow became a country singer at Callaghan's Bar, but she got booed off stage one too many times. General fired her and then rehired her to help out in the pizza parlor, where she was let go again due to laziness and eating up the profits.

I furrow my brow and stare at him. "Why in the hell would you think I give a shit what happens to the bitch?"

"You've been fucking around with her on and off for the past three goddamn years," he bites out, glaring back at me. "Honeypot and Marshmallow practically moved into the motel with you."

Fuck—fuck—fuck! I can't believe I was that screwed up. Jewel saw it all during her pregnancy with Finlan.

I clear my throat. "How much does Jewel know?"

Pick snorts. "I think we're long past what Jewel knows about you. For three months, the woman watched you fuck around with Honeypot and Marshmallow, *while* she was pregnant with your baby. Jewel cares about you, but not in the way a woman cares about her man."

Fucking Christ. That's Pick, laying it out. I know it's not to be cruel. It's his way of telling me not to hope for things that won't happen.

"She gave me the protein bars and Jackie's hair." I caress my cylinder charm. "She shared her pictures with me."

"High asked Jewel for Jackie's picture and his hair." Godfather tilts his head toward CJ. "He told her you were sick. The woman has a soft spot for you." Then he looks at me. "Joke, I learned through my mistakes not to get involved with other people's relationships. If you want Jewel and your son, it's going to take a hell of a lot of work. She's leery of men, with good reason. Jewel lives for her son."

I get that. I think in my subconscious, I stayed alive for our child, too. Honestly, I didn't know how to swim through the murky waters of life. What happened to Jewel and our eldest son pulled me under. I can't explain Honeypot or Marshmallow. I was drunk, and they were there. There was no love, commitment, or friendship between us. It was just sex. Ninety-nine percent of the time, my mind wasn't present.

I clear my throat and run my fingers across my lips. "Do you know where Jewel lives? I need to thank her and give her something."

"Joker," says General, looking at me like I have three heads. "It's just through the woods. She is High and Cookie's neighbor."

"That's"—I moan—"the Jewel property."

General nods slowly and sucks air through his teeth. "Jackson Sawyer put it in his wife's maiden name, for privacy. Jenna Reagan Jewel."

I ball my fists against my thighs. The goddamn tremor is back. I'm beyond pissed. General, Pick, and Beau knew Jewel was Reagan Sawyer, an heiress to a fortune. They knew she had a house on the mountain, yet they allowed her to come into the club as a *SWEET BUTT!*

I glare at General. "WHY?! Why would you do it? Jewel wasn't some gash off the street."

General's eyes are blazing back at me. "Do you think Beau and I wanted her to be a sweet butt? Fucking get a grip, brother. Christ!" he barks; all his frustration aimed at me. Then he blows out a quick breath. "What that fucker did to her came straight out of hell." He points at me. "You would have known that if you'd attended the trial. The pictures were right out of a horror show."

"I was there!" I go on to explain my plan to kill Briggs.

He furrows his brow. "That's what fucked you up?"

I harrumph. "Christ, everything screwed with my head. But the trial sent me over the edge."

General pinches the bridge of his nose and pulls in a long breath. "Reagan had lost her parents and her career. She spiraled into a deep depression. Beau had been worried about her for months. After she came out of rehab, she just wanted to hide. She was fucked up, Joker. Briggs was in the wind. Reagan told Beau she just wanted to be someone else. She wanted to feel safe." He snorts. "A sweet butt. Beau and I discussed it. We agreed to let her try it. It was her Jack Daniels."

I nod, looking down at my hands. "Then I happened."

"Aye, then you happened." General puts a hand over my fist. "After Finlan passed, we thought Jewel was going to follow him. For three months, she laid in bed, not speaking and barely eating. Maggie said she'd lost her will to live. None of Maggie's voodoo magic worked." He grins. "Or maybe it did. You showed back up and did what you did."

Those three months, I was living in my own misery. I left the club in search of Briggs. All I wanted to do was find the motherfucker and put him to ground. I'd gained intel from a few of his ex-military buds; Briggs liked the dark side. I searched for two and a half months. I hit every seedy bar, every strip club, and every underground BDSM establishment between Pony, Montana, and Los Angeles, California. Briggs was the invisible man. When I returned to the club, Maggie told me that Jewel wouldn't live another month. Maggie's spirits weren't helping quickly enough. That motherfucker wasn't going to take Jewel, too. On some level, in my screwed-up brain, I knew I loved Jewel.

I snort. "Angry sex." I yank down my tee and show them my shoulder. Jewel's teeth marks: I had Rocky tatt them onto my skin. I chuckle, remembering his face. "Bro, you want me to trace her fucking bite mark?" He thought I had lost my mind. I did, after the trial. I put the memory away and blow out a breath. Then I run a hand around the back of my neck. "She cursed me, bit me, hit me, and had a death grip on me through it all. After, she cried in my arms until she fell asleep."

Godfather nods. "That's what Jewel needed, a release for her grief. The baby you put in her belly gave her someone to live for. She was determined to send Briggs to prison. She was eating healthy, surfing, and jogging. She started drawing again."

Briggs was found in a Los Angeles drug den a week after Jewel and I had sex. She and Beau left for Malibu two days later. I didn't have any say; I wasn't her man. Our child was dead. And I was riddled with guilt. All I thought about was killing the bastard. I left a few days later and rented an apartment. I planned Briggs's demise.

Briggs's attorney filed for delay after delay. The fucker pled insanity: he needed a psych eval. Then we needed to wait for the government to turn over his service records. It took Princess and Briggs's attorney a week just to choose the jury. To me, it was a cut-and-dried case: the asshole beat Jewel and killed our son.

The trial finally started; it lasted for a week. I watched Jewel suffer through the most horrendous testimony. Briggs's attorney brought up Jewel's promiscuity in Italy, the club, and me.

Christ, Princess painted me as a war hero. She had my service records and pointed out I received the Medal of Honor and a Purple Heart. She deemed the Sinners a motorcycle club composed of professional people, doctors, lawyers, teachers, and business owners. Everything else, she got ruled as irrelevant.

I listened to my son's autopsy results: Finlan died of exposure between his mother's legs—early labor brought on by repeated blunt force trauma to her stomach. I knew that; I was the one who found them.

I viewed the most gruesome pictures of the woman I loved. And listened to the doctors' testimony as they methodically went through each x-ray, pointing out Jewel's fractures. I counted them—an even dozen.

Christ, if Princess hadn't told the jury it was Jewel, I wouldn't have recognized her. Her face was swollen and bruised so severely she couldn't open her eyes. She had a metal brace drilled into her skull. Then Princess showed the jury a picture of Jewel's left hip—fifty staples. Her right arm was in a cast from her shoulder to her palm. Her fingers looked like purple sausages.

"Joke," says Godfather softly, giving my shoulder a shake.

I turn, looking at him dazedly. Then I rub my eyeballs and clear my throat. "I need a ride to the motel. I need to get my bike."

"Your Dyna and your truck are in High's garage." General pins his blues onto me. "I don't think you're ready for an outing yet, brother. Take a few days." He takes a sip of his coffee. "Let your body heal. Thank god you didn't need to endure the DTs. Doc said your electrolytes were out of whack. You're malnourished and totally exhausted."

Rest? Christ, I've been living in a goddamn drunken coma for over a year. I'm not resting. I'm moving forward. Jewel, Jackie, and I need to be a family. I'm ready to work for it.

"I wonder if I have any money left," I mumble. "I need to check my bank accounts." I rub my forehead. "Where in the hell did I leave my checkbook and wallet?"

I need to write Jewel a check for our son's expenses. *The Wall Street Journal* did an article about the cost of raising kids in America: birth to four costs in the neighborhood of twenty grand per year. Double that; Jackie lived in Malibu. Then there is the bill for the motel.

Godfather laughs. "Joke, my son has been overseeing your green. You have a healthy bank account and an even healthier stock portfolio. Relax, rest."

Mafia Man would do that for me. He is my Sinners' brother—*ride free, die free, in brotherhood*. He's also the MC's accountant: He's all about checks, balances, and investment portfolios.

Pick takes a gulp of his coffee. "Why in the hell are you worried about money? Even if you didn't have any, we would cover you. You're flush, brother."

General gets up, walks over to the counter, and pulls open a drawer. He tosses my checkbook and wallet onto the table. "Cookie found them when she was cleaning out the motel room. You had hidden them under the sink."

I caught Marshmallow "borrowing" my bank card. I was too drunk to throw her ass out. but I wasn't too drunk to hide my shit.

I rattle off my expenses, using the calculator on my phone to add them up. "Motel and Jewel." I pause to think. Maggie, Princess, White Dove, Cookie, and Raven took turns cleaning my motel room. Maggie had Mafia Man bring in a fridge and microwave. They kept it stocked in hopes I would eat. "The women need compensating—"

General stares at me. "Christ, slow your roll. No one needs any fucking money."

I push back my chair. "Thanks for keeping me alive," I say, almost euphoric because, for the first time in two years, I know my path. "I need to take a shower. I have shit to do." I head to the stairs on steadier legs with three sets of worried eyes on me.

CHAPTER 6

I CAN'T BE THAT WOMAN – JEWEL

Buzzzz…buzzzz…buzzzz! God, no, ignore the bell; whoever it is will go away. I'm super freakin' late. I should have been at Sinners Biker Babe Boutique two hours ago; Mika picked up the furniture from our Malibu workshop and arrived this morning.

I grin. I love Mika. General's son, Tristen, joined the Army with his three friends, Mika, Cole, and Robbie. When they were discharged, Mika was looking for a business. The four of them came to LA to support me through the trial. All the Sinners came with their families, and everyone stayed with me at my Malibu home. When the trial was over, the Sinners went back home to Pony. Mika stayed with Beau and me.

I had been fooling around with the idea of making furniture and accessories out of vintage motorcycle parts. The inspiration hit me when I saw Tank working on his bike in my garage. I left the designs on the coffee table. Mika saw them and became excited: "You design it, and I'll build it." Mika transformed my garage into *"our"* workshop. It's his workshop; I know nothing about welding metal or cutting glass.

In reality, it's all Mika. I sketch the designs; Mika modifies them, making the pieces into artistic, functional furniture.

Among my favorites are his bars: Mika uses a vintage Harley as the base. His barstools are so cool: he makes them from Harley saddles. The coffee tabletops are four-inch beveled glass; Mika uses Harley engines and springs for the legs—super rad. He searches high and low for "our" supplies: Jackie and I have been to more than our fair share of junkyards, garage sales, and swap meets. We've even accompanied Mika to a few dumps. One man's trash is another man's treasure.

After we get the furniture set up at the boutique, Mika will come back here and set up "our" second workshop in the barn.

Buzzzz...buzzzz...buzzzz! I sigh and look down at my son. He's banging a Tupperware bowl against the floor. Damn, they're not going away. I grab my robe and quickly slip into it. Then I scoop up my son and run down the stairs. I set Jackie onto his feet in the kitchen and sprint for the door.

I whip it open. I'm met with the one person who I thought would never grace my doorstep—Joker. My heart picks up speed just at the sight of him. He's thin...too thin. But, lord almighty, he's still gorgeous in his white tee and dark blue jeans. His blond hair is pulled back into a ponytail. Good heavens, one look and my lady parts decide to go bonkers over the guy. *Ridiculous.* I pull my robe tighter around me so that I don't embarrass myself—freakin' pointy nipples.

Joker's blues are just staring at me. *Why isn't he saying anything? He's the one who laid on my doorbell.*

I clear my throat. "Joker." Good god, it came out in a croak.

He grins that insane, panty-dropping grin of his. Now my lady parts are singing—my panties are wet. *No, this is not happening. You're in full control. He wants nothing to do with you or your son. He only wanted the pictures of Jackie and his hair to satisfy his curiosity. Don't read more into it; he's with Marshmallow and Honeypot.*

"I stopped over to thank you for the peanut butter protein bars, the pictures, and this." He fingers the silver cylinder lying against his chest.

See? Cool it, lady parts; he stopped by to thank you.

Before I can say anything, Jackie totters up to the screen door and bangs on it with his Tupperware bowl. "Numm-numm-numm!"

Joker's grin splits into a huge white-toothy smile. He drops down onto his knees. "Numm-numm-numm," he echoes to my son and puts his palm against the screen.

I smile when Jackie goes into a fit of giggles. I don't know why, but my eyes start to sting from seeing Joker play with my son. It's absurd. *Lord, get yourself together. Jackson Frazier doesn't want to be Jackie's father.* Yeah, I named Jackie after Joker. No one knows that; everyone thinks I named him after my dad. Weirdly, they have the same first name.

I should send Joker away. It's crazy, but I want to give Jackie his father, even if it's only for five minutes with a screen between them.

Then Jackie does it. He starts chanting, "Jo-Jo-Jo." Jackie knows his father as Joker because of a picture I keep by his crib. I wanted Jackie to know he has a daddy, even if his dad doesn't acknowledge him. Every person has the right to know who fathered them and what they look like.

Joker looks up at me. His brow furrows. "Is he saying my name?"

I can't read his look. Is he pissed or surprised? Who gives a rat's ass?

A surge of anger bolts up my spine. *Screw him!* "Every person has the right to know who fathered them, Joker," I bite out. I leave out: *whether they're wanted or not.* I never want Jackie to hear those words. Yeah, he was a surprise. But I loved him from the second I found out I was pregnant.

Joker nods, smiling at my son. "I'm happy. Though Daddy is my name to him."

Daddy? That's a title for fathers who are there for their children. Joker is not a daddy. I bite my lip to keep from saying it. He's only here for a few minutes. There is no sense fighting—not that I've ever fought with Joker. He did whatever he wanted to do, and I kept my mouth shut.

To keep from saying more, I take the Tupperware from Jackie. I open it and hand Jackie a peanut butter ball. "Numm means hungry."

Jackie fists the treat into his mouth.

Joker laughs. "You're a munch monster." Then he stands, pulls out his wallet, and holds up a check between two fingers. "I want you to have this. I'm sorry I'm delinquent. Things have been fucked up for a couple of years."

I stare at the blue check. Then I look at him, and my anger flares again. *How dare he!* "I don't need your money, Joker. I have the house with the white picket fence. Thanks."

Bullseye. He flinches.

"I know that," he says softly. "I should have never said all that shit, Jewel. And I should have never thrown the pregnancy stick at the wall. I—" He blows out a breath. "I have no excuse, other than I was an asshole. It will never happen again."

How many times did Ricky apologize for his quick temper? How many times did he tell me the same thing? But Joker isn't Ricky. He may be a selfish man, but I know he didn't mean to hit me. The damn thing bounced off the wall and cut me.

"I want to support my son."

He doesn't want a relationship with his son. No, he wants to *support* his son. *Be civil and get rid of him; you're mega-late.*

I paste a fake smile on my face. "Thanks for dropping by. I'm glad to see you're over your illness. I need to run. I'm late getting to the boutique," I explain and move Jackie back so that I can close the door.

"Wait!" shouts Joker.

Jackie startles. He looks at me, scrunches up his face, and starts crying. I scoop him up and coo to him, "It's all right. Shh, we're good."

Joker's eyes dart to Jackie and then to me. "Oh god, fuck, I'm sorry. I didn't mean to yell. I didn't mean to scare him."

I put Jackie to my shoulder. "No worries, he's fine. Jackie's cutting his twelve-month molars, so he hasn't been sleeping through the night."

Joker looks all kinds of flustered. "Is he in pain? I'll go get Doc. Or I'll call Doc and have him come right out." He whips out his phone, fumbling with it.

"Joker, stop. He doesn't need Doc. He needs some Orajel, Tylenol, and a nap."

Jackie looks at Joker. His bottom lip wobbles; tears are hanging off his long lashes.

"Hey, baby boy," coos Joker, putting his palm against the screen.

Jackie reaches out, touching Joker's palm.

Then Joker breaks down. He looks at me, his blues brimming with tears. "I want to hold my son."

Lord knows I have every reason to send him away. I should, but I can't; he's Jackie's father. I can't be *that woman*, the one that uses her kid for revenge. Jackie is loved by the Sinners. If Joker cuts and runs, I'll have a plethora of men and women to help me pick up the pieces.

I exhale and open the door. "Come in."

CHAPTER 7

THE PAST IS IN THE PAST – JOKER

When I first saw Jewel, I just about busted a nut. Fuck me, she opened the door in her short robe. She looked like a goddess straight out of a fairy tale. My cock went solid, and I didn't feel an ounce of pain at the tip. My eyes went from her gorgeous legs to her V, to her huge tits, and then to her beautiful face. I locked onto her violets, drinking her in.

That is, until my son caught my attention. Then it was all about him.

I loved my child from the day I found out Jewel was pregnant with him. My messed-up head prevented me from admitting it to anyone. Now that I've met him, there is no way anyone is keeping me from being his father.

Jewel took pity on me and let me into her home. Now all I need to do is figure out how to stay.

I untie my boots and toe them off. "Nice crib." I clock Beau's boots and running shoes in the tray by the door. "Does Beau live with you?" I know he does, but I need an icebreaker.

She nods as I follow her into the kitchen. "Beau has lived here for twelve years. He took care of the place when I got accepted to Parsons."

I just about trip over a dump truck.

"Sorry, I usually have all Jackie's toys picked up by now. Pour yourself a coffee. Mugs are in the cupboard above the pot. We'll be right back. I need to grab Jackie's Tylenol."

I watch her disappear into a bathroom off the kitchen. "Parsons is a design school. Right?"

"Yeah," she yells back.

I walk over to the coffeepot, grab a mug out of the cupboard, and fill it. Then I lean against the counter and sip the heavenly brew. I'm fucking exhausted, but I'm not giving this up.

Jackie screeches, crying, "No-no-no! Ma-Ma-Ma!"

Christ. I set down my mug with a clunk and walk quickly to the bathroom door.

Jewel is wiping Jackie's face with a washcloth. She sighs. "Jackie doesn't like to take the Tylenol or have his nose wiped. The Orajel is going to be a fight."

"Jo-Jo-Jo," he cries, cocking his body to the side. His mother needs to sidestep to keep her balance.

I take him from Jewel and cuddle him to my chest. "Hey, son, Mommy is trying to help you," I coo, rubbing circles over his back. He settles, sniffling into my neck.

Jewel looks at us; worry is in her violet eyes.

"Jewel, I'm not going anywhere. The past is in the past. Jackie comes first," I assure and kiss his crown.

She nods, giving me a smile that doesn't reach her eyes. Nope, her eyes are filled with a mother's fear. I get it and need to fix it.

"We'll try it. That's all we can do. If things get too much for you, let me know." I don't miss the doubt in her voice.

Christ, Jewel thinks I'll cut bait and run. *You've done it twice before, asshole. Be thankful she's giving you another chance.*

"Here"—she holds out her arms—"let me carry him. Your arms are shaking. Jackie's solid; he's heavier than he looks."

"I'm good, Jewel. I won't drop our son." It takes everything I have to keep the irritation out of my voice. Christ, she's five eight and weighs a buck ten.

Jewel goes over to the fridge and grabs a pitcher of water. "I weaned him a month ago. Then he started cutting teeth and wanted my boob." She laughs. "I'm as dry as a desert, so I gave in and let him have a bottle of water. Milk will rot his teeth. He only gets that in a sippy cup."

I chuckle. This is the second personal thing Jewel has ever told me. Parsons was the first. When we were together, it was sex, drinks, and food. I knew she loved books. Her room was filled with them, but we never talked about them—or anything of value. I want her to tell me about herself, but it's too soon.

Jewel's at the counter, filling Jackie's bottle. Her cell rings. She looks at the caller ID. "Damn." She picks it up and hits the answer button. "Hey, Beau. I'm running a bit late. Yeah, everything is good. Joker stopped by to thank me for the peanut butter bars, pictures, and Jackie's hair. Hold on a sec." She quickly screws the nipple onto the bottle. "I'm back. Yup, Joker is out and about."

Phone cradled between her shoulder and ear, she comes over to me. She holds out her arms for Jackie. I shake my head no and take the bottle from her.

"He's here giving Jackie a bottle of water. No, you don't need to come home. Everything is fine. I just need to get dressed. I'll be there in an hour. Beau"—she sighs—"Joker is Jackie's father."

Damn right, I am. What the hell?! Is Beau trying to butt into our business?

"No worries, I have everything under control. Just have Mika put the furniture anywhere, and then he can take off. I'll arrange it when I get to the boutique. You can head for Margo's. Don't worry about us. Yes, I'll set the alarm. No, I don't need a brother to stay with us. We're safe. We love you, and we'll see you tomorrow. Kiss Margo for us. Later." She hits the end call button and sets her cell onto the counter.

"Beau isn't coming home tonight?" Christ, I don't like them being left alone up here.

"No." She smiles. "He's spending the night with Margo. She still

44

lives in Butte. Will you be all right with Jackie for a few minutes? I need to run up and get dressed."

I look down at my son. His eyes are closed, and he's stopped sucking on the nipple. I set the bottle on the table.

"Go. We'll hit the living room and wait for you."

I watch Jewel run up the stairs. Her robe separates, leaving me with a view of her bra-covered, bouncing tits. My cock chubs up, and I need to look away.

"Mommy thinks she's going to stay here alone tonight. Daddy's not going to let that happen," I whisper to my sleeping son. Now all I need to do is convince Jewel to let me spend the night.

CHAPTER 8

INSUFFERABLE MAN – JEWEL

"Joker, geez, please listen to me. You've been sick; you can't move the bar alone. Lord, you're about to keel over."

For the last three hours, all my pleading has fallen on deaf ears.

I found Joker softly snoring on the couch with Jackie asleep on his chest. When I tried to lift Jackie off him, he awoke startled; his fingers made an iron grip around my bicep. Joker's protective daddy mode slightly confused me. Can a parent bond with their child in less than an hour? I needed to remind myself he's Joker—the man who does what he wants, when he wants, to whom he wants—a badass biker.

I told Joker to stay and rest. Would he listen to me? No! He insisted on coming to the boutique with us. Then I told him to watch Jackie, and I'd arrange the furniture. What did the insufferable man do? He handed me Jackie and started moving the furniture. Now he thinks he can push a thousand-pound bar alone in his condition. The base of the bar is a vintage Harley encased in plexiglass. The top is a four-inch-thick piece of glass, four feet wide and twelve feet long, with beveled edges—so cool. The bartop alone weighs four hundred pounds. Yeah, Mika left it on the leg dollies, but it's still heavy.

"I'm not going to fucking keel over. Tell me where you want to set up the bar."

Cookie is at a rack, steaming clothes. She lets out a volley of French. Then she points to CJ. "Do not translate."

He giggles, zipping his lips.

High comes in, chuckling. "I can hear the two of you all the way out in the parking lot. What's wrong?"

I throw my hand toward Joker. "He won't listen to reason. Look at him. He's all sweaty and exhausted."

"Nothing is fucking wrong with me, other than I might goddamn die of old age waiting for you to tell me where you want the bar."

"Hey, baby," chuckles High to Cookie. He gives her a kiss. "How long have they been going at it?"

"We're going on our fourth hour. First, it was the boxes, and then the chairs and coffee table. After that, it was the dressers and display cases. Now, it's the bar." She grins up at High. "If he didn't get a hernia or have a heart attack by now, we're good."

"Cookie," I whine. "You're supposed to side with me." I throw up both hands and stomp over to the boxes. "Fine! If you want to collapse in front of your twelve-month-old son, then go ahead and move the bar. I'll just tell him his father died of *PIGHEADEDNESS*!"

High walks over to Joker, laughing. "Where does she want the bar?"

"Who the hell knows?!" bellows Joker. "Christ, for the last four hours, I've been fucking *HENPECKED* for sliding around furniture."

I pivot slowly on the balls of my feet. *Henpecked! How dare he!*

"Forgive me for expressing my concern for my son's father's health," I say through gritted teeth. "You're a liar!"

"I'm a liar?! Christ, woman, how in the hell did I lie?" barks Joker, throwing up a hand.

I pick up the box, walk two feet, and set it down. "That was lifting." Then I give it a hard kick; it goes sailing across the floor. "That was sliding. You *LIFTED* the furniture because you didn't want to gouge the floor!"

General, Horse, Godfather, and Pick are standing just inside the doorway. All their eyes are pinned on me. Pick is holding Jackie. Amusement dances in his eyes.

"Lady drama," sighs Horse.

CJ firms his lips, nodding his head. "Aunt Jewel called Uncle Joker pigheaded, and Uncle Joke called Aunt Jewel a hen."

The men throw back their heads, laughing.

"None of this is funny!" I toss a hand toward Joker. "He won't listen, and now he's going to get sick again." I glare at Joker and rant, "Exhaustion, dehydration. Remember? Have you drunk a sip of water since we've been here? No! Have you taken a break? No!"

Joker stalks over to me. Taking me by surprise, he places a soft, lingering kiss on my lips.

My freakin' girly parts betray me—pointy nipples and wet panties.

Joker gently bumps his nose with mine. Damn! His Eskimo kisses always made me melt into a puddle of mush. "Babe, give me a bottled water, and I'll drink it," he acquiesces in his whispery, sexy tone of voice. "Then tell me where you want the bar, so we can get the hell out of here and feed our son."

Right now, I don't care where Joker puts the bar. I want to kick everyone out and… *Girl, just wipe that thought right out of your mind. You and Joker are building a friendship for your son.* I need to remind myself that bumping uglies is off-limits, out of the question, a no-go.

"Babe," drawls Joker, chuckling.

I slowly look up at him. He grins down at me. And, geez, it's his panty-dropping grin. *Good lord, God help me.*

I clear my throat, close my eyes, and wave my hand toward the window.

Joker chuckles low. "Words would be helpful, babe."

"Helloooo!" calls Honeypot. "Hey, everybody. I just got off work and stopped by to see how the place is coming along."

Just in the nick of time. Honeypot is like a bucket of icy water tossed over my body. The sizzle is extinguished. The friend zone has been re-established.

"Hey, cutie," she coos, running a finger down my son's leg.

I clench my teeth to keep from shouting, *Don't touch my son!*

She moves further into the room and runs her skanky hands over everything. "Jewel, this place is incredible."

"Fucking leave, now," growls Joker. "And don't ever touch my son." Joker takes Jackie from Pick. He walks over to the hand sanitizer and squirts some into his palm. Then he rubs it onto Jackie's leg.

"I don't have cooties, Joker," sneers Honeypot. She turns, stomping out the door.

I walk over to the bar. "High, can you help me move this? Then Jackie and I are heading home."

His eyes dart to Joker and then to me. "Sure, Jewel. Where do you want it?"

"Move," orders General. "We'll help High."

I give General a fake smile. "By the window is good. Tomorrow, I'll stage the display."

In my peripheral vision, I catch Joker walking toward me. *God, please, just let me get this done and go home.*

"Jewel, you're upset," he murmurs. "Please don't let Honeypot wreck our plans. Let's go to the diner and have dinner together."

I shake my head. Again I plaster a fake smile on my face. "I'm not upset. I'm tired; it's been a long day." I'm not lying; it has been an extremely long, emotional day. Jackie spending time with his father was great, but I need to slow this crazy train down. "We'll do it another time. Cook, can you lock up? I need to get Jackie home."

She gives me that look. The one that says, *I know you're not okay, sister.*

I can't do it; I can't make myself smile another fake smile.

Cookie nods. "We'll lock up. I'll give you a buzz after you put Jackie to bed. Go."

"Thanks," I murmur, giving her a hug. "Love you, sister." I hold my arms out for Jackie.

"Hit the SUV," growls Joker. "I'll carry Jackie out."

Good lord, I know what's coming. I follow him out, but he doesn't stop at my vehicle. He's heading for the diner.

"Joker, stop. I need to go home and feed Jackie. I want a glass of wine and a bubble bath," I half yell, running to catch up to him.

"We are not missing out on family time because of an inconsiderate dumb bitch. You can have a glass of wine here, and I'll drive us back to your house. Then you can take a bubble bath, and I'll put Jackie to bed." He holds open the door for me. "Step in, babe."

Before I can get a word out, Becca comes running up to me. "Jewel, I thought I saw you." She gives me a hug. "Welcome back."

"Thanks."

"Becca, we need a table with a highchair. Make sure you wipe it down with those antibacterial wipes," orders Joker in all his badassness. "I don't want my son getting any germs from another kid."

Becca does a slow blink. Her eyes go to Jackie and then to Joker. Slowly, she forms a wide grin, recognizing father and son's similarities. She nods, still smiling. "You got it, Joker. Pick your table."

Joker tilts his head. "Babe, after you."

I squeak out, "What is happening?"

Joker chuckles. "We're having a family dinner. Pick your table, babe."

In a daze, I walk to the back of the diner.

Joker pulls out my chair. "Sit, babe."

Entirely unladylike, I plop down onto it. Joker laughs. Using his thigh, he pushes me in.

Becca comes over with a highchair. "All sanitized." She sets the menus down on the table. "Can I get you drinks before you order?"

"Jewel will have a bottle of cab. I'll have a club soda," orders Joker. He settles Jackie into the seat. Then he grabs a bunch of napkins and wipes the table. "Bring us a seafood platter to start. Jewel likes Tabasco with her oysters." He looks at me. "Babe, what would Jackie like for an appetizer?"

I rub my forehead, trying to clear my mind. I feel as if I've been transported to a different realm. Or maybe I'm in the dystopian TV show Beau likes—*Westworld*. Perhaps Joker is an android. I reach over and pinch his thigh. Hard.

"Ah, babe, what the hell?"

I giggle. "You're not an android."

Becca laughs. "You are acting a bit strange, Joke. But it's a good strange. Can I make a suggestion for Jackie's appetizer?"

"You'd better," snorts Joker. He wipes the drool from Jackie's mouth. "By the time his mother orders, he'll be old enough for a beer."

Becca giggles again. "Chicken noodle soup. I made it this morning. It's not too spicy, the veggies are soft, and it's easy on the tummy. Jackie looks like he's teething."

"He is. My son's twelve-month molars are coming in. It's very, very painful. The soup sounds great," nods Joker. "He'll have milk. Oh...in a sippy cup."

I blink and then make my eyes focus on Joker: he looks the same, but someone must have switched him out. Joker is talking about *his son's* molars.

"Right." Becca looks at me. She's biting her lower lip. I know she's trying not to laugh. "Maybe you should pinch him again, just to make sure." Then she walks away, guffawing.

"Numm-numm-numm," shrieks Jackie. His eyes are pinned to the table in front of us.

Joker chuckles. "We'll get you a sundae for dessert, baby boy. You need real food first."

I grin. "I haven't taken Jackie to many restaurants." Reaching over, I grab a package of saltines and open it. I hand Jackie a cracker. "Beau likes my cooking, and I love to cook." I shrug. "I cooked."

Joker smiles at me and takes my hand. "You're nervous. There isn't a reason to be. Let's get to know each other. I'll go first."

Becca brings over the wine and appetizers. I squish up a few crackers and put them in Jackie's soup.

Joker dips his pinkie into the broth. "Too hot." He spoons a few ice cubes from his drink into it and starts feeding Jackie.

While eating scrumptious seafood and drinking delicious cab, I learned that Joker grew up in Hawaii with his two parents and his sister. He met Flame in the service and came to Pony a few years after he was discharged. Surprisingly, he likes to read historical nonfiction. He loves to watch sports, which I knew from my sweet butt days. He loves to fish, hunt, and work on bikes. I knew that, too. He hates movie theaters because he can't kick back and relax with a beer. He loves my dad's movies. Of course he would; most of them are action films.

Becca sets our entrees down. "Would you like another bottle of wine?"

I stare at the empty bottle. Lord, I drank an entire bottle of wine.

"Bring her another—"

"Joker, no. I need to take care of Jackie."

"She'll have another." He smiles. "Babe, you've taken care of Jackie for a year. It's my turn. Eat, drink, and enjoy." He cuts Jackie's burger into tiny bits. Then he pops a piece into Jackie's mouth. "Chew." Joker saws through his steak. "Tell me about yourself."

I fork a piece of rare beef into my mouth. The succulent juices wash over my tastebuds. I roll my eyes. "So good."

"Babe, are you having an orgasm over your food?" he laughs.

I giggle. "Yes. I don't eat beef often. But I'm a carnivore at heart." I chew and swallow. "My mom had borderline high cholesterol, so Dad and I ate what she ate: fish and chicken. If she wasn't at home, we'd sprint to the closest steak house." I stick another piece of beef into my mouth, humming.

Joker nods, chuckling. "I always wondered why you never ate red meat." He forks another piece of steak into his mouth. "You were close to your mother and father."

"Hm." I swallow and take a gulp of my wine. "It was just the three of us."

"In NYC, were you some kind of fashion diva?" He gives a piece of burger to Jackie.

"I designed urban clothing. It's the same stuff I design now, except out here there's a lot less pressure. I make what I want, when I want." I take another drink of my wine and push my plate to the side. "My schedule revolves around Jackie. Mika and I don't have time to manage the boutique, so High will do it. I'm not sure if he's planning on the brothers working in the store, or if he'll hire it out. I suppose he'll take it to the table."

Joker grins. "My munch monster ate all his burger and carrots."

Becca comes over to the table and clears away the dirty dishes. "Jackie, is your tummy full, or did you save room for dessert?"

Joker laughs and wipes Jackie's face. "He'll have a hot fudge sundae."

I shake my head no.

"Babe, I promised him one."

"How about I make you a tiny hot fudge sundae?" She swings her eyes to me. "How about you, Jewel? Did you save room?"

"No thanks, I'll just have a coffee."

"Joker? How about you? Annie made her coconut cream pie."

"Babe, you love coconut cream. Split a slice with me. I'll have coffee, too."

"How do you remember the food I like?"

"Babe, it was our thing. Food and..." He gives me big eyes.

Becca bursts out laughing. "Coconut cream it is. I'll bring the coffees."

Joker takes my hand and runs his thumb across my knuckles. "Thanks for this. It's normal."

I've known Joker for six years. He's never done anything normal. That's what I loved about him: his spontaneity, his wittiness, and his who-gives-a-damn attitude. One time he woke me up to ride his bike, so we could see the stars from the top of the mountain. I was afraid to go because of Ricky, but I went because he was Joker. Another time, he woke me so we could watch a lightning storm. And another time, he dragged me out into the rain because he thought he'd found a two-headed snake. To his disappointment, it was two snakes mating. That was him; the world excited him. Until I came along, life was a party, and sex was a group affair.

My eyes fill with tears. I blink them back and look down at our linked hands. "I didn't want to ruin it for you."

"Ruin what, Jewel?"

"Life. You loved life and all the things it had to offer."

"You didn't ruin anything. I was screwed up from the war." He runs a finger down my cheek. "We'll talk about all the heavy shit, but

53

not tonight. I want to enjoy you and our son. Let's eat our dessert and head for home."

Home with Joker. Can that be possible after everything we've been through? Will I regret getting involved with Joker again? My dad used to tell me regret is a double-edged sword. If you don't do something you want to do, later, you'll regret it. You'll always wonder how it would have turned out. Then there is the other side: you do something you want to do. If it turns out bad, you'll regret doing it. But at least you had the experience. There is always the possibility of no regret, and that's why you can't overthink things. The Sawyers are doers, regret be damned.

CHAPTER 9

TOGETHER WE RELEASE OUR GRIEF – JOKER

For the last two hours, Jewel's words have been playing on a loop in my mind: *I didn't want to ruin it for you. Life. You loved life and all the things it had to offer.*

I punch the pillow, willing my mind to shut off. I need blissful sleep to come. It's impossible with Jewel sleeping two rooms away from me.

When we made it back to Jewel's house, we argued about us becoming a family. It isn't lost on me that Jewel is afraid to let me back into her life. "This is going too fast," she said. This, meaning her and me. "We were never a couple. We don't know each other," she argued. I reminded her we were getting to know each other. "This is ridiculous," she whisper-yelled. "You were with Honeypot and Marshmallow a week ago." I had nothing to say to that. It wasn't the time to explain my screwed-up head. "You like your freedom," she informed me. "Jackie and I are something new. It seems exciting now, but you'll quickly become bored with us. Just go to High's or the club or the motel. Jackie and I are fine." I flat-out refused to leave. That's when Jewel decided she should try to make a deal with me. "I'll make you a deal," she said. "You can see Jackie whenever you want. Come over and spend time with him. If you feel the same way in six months, we can revisit the family thing." I refused the deal. Jewel became frustrated. She threw up her hands. "You want to live with us? Fine, take the guest room." Then she stomped off to her room.

I didn't want to sleep in the guest room, but I knew if I pushed her, she might take Jackie and bolt back to Malibu. I acquiesced, and now I'm in the goddamn guest room with a raging hard-on at three in the morning.

Jackie's screeching cries cut through the silence.

"Shit!" My goddamn legs tangle in the sheets. I quickly roll out of bed and thud to the floor; my hip bone takes the brunt of my weight. "Ah, Christ," I bellow. Pain is shooting down to my ankle. I free my feet and grab the mattress, hefting myself up. I awkwardly hobble-run to the door.

"Shh, Mommy is here," coos Jewel from the room one down from mine. "Those teethers are hurting you."

I make it to Jackie's room just in time to see Jewel disappear with Jackie into the en suite bathroom. I follow them in, hoping I can get Jackie to take the Tylenol without a fight.

"Hey." I whisper so that I won't scare them. "His teeth are paining him?"

"Hm." Jewel nods. She reaches into the medicine cabinet for the Tylenol.

That's when I notice her sleepwear. A satiny black tank that barely covers her tits and a pair of silky black shorts, showing off the roundness of her ass. *Christ—save it.*

Jackie takes one look at the medicine and hits the stratosphere with his crying.

I hold out my arms. "Give Jackie to me. I'll cuddle him while you give him the Tylenol."

Jewel puts him in my arms. I cradle him against my chest and bounce from foot to foot. "Daddy has you," I coo and kiss his temple. My eyes widen at the feel of his hot, sweaty skin against my lips. "Babe, I think he has a fever."

Jewel takes a thermometer out of the cabinet and runs it along Jackie's forehead. It beeps: "One hundred and one."

I furrow my brow, looking at her. "Should we call Doc? Sinners Urgent Care isn't open until seven."

Jewel squeezes the dropper. The pink liquid rises to the teaspoon mark. "Kids get fevers when they're cutting teeth," she informs me.

I drop down on the toilet. "Daddy first. Watch Daddy take his medicine, baby boy."

"Joker, you're not going to take Jackie's Tylenol. Just hold him and tip him back a bit."

Jackie looks up at me. Tears are on his bright red cheeks and hanging off his long lashes—snot is running from his tiny nose to his lips.

My heart pounds painfully in my chest. Like every Sinners' parent, I want to take the pain from my child.

I plaster a bogus smile on my face. "Daddy is first, and then it's your turn." I tilt my head back and open my mouth.

Jewel sighs. She squeezes the dropper of medication into my mouth. It tastes like shit: cherry my ass.

I grin. "Numm-numm-numm," I say and smack my lips. I laugh when Jackie opens his mouth.

Jewel smiles, hurrying to get another dropper filled with medicine. When she squirts it into Jackie's mouth, I can tell he's about to spit it out.

I tip him back quickly. "Numm-numm-numm," I coo, and he swallows. I hold out my hand for the Orajel, not taking my eyes off Jackie. "Baby boy, let Daddy see your gums."

The numbing medication turned out to be a challenge. Jackie didn't want either of us touching his swollen red gums. He screamed bloody murder when I finally was able to get my shaky pinkie into his mouth with the gel.

My baby is hurting, and I feel like blatting, too. I have him cuddle to my chest while I pace the floor. Jewel is downstairs, fixing him a bottle of water.

Jewel comes running up the stairs. "I'll take him to bed with me."

I shake my head no. "He'll sleep with us." I take the bottle from her and march into her room.

Tough shit. My son isn't feeling well; I'm not leaving him. I slide into Jewel's king-sized four-poster bed and give Jackie his bottle. He's sniffling and snuggling into me.

"Babe, get the light," I order, half reclined.

Flopping my head back, I listen to my son sucking and his stuffy snorts. Jewel is rubbing circles over his back.

"Thank you," she whispers in the dark.

It's fucked up she's thanking me. A tear runs down my cheek. I left her alone to fight through so much shit. There is nothing I can do to make up for the past. I can only push forward and make a better life for us.

I brush my tear away and clear my throat. "You have nothing to thank me for, Jewel. I have everything to thank you for. I don't think there is a woman alive who would have let me back into their life after everything I've done."

She snorts. "I don't think you did anything bad. You are you, Joker."

"That wasn't me, Jewel. That was a fucked-up man who didn't take responsibility for his family. Finlan would be alive if it weren't for me."

"You had nothing to do with Finlan's death, Joker."

"Yeah, I did, babe." I sniff. "When you were being attacked, you called me. I didn't hear my phone. I was at Callaghan's listening to Cookie sing. My phone clicked over to voicemail and recorded for three minutes. You were fighting for our son's life." Tears are streaming down my cheeks, dripping off my chin. "If I would have answered, Finlan wouldn't have died on the fucking floor between your legs. The autopsy proved he lived for an hour. He struggled for an hour while you laid beaten and unconscious, Jewel," I cry.

Jewel cuddles into us, crying with me. Together we release the grief we should have released over two years ago.

After a few minutes, she wipes away her tears, and then mine. "You can't blame yourself for not hearing a phone or being at

Callaghan's. Just as I can't blame myself for not fighting harder or for my body giving up." She kisses my shoulder. "When I found out I was pregnant with Jackie, I made the decision to get healthy and strong for him. I also decided he would never live his life under the shadow of Finlan's death. Finlan is gone, and he took a piece of my heart with him. Maggie told me my mom and dad are taking care of Finlan. I will meet our son again."

I sniff and blow out a breath. "Yeah, I should have guessed Maggie would have checked in with her spirit."

"Jackie is alive, and he deserves two whole parents who love him, Joker."

"I'll get healthy for you and Jackie, babe. Jewel?"

"Hm?"

"I never told you that I loved you. I don't know why. Fear, maybe. But I'm telling you now. I love you, babe." I kiss the crown of her head. "Marshmallow and Honeypot meant nothing."

Jewel sighs. "Joker, what you did with Marshmallow and Honeypot isn't the reason I'm angry at them. *You and I* led a life of frivolous sex. Sex isn't love. Making love is love. Sex is an activity."

I chuckle. "*An activity.*"

She giggles. "Well, with you, it was more like a sport." She exhales. "Honeypot and Marshmallow were never my friends. Honeypot is ditzy. She probably figured she was helping you with brain-numbing alcohol. Marshmallow is malicious and devious. She will do anything and hurt anyone to get what she wants. To her, becoming your biker babe—or, better yet, your wife—is the ultimate prize."

"That would never fucking happen."

Jewel turns over onto her back. "Cookie had a songbook."

I snicker. "'My Religion.' No one will ever forget that one, babe."

Jewel looks up at me and giggles. "Yeah, Cookie loves and worships High. He is her religion." She laughs. "His partner in all things. Do you remember High's sex analogy when he taught Cookie to hook up the plow to the truck?"

"Yup." I need to bite my bottom lip to keep from guffawing.

"Anyway"—Jewel sighs—"do you remember several years back when Marshmallow was getting booed off the stage at Callaghan's Bar?"

"Yup. General needed to give away free drinks to keep the customers happy."

"Well, Marshmallow blamed it on the songs and wanted Cookie's songbook. High hates her."

I snort. "I'm aware."

"He told Marshmallow to go to hell. The next day, Cookie and High went to the barn to feed Puddin'."

"Puddin'?"

"He was Cookie's bobcat. She found him when he was a few weeks old. Anyway, Cookie and High found him dead. He was stiff as a board and frothing at the mouth. High said Puddin' had been poisoned. He believes Marshmallow killed him because of the songbook."

"No shit. I'm surprised High didn't put Marshmallow to ground."

"Oh, he would have if Cookie let him. Cookie said they couldn't prove it was Marshmallow. But Marshmallow was friends with Dyson and Josie."

I furrow my brow. "I didn't know that. Christ, the woman gave up Dyson to Mafia Man."

Dyson infiltrated the club as a sweet butt two weeks after Mafia Man moved to Pony. It turned out she was Darlene De Luca, the daughter of Dominic De Luca, second in command of the Italian Mafia. Dyson was sent to Pony to gather intel on the Kincaids. Tony Rossi, the kingpin of the Italians, wanted to kidnap Maggie and use her as a pawn in a business deal with Jesus Hernandez, drug lord of the South American Cartel.

"Yeah, Marshmallow did. There was talk of General putting her on a bus to nowhere because she was lazy. Marshmallow gave Mama Cass a hard time about everything. She gave up Dyson's burner phone, which was a good thing, but she did it to save herself. And she perpetuated what Tank said about Princess. Tank was angry and drunk when he called Princess a maneater. He only said it once. Marshmallow spread it all over the club and kept it going for Josie. Josie didn't like

Princess because she was Tank and Jillian's childhood friend. She feared Tank would dump her as his old lady. Marshmallow was the one who told Jillian about Josie."

"Christ," I drawl.

Jewel puts her hand on my thigh. "Tank has always loved Jillian and their boys. Josie and Marshmallow manipulated him. Thank god Tank woke up, and Jillian forgave him."

"Babe, no worries. Tank and Jillian are as solid as a couple can be."

"Yeah, I know. I just need to give you the heads-up." Jewel yawns. "Marshmallow won't give up on you."

"Babe, I am committed to you and Jackie. You're tired. Drift," I order and take the bottle out of Jackie's mouth. He's sound asleep. I slide down in the bed, taking him with me.

"Joker?"

"Hm?"

"I love you, too."

"I know that, babe." I kiss the crown of her head. "You came back and saved me. Love you. Sleep."

I close my eyes and smile. For the first time in two years, I'm entirely relaxed. I've locked down my future with my son and my woman. Tomorrow, I'll start to get healthy. Making love to Jewel will take stamina.

CHAPTER 10

COWBOY - JOKER

I roll over and feel for Jackie and Jewel. My palm hits cold sheets. Cracking an eye open, I look at the alarm clock—7:00 a.m. Inhaling, I stretch my arms over my head, listening for a sound. No voices—total silence, except for the birds squawking and the squirrels chattering outside.

I take a minute to look around the room. It's Jewel: light and dark wooden furniture, mirrors framed in silver scrollwork, carved wood figurines, and blown glass. Layers of flowing, colorful silk curtains cover the room. I snort. She has enough candles to burn the place down. Pictures cover every surface, the Sinners, the Sinners' kids, the Native Americans, the Native American kids, Jackie, Beau, Margo, Willie, Jackson, Jenna, and me. Lots and lots of candid shots of me. It's more proof she loves me.

In the east corner of the room is a massive bookcase overflowing with books. I smile. On my nightstand—yes, I've claimed it as mine—there are Jackie's books and his bottle of water.

I roll out of bed and grab the bottle. Halfway to the bathroom, I bend down and swipe her tank, shorts, and Jackie's pajamas. I grin, looking at the wicker hamper. She was going for a basket and missed.

Last night I learned something about Reagan: she doesn't mind chatting on the phone. When we got home from dinner, Cookie, Mika, Raine, Maggie, Princess, Jillian, and Raven called her. She was running around the house cleaning and taking call after call. I had mixed emotions about it. At the club, she was reserved. Honestly, I could probably count how many words she'd spoken until Maggie came to Pony. The girls would have many hushed conversations. Now I know why. Maggie recognized Jewel as Reagan Sawyer. Maggie is the ultimate mama bear and a devoted friend. She was determined to help Jewel get back to being Reagan.

I took the phone away from her and turned it off. Then I checked to make sure she didn't have a permanent indentation in her shoulder.

I chuckle at the memory and just about trip over a basket of folded laundry Jewel left in the bathroom doorway. On the top of the pile are a pair of Beau's sweats and his tee. I swipe them up to wear and put the basket on the chair. I'll put them away after breakfast.

The bathroom is enormous. There is a whirlpool tub with a view of the mountains, a walk-in shower, and a double-sink vanity. I do a slow blink at the makeup vanity. There is so much shit on it I can't see the top. Then there is the walk-in closet. The room is big enough to be a goddamn bedroom, and it's stuffed full of clothes and shoes. I'll need to weed it out ASAP.

I take my piss. Thank god the head of my cock is pink again. I wash my hands and grab my woman's toothbrush. We've swapped every bodily juice; using her toothbrush isn't a big deal. Squirting a large amount of toothpaste onto it, I brush vigorously. Then I bound down the stairs and enter the kitchen to find my woman and kid.

It's a large country kitchen with the usual stainless steel appliances. The counters are white marble, and the cabinets are oak. The walls are painted a soft mustard yellow.

"Jewel," I shout and get nothing.

Christ, she left me a note. Why didn't she just wake my ass?

Cowboy,

"Cowboy." I chuckle at the name she called me when we fucked.

Coffee is in the pot. I left you a banana strawberry protein shake in the fridge. Please drink it. I went for a run with Jackie. Be back in an hour.
Love you,
Jewel

"Christ," I bark. I don't like her running alone with Jackie. Anything could happen. She could fall or twist her ankle or meet up with a grizzly or a moose. Moose are dangerous, aggressive mother-fuckers.

Ring...ring...ring. I follow the sound to a landline phone on the wall.

I clear my throat and lift the receiver. "Hello?"

"Joker?"

I groan. It's Beau; he's probably calling to bitch at me.

I sigh and walk over to the coffeepot. "Hey, brother."

"I need to give you the heads-up about a few things."

Here we go. "Oh, yeah? What?" I remind myself Jewel loves Beau. I need him as my ally. I pour myself a mug of coffee and wait him out.

"Jewel called me and told me she was going to try with you. I'm glad, Joke. Keep your goddamn temper in check, and don't ever throw shit at her."

I take a sip of my coffee. "I was fucked up to the max, Beau. But I have my head on straight. I will never, ever do that again, brother."

"Good. Jewel is out jogging with Jackie. I know she said she'd be an hour. I didn't want you to freak out when it turned into two. She jogs, walks, and then jogs. Jewel shouldn't be running on her titanium hip with Jackie on her back."

Furrowing my brow, I set my mug down. "What the fuck, Beau? Is the metal going to bend or break or something?"

"No, brother. It becomes sore and causes her to limp. She wouldn't listen to me about the terrain being different than Malibu's. There, she runs with Jackie in a stroller made for the sand. Jewel thinks the muscle will strengthen in time. I'm tracking her. She's good."

"Tracking her? How are you tracking her?"

He chuckles. "Jewel takes her phone. I have an app."

I laugh and pick up my mug. "I need that app."

"I'll send you the link. Now we need to talk about living arrangements."

"Brother, this is your home." I take a sip of my coffee. "Me being here isn't going to change that."

"Cheers, Joker. I'm glad you're off the sauce and got your head out of your arse," yells Willie in the background.

"Christ," breathes out Beau. "Sorry, brother. Willie is eighty this year, and she hasn't a filter."

"Hello, darling Joker. Kiss, kiss. Glad you're feeling better," yells Margo, her voice fading, as if she's running past Beau.

Beau sighs.

I chuckle, knowing Beau is irritated. He became a brother after he was discharged from the Royal Canadian Air Force. Hunting, fishing, flying planes, and riding bikes are his passions. He's a badass at age fifty, but he's set in his ways. Beau loves Margo and Willie, but he doesn't like them poking their noses into his business.

I grin and take a gulp of my dark roast. "You've only been there for a day, brother."

"I'll be home tonight. We'll start training tomorrow. Doc said you've lost a lot of muscle."

I'm not surprised Doc told him that. Doc is Beau's best friend. I'm sure he kept Beau apprised of all my fuckups. Beau is a Sinner; judging me isn't in him.

"See you tonight. Later, brother." I hang up the receiver and grin.

I walk from room to room. Shit, this place is massive, but not ostentatious. It's homey. My favorite room is the game room. It's masculine with a large pine bar, billiards table, and eighty-five-inch flatscreen TV. Dark brown leather sofas and recliners are placed strategically around the room for a comfortable view of the TV and pool table. Unlike the other rooms, this room has pine logs for walls. They're covered with heads of bear, deer, moose, and elk. Framed pictures of Jewel's dad and Beau are interspersed around the room.

I get close to a photo of Jewel and her father. He's holding Jewel in his arms, his foot on a moose, and both are smiling big for the camera. Jewel was young, maybe six or seven. Looking at this picture, there's not a doubt in my mind: she adored her dad.

Jackson Sawyer was a tall, muscular man with black hair and blue eyes. I'd seen pictures of him in magazines. They always seemed staged. This picture elicits his real personality—a loving father. I grin. Jewel got his smile.

I stroll over to the twelve-foot-long locked gun cabinet and tap on the glass doors—bulletproof. Jackson was a collector. There are rifles for large and small game, and pistols in all different makes and models. I clock Beau's hunting rifles and M4A1. There are several empty slots at the end; I'll add mine to the mix.

The south wall has two doors: one leads into a full bath, the other is a set of stairs leading down to the basement. I flip on the light and head down. *Wowzer, super rad.* It's a workout room with all the equipment: free weights, bench press, elliptical, treadmill, speed bag, heavy bag, and weighted ball. The room is covered in pictures of Jackson with famous MMA fighters. I chuckle at another eighty-five-inch flatscreen TV. Beside it is a glass door to an extensive, nearly empty wine cellar.

I clock the stereo system with surround sound. *Fucking awesome!* Jackson had excellent taste in music. I tap the icon. Pink Floyd, "Another Brick in the Wall," comes blasting through the speakers.

I smile, set down my mug, and grab the gloves off the bench. Time to get healthy.

CHAPTER 11

COMMUNICATION – JOKER

For two hours, I pushed myself: dead lifts, back squats, bench presses, dumbbell Romanian dead lifts, push-ups, pull-ups, sit-ups, and I ended with the speed bag. I was pissed for allowing myself to become so rundown. I could only lift half the weight, do half the reps, and I needed to take short breaks. Still, it felt great to push my body.

I grab a towel, wipe the sweat off my face, neck, and abs. Then I head to the kitchen.

"Jewel," I shout and get nothing. Christ, where in the hell are they? I check the time—9:30 a.m. I got up at seven; they were gone. It's been over two hours.

I grab the protein smoothie out of the fridge and walk out onto the porch with my phone. My nerves are buzzing with anxiety. *Calm your ass. Download the fucking app and go look for them.*

I guzzle the smoothie in five gulps and set the glass on the log end table. I hit the message icon, then follow Beau's instructions. The goddamn circle goes around and around. *Come on, you fucker.* As I wait, I look down the driveway. In the distance, I catch Jewel with Jackie on her back in a carrier. She's walking with a pronounced limp.

"Shit!" I roar and leap off the porch, sprinting toward them. "Babe, are you hurt?" I yell, pushing myself to go faster.

"No," she yells back. "I got a stitch in my hip."

A stitch in her hip. A person can get a stitch in their side, not in their goddamn hip.

When I get to them, Jackie decides now would be a great time to throw his old man for a loop.

"Da-Da-Da," he shrieks, banging his hands onto Jewel's head.

I used to make fun of the brothers who would make a big deal over their kids' firsts. Now I'm laughing at myself, because I want to tell the world my kid just called me daddy for the first time. Christ, next I'll be saying potty, poopy, and pee-pee.

I quickly remove the carrier from Jewel's back. "Yeah, son. I'm your daddy." Then I laugh at him in his mirrored shades and baseball cap. I swing his carrier onto my back. Hardening my jaw, I swing Jewel up into my arms. Two years ago it would've been a piece of cake to carry them. Today, I steel myself and lock down the pain.

"Joker, I can walk! I'm too heavy for you to carry."

"Shush." I start walking back to the house. It's slow, but I'm doing it.

Once I get them inside, I'm ecstatic that we made it. I set Jewel on a kitchen chair and swing the kid's carrier off my back.

I take Jackie out of it, wipe the drool off his chin, and take off his shades and cap. "If you want to jog in the morning, I need to be with you."

"Joker—"

"Jewel," I say, cutting her off. I push down my irritation and keep my tone even. "The road is rocky and rutty. Jackie is too heavy for you. He adds pressure to your hip. It's jog with me or don't jog at all." I lean down and give her a kiss. "I love you, babe."

She stares up at me and rubs her left hip. "Are you going to be a bossy badass, Cowboy?"

"When it comes to you and Jackie, yup," I nod, chuckling. I set Jackie onto his feet and drop to my knees. I lift Jewel's left leg, stretching it gently.

She closes her eyes, hissing.

"You need a couple of Motrin." I examine the area around her scar. It appears a little puffy, but there isn't any redness. "I'll connect with Bluebird for some ointment." I get to my feet, walk over to the fridge, and grab her a bottled water.

She smiles up at me. "Did you work out this morning?"

Her violets are slightly dilated. My cock thinks it'd be a great idea to get a little midmorning action. There is no hiding my wood. There is also no way I can make my woman happy with our one-year-old awake. So I ignore it.

I yell from the bathroom, "I found your dad's workout room in the basement." *Motrin. Where's the fucking Motrin? Ah, there.* I grab the bottle and bring it back to the kitchen. I shake out two tablets. "Open."

Jewel rolls her eyes and opens her mouth. I drop the tablets in, and she swallows.

I stare at her. *Who in the hell takes pills without liquid?*

"No water?" I ask, holding out the bottle to her.

"Nope, I don't need it, thanks." She gets up, goes over to the fridge, and pulls out eggs, cheese, and veggies. "Are you planning to live with us?"

I thought we'd already established that last night. Guess not.

I lean against the counter and watch her chop the veggies. "Any objections?"

She smiles and shakes her head. "No." Then she stops chopping and turns to look at me. "Joker, I'm not the same woman I was at the club."

"Not the same woman," I echo. What the hell is she getting at?

"No, becoming a mother changed me. I'm not a mainstream thinker, per se. I mean, I think people should be themselves, do whatever makes them happy without being judged. Communal living and multiple partners were great before I had Jackie."

I stare at her, entirely confused.

Jewel goes back to chopping. "I want Jackie to grow up in the Sinners family. Their beliefs are on point with mine: family comes first, and then God, or a higher power, and then, of course, country, and then, whatever else"—she swirls the knife around in the air—"comes after." She grabs another red pepper.

"Jewel—"

She blows out a breath. "You said you want us to be a family. If you're planning on sharing my bed, we need to be exclusive. If you don't want that, it's fine. You can take the guest room as yours." She deseeds the red pepper and starts chopping. "But overnight guests are off-limits. I don't want to deal with them."

"Jewel—"

"Please let me finish. You can be you, but I also need to be me. That means I'll have a total say over Jackie and me—where we live, here or Malibu, and who Jackie is exposed to." She says under her breath, "It isn't going to be Marshmallow or Honeypot. That's for damn sure."

I tilt my head up to the ceiling, keeping my anger in check. Does she think I'd move into her goddamn house and bring women home while my son slept in the next room? *Actions have consequences, asshole.* I look down at my son. He's busy pulling his toys out of the toybox. I take the knife out of her hand and lead her to a chair.

"Joker, I need to finish cooking breakfast."

"It'll wait." I drop down onto the chair. "Straddle me, so you can see me when I tell you this."

She throws her leg over me and nestles her pussy against my cock. I stifle a moan. My cock is as hard as granite. Jewel's reaction is to wiggle against it. I know she's sexually aware of me. It would be easy to make love to her, using my words and my body. But that can't happen with our son a few feet away from us.

I clear my throat, take her cheeks between my palms, and look her in the eyes. "I'm committed to you. We're exclusive. I want a life with you, whether it be here or in Malibu. I prefer it to be in Pony. I'm a Sinner, and I work here. But if you prefer Malibu, we'll move. One day soon, I'd like for us to get married."

She furrows her brow. "*Married?*"

"Yeah, Jewel. That's what people do when they love each other and have a kid together. They put a ring on each other's fingers and say a bunch of words. Vowing to love each other for eternity. Bam, married," I chuckle.

"Whoa, Cowboy," laughs Jewel. "You need to slow your roll. We need to live together to see if we're compatible. I just explained to you I'm not the *Jewel* from the club, Joker."

I grin. "So I've noticed. You like to fucking talk."

She nods. "I do. And I need communication."

I grin wider. "*Communication?*"

"Yes." She nods. "Where two people talk about their day. They decide on things together."

"*Things?*" I chuckle and rub the sides of her ass.

"Life things, Joker. Like where will Jackie go to school and if I should sell the apartment in Manhattan and—"

"You have an apartment in Manhattan?"

"Yes. I'm thinking about selling it. The Sinners don't want it: Godfather, Mrs. Fitzpatrick, and Mac's houses are in Brooklyn. And, you know, Mafia Man and Maggie have the brownstone. But then I thought, what if Jackie wants it when he gets older? It overlooks Central Park, so it won't go down in value. But it's just sitting there empty. Mafia Man told Beau the taxes are going up."

"Mafia Man?"

"After Dad died, Beau took care of my money." She stares at me. "I don't know anything about money or the stock market, Joker. Dad always took care of it." She throws up a hand. "I was young and an artist." Her voice elevates, and her words speed up. "I'm not stupid; I have a master's in fashion management. But I don't care about the money. I care about designing clothes."

"Okay, you're getting worked up. So Beau and Mafia Man oversee your money."

She nods. "And High."

I blow out a breath and lock down my irritation over my best friend's involvement. "And High. Do you know how much money you have? You know, to keep all the properties afloat?" I sigh. "I have money, babe, but I don't think I have enough to carry three homes."

"Um." She squints and tips her face to the ceiling. "The last time I talked to Beau, he said I had somewhere in the neighborhood of nine hundred and seventy-five million. That number didn't include the real estate, my mother's jewelry, or the royalties from my mom's books and my dad's movies. It fluctuates with the U.S. and foreign markets and interest rates."

I know I have my mouth hanging open, but I can't get my muscles to function. I'm stunned speechless. She's worth over a billion dollars. How in the fuck did Beau and General allow her to become a sweet butt?

"Joker?" She taps my cheek. "Are you all right?"

I nod, swallow, and exhale. "Communication." Then I start laughing.

"What's so funny about wanting communication?" She snaps, "Couples communicate, Joker."

I kiss her lips. "That's not what I'm laughing about. Jewel, you should be a pompous, arrogant asshole with tons of servants kissing your feet. But you're not."

"Why would I be like that?" she says incredulously. "We didn't have any servants. Well, Maria, but she doesn't count. She was my mom's friend. Maria fell on hard times when her husband died suddenly. Mom wanted to give her money. Maria wouldn't take it unless she earned it, so mom hired her as our housekeeper. My mom did our laundry and cooked every meal, Joker." She smiles. "Dad grilled."

Christ, the Sawyers pulled it off: they gave Jewel an everyday life in the whirlwind of Hollywood. Then they fucked her up by dying.

"We'll communicate, babe." I put my lips to hers and run the tip of my tongue along her seam. "Open." She opens for me. I groan, tangle our tongues, and push my cock against her pussy. She moans and threads her fingers through my hair, moving her hips ever so slightly. I deepen our kiss and add pressure where she wants it most—her clit.

"Mommy and Daddy are giving you a PG foreplay show, Jackie," chuckles High from behind us.

Christ, I didn't even hear him come into the house.

Jewel laughs and slides off my lap. She walks over to the drawer and pulls out a stack of papers. "Beau is old-fashioned; he likes hard copies." She drops the documents in front of me. "Do you want some breakfast, High?"

"Sweetheart," he drawls, "it's 10:00 a.m.; it's almost lunchtime. I came over to see your man." High walks over to the coffeepot and pours himself a mug. He strolls back and drops down on the chair next to mine. High chuckles and tips his chin to the papers. "Those are Jewel's checks and balances for the month. Beau doesn't like hard copies; he wants her to go over them. She files them."

I look over at Jewel.

"I review the accounts, High," she scoffs, beating the eggs to death. "I just don't spend hours going over every detail. Who cares if Microsoft went up or down two points?"

I chuckle and take a sip of my coffee. "Bill Gates and a billion other people in the world."

"Joker, it isn't as if Beau is going to sell it." She makes quotation marks with her fingers. "'It's a keeper.' So why do I need to know about it? And I can't do anything about the price of oil, the price of the dollar, or inflation. I *can* raise a healthy kid, make Sinners Biker Babe Boutique a success, and make sure the people I love are taken care of by sharing my money." She puts the eggs in a pan. "And, of course, the charities. Pony Library, that's the most important one. It was my mom's heart. Children's Literacy—for my mom. Filmmakers for a Cause—for my dad. The Cancer Society—for Maggie and Mafia Man." She looks over at me. "Their mothers died of cancer." She continues. "No Kid Hungry—for Patriot, Brainiac, Scottie, Jonas, and Abel." She looks at me again. "Their biological mothers were a piece of work. Rotten to the core." Jewel goes back to cooking and continues. "America against Domestic Violence—for Cookie, Patriot, and the kids. Say No to Drugs—for Cookie, Patriot, and the kids. The Women Shelter—for Cookie."

I bite my bottom lip to keep from laughing.

"The Irish/Native American Scholarship Fund"—she looks at me—"that's our charity."

I widen my eyes at the continuing litany of charities.

"The Kincaid Foundation"—she looks at me again—"that's another one of our charities. Coats for Kids, Toys for Tots. And, um—"

High sighs. "International Child Art Foundation, The Dreaming Zebra Foundation, Healing and Education Through the Arts, St. Jude Children's Research Hospital, The Ronald McDonald House, and The Veterans Foundation."

I do a slow blink and run my hand around my mouth. "You, Mafia Man, and Beau take care of all that?"

"Yup." High takes a gulp of his drink. "With all the brothers' help. We try to keep her away from the TV. She sees a sob story and adds a charity. Beau said she's like her mother—every cause deserves funding."

"They're all worthy causes, High. You vetted them," says Jewel. She sprinkles veggies onto the eggs.

High glances at her and lowers his voice to a whisper. "Mafia Man, Beau, and I have full disclosure with the brothers when it comes to Jewel's finances. When Jackson was alive, he took care of everything with a lawyer and an accountant. He stayed on top of all their assets and controlled his wife's charity gifting. Jewel's father knew she wouldn't have an interest in managing her money. He also knew Jewel was like her mother; that's why he made Beau the fiduciary if something happened to him."

I furrow my brow. "Why Beau? The man must have had people he was close to, trusted."

"You need to read Jenna's book, *Self-made Man: Rags to Riches.* It's an autobiography about her husband. Jackson Sawyer grew up in the Blue Ridge Mountains of Kentucky. He came from a hillbilly family. He was too well-known in Kentucky to have a hideaway. I suppose Pony reminded him of home. His family died in a moonshine still explosion when he was eighteen. Jackson was the only survivor. Beau, who knows, maybe he reminded Jackson of someone."

I take a gulp of my coffee. "Jewel's mother? She didn't have any family?"

High grins. "There's another book for you to read, brother. *Flower Child: The Life of a Hippie.*"

I smirk. "Let me guess: it's Jenna Sawyer's biography."

"Cookie said it's a page-turner. Jenna Jewel's parents were hippies. They died in a car crash when she was a tween. Jenna was raised by their hippie friends. I suppose that's what inspired her to write about subcultures in America. Cookie has read them all. She said she totally got Jewel after she read them. Cookie said Reagan's transformation into Jewel wasn't difficult to understand, given her mother and father's background: family, God, country, and fuck the government. Politicos weren't to be trusted." High takes a slug of his coffee. "Anyway, after Jackson died, Beau caught the two assholes dipping their hands into the cookie jar. He fired them and took over. He needed help, and I stepped up. Now Mafia Man, Beau, and Pick do most of the complicated stuff. We vote on the important issues." He chuckles. "I read Jenna's book, *Welcome to the Jungle*. It's about Jenna and Jackson's experiences navigating mainstream culture within the business world. It paints a fucking ugly picture."

I smirk. "Thanks for stepping up, brother. It sounds like the goddamn vultures would take advantage of Jewel, and she'd give it all away."

High laughs. "Jewel told Beau and me just to put it into the pot with the family's money—she meant the Sinners." He snickers. "When I told Cookie, she said, 'Read the books; you'll get it.'"

I chuckle. "Christ, I'll read the goddamn books."

"General texted. He wants to do church at eight tonight. He wants you there. You didn't text back. He got worried." He tilts his head to Jackie. "I brought you a helmet and harness for Jackie."

I chuckle at my son. He has a wooden spoon he's using to bang on the helmet.

"Cowboy, you need to go. Jackie and I will be fine," says Jewel. She slides a veggie omelet in front of me.

There is no way in hell I'm leaving them alone.

"Nope, not unless you and Jackie come with me." I pull my phone out of my pocket to see if I missed any other texts. All the brothers have sent their greetings and congrats. I grin. News travels fast, and I'm back in the fold.

Jewel sits Jackie in his highchair. "Joker, none of the girls are going to be at the club. They're all in Malibu. Just go to church, have *a* beer with the brothers, and come home after."

"*A* beer," chuckles High. "Joke is not an alcoholic, sweetheart."

I snicker and cut up Jackie's omelet.

She nods. "I know, but I want Joker to eat healthy, High. Beer is empty calories." She pauses for a beat. "Though, I did read there is a new study that beer stimulates a person's appetite."

I roll my eyes and pop a piece of egg into Jackie's mouth. "Chew," I order.

High stands and stretches. "I'll bring Cookie and the kids to the club tonight. You can hang with them while we meet. The brothers will be over at 7:00 a.m. tomorrow to work out with you, Joke." He walks over to Jewel and kisses her temple. "Later, sweetheart. I need to beat feet to Ace to pick up the take from last night. Mika is coming by with his equipment. If he can't get it off the trailer, tell him to leave it. I'll get it tomorrow with the brothers."

"All right, High. I'll stick around and help Mika. Then I need to go to the boutique and start staging the furniture."

"Babe, you're not lifting that heavy shit," I growl and take a bite of omelet. "I'll help Mika when he gets here."

High laughs. "He's back, thank fuck. Later, brother."

Damn right, I'm back. "Lord, babe, you can cook." The omelets are light, fluffy, and cheesy. I chuckle. *Yummy for my tummy.*

CHAPTER 12

COMING HOME – JEWEL

Entering the club feels surreal but also like coming home. I lived three years of my life here. Memories of the hog roasts, the free-flowing booze, and the carefree sex are swirling in my mind. For the most part, it was fun to be a sweet butt. Like all things in life, nothing stays the same. In my wildest dreams, I never suspected I'd be walking back into Sinners as one of the coveted biker babes. Here I am: Jewel, Joker's woman.

Joker rubs my back. "Babe, are you all right?"

"Yes, I am." I smile up at him. "I really am. I'd like to see my old room."

General laughs. "It's still your room, Jewel. You and Joker need to make a decision about which room you're going to keep. I'd suggest yours. It's quieter upstairs."

Cookie squeezes me. "Keep yours. You'll be next to High and me. We can take turns watching the kids, so we get *alone time*."

I haven't had sex since Joker and I made Jackie. Mr. Sizzle, my purple vibrator, takes the edge off, but he's not Joker. We rode the bike to the boutique, which set my girly parts on fire. Joker is sexy as heck on the bike. He might have lost some of his muscle, but he's still solid. He has the body of a god. And his package is magnificent—a full eleven inches and as thick as…I moan. *He's thick.*

If Cookie knew how many times I wanted to drag Joker's gorgeous butt into the supply closet, she would have asked me what I was waiting for—ride that cowboy.

Joker's smiling down at me. "Babe," he drawls.

Oh god, he knows. Does everyone know? General, High, and the brothers all laugh. *Yup, everyone knows.*

I clear my throat and smile up at Joker. "It's up to you, Cowboy."

He grins the panty-dropping grin down at me. I quickly reach up and cover his mouth. Having a spontaneous orgasm in front of the brothers and my son isn't happening.

What does my cowboy do? Sticks the tip of his tongue out and circles my palm lightly. And good god, it happens, I have a glorious mini climax right in the game room. The old Jewel wouldn't mind. The new Jewel is much more reserved: motherhood will do that to a woman.

I pull my hand away as if I'd touched a scorching pan. "Stop that," I say through smiling, gritted teeth.

"You just had a tiny O," he whispers into my ear. "When we get home, I'll give you the big, triple O."

Jesus, Lord, and all that's holy, help me. My toes are curling in my biker boots. And my panties are now drenched. I'm sure my nipples are freakin' beacons in this slinky silk crisscross top.

When I manage to look up at Joker, it isn't his eyes pinned to my boobs. It's my son's, making his "Numm-numm-numm" sounds.

The brothers break out in loud laughter.

"He's Joke's kid all right," snickers Cue Ball.

"Fuck you, asshole," chortles Joker. "Here, babe, take him, so we can get this done."

He hands me Jackie, kisses my lips, and then he whisks off to the war room.

CHAPTER 13

ANGRY WOMEN ARE FUCKING VICIOUS – JOKER

I had mixed emotions over coming back to the club. I hadn't been here in two years. I took one step in, and it was like coming home. All my brothers greeted me with bro hugs and back slaps. When Beau walked in, I was a little worried it would be weird between us. It wasn't. He walked over to me, pulled me in for a hug, and kissed my temple. Then he told me he'd kick my ass if I fucked things up.

There is no chance of that. Once you've been to hell, you don't want to go back.

After we shot the shit and teased Jewel, we headed to the war room. I took my old seat and needed a minute to get my emotions under control. Christ, I made it through the fires of hell, and I'm home.

General bangs the gavel down. "Let's get to it. Doc, do you have the brothers on the line?"

"We're here," confirms Flame. "Welcome back, Joke."

"Congrats on Jewel and Jackie, Joke," says Mafia Man.

"Get your ass back to work. The customers miss your ugly mug," laughs Tank.

"If you're bored, I left an engine that needs a rebuild," chuckles Tristen.

"Thanks, brothers. Tristen, I'll check out the engine tomorrow." I grin and look down at my hands. *Christ, I'm not going to cry like a pussy.*

"I'm sending you a video of Grandma Dove, Grandma Hi, and Grandma Raven on a surfboard. It's funny as shit," guffaws Brainiac.

"Don't let your grandmothers fucking drown," barks Pick. "We're headed back in the morning."

"Beau, you're up," says General.

A thick binder thuds onto the table in front of me. Beau grins. "Welcome to our life." He points to the binder. "That's everything concerning Jewel's finances. Good luck; it'll take a week of continuous reading for you to get caught up. We all try our damnedest to make the best decisions for Jewel and Jackie. All her personal and household bills come to me electronically. I've added you as a user."

"Thanks," I mumble. I thought the Sinners' and Native Americans' finances were challenging. I'd need a master's in finance just to read the damn thing.

"There are a few things to be aware of: Jewel uses her American Express card for almost everything. If the store doesn't take American Express, she'll use her MasterCard. She shops mostly at the same places. Learn them. You need to know the types of things she buys. If something is in question, ask her. Hackers are a pain in the ass. I've needed to replace her plastic ten times in the last three years. If she needs cash, she'll ask High or me to hit the ATM. Her mother was robbed at one, and Jewel was with her. The asshole pointed a gun in Jenna's face. Jackson never allowed them to go to an ATM again. Their safe became Jenna and Jewel's cash machine."

I nod and thumb through the binder. "I'll give her cash."

"Right now, we're working on the library's endowment," informs Mafia Man. "The asshole accountant and attorney were siphoning money off it to fill their own goddamn pockets. It'll run out of green by the end of the year. We're juggling a few assets around and setting up a nonprofit like the one we have for the Kincaid Foundation."

I flip to the library's account. The assholes ripped off the library for millions before Beau caught them. "Were the fuckers dealt with?"

"They're goddamn bankrupt, brother. Pick, Devilan, and I wiped them out. We recovered most of the stolen money. All the other assets are solid. The binder was Jackson's." Liam laughs. "We've sent you the spreadsheets and the online links."

I chuckle and close the binder, pushing it aside.

"Maria," shout ten kids in the background. "We want tacos with nachos."

I grin and drag a hand down my face. "I need to up Maria's wages."

"That's part of what we're discussing," says General. "So let's start with the easy shit."

I kick my legs out and fold my arms over my chest, ready to listen.

"Jewel's taxes on the beach house are in the neighborhood of thirty grand a year. There is the upkeep, which is another twenty. Maria makes a grand a week. Over the past two years, we've tried to give her an increase. She's refused. Maria loves the kids," explains Mafia Man. "Jewel has a lot of bank, but that doesn't mean she should pay our way. I ran the numbers. We can swing the taxes and the upkeep. This needs to be on the down-low; Jewel will never go for it. We're her only family, and she likes to share."

"Agreed," nods High. "One or more of our families are in Malibu just about every month."

"Everyone who agrees, say aye," orders General.

All the brothers say, "Aye."

"Nay." I look at my brothers. "I can't lie to Jewel. I'm all for paying the taxes, upkeep, *and* Maria's wages. But Jewel needs to know we're doing it."

Beau frowns. "Christ, Joke, she won't agree. We had an argument about the gasoline for my boat and the jet skis."

I nod. "She will. We have this thing about communication. I'll get her to agree. As far as Maria goes, we can pay her taxes or her lease. That way, she can't refuse."

"Joke, we moved Maria into the beach house," says Liam. "Her lease was up. We didn't want to leave it empty when we left. There's been an increase of vandalism in the area."

I nod again. "That's good. We'll leave it for now. When Jewel and I go to Malibu, I'll convince her."

"Uncle Liam," yells Keeley in the background. "Maria wants to know if you want another margarita with your fish taco."

Liam is Mafia Man's badass eldest blood brother. It's funny as shit he'd be drinking margaritas. He's usually nursing a glass of Jameson or a beer.

Godfather chuckles and leans over, showing me a picture of Liam in his boardshorts sipping on a margarita. Christ, I just about piss myself. He looks like a guy straight out of Brie's *Teen* magazine.

I laugh. "Who's the chick hovercrafting him?"

Godfather grins. "Some beach bunny looking for a good time."

I grin back. "Did she get it?"

He slides his thumb over the screen to the next picture. Keeley is wrapped in a towel, curled up on Liam's lap. "Nope."

I snicker. "Keeley, the six-year-old cockblocker."

General interrupts, "Next up is the boutique. High is going to manage the day-to-day shit. We need to figure out who is going to work the store and take care of the online orders."

Sly pipes up, "Cutter has expressed an interest. He needs a break from bouncing at Ace. The strippers are a pain in the ass."

"Dad," says Tristen. "Cole also expressed an interest. We can move a prospect to Ace."

He looks at me, Beau, and High. "Will Jewel be happy with that?"

I tilt my head toward High. "She left the decision to him."

"High?"

He nods. "Agreed."

"Done," barks General, slamming down the gavel. "Tristen, pick two prospects and train them for Ace."

"Okay," affirms Tristen.

General sighs. "Marshmallow has become a huge problem. She hasn't paid rent in the last year and refuses to pull her weight around here."

"Put her on a fucking bus," I sneer. "Why are we stressing about her?"

The war room fills with a woman's enraged scream. I leap up and run for the stairs.

"You know, *Miss Thing*, you weren't so high and mighty when you were a sweet butt. You're a real sicko, Jewel. Who in the hell would become a sweet butt when they have more cash than God? An ungrateful bitch who's fucking nuts. I'm sorry your brother didn't do your ass in," shouts Marshmallow at Jewel.

"Fuck no!" I sprint down the stairs.

Jewel holds her hand up, stopping me. Her violet eyes are ablaze with fury. "My brother?" she asks in a cold, stern voice.

"Yeah, Jewel, your brother. The Army guy. The guy who beat you up and killed your baby." She juts out her hip with her hand on it. "At the time, I felt bad for letting him into the boutique."

I growl, "I'm going to fucking kill the bitch."

Jewel shakes her head no. "Let her talk, Cowboy."

"*Let her talk?!*" Marshmallow just admitted to letting Briggs into the goddamn boutique two and a half years ago. He beat Jewel and killed our son!

"You were such a bitch, Jewel. I found the pregnancy stick you were trying to hide. I left it on the bathroom vanity for Joker to find. I knew Joker would flip out. He didn't want you. And he didn't want your kid. Joker wanted me. I don't believe for a second the stick *bounced* off the wall and hit you in the eye. Joker is badass with a temper. He was an Army Ranger, a sniper. He aimed and hit a bullseye." She laughs sadistically. "Get it? Bullseye?"

Cookie inhales sharply.

Marshmallow sneers and looks at Cookie. "Yeah, Cookie, Joker almost blinded her. Right?" She swings her eyes back to Jewel. "Did you take the fucking hint?" Marshmallow snorts. "No. You strutted around with your pregnant belly on display, making Joker feel all guilty and shit. He started to question his decision about cutting you loose. I overheard him talking to High. How he needed to have a private conversation with you...blah, blah, blah." She rolls her eyes.

"Joker accepted Finlan as his son. He was ready to step up. Fucking disgusting. I told Joker after he cost you four stitches, you'd never talk to him."

"You are fucking dead," I snarl at Marshmallow.

Jewel is standing statue still, blank-faced, just listening. I'm seething, with every nerve in my body zapping me. I'm ready to snap Marshmallow's goddamn thick neck.

"Your brother showed up outside of Callahan's asking about you. He wanted to take you home. Well, he seemed sincere. The dude was Val Kilmer *Spartan* huge. I borrowed Joker's phone so I could call for help if I needed to: I didn't want to take the chance he was a nut job. I thought I was doing you a good turn. I mean, Joker was never going to step up and take care of your kid." She tosses her hand out toward me. "Come on, he's Joker: he likes threesomes with Honeypot and me. And hunting and fishing with High. He *is not* the fatherly type." She huffs out, "After everything went down, Honey and I found out you're some rich bitch from *Ma...li...bu.* You brought your psycho killer brother to our door to save your own ass."

"You wickedy old witch," yells Cookie. "That animal wasn't Jewel's—"

Jewel shakes her head. "Cook, no. Let her talk."

I look over to the kitchen. Merrill is holding my son, and he looks like he's about to come unhinged. Honeypot is as white as a sheet. She's holding on to Merrill's arm. Christ, she's going to pass out.

"You know, you invited everyone but Honey and me to your beach house. Now I just heard Joker say to put me on a bus to nowhere. *WHAT...THE...FUCK?* He was a smelly-ass drunk who couldn't keep a hard-on for more than a minute. The one-minute wonder," she laughs sarcastically. "As soon as you hit town, he threw Honey and me out and cleaned himself up. Yeah"—she nods slowly—"it makes you think. Right? He didn't want you as a sweet butt. Now that he knows you've got some dough, he's kissing your ass. Wake up, Jewel! Joker only wants your money. He doesn't give a shit about you or your son." She swishes out her arm. "None of the Sinners do. You pay, they play!"

I was wrong. It wasn't Merrill who was coming unhinged; it was

84

my woman. Jewel launches her body at Marshmallow. She wraps her hands around Marshmallow's throat; they both thud to the floor, screaming.

"*YOU HELPED RICHARD BRIGGS KILL MY BABY!*" screeches Jewel. She's sprawled out on Marshmallow, leaving herself open. My woman isn't a fighter. Marshmallow is a different story: she's snarling like an animal. The goddamn bitch is battling like she's an MMA fighter going for the UFC heavyweight title.

Quick as lightning, Cookie is in the fray: she's pulling Marshmallow's hair and shrieking in French.

"Fuck!" I push off and run for Jewel. Suddenly, I'm body checked by Honeypot. I fly into High. He takes down Sly, Hawk, Doc, Horse, and Beau—falling dominos.

"Cowabunga!" shrills Honeypot. She leaps onto Jewel's back and starts bitch slapping Marshmallow. *Smack! Smack! Smack!* "Take that, you mother-f-ing lazy ass biatch! Cookie, use your fists. Punch her!"

It's total pandemonium. The brothers are shouting, the girls are screeching, and my baby is screaming for his mother.

I'm trying to scramble off the pile of brothers. Their arms and legs are everywhere, trapping me in place.

"Ah, goddamnit," curses General. Blood is streaming from his nose.

Christ, he caught Honeypot's shoe in the face.

"Ah, fucking Jesus, that's my goddamn arm you're biting, Cookie," bellows Godfather. "Jesus Christ, stop!"

I finally make it to my feet. Beau trips over Doc's foot and takes me down again. My head connects with his face. I see white sparks of light behind my lids—fucking stars.

Sly and Hawk are the ones who drag Honeypot off Jewel's back. Both of them are taking punches and kicks meant for Marshmallow.

"Fuck!" yells Sly.

Ouch. Cookie's foot cracked him in the balls.

Beau and I crawl on all fours, making it to the pile. I manage to get my arm around Jewel's waist. Beau drags us back. High lifts Cookie into the air; she's kicking and punching with her eyes squeezed shut.

"Marshmallow is dead," shouts Doc. His two fingers are against her neck.

It's like the YouTube video—*Frozen Grand Central*. Everyone freezes in place and stares at Marshmallow's limp body in disbelief.

"I killed her?" whispers Jewel. She gazes up at me. Her body starts to tremble. "I'm a murderess." Jewel starts crying hysterically. "I...won't...see...Finlan...in...Heaven."

"Shh, you'll see him," I coo and rub circles onto her back with my eyes pinned to Marshmallow. I can't believe the girls killed the bitch.

"Finlan?" asks Beau. Blood is dripping down his chin. My skull split his lower lip wide open.

I shake my head and keep rubbing.

"No," says Doc. "She had a goddamn heart attack. The woman was overweight. She ate all the wrong foods, drank like a fish, and never exercised. No one fucking killed her."

"A heart attack," sneers Honeypot. She stares at Marshmallow's body, shouting incredulously, "The biatch died from eating too many of Raine's doughnuts?"

Jackie is still screaming in the kitchen.

"Babe, let Beau hold you. I need to go to Jackie." I kiss her lips and give her to Beau.

Standing on shaky legs, I stiffen my body and limp into the kitchen. The room smells as if it were doused in sour milk. Merrill is bouncing Jackie, trying to calm him. My son has curdled milk puke down his chest. Snot is running from his tiny nose to his lips. He's wailing at the top of his lungs; tears stream down his bright red cheeks.

"Hey, Daddy is here," I whisper and take him for Merrill. "Mommy is all right, Jackie. Shh, calm for Daddy."

He wraps his puke-covered hands in my hair, trying to climb up my body. I take him outside, onto the back deck, where it's quiet. His skin is hot...too hot. His little body is covered in sweat. After five minutes of walking and cooing, he begins to settle.

Just when I think it's over, Jewel and Beau come out, and Jackie starts all over again. Jewel takes him from me. She sits on the step, rocking him and cooing to him. He snuggles into her neck, snorting, hiccuping, and shivering. I take my tee off and wrap it around him. Beau and I drop down on each side of her. With our arms locked together, we support Jewel's back. Beau and I take turns softly talking to Jackie, reassuring him we're here, and everything is all right.

The brothers quietly come out onto the deck. Frozen bags of peas and corn are passed around. No doubt, it looks as if we've all been through a battle and got our asses kicked.

I take a bag of peas and hold it against Jewel's left eye. She's going to have a shiner. Beau holds one to his lip. General is holding a bag of corn to his nose and another to my head. Godfather has frozen peas on the bite on his arm. I look over at High and Cookie. High is holding corn to the side of Cookie's right temple and another to his cheek. Cookie headbutted him. Hawk's holding a bag of peas to his left eye, and Sly has a bag tucked down his jeans. Honeypot was the only one who came out of it unscathed. I snort. She was on top. Jewel and Cookie took all the return punches before the bitch bought it.

I've learned my lesson. By the look of my brothers, they have, too: shut the shit down before things escalate. Angry women are fucking vicious.

CHAPTER 14

LIKE FATHER, LIKE SON – JEWEL

I open one eye and look at my son sleeping on his father's chest. Marshmallow's words play in my mind: *Wake up, Jewel! Joker only wants your money. He doesn't give a shit about you or your son.* It never entered my mind that Joker wanted my money. He offered me a check for Jackie's living expenses. He was sincere in his concern for my real estate: *I have money, babe, but I don't think I have enough to carry three homes.* To me, that meant he was willing to share.

Joker had a surprised look on his face when I told him the amount of money my parents left me. For Christ's sake, his mouth was hanging open. A man can't fake that. No, those were just ugly words from a jealous woman.

My son snorts in his sleep and rubs his cheek against Joker's chest. I reach out one finger and run it lightly around the shell of Jackie's ear. Like his father, Jackie is perfect.

I sigh and roll out of bed. It doesn't matter the reason Joker came to us. He's here, and Jackie loves his daddy.

Who are you kidding? You'd give Joker your last dime if it meant

Jackie could have his father. Whoever said you can't buy love is full of crap. I've seen lots of top-notch designers purchase themselves a whole lot of love.

I look over my shoulder. Joker has his huge hand covering Jackie's diapered bottom. No, Joker didn't come for money. God granted me my secret wish—Joker came for his son.

I limp into the bathroom. Every muscle in my body is aching; my left hip throbs with each step. My left eye feels gritty, like there's sand in it. Then I remember Marshmallow's limp body lying on the game room floor. Good god, at least I'm alive to feel the minor discomforts. Lord have mercy; I caused the woman to have a heart attack and die. I do a quick sign of the cross, asking God to forgive me. I need to see Finlan in Heaven.

How old was Marshmallow? Older than me, but still too young to have a friggin' heart attack.

I giggle as if I'm half-cracked recalling Honey. She yelled, "Cowabunga!" with all of her two hundred pounds crashing down on my back. I glance down at my left hip. It's as purple as an eggplant and the size of one, too: the bruise is covering my four-inch scar. Honeypot's weight caused me to slide to the left and smash my hip into the floor, which opened me up to take Marshmallow's elbow to my left eye.

Honey paid me no mind. She was bitch-slapping Marshmallow, screaming, "You twat! You killed my nephew!" I exhale. Honey thought of Finlan as her nephew. It's time to let the past go. Cookie and I need to forgive Honey and move on. No, we'll never be besties with Honeypot. Forgiveness is all I have to offer.

Cookie. I snort. Good lord, my best friend had her eyes squeezed shut, kicking, punching, and biting. I grimace, recalling Godfather's forearm: Cookie broke his skin and damn near took a chunk out of him. The poor guy needed to have a penicillin shot. Doc said human mouths have a high level of bacteria. He said human bites are more dangerous than animal bites. Who knew that? Animals eat their own poop!

I look into the mirror and examine my eye. It's purple and swollen.

I hiss and open it. The globe is blood red without any white. *Grotesque.* I close my right eye. Well, at least I can see out of it. I take the Motrin bottle out of the medicine cabinet. *Girl, you've been through worse crap.* Shaking out four tablets, I pop them into my mouth and swallow. I'm so used to taking pills, I don't need liquid. Then I grab the Natural Tears and squirt a couple of drops in my eye. "Ah, sugar-honey-ice-tea," I hiss through gritted teeth and fan my eye. It stings like a bee. I hold my lid closed and wait for the sting to go away.

Exhaling, I glance at the tub. After we got home from the club, I was exhausted. The adrenaline rush was gone, leaving me with barely enough energy to make it into the house. Jackie was clingy: he only wanted me. He needed a bath; I needed a bath. We were both sweaty, pukey, and snotty. Joker swept us up into his arms and carried us upstairs to the bathroom. He set us down on the vanity and filled the whirlpool tub with warm water. Then he took off our clothes and stripped himself.

Joker isn't the type of man to be self-conscious of his body. I've never been self-conscious of mine. I modeled my clothing line. I stood naked in front of many people; there's no time for embarrassment. Jackie's a baby: he loves to run around naked. And, like all males, he loves to play with his cock.

I lay back, enjoying the jets of the whirlpool tub with Jackie lying on my chest. Joker spoke softly to our son, counting his fingers and toes, playing the eyes, nose, mouth, belly button game until Jackie gave me up and went to him. I dozed off and awoke to Joker coaxing Jackie into letting him brush his teeth. *Watch Daddy brush, Jackie.* Joker managed to brush his teeth without too much of a fight. Then Joker snuggled us into bed and held us until we drifted.

The way Joker took care of us last night, no one would believe he was deathly ill less than two weeks ago. I know Joker's inner strength...his capacity to love. Joker fought by his fellow soldiers in Afghanistan. He has fought by the Sinners' sides more than once. He loves all the Sinners and the Sinners' kids. He's never hesitated to kiss them, hug them, and comfort them when they were hurting. In a pinch, he's even changed a few diapers.

I wanted that side of Joker for Jackie—secretly prayed for it. That's why I let him into our lives so quickly. I could have held off for six months, but there wasn't any sense in that. When Joker wants something, he's tenacious in getting it.

I grab my pink toothbrush and make quick work of getting my teeth brushed. I sigh and look over at my makeup vanity. Even my waterproof body makeup won't cover up these bruises. *Screw it.* I leave the bathroom and quickly dress in my yoga outfit. I glance at Jackie and Joker. They're snuggled together, still snoozing. *Let it go, Jewel. It doesn't matter why Joker had a change of heart. He did, and that's what counts.*

I walk down the stairs, no longer feeling the ache in my hip. Now it's stiff as a board. I need to remind myself not to swing my leg out. I amble over to the coffee maker, fill it, and jab the on button. The grinder worries, filling the room with the rich aroma of expresso beans. I hit the fridge for strawberries, yogurt, and milk. On my way back, I grab three bananas off the table. I toss everything in the blender with the raw organic protein powder and jab the puree button.

"Mornin'." Beau kisses my temple. He reaches for two mugs and waits for the carafe to fill. Then he pours us two cups. Mine, he adds milk to. He struts over to the table and grabs the computer, logging into *The Wall Street Journal*. I sip my dark roast and take three large glasses out of the cabinet. I fill them with the smoothies, plastic wrap the mouths, and walk over to the fridge.

"Your hip is stiff today." He tilts his head toward my leg. "You need to stretch it out." Then he sees my bruise through the white mesh. "Fucking Christ, we need to go to Sinners Urgent Care for an x-ray. You might have damaged it."

I smirk. "It's titanium. I think it can take a little fall, Daddy Beau. I'll stretch later."

"That eye." He sighs. "Did you put drops in it?"

"Yup," I affirm. "Did the brothers take Marshmallow to the canyon?"

Beau takes a gulp of his coffee. "Nope. Doc has a friend at Butte Hospital. He wants to do an autopsy. The guy is participating in a study on early death related to obesity."

"Huh." I down my dark roast and grab my sneakers. "I left the smoothies in the fridge. Strawberry banana, your favorite."

Beau narrows his eyes on me. "You are not going to fucking jog today."

"Mmm," I hum. "After my run, Jackie and I need to hit the boutique." I hiss at the need to bend and quickly tie the laces of my sneakers. "I also need to go through Mom's things in her office. I had Mika and Joker put my sewing machine and materials in there. I want to make it my design room. I think Joker is going to Sinners Bike Shop. Tristen left him an engine that needs fixing."

Beau takes another drink of his coffee. "Joke seems to be doing okay in the daddy department."

I smile. "Joker is wonderful with Jackie."

"Let me know if that changes," he mumbles and goes back to reading his online newspaper.

I grab my shades and baseball cap. I'm just about out the door when Joker comes down the stairs with Jackie on his hip. Jackie has his fingers in his father's mouth, trying to see his teeth. Best guess, they brushed before coming downstairs.

Joker eyes me up and down. "Babe, you're not jogging on that hip."

I grin and walk over to kiss him. "Cowboy, how about a good morning before you start bossing me around."

"Mornin', babe," chuckles Joker. He kisses me.

"Yo!" shouts High. He walks into the kitchen with Sly, Cue Ball, and Hawk trailing him. "Your old man is standing in the kitchen in his boxers, sweetheart," laughs High.

I grin and scan Joker's body. Lord, he even has sexy feet. No man should have sexy feet.

"Babe," drawls Joker, chuckling.

"Fuck me, there's a pool in here," yells Sly from the four-seasons room.

"Don't walk through my house with your dirty goddamn boots on, asshole," shouts Joker. "My kid crawls around on these floors." He puts his hand on my butt and gives me a rub. "Jackie needs to eat, babe."

Why does his possessive, domineering, badass side cause my girly parts to go on full alert? Maybe because it's his house and his kid. *Every time he touches you, it sends your girly parts into overdrive.*

Beau chuckles, not looking up from the computer screen. "Have your coffee, Joke, so we can get to training."

I open the fridge. Cue Ball's head pops under my arm. "Ooh, is that a strawberry banana smoothie?"

Joker puts Jackie into his highchair, growling, "Not for you, shithead. Jewel makes them for me."

High snickers and pours himself a mug of coffee. "Possessive much, bro?"

I roll my eyes and hand Cue Ball the smoothie. "I can make more." I take out the yogurt from the fridge. As I pass, I grab a banana off the table. "Love you, Cowboy."

"Love you, too," he mumbles and watches Cue Ball slurping *his* smoothie.

"Delicious," grins Cue Ball.

"Don't antagonize him, Cue Ball," I chide.

I learned early on that the Sinners' brothers are "real" brothers. They love each other, play together, fight together, and argue, as brothers do. I grin. All the wives intervene when the brothers argue. I just did my first intervention. *Clink for me!*

"Fucking awesome weapons collection," yells Hawk from the game room.

Joker moans and lays his forehead onto the table.

I walk over and rub his back. I need to bite my bottom lip to keep from laughing. He's like his son, or his son is like him. They don't like to share.

Jackie screeches, "Paa-Paa-Paa. Numm-numm-numm," with his eyes on the bananas.

Beau reaches over and grabs a banana. He peels it, breaks it in half, and hands it to Jackie. He's about to stick the rest into his mouth when Jackie shrieks, "NO!" waving his hand for the other half.

"Like father, like son," I sigh and kiss Joker's head. "Jackie, share with Papa." I walk back to the counter and snatch the homemade granola. I add milk to soften it and mix it with Jackie's yogurt. I forgo the banana; he's already eating one.

"I'll have mine crunchy with sliced banana," says Sly. He plops down on the seat next to Joker.

I look over at Joker. He appears as if his head is going to pop off. I snicker and prepare two more.

I hand Beau his bowl and Jackie's and then slide the other two in front of Joker and Sly. "Anyone else for yogurt and granola?"

Joker tilts his head up for a kiss. "Thanks, babe. No one needs anything else."

I kiss him and whisper onto his lips, "Be nice and share."

Beau is feeding Jackie, chuckling.

Joker shovels a spoonful of yogurt into his mouth. "Did General, Pick, Buck, Horse, and Godfather leave for Malibu?"

"Hm." Sly swallows. "Six this morning, on their bikes. They're hoping to make it most of the way through Utah. Flame, Tank, Buck, and Mafia Man are taking their women to wine country when they get there." Sly chuckles. "The grandparents are babysitting for a week."

"Wine country is so beautiful this time of year." I wipe Jackie's face and set him on his feet. "High, you should take Cookie."

"Nope," he chuckles. "She wouldn't go with you here in Pony. Besides, who the hell wants to walk through a bunch of grapevines and eat expensive food that doesn't fill you up? They're going to sweat their balls off and pay a hefty price while doing it."

I roll my eyes. "It's romantic, High."

"Cookie is romanced between the sheets." He laughs. "She doesn't need a four-hundred-dollar-a-night room."

Joker pushes back his chair. He grins. "Babe, I'm going to take the brothers down to the workout room. Don't run today. Let your hip rest. When we're done, we'll head to town."

I tip my face up for a kiss. "Okay, Cowboy."

"*We* need to find time to be romantic between the sheets," he murmurs onto my lips.

I watch his sexy butt walk to the game room. Lord, I'd love to be romanced between the sheets. I laugh. I don't even need the sheets.

CHAPTER 15

MR. SIZZLE – JEWEL

Joker pulls up to the boutique. I slide off the back of his bike and take Jackie out of his harness.

Jackie screeches, "Daaaddeee! Daaaddeee," reaching for Joker.

For the past month, everything has been "Daddy." It's understandable; Joker gives Jackie everything he wants. When I protest, Joker's rote answer is always: "He's my baby, Jewel."

I get it, but Jackie needs to have a bedtime, and he needs to sleep in his own bed. Mommy needs a little romancing between the sheets.

"Daddy needs to go to work, baby boy. I'll pick you and Mommy up when I'm done." He puckers. "Kiss."

Jackie gives Joker a lip-quivering kiss.

I sigh. "Go. He'll settle."

"Jewel," Joker murmurs and runs his finger down my cheek. "Tonight, it'll be just you and me in our bed."

I plaster a fake smile onto my face and give him a kiss. "Go."

Joker gives me a quick pat on my hip, then he pulls away. I sigh, walk into the boutique, and set Jackie down by his toybox. Then I check the time—nine. *Damn, it's too early for wine.*

I start unpacking the boxes, and Cookie comes buzzing in.

"Sorry I'm late. High and I slept in, and then we got our groove on."

I'm glad someone is getting their groove on. I've been thinking seriously about giving Mr. Sizzle a go. Though he might have lost his sizzle—dead batteries.

"High told me Marshmallow's autopsy came back. Her freakin' arteries were all clogged up. Did you know she was forty? What the heck is a forty-year-old doing as a sweet butt? High said she had a lot of work done before coming to the club. The woman had her vag tightened up."

I burst out laughing. "How does High know that?"

"Medical records. She had it done in Nashville, along with her boob job. Maybe she tried to be a Dolly look-alike."

"Too bad she couldn't sing like Dolly," I mutter and pull the tape off a box.

"She was pitchy. You know, flat on some notes and sharp on others." Cookie pulls a silk scarf from the box. "This is gorgeous. Are those Jackie's handprints?"

I nod. "Pretty cool, right? I shadowed his prints to make them look more badass. They glow in the dark. I'm going to display them hanging off the drawer of the dresser. Sort of a teen-girl messy look." I giggle. "I got the idea from Raine. She was complaining the girls leave their clothes half-hanging out of the drawers."

Cookie laughs. "It drives Raine crazy. Maggie said Buck sneaks in and straightens up before she can see it."

"No way," I giggle.

"Oh, yeah, he does," nods Cookie. She opens another box. "Mafia Man told Maggie that Buck wants another kid. Raine told Buck she was too busy picking up after the ones they already have. Jillian said that's why Buck agreed to go to wine country. She also said they didn't come out of their room for three days. A twelve-hundred-buck baby. Get it? Buck and Buck!" She laughs at her own joke.

"You're such a dork." I laugh and fold the scarf.

I inhale deeply and then exhale. What would it be like for a man to want you to have his baby? I snort. Dote on you? Rub your swollen feet? Kiss your pregnant belly? Tell his unborn child he can't wait for him to come into the world? I harrumph. And want to be there when he does. I wonder what it would be like to have your husband make a midnight run to the store because you're craving Häagen-Daz. I wonder what it would be like to be made love to…to be cherished and loved. *Girlfriend, you love hot, sweaty sex.* I furrow my brow. *There must be a way to have hot, sweaty sex and still feel loved: pipe dreams. You can't get Joker alone to have any kind of sex.*

"Okay, spill it, Jewel," orders Cookie. "Something is bothering you. You've been folding that scarf for the last ten minutes."

I open the dresser drawer and hang the hand-painted scarf. I exhale. "It's just"—I pinch my forehead—"it's been difficult. Jackie has been teething, and the thing with Marshmallow freaked him out."

Cookie takes my hand. "Come with me."

I look over my shoulder. Jackie is pulling hats out of a box.

Cookie uncorks a bottle of cab. "It's noon somewhere." She smiles and pours us two glasses.

I drop down onto the chair, take the glass, and gulp.

Cookie raises one eyebrow. "Okay, it's going to be get-your-buzz-on day-drinking." Cookie smirks and takes a drink of her wine. "Spill it."

I inhale, loosen my shoulders, and take another gulp. "Joker and I haven't—"

Christ, am I undesirable? Or maybe I'm not sexy to him because I'm a mother? When I was in Malibu, I used to get hit on by good-looking guys. Not as hot as Joker, but they were decent-looking. The backs of my eyes start burning, and my nose is tingling. I'm not a crier. *Girl, you will not cry over this crap.*

"Jewel," drawls Cookie. She waits for me to say something.

"Joker's committed to being healthy. He works a lot. He's devoted to Jackie, and that's a good thing," I babble and take a big, big drink of wine. "He's tired—"

"You and Joker haven't done the dirty for how long?" inquires Cookie. She drains her glass.

I shake my head, my eyes brimming with tears.

Cookie raises both eyebrows. "Since you've been back?"

I shrug my shoulders and guzzle the rest of my cab. "Nope."

Cookie blinks a few times, bites her bottom lip, and refills our glasses. "Do you know why?"

I take a drink of wine. "Everything I said, plus Jackie sleeps with us."

She furrows her brow and gives me her oh-my-god look. Which is pretty funny. So I laugh. "This isn't funny, Jewel," chastises Cookie, all serious. "People who groove together stay together. Why does Jackie sleep with you?"

I snort and take another gulp. "Because he wants to, and Joker says, 'He's my baby.'" I sigh. "Honestly, Cook, I don't think Joker finds me desirable. He gives me quick kisses and tells me he loves me. He promises, 'tonight's the night.' But somehow, 'tonight' is never 'the night.' High touches your boobs, right?" I don't wait for her to answer. "Joker doesn't touch my boobs, Cook. Like, never, not once. And when I'm all"—I shake my head—"for lack of a better word, *hot* for him, he'll drawl, 'babe,' and chuckle. Joker's just not into me."

"That's ridiculous." She laughs and throws her hand toward me. "Look at you! You have a face and body that any woman would die for, and any man would want. And your hair!" She makes big eyes. "Sister, your hair is gorgeous." Cookie refills my glass and grabs her phone, texting.

I watch her and wonder how people have that kind of dexterity. When I tried holding my phone with one hand and texting with my thumb, I dropped the damn thing in the toilet and needed to purchase a new one. I take another long drink of my wine.

Jackie comes walking over. "Maa-Maa, numm-numm-numm."

I hold out my arms. Jackie runs into them. I breathe him in; he smells like Joker's spice cologne. *Daddy loves you, and that's all that matters.* I dig around in my bag and find the Tupperware bowl of cheese. Opening it, I give him a square of organic mozzarella.

"Where are CJ and Pete?"

"Jewel, you're trying to change the subject." Cookie sighs.

99

"They're with Faith. She misses the kids." She takes a sip of wine and a square of cheese. "So what are we going to do to get your groove on?"

I shrug. "Nothing. If Joker doesn't want me, I'm left with Mr. Sizzle."

"No," drawls Cookie in horror. "Your vibrator?"

"Yup." I giggle. "He's dependable, and he's there when I need him." I giggle again. "He never lets me down."

Cookie furrows her brow, taking a gulp of her wine. "There must be something wrong with Joker."

I roll my eyes. "Joker didn't have any problems doing Honeypot and Marshmallow."

Cookie snorts. "I don't know about that. Marshmallow called him the 'one-minute wonder.'"

"She lied, Cook. Doing the dirty with Joker is like a triathlon event." I guzzle the rest of my cab and pour myself another glass. "He'd take me to a subspace in my brain where my body felt as if it were riding on a fluffy white cloud. I was suspended in a bubble of pure pleasure. It was a beautiful haze—heaven. I forgot who I was, where I came from, and what I'd been through. All my fears were gone. His touch would send my body into yet another blissful orgasm."

"Lord have mercy," breathes out Cookie in French. She fans her face. "Don't get mad, but I think I just had a little O listening to you."

We both giggle drunkenly.

I hold up my glass and smile. "Clink to Mr. Sizzle. He's going to get lucky tonight."

"I love you, sister," says Cookie with a bit of a slur.

I down my drink and flop my head on the back of the chair. "I love you, too, Cook."

CHAPTER 16

MR. SIZZLE, HER VIBRATOR – JOKER

The soundtrack changes. Tim McGraw, "It's Your Love," blares throughout the garage. I throw my wrench down and close my eyes. The image of Jewel consumes my thoughts. It isn't just her gorgeous body that sends my cock stirring in my jeans. It's the way she smiles up at me as if I'm some kind of miracle God gave to her. It's the way she gives me soft kisses and calls me Cowboy. It's the way she looks at me with wanting violet eyes. It's the way she puts Jackie and me first...the way she makes sure all our needs are met.

"Hey, brother."

I snap my eyes open. High is strutting into the garage, carrying Jackie.

I leap to my feet and turn off the tunes. "Why do you have Jackie? Is Jewel all right?" I jog to the sink and scrub the grease off my hands.

"Jewel's at the boutique, day-drinking with my woman, brother." High drops down onto a chair. He pulls out a bag of Cheetos, opens it, and hands Jackie one.

I walk over and take Jackie from him. "Jewel doesn't feed him processed shit."

High chuckles. "I know. That's why his uncle does."

Jackie holds his half-chewed Cheeto to my mouth.

I push his hand down gently. "It's yours, baby boy."

"You're the only one he will share with," grins High. He tilts his head to the chair next to him. "Take a seat, brother. We need to conversate."

A shiver runs up my spine, setting my nerves on edge. The last time High said that to me, he told me Jewel had left for Malibu, and she wasn't coming back. No, the last time he used those words, he told me Jewel was pregnant again. Jewel is day-drinking—it's fucking bad news.

High pats the chair. "Joke, it's nothing bad. I just want to converse."

I roll my eyes. *Conversate. Converse.* Who the hell has he been hanging out with? Princess is the only person I know who would use those words. Ordinary people say "shoot the shit."

I drop down onto the chair with Jackie on my lap.

Jackie yells, "Heee!" demanding the bag of Cheetos.

I take the bag and hand Jackie a Cheeto. "Mommy wouldn't like you eating shit," I whisper and kiss his crown.

High sits up with his elbows on his knees. He gives me a sideways glance. Fucking great, he's uncomfortable. Now I'm uncomfortable.

He exhales and sits back. "I just need to know how you're handling things. You've had some life-altering changes this past month." He pauses for a beat. "You know, moving in with Jewel, being a daddy to Jackie, living with Beau, and coming back to the club and the garage."

I furrow my brow, staring at him. Exhaling, I move my head from side to side, cracking my neck. *He's trying to get at something. What?*

"You're at my house every morning, brother. You see me with Jewel, Jackie, and Beau. You know things are going fucking fantastic. Why is my woman day-drinking? Jewel doesn't do that shit."

Jewel has a screwed-up rule she imposed upon herself: no drinking until 6:00 p.m. That's the time she makes dinner. I smile. *It's six o'clock. Wine time.* Jewel always says it as if it's a treat she never gets. But she always enjoys a glass of cab while she cooks.

High drags a hand down his face. "I'm just gonna ask. Christ, Joker, is your cock working?"

I choke, coughing on my own spit. "Is my cock working?" I repeat. "Yes, my cock is working. What the fuck, High?"

He pinches the bridge of his nose and blows out a long breath. "Then you don't find Jewel sexually attractive."

"What?!" I yell incredulously.

He throws up a hand. "That's the only goddamn explanation for not fucking your woman. Your cock works...you live in the same goddamn house as she does. You're sleeping with your kid, using him as a cockblocker."

"You've got to be fucking kidding me," I bark. "Jewel has been complaining to Cookie."

"No, not complaining," says High softly. "Jewel wouldn't do that shit. Cook noticed Jewel wasn't herself today and pried it out of her." He snorts. "Jewel is okay with it, Joker. She's planning to use Mr. Sizzle."

"Mr. Sizzle," I echo angrily. "Who the fuck is Mr. Sizzle?"

High smirks. "Her vibrator. She needs batteries." He takes them out of his pocket and tosses them onto the table. "Cook texted me to pick them up. Take them home with you."

I stare at the batteries as if they're my nemesis. Christ, Mr. Sizzle, her vibrator.

I close my eyes and exhale. "High, I find my woman off-the-charts sexually attractive. Shit, I've been walking around with a goddamn hard-on for the last four weeks." I turn my head, staring at him. "Jackie was teething, and it was damn painful. Then he was traumatized by Marshmallow. I don't know; he started sleeping with us and didn't want to go back to his crib."

"I get that," nods High.

"No, you don't," I sneer. "CJ and Pete had you from the moment your seed entered Cookie's egg. My kid didn't get that because of my fucked-up head. You didn't need to gain your babies' trust. You didn't need to coax them away from their mother so she'd get a break. You didn't need to teach your kids your name is Daddy, not Jo-Jo."

"Daddy," says Jackie, patting my face.

I chuckle and look down at my son. "Daddy."

"Right," nods High. "So tell Jewel all that, and she'll understand. It's not a big deal, Joker. Jewel will use Mr. Sizzle until you get to a good place in your head. Then you can romance her between the sheets, and life will be splendid."

I roll my eyes. "Where in the hell are you getting these words?"

He snickers. "Cookie gets them from Princess and passes them on to me. I'm broadening my vocabulary."

I inhale and exhale a frustrated breath. "I need to figure out how to get Jackie to sleep in his crib without him screaming his goddamn head off. I need to take care of my woman tonight."

"It's tough, bro. Sometimes you need to lay down the law with your kids. The right kind of discipline is love, Joker."

I nod and look down at my son. He gives me a Cheeto smile. *Fuck me.*

CHAPTER 17

IT'S TORTURE – JEWEL

A soak in the tub will be my excuse for alone time. Mr. Sizzle is water-proof, and the jets of the whirlpool will drown out the buzzing. I put my wineglass to my lips and take a swallow. Then I look back down at the design I was drawing on my iPad. It's garbage. I hit the delete icon. "Lord," I moan; I need to get my head in the game. I haven't designed anything worth a damn in weeks.

"Babe, are you all right?"

I look over at the couch. Joker is lying with Jackie, watching a baseball game.

"Yeah." I try to keep my voice light. "Why do you ask?"

He sits up with Jackie. My son's eyes are glassy and heavy-lidded. "You moaned, babe. Are you in pain?"

Pain? I wouldn't call being horny as heck for the last four weeks pain: it's torture! *Lie. And for god's sake, don't look at him.* Joker has developed the annoying superpower of looking at me and knowing what I'm thinking.

"Just a tad of muscle soreness. The boxes were heavy." I doodle on my iPad. "I think I'll soak in the tub for a bit before bed." *Good lord, I suck at lying.*

Joker stands. "I'm going to head up and put Jackie to bed early. I'll run your bath."

That's just GD irritating: It's nine o'clock, a freakin' hour past Jackie's bedtime. When we lived in Malibu, I had Jackie on a schedule —in bed by 8:00 p.m. sharp.

I school my voice, not taking my eyes off my iPad. "No thanks. I'll run it when I come up. I need to finish this sketch. I'll lock up down here and be up shortly."

"Babe," calls Joker. He's leaning down. "Kiss Jackie goodnight."

I smile at my son and kiss his tiny lips. "Mommy loves you, Jackie. Sweet dreams, baby boy."

Joker gives me a lip touch. "Is Beau coming home tonight?"

I shake my head and smile. "He's fly-fishing with Running Deer. He took his satellite phone with him. The number is by the landline."

"Don't stay up too late, babe." Joker retreats through the kitchen and up the stairs.

I roll my eyes and guzzle the rest of my wine.

CHAPTER 18

MR. SIZZLE JUST FIZZLED OUT – JOKER

What the hell happened to communication? I snort. Jewel's doing all her communicating with Cookie. She's taken up lying to me: *Just a tad of muscle soreness. I think I'll soak in the tub for a bit before bed.* As if I don't know she's planning to get off with Mr. Sizzle in the tub. I found Mr. Sizzle in her goddamn makeup vanity, batteries fresh and ready to go. I'm all for toys...I love toys—when we're using them together.

I march down the hall with a bottle of water in hand, Jackie cradled to my chest. Christ, I just need him to sleep in his crib before my life goes to shit. Jewel is young—twenty-eight. I read in Honeypot's *Cosmopolitan* magazine that a woman's sexual peak hits at thirty.

Now that she has her head on straight, her sexual frustration will lead her to stray. There are plenty of townies and Native Americans who wouldn't mind helping her out with that.

I make the turn into Jackie's room and drop down onto the rocking chair. Jewel would go apeshit on my ass if she knew I was giving Jackie a bottle. But desperate times call for desperate measures. I glance at the door. I hope she keeps her ass downstairs until I get him to sleep.

Snuggling Jackie close, I give him the bottle. I start humming. I pray like hell it works for me like it does for Jewel. After five minutes, I think I'm home free. I carefully remove the bottle from his mouth and go to stand. Jackie pops his head up and stares at me. I groan and sit back down, repeating the process.

Christ, Lord Jesus, send me a little help down here.

After another fifteen minutes of rocking, I try again. Holding my breath, I ever so gently pull the bottle from Jackie's mouth. Then I stand at a snail's pace and tiptoe over to his crib. I slowly...slowly... slowly lay him down. He sniffs and scrubs his head against the mattress. I stop and don't dare to move. Once he settles, I back out of the room and close the door with the tiniest click.

I throw my arms up into the air. "Yes!" I hiss and quickly move down the hall. I practically run into the bathroom—no Jewel. Strip and greet her naked in bed? No, she's upset. She might not come upstairs for a while. Strip and go downstairs naked? Let her see the hard-on I've been sporting for four weeks? If we do our initial lovemaking downstairs, there will be less likelihood of us waking Jackie.

I shed my clothes in record time and stare down at my massive erection. *We're getting lucky tonight. Mr. Sizzle, you just fizzled out.*

I jog down the stairs. Jewel is at the sink, washing out her glass.

"Babe," I call softly.

"I'll be up in a sec," she says without turning around.

My cock twitches at seeing her in her low-rise white short shorts. I walk over to her, wrap my arms around her waist, and push my cock into her ass. Then I whisper into her ear, "I heard you had a date with Mr. Sizzle. I canceled it. You'll take your man instead."

She turns her head, trying to look at me. "How did—"

"Babe," I drawl and unbutton her shorts. "I fucked up," I murmur into her neck and push her shorts down, taking her panties with them. "I didn't take care of us." I nuzzle her ear and kiss her neck, running my hands over her abs and pussy. "I thought you knew how much I wanted you." I hum, breathing her in. "You're right; I haven't touched your tits." I slide my hands up and glide them under her tee. I knead her large, firm globes.

"Joker," whispers Jewel. She drops her head onto my shoulder and pushes her breasts into my touch.

"If I would have touched you, nothing would have stopped me from taking you. It wouldn't have factored where we were or who was in the room." I slowly pump my hips, gliding my shaft against the crease of her ass. "It was a mistake I won't repeat. Without me showing my desire for you, there won't be an us. That won't work for me, because I love you. My precious Jewel."

"I love you, too, Cowboy." She turns her head and kisses the bite mark on my shoulder.

"I need you to know." I nip her lips. "No matter what I do to your body." I nuzzle her with my nose. "No matter how hard I take you." I lick her plump lips. "I'm making love to you," I breathe out onto her neck, pumping my hips slowly.

"I know that, Cowboy," she murmurs. Tilting her head, she gives me more access.

A tear runs down her cheek. I lick it away. "Babe, I need you to know another thing: Finlan and Jackie were made with love," I whisper and kiss down her neck. "I didn't say it. I didn't show it. But in my heart, babe, I felt it." Tears run down my cheeks. I hold her tightly, her back to my front. "I don't ever want you or our son—" I shake my head, swallow, and sniff. "I'll rephrase that: Finlan is always with us. I don't want you or our *sons* to ever think I didn't love all of you." I nuzzle my cheek against hers; our tears mingle. "I held our baby and told him, Jewel. I told Finlan how much we loved him and wanted him, babe. I pray our baby boy heard me."

She sniffs and puts her shaky palm to my cheek. "I'm sure he did, Cowboy."

I cup her pussy tenderly. Using my thumb, I run circles around her clit. I let out a tiny chuckle. "I don't know how to do this…I mean, make love to you. Soft and slow, or hard and fast?"

"You be you, Cowboy. You're in charge," whispers Jewel. She turns her head, wanting a kiss. I put my lips to hers. We find our rhythm, entwining our tongues. My groans meld with her moans. Soft kisses turn into open-mouthed, fevered, hungry kisses. Breathily, I tell her, between nips and bites, "I love you…want you…and need you."

Jewel pants into my mouth, "I've always loved you, wanted you, and needed you, Cowboy."

I cup her pussy and inhale deeply. A slight hint of daisies mingled with her sweet pussy perfume fills my nose; I love her scent. It's been over two years, but my cock remembers the feel of my woman's tight warmth. It's rutting between her cheeks with a mind of its own.

I glide two fingers into her, my thumb circles her clit. Jewel throws back her head, gasping.

"Tight…so fucking tight," I growl onto her lips.

Jewel's pussy walls flutter. Her silky cream is flowing, coating my fingers. Her clit pebbles under my thumb. Her breaths turn into short gasps against my shoulder. It's my woman's body calling to me, enticing me to take her.

"On your toes and tip. You need to come," I order and position my cock. In one smooth, powerful thrust, I sheath myself to my root. We both cry out together. Jewel's pussy walls spasm, milking my granite shaft.

My cock thickens, lengthens, and twitches. A light tingling sensation starts at the base of my spine. *Fuck no, I'm not the goddamn one-minute wonder. Not with my woman.*

I stay still and put my forehead between her shoulder blades. I slow down my breathing and take a minute to savor being with my woman. An awareness runs through me: I'm where I should be—home. I kiss her spine and run my tongue around the ridges, tasting her heated skin.

"Cowboy," drawls Jewel breathily. She rolls her head against my shoulder.

I recognize my woman's tone. I've heard it a thousand times. I failed to understand its message—unconditional love for me. After everything I have done and haven't done, my woman still loves me.

I give her spine another kiss and grip her hip. My other hand cups her breast. I do what she loves: give her my cock in powerful, long strokes with a gyration at the end.

"Fuck, I love your tits," I growl and squeeze her left firm globe.

"Ooh, my lord, Jesus," cries Jewel, as her body tightens.

"Go again, babe. Go now," I yell, making my hips fly.

Jewel has one hand white-knuckling the sink. The other she has on my ass cheek, digging her nails into my skin.

"Cowboy!" she screams. Her pussy's clenching around me.

I pull out and carry her to the table. My eyes catch the butter. Her cowboy would butter her up and take her ass. My woman's words run through my mind: *You be you, Cowboy.* I bend Jewel over the table. "Grip the edge, babe."

As Jewel has always done, she does as she's told, with her cheek resting against the cool, smooth surface. My woman doesn't question me. She never has; she trusts me.

I scoop up the butter with four fingers. Spreading her ass cheeks, I place a kiss onto her rosette. Then I slather it with the butter and work two fingers in and out of her...preparing her to take me. Her rosette blooms from my touch. So beautiful.

"Oooo," she hisses and pushes back on my fingers.

I grin. My woman loves her ass fucked by me...only me.

I scoop up another glob of butter and grease my cock with it. "Jesus, fuck," I growl and look down. Christ, it's a goddamn titanium rod. Slow and steady is the way to go.

I spread her cheeks and place a kiss on her tailbone. "Love you, babe."

"Love you, Cowboy."

I grit my teeth, push past her sphincter, and keep going. We both cry out at the extreme pleasure of being coupled in our intimate way.

Jewel's body shutters. She moans, tightening around me.

"Relax," I order through gritted teeth. "Feel me loving you, babe."

I get to my root, deep breathe, and run my hand over her cheeks, hips, and back. Jewel wiggles her ass. It's an unconscious thing her body does, letting me know she's ready for me to ride.

Covering her with my body, I link my muscled arms around her neck. She rests her cheek against my forearm. I learned long ago she likes to be covered by me. Feeling my weight and being held tight during ass-fucking makes her feel safe. I send my hips into action.

"Babe, I feel you. You're getting ready to go." I breathe out into her ear. "If you want to be finger-fucked through your orgasm, you need to lean up."

She shakes her head no. Taking one hand off the table, she reaches up and wraps it around my neck. I kiss the side of her head. Staying deep, I gyrate my hips. She screams my name. Her ass starts sucking my shaft with a vise-grip intensity.

A primal feeling infuses me: I need her pregnant again. I need to be with her from the beginning. The tingles hit my lower spine. I rip out of her ass and plunge into her pussy. Fucking hard and deep, my balls tighten, and my cock jerks. I stop and stay firmly planted. I release my jizz and bellow like a goddamn bull. "Take my fucking seed!" I hump deep, trying my damnedest to impregnate her.

I tremble from the aftershocks of our lovemaking. My cock kicks with each squeeze of Jewel's pussy. I drag in deep breaths, trying to slow my breathing. "Christ." I blow out a long breath and place a soft kiss onto my woman's lips. I nuzzle her and tighten my hold around her neck, giving her the security of my body. Gliding slowly in and out, I murmur, "I love you, babe." I whisper into her ear, "I'm entirely devoted to only you."

She shudders beneath me, her pussy ripples around my sensitive cock.

I drag my nose over her damp heated skin and give her tiny nips and kisses, loving her through her euphoria.

After a few minutes, Jewel inhales and tightens her hold on me. "Cowboy, I love you, too." Then she emits a tiny giggle. "I'm as limp as a buttered noodle."

I laugh. "That was bad, babe." I pull out gently and carry her to the pool. I'll add more chlorine if I need to. I carry her down the steps and sit on the bottom with Jewel leaning against my chest. The warm water laps against us, relaxing us.

"Do you get that I desire you?" I kiss her temple. "That I'm hoping we made our third child?"

Jewel tilts her head up to look at me. "I'm on the pill."

"Come off the pill, babe," I growl, grinning.

"Give me one year, Cowboy." She sighs and relaxes back into me. "Jackie is only thirteen months, and we have the boutique."

"Nope. I'll give you three months," I murmur onto her crown.

She runs her hands up and down the sides of my thighs. "Three months."

I laugh and hold her tight. Two years of drowning in a sea of agony has finally ended: I can breathe.

My mind drifts to Finlan, as it does on most days. Why now? Probably because we're planning for another baby. I don't have as much guilt over everything I've done and haven't done, but I still have enough to cause an ache in my chest.

We didn't find out Jewel was pregnant until she was four months along. For the next two months, I was in a state of denial. High was my voice of reason. He had told me to knock it off; the baby was mine. Six months into Jewel's pregnancy, I had come to my senses. I accepted Finlan. I wanted his mother and him.

I'd catch glimpses of Jewel in those days. Her belly wasn't big, but she had a notable baby bump. I never understood why people said a pregnant woman glowed until Jewel. She was radiant, and the blue strands of her hair shined without the sun. Her eyes appeared to become a deeper violet.

I was aware that, in order to get what I wanted, I needed to get close to Jewel. I needed to apologize for all my mistakes—Honeypot and Marshmallow were among the biggest. But Jewel spent most of her time at Sinners Biker Babe Boutique. She had a studio on the top floor where she'd make her creations. And she avoided me as if I were the plague.

I tried to coerce High into helping me get Jewel alone. He refused. Cookie was Jewel's best friend. High knew it would piss off Cookie; it would cost him his wife's pussy.

I should have kicked Honeypot and Marshmallow out of my bed. Then I should have fallen on my knees and begged for forgiveness. I didn't do that; I went about my business as usual. I was pissed off no one would help me.

When Jewel was seven months pregnant, I received a mass text. Maggie, Cookie, Jillian, Raine, and Princess were planning a surprise baby shower at the club. It irritated me I wasn't told in person. I was unsure of how many people knew I was the baby's father. I learned later, not many. Jewel had only told Cookie, and Cookie told High.

I procrastinated about a gift. When I finally got around to asking Maggie, she pulled out a list. "Sorry, Joker, I don't know. Everyone has signed up for the things on the list." Christ, he was my kid. So I asked about a crib, a dresser, and changing table. Maggie shook her head. "General and Raven have the furniture covered. I'll let you know if I think of something." Turned out, Jewel never got her baby shower. The fucking asshole killed my baby the night before the party.

It was a shitty night—cold and rainy. Cookie was singing at Callaghan's. We all decided to go. Marshmallow was excited because the band had agreed to let her sing one song during Cookie's break. She convinced me to drive her and Honeypot in my truck.

I came into the game room, and Jewel was standing by the bar. Cue Ball had his hand on Jewel's belly, smiling. I saw red; he was feeling my baby move.

I stalked over to the bar and asked him to leave. He went without an argument. Jewel took several steps back, putting distance between us. I asked her if I could feel my baby. She just nodded and didn't move when I came closer to her. I put my hand on her belly. I was amazed at its firmness. Then I felt my son's foot kicking against my palm. An electrical current went straight to my heart: I had an over-whelming love for my son. Marshmallow ran over to us and said we needed to leave. I asked Jewel if she'd let me drive her. She shook her head no. "I have my SUV. I'm not going to Callaghan's. I need to go to the boutique."

During Cookie's break, I went outside and looked over at the boutique. The lights were on. I could see the shadows of two people. I thought it was odd, so I was going to head over. Then High came out and said Marshmallow was getting booed off the stage. He hated

Marshmallow, so he thought it was hilarious. I went back inside with him.

Hours later, we were leaving Callaghan's. The lights were still on in the boutique. I thought it was weird, being after 2:00 a.m. So I ran over to check it out. I thought Jewel had accidentally left them on. I let myself in and found Jewel beaten and unconscious. My son was lying between her legs, bloody, stiff, and blue. Finlan had a full head of wavy blonde hair—my hair.

I totally lost my shit. I tried doing CPR. My screams brought the brothers. I told my son Mommy and Daddy loved him and wanted him. I pleaded with my cold, dead son to come back to us, if not for me, for his mother. I don't remember much else. I was told I wouldn't give up my son's body. The brothers needed to drug me and lock me down for a week. The same amount of time Jewel spent in Butte Hospital. Jewel sustained a hairline fracture to her temporal bone and several cracked ribs at the hands of Briggs. I don't remember begging High to stay with Jewel, but High told me I did. He and Cookie never left Jewel's side.

Tears are streaming down my cheeks. I sniff and wipe them away. I've been given a third chance to be a good father. I don't know why. I am a Sinner—Sinners take care of their family. Above everything else, our women and children come first. I didn't adhere to the code; I didn't take care of mine. Yet I'm being granted a gift—the third time is a charm. I won't fuck it up.

CHAPTER 19

PILL-POPPING THIEF – JOKER

Young people's giggles come from upstairs. Brie and Keeley are fooling around with Jackie. Mafia Man's two girls came over to get ready with their aunt for the grand opening of Sinners Biker Babe Boutique.

"Babe, if you don't want to be late, shake your ass," I yell up the stairs.

Beau chuckles and pours himself a mug of coffee. "I wonder what made her late? It couldn't have been the dirty deed in the shower?"

I chuckle, grin, and adjust my cock. Since Jewel and I "broke the seal," making love has become an essential part of our morning, noon, and nighttime *activities*.

"Cowboy, I can't find my pills...*again!*" laughs Jewel from upstairs.

I snicker. "Babe, don't worry about them. Get a move on." I pull the circular disc from my pocket. Walking over to the sink, I pop the yellow pills into the garbage disposal. I'm aware I agreed to wait three months to make our baby. I've given Jewel one. It has been long enough. Our life together is on track. Jackie is in an excellent place, and the boutique is opening today—it's time to make our third child. Jewel has been going crazy in preparation for the boutique's opening. She didn't need one more thing to fixate on. I'm just taking care of my woman by ditching our birth control.

Beau shakes his head at me. "When are you going to tell her you're the pill-popping thief?"

I chuckle. "My woman knows. She's laughing."

Beau smirks, glancing at me. "Did you get the ten cases of champagne and the flutes to the boutique?"

"Yup. High and I also picked up all the hors d'oeuvres from Raine. Everything is set." I take a gulp of my coffee. "Maggie got the word out to several biker clubs. We set up a display of our custom builds in front of the building. She said the guys can look over the bikes as their women shop—a twofer."

Beau chuckles. "Sounds like her—always the marketer. I hope you put a barrier around the bikes. You don't want people knocking them over or kids climbing on them."

"This morning, Tank, Flame, Tristen, and I strung up a couple of ropes to act as a fence. We'll stay outside to watch over them."

Sinners Bike Shop has gained popularity. Our custom builds have been featured in all the chopper magazines. The Sinners have been offered a reality TV series. We turned it down. We're a one percent biker club with skeletons. We don't need prying eyes poking around in our business.

Beau nods. "Remember, Jewel doesn't want Jackie or herself in any of the photos."

The Sawyer name has died down among the public gossip. However, there are still people who will recognize Jewel as Reagan Sawyer, the urban fashion designer. We're determined to keep Pony as her sanctuary and give our kids a "normal" life. Keeping the name Jewel was a vital component to that—"Reagan" would draw too much attention. The fashion industry would pounce if they knew she was designing again.

Brie comes running down the stairs and twirls all the way over to me. My eyes practically bug out of my head at the look of her. Sinners are not prudish unless it has to do with our female children. Brie is wearing a black tutu and a bedazzled white band around her chest. "Sinners Biker Babe" is splashed in multicolored beads across her budding boobs—they're not breasts. Even so, there's no way she's leaving my house in that getup. She's wearing tons of jewelry: multiple silver chains around her neck, and her wrists are covered in bangles. Good lord, her makeup matches the beads. And her beautiful hair is done up into a sprout of cascading red curls.

"Fuck no! You're thirteen, not twenty-three," I bark and point to the stairs. "Go put on the body thingy Aunt Jewel made for you."

Beau chuckles. "Stocking."

"Bodystocking," I clarify.

When Brie picked out the outfit from Jewel's collection, my woman agreed she could wear the outlandishly provocative getup if she wore a leotard beneath it. Jewel made her one, calling it a bodystocking. Her mother, Maggie, was grateful she didn't need to listen to Mafia Man and Brie battle.

"Uncle Joker," she whines. "It's going to be too hot. It's eighty-five degrees outside. This covers me more than my bikini does."

"I don't give a shit if it's one hundred degrees outside; it's not happening," I growl. "We're the only ones who see you in your bikini. You're not leaving this goddamn house without the bodystocking."

"Papa Beau, tell Uncle Joker I don't have to wear it!"

Beau looks at her, shakes his head, and chuckles.

"Aunt Jewel!" she yells up the stairs and stomps her foot.

"Listen to your uncle. Wear the bodystocking, Brie," yells Jewel down the stairs.

I snicker and watch her stomp back up the stairs.

Keeley emerges on the upstairs landing. She's holding Jackie's hand, getting ready to walk him down.

"Christ." I set down my mug with a loud clunk and run up the stairs. I lift Jackie onto my hip and take Keeley's hand, walking them down.

Keeley's long brown curly hair is wild and free-flowing. I look at her and grin; now that's a cute little Sinner. She's wearing a white tank with "Sinners Biker Babe" printed in colorful beads. Her white shorts have the same-colored handprints covering the legs and butt, with colorful beading surrounding the cuffs. I chuckle at her high-top black Converse sneakers. Obviously, her choice—Keeley is a tiny tomboy.

"I'm not showing anyone my tatas, Uncle Joker." She leaps off the bottom step.

I chuckle and set Jackie onto his feet.

Jackie throws back his head, giggling, "TATA!"

When the kids returned from Malibu, Jackie started talking and hasn't stopped.

Liam laughs as he enters the kitchen with Rocky at his side. They're carrying two small helmets.

"You don't have any tatas, baby doll," chuckles Rocky. He walks over to the coffeepot and pours himself a cup of dark roast.

"Let me guess," snickers Liam. "Brie gave you a hard time over the bodystocking."

"Hm," I hum and check out my son's outfit. My large handprint is covering his butt. I laughed my ass off when Jewel stuck my hand in robin's-egg blue glittery paint and placed it on Jackie's black shorts. It covered the entire backside. Jackie's tee says, "Daddy's Little Biker Boy." The calligraphy is in the same robin's-egg blue glittery paint.

Brie bounds down the stairs. She does a spread eagle with her arms and snaps them down by her side. "Happy, Uncle Joker? I'm going to mega-roast."

I chuckle.

"Lose the attitude, Brie, and get the helmet on," growls Liam. "We need to make tracks. Your mother will be at the boutique."

"OMG, I can't wear the helmet!" shouts Brie. She does the bendy pointy finger thing at her head. "It will smoosh down my hair, Uncle Liam."

I need to bite my bottom lip to keep from laughing. Brie said it as if Liam doesn't understand the importance of looking model perfect.

"Christ," barks Rocky. "Put the goddamn helmet on and move your ass to my bike." He points at her. "That's the end of it, Brie. Not another word."

Keeley rolls her little eyes and runs for her helmet. She removes her shades from inside and yanks it down on her head, not giving a shit about her hair. Then she slides on her Wonder Woman sunglasses and stares up at Liam, waiting for him to buckle her chin strap.

Jewel comes bouncing down the stairs. Christ, she looks sexy as hell. Being my biker babe, she dresses the part: low-rise dark short shorts with a *phat* as hell scalloped silver-studded waistband. Her famous bustier is made of leather and pink silk. She paired it with the wildest hair I've ever seen. Her dark purple makeup makes her violet eyes pop. My cock decides now is the perfect time to become a steel rod in my jeans.

"Aunt Jewel, you'll need to fix my hair when we get to the boutique. Uncle Liam and Uncle Sean are making me wear the helmet!" huffs Brie, her she-devil attitude in play.

That takes care of my hard-on. Lord, when I get Jewel pregnant, I'm praying for another boy.

"Let's beat feet." I grab the harness that tethers Jackie to my chest. Jewel snatches up his helmet, and we're all out the door.

Getting Jackie ready to ride with us is a production. I pop his helmet on his head and buckle his chin strap. Then I slide his mirrored shades onto his tiny face. Next comes the harness that allows me to ride with my hands free. I thread Jackie's arms and legs into the leather straps and then slide my arms into the shoulder straps. Jewel buckles them around my chest and waist. She slides mirrored shades onto my face and then puts on her own. I mount my Dyna and hold out my hand to her. She swings her gorgeous leg over and snakes her hands under Jackie's butt, cupping my junk. I chuckle—her perfect handle.

I look over at Rocky. Brie is bitching at him about needing to wear the safety belt that tethers her to him. "I'll hold tight and won't fall off, Uncle Sean!" I chuckle at him growling and buckling the belt around his waist. Brie didn't get her way again. I don't know why she argues continuously with the adults. She never wins.

Liam has Keeley sitting in front of him, belted against his chest. Nope, she doesn't bitch; she just likes to ride.

I pop the clutch, and we're off. Jewel does several whooping howls. Brie and Keeley answer with their loud, high-pitched shrieks. I laugh, hearing my fourteen-month-old son joining them. He is mimicking Keeley with his tiny fists in the air.

CHAPTER 20

PONY IS A VACATION DESTINATION – JEWEL

Joker swings into the parking lot of the boutique, which is just one big dirt lot for the clapboard buildings: Sinners Bike Shop, Top Gun Securities, and Under the Gun Tattoo, Callaghan's Bar, Sinners Biker Babe Boutique, Sinners Beauty Salon, Pony Motel, and Pony Diner. The buildings are in a horseshoe shape—the property is owned by the Sinners. Butch and Annie lease the space for their diner. Butch's daughter from a previous marriage, Becca, helps the couple run it.

Pony has become somewhat of a destination: Diva Mountain Native American Village opened and brought in scads of visitors.

Tucker-Adams Ranch offers three-day chuck wagon camping excursions, trail rides, and riding lessons, in conjunction with breaking, training, and selling horses. Two of the Sinners' brothers, Robbie and Rascal, manage the ranch because, in reality, it's owned by the Sinners. Herb and Burt managed it up until this year. It became too much for them—not that they would ever admit it. It was their wives who went to General with their concerns. The two men are in their late seventies. Bess and Mable wanted to keep them around as long as possible—their true loves. Now Herb and Bert do what they want, when they want: it isn't unusual to pass by the ranch and see them mending fences.

Running Deer manages the fishing/hunting guide business for the Sinners. More than once, he's called Beau to help him out with the "city slickers." Running Deer says he spends most of his time untangling their lines, removing fishhooks from their hands, and preventing them from shooting each other.

The Sinners and Native Americans aren't overjoyed that Pony is a vacation destination. But it takes a lot of money to keep the Sinners and the Native Americans running in the black. The chief of the Cherokee, Running Bear, said, "It beats having a casino." It irritates Running Bear that they're popping up all over Montana. He fears the Native American culture will one day disappear.

"Babe," calls Joker. He's holding out his hand for me.

I take it and dismount. Multiple bikes are whizzing by us; we should have posted a speed limit. *Right, they're freakin' bikers—rules don't apply.*

"Cowboy." I tilt my head to the Sinners' motorcycles displayed in front of the boutique. "You have several men interested. I don't think you should let them behind the ropes without you."

The bikes that Tristen, Tank, Flame, and Joker custom design are works of art—hand-painted tanks of mountain scenes, half-naked girls, flames, wildlife, or whatever inspires them. Souped-up engines and sweet chrome or black pipes. They cost big bucks, starting at fifty grand.

Joker chuckles. He yells over to Tank and Tristen. Then he tilts his chin toward the bikes.

"On it, brother," shouts Tank.

I take Jackie out of his harness and set him on the ground.

"Me, pop, too," yells Jackie.

"No, Jackie," shouts Joker. He lunges for Jackie and just about topples us both to the ground.

I grab for Jackie as I sidestep to maintain my balance and miss. He's too fast: Jackie's running for the kids who came out of Callaghan's Bar with freeze pops.

Beau manages to catch Jackie by his tee without face-planting into the dirt. "Jesus Christ, grandson," he breathes out and holds Jackie to his chest. A motorcycle races by mere inches from where they're standing.

"Papa, pop, kids," points Jackie.

Flame holds up a handful of freeze pops and yells for the kids to stay together and close to him.

"Unk Fame...Unk Fame," screeches Jackie. His hands are waving high in the air. "Down, Papa!"

"Nope, you're with me for the rest of the day," growls Beau. "There are too many people here and too much traffic for you to be fooling around with the kids. We're going to stay for a bit and then head over to Callaghan's."

I kiss Beau's cheek. "Thanks, Daddy Beau. See if you can work on Jackie's L's."

Beau chuckles. "They'll come when they come."

I look at my badass biker; he's pale. "Hey, Jackie's okay, Cowboy." I run my hand up and down his arm. "I need to head inside. Love you."

Joker kisses my lips and gives me an ass pat. Just like always, my girly parts do a happy dance.

"Babe," he drawls, chuckling. "Do we need the supply closet, or can you wait?"

Lord knows the boutique's supply closet has seen a lot of action in the past few weeks.

I giggle. "I can wait."

"Hm," he hums skeptically. Then he gives me a chaste kiss and walks toward Tristen and Tank.

Yum, lord, he's a sexy hunk of a man. I need to rethink the supply closet.

"Sister, you'd better bring your butt in here before people notice you're drooling over your man's buns," laughs Cookie.

Joker gives Cookie an ass wiggle and a wink.

I laugh and run up the three steps into the boutique.

The store has two levels. The bottom is home furnishings mixed with some clothing. The upper level is all biker babe outfits. Everything in the store is based on the biker theme. Biker babe clothing is sexy, wild, and meant to show skin.

All my biker sisters are here: Maggie, Jillian, Princess, White Dove, Raven, Raine, Cookie, Hialeah, Dana, and, yeah, Honeypot. She's somewhat back in the fold. The Native American girls are also here: Faith, Bluebird, Cottonwood, Awenasa, and Aveline.

Raven hands me a flute of champagne. "Sweetheart, this place looks gorgeous. You and Mika make a great team."

Maggie holds up a tee. "Freakin' fantabulous."

"Sister, that is not going to cover your gargantuan boobs," laughs Princess. She rolls her eyes and takes a sip of her champagne.

I split the tee in half and half-mooned the inner seams, showing off the upper chest and the entire abdomen. Then I made a massive button out of a Harley medal. It holds the tee together at the nipple-line.

Maggie furrows her brow and holds it up to her chest. She examines herself in the floor-to-ceiling mirror.

Jonas stalks over and takes the tee from his mother. He hangs it back on the hook. "That isn't going to cover your pillows, Mom!" he barks in disgust. "It's for Aunt Corrie. She has pancakes." Then he walks off, shaking his head.

We all burst out laughing.

Princess looks at us, giggling. "Should I be offended? My nephew called my boobs pancakes. It didn't sound like a compliment."

Joker comes in and strolls up behind me. "Who called whose tits pancakes?" He slides his hand into my bustier and squeezes my breast. "These are firm, ripe, sweet-tasting melons," he growls into my neck.

"Lord, I don't think Buck has ever equated my boobs to fruit," giggles Raine. She downs her champagne. "It's kind of hot."

I turn in his arms and hug him around his middle. "Did you get an order for a bike?"

"Yeah, a couple." Joker kisses me. "I'm going to open up the doors. High, Mika, Cutter, and Cole will be right in. I told Cutter to take the upstairs with the kids. High and Mika will stay downstairs with you. Cole is on the register."

"Thanks," I say and pucker.

As is Joker's way, he lays a hot, wet kiss on me.

"Lord," says Cookie. She fans herself. "High and I are going to need to borrow your closet if this keeps up."

Joker laughs and cracks my butt on his way to the door.

As soon as Joker opens them up, the place floods with girls and women. I laugh at Brie and Keeley running around with flutes of sparkling apple juice, showing the younger crowd the tees and shorts. High is standing at the door, greeting people, and telling them most of the clothing line is upstairs. Mika is showing off his creations, explaining what materials he used to make them.

Cole is running the cash register. The beeping is continuous. I run over to him; he's fallen behind due to needing to fold, box, and bag the women's purchases. I take up my position and start packaging the items. Then there is a flash. Damn! Someone took our picture.

"Sorry, ma'am, you'll need to delete that," says Cole. "We're not permitting pictures."

"She's Reagan Sawyer, the urban fashion designer from NYC. I'm not deleting it. My friends need proof I met her."

"I'm sorry," I apologize. "I get that all the time. I'm not her. I'm Jewel Frazier." It's a tiny white lie—Joker and I will be married when the time is right.

The woman looks at me, and then the witch googles an old picture of me. She stares at me again. "You are *way* too old to be her." She frowns and deletes the photo.

I'm used to the public being judgy, but Jesus, I'm only twenty-eight. The woman said it as if I have one foot in the grave. *Screw you, lady.*

I package her purchases with a fake smile plastered across my face. "Enjoy the scarves," I say with an airiness to my voice.

The next woman steps up. "Viv is such a bitch. She's always trying to one-up me. You know, because I have a picture of Mick Jagger. I snapped it in the Helena airport." She whips out the photo, showing Cole and me.

I need to bite my lip. I've met Mick Jagger, and that isn't him. I take a closer look. I think it's a woman in drag. I can see the shadow of her boobs.

"Nice," I nod and wrap the outfit she purchased.

"Mommeee," shouts Jackie. He's pointing to the tray of hors d'oeuvres.

I nod. "Papa will help you, Jackie."

The woman stares at him and looks back at me. I see the wheels of recognition turning.

I grin. "Sorry, I'm still not Reagan. Enjoy the outfit, and make sure to check out our website. It's on the card. Next in line, please."

Cole just about ruins the entire thing by choking back a laugh. I elbow him and nod to the woman next in line. She's in her late fifties to early sixties, and she screams old lady: piercings, necklaces, bangles, and rings on every finger. The leather catsuit open to her navel and gray hair tied back with a skull bandana is fabulous—an inspiration for design catsuits with a twist.

The woman hands Cole a card. "It's for the bar and stool set, baby." She turns and points at it.

"Mitzi," calls General from the door.

"Hey, General!" She waves. "Is Raven here?"

Cole and I look at each other. *Okay, they know one another.*

General comes over and gives her a hug. "Raven's at the bar with the grandkids. Is your old man here with you?"

She nods. "Do you think my hunky honey would let me travel this far without him? He's outside with Joker and another young biker. Wait." She shakes a two-inch blood-red fingernail at him, grinning. "The young biker is Tristen?"

General nods, smiling.

"Handsome fucker, like his old man."

I blink and swallow my laughter.

General chuckles.

"Geronimo is buyin' another bike. I figured if he could get a bike, I can get a new bar." She turns and points to the set. "It's cool as fuck, and it'll look badass in the clubhouse." She glances at me. "Who is this dynamo of a designer?"

"Jewel is Joker's woman," grins General.

I hold out my hand. "Hello, Mitzi. It's a pleasure to meet you."

"Joker caught himself a pretty hot piece of ass," cackles Mitzi. "It's nice to meet you, too, hon. General, give me two secs; I'm holdin' up the line." She turns to Cole. "Will you take a check, baby?"

General chuckles. "Give me the tag. I'll settle up with Geronimo."

"Thanks, sweets." She hands General the tag. "I need to ask Mr. Handsome behind the register about delivery." She turns back to Cole. "We're on the bike."

"Mitzi, you're covered," laughs General. "Go see Raven. I'm going to shoot the shit with your old man."

Mitzi gives General a quick hug, and then she struts off on her three-inch high-heeled biker boots. The way she's swaying her hips, I hope she doesn't dislocate one of her joints. I pull out a sold sign and hand it to General. "There you go, sweets," I laugh.

General rolls his eyes and looks at the tag. He whistles low. "Give me two more for the Harley sign and the tire chandelier. They're on us. Geronimo is dropping a ton of green today."

I grin and hand him a pair of scissors to cut the tags and two more sold signs.

"Sir," says the woman standing next to General.

The lady is probably in her thirties. She's a pretty, blonde-haired, big-boobed, heart-shaped-ass woman.

General turns. The lady dumps the pile of clothes she's holding into his arms. Then she intertwines her arm with his and drags him over to the dresser. "The candelabras, do they come with the candles?" she asks in a wispy voice. Her eyes are all over him. They linger a bit too long on his crotch.

It's not surprising the woman would be interested; General is a muscled, handsome, Irish, badass biker. But the look he's giving her is hilarious. Cole and I burst out laughing.

Joker, Tristen, and Geronimo come through the front door. They stop and stare at General with the woman. The lady's lust-filled googly eyes are staring up at General as if he's the man of her dreams—her biker prince charming. Joker, Tristen, and Geronimo break out in a fit of laughter.

"Jewel, Christ," barks General. He's trying to get loose from the woman's grasp.

"Coming," I sing, still laughing. I remove the woman's arm and take the clothes from General. The poor lady looks deflated. "The candles are included with the candelabras. Very romantic, don't you think? Would you like both of them?"

She nods and looks around for her next target. Her eyes land on my man. *Oh, no, honey, he's taken.*

"Sorry, they're all married," I lie and smile. "Let me ring up your purchases. Cowboy?" I tip my head toward the candelabras. "Ask one of the *girls* to bring me those."

She sighs, grabs a flute of champagne, and follows me to the register. "These men, they're all Sinners?"

I look at Cole. He's keeping his head down and his mouth shut. He doesn't want to be her next victim.

"Hm," I hum and ring up her items.

She smiles at me. "Do you live in Pony? With the Sinners?" She leans her hip against the counter. "I see how you stay in shape. The sex must be off the charts with these gorgeous bikers."

Keeley comes over and points to a young teen. "These are hers." She flops an outfit down onto the counter. "She wants them saved while she looks around for more stuff." Then Keeley glares up at the woman. "My Aunt Jewel jogs every morning to stay in shape. She doesn't do the dirty." Keeley spins on the balls of her feet. She's off, finding another customer to help.

"I need a minute," chokes out Cole. He turns around and laughs into his arm.

"Too bad for you, Aunt Jewel." The woman goes back to ogling the men while sipping her champagne.

I refrain from rolling my eyes. *Good lord, horny women.*

CHAPTER 21

JEWEL'S MISSING – JOKER

Sweat is pouring off me as I pace and stare at the tracking app on my phone. Jewel has been gone for two and a half hours. According to the app, she hasn't moved in ten minutes.

Every nerve in my body is buzzing on full alert. Jewel and I are connected; it's like some freaky sixth sense we've developed. I know something happened to her. I run my finger over the image of the trail High, Beau, Rene, and I cut through the woods. It leads to High's house.

I hit the call button again. "Come on, answer. Just answer the goddamn phone."

Beep...It's Jewel. I'll get back to you after I'm done loving on my hunky Cowboy. She giggles. *Leave a message. Beep...*

I close my eyes. *Find your fucking center.* I deep breathe, filling my lungs with the pine-scented mountain air, and lock down my fear. I walk back inside to the game room. Unlocking the cabinet, I grab my M4A1 rifle. Then I do a mass text to the brothers and Native Americans:

Me: *Jewel went for a jog, and she's missing. I'm headed out to find her. LKL-trail to High's house.*

Texts come in from the brothers and Native Americans:

General: *The lads are on horseback. Brothers are on bikes.*
High: *Keep it tight, brother. I'm running. Meet you in the middle.*
Flame: *The old man and I are on horses.*
Burt: *Cowboys are riding.*
Running Bear: *Braves are on their way.*

I grab the kid carrier and run upstairs for Jackie. He's napping.

Jackie doesn't usually take morning naps. We went to the club to celebrate after we closed Sinners Biker Babe Boutique. The grand opening was a huge success.

Geronimo, Mitzi, and the Red Devil brothers were invited back to spend the night. Blade and the Whitefish Sinners were there. We partied until 2:00 a.m. and then came home. Jackie was exhausted from playing with the kids. Jewel didn't want to interrupt his usual routine— sleeping in his own bed.

There's no help for it; I need to wake him and look for Jewel.

I lift Jackie out of his crib. "Hey, baby boy. We need to go for a jog and look for Mommy," I say softly.

He rubs his eyes and looks at me. "Daddy, wunch."

I kiss his forehead. "We'll have lunch after we find Mommy." I grab his baseball cap and shades and quickly put them on him. Then I settle him into the carrier, swing it onto my back and run back down the stairs.

"Beau," I breathe out, glancing at the number taped by the landline. He left this morning to help Running Deer and ten "city slickers" fly-fish.

Call or wait? Wait 'til I have intel. I grab my rifle and jog out the door, down the steps, and onto our driveway.

"Hold on, Jackie. We're running," I order and pick up my pace.

Jackie is bouncing on my back with his little hands gripping my hair. I make the right turn into the woods. The path is four feet wide and worn from High, Beau, Rene, and me running it every morning.

High's parents, Rene and Dana, love Jewel. They hate when she runs alone. I do too, but Jewel insisted on us guys running together. "Cowboy, the four of you push each other. I jog slower. I'm good with running alone. No worries."

I made my woman a deal: if she stopped jogging with Jackie on her back, she could run the trail solo. Jewel agreed, and we fell into a routine. In the morning, Jewel and I make love, and then Beau, High, Rene, and I go for a morning run while Jewel gives Jackie his breakfast and does what she calls a "spot clean" to our home. When I get back, she goes for her morning run while I get Jackie and me ready for the day. When Jewel returns, she showers. Then Beau, Jewel, and I discuss what we have going on for the day as we down our smoothies and protein bars.

We're out the door by eight o'clock—Jewel and Jackie at the boutique, Beau at the club (unless he decides to take a job as a guide, or hunt, or fish, or fly his plane or his helicopter), and me at the garage.

My feet hit the earth in a rhythmic pattern, heel to toe. I inhale for three strikes, exhale for two strikes. I concentrate on the sounds around me, listening for Jewel. The breeze rustles the leaves on the trees. The birds are squawking, and the animals are chittering.

A mile into the woods, I stop. "Jewel!" I shout and glance at my phone. Nope, she hasn't moved; the dot is four more miles up the path.

"Mommeee! Wunch!" screeches Jackie.

We wait for a beat and get no answer. Dread creeps up my spine. For some goddamn reason, I can't get Briggs's name out of my mind. Fuck, the asshole is in prison; he can't hurt her. I wipe the sweat off my brow with my forearm and force myself to focus.

"Let's go, Jackie." I start running again, only this time, I force myself to pick up the pace.

Every mile marker, I stop and call out to Jewel. Jackie does the same. We wait and get nothing.

I need to tamp down my rising panic and control my nerves. Losing it with my son on my back isn't an option.

I exhale and scan the ground. I look for any clues: blood, hair, broken branches, or trampled foliage. Nothing!

We get to the five-mile mark. I drop to my knees and stare at Jewel's phone. It's in the middle of the trail, lying faceup with a cracked screen. A foot away, there is a darkened clump of earth, six inches in diameter. I pick up Jewel's cell with a shaky hand. My heart is thudding painfully; my chest tightens, making it impossible to take a deep breath. Bile rises in the back of my throat. I force it back down and spit.

"Joker!" shouts High.

I look up the trail; High is almost to us.

"Don't move, brother. Just stay where you are and give me a minute to survey the area."

Right, I need to look for clues.

I cup my hands around my mouth. "Jewel! Babe, answer me!" I wait a few seconds and get nothing. I call her name repeatedly. Jackie is echoing my call, adding, "Wunch time!"

"High, take the right side of the forest. I'll take the left."

He nods and gives me a shoulder squeeze. "We'll find her."

High and I push through the foliage, careful not to disrupt any clues that might lead to Jewel's whereabouts.

The whine of dirt bikes, the rumble of Harleys, and horses' hoofs are coming from each end of the trail.

High and I come out of the woods to meet the brothers, Native Americans, and cowboys.

Jackie starts bouncing, excited to see his grandfathers, uncles, and cousins on horses.

High walks over to the men, giving them what we know, which isn't much. "There's a darkened area a foot from where Joker found Jewel's phone. I think it might be dried blood. That's the only blood we found. There aren't any drag marks, and the foliage hasn't been disturbed, so I'm reasonably sure Jewel wasn't attacked by an animal."

Hawk leaps off his horse and walks over to the clump of darkened earth. He crouches and takes a bit, rubbing it between his two fingers and thumb. I crouch next to him and watch as he checks the color—red. Then he tastes it. He nods. "It's human blood."

General's looking around. "If Jewel is hurt and disoriented, she might have gone off the trail. She could be lost in the woods."

Flame leaps off his horse. "We need to do this on foot. If Jewel passed out, we don't want to trample her or ride over her. Spread out, six feet apart, comb the woods. If you see something or hear something, stay where you are, shoot off three shots, and text. A tracker will come to you."

The men dismount and tie their horses to the tree branches. I glance at them. They're heading into the woods six feet apart with their eyes darting around them. I catch a glimpse of Becca, Butch, and Annie.

Becca looks at me. She gives me a reassuring smile and a thumbs up.

Tristen leaps off his horse. "Hey, Jackie. Let me take you from Daddy."

"Triz, wunch," says Jackie.

"S's and L's are a bitch to pronounce," chuckles Tristen. "What do you say I have Brainiac take you back to the house? Grandma Raven will give you lunch."

"Daddy run...Mommy wunch," he explains and pats my head. Then he screams, "Mommeee, wunch time. Mommeee, come, wunch."

I bow my head and put my face into my hands, deep breathing. Tears are stinging my eyes; my nose starts to run.

"We're going to find her," growls High into my ear.

I swallow and sniff. I wipe my eyes on my forearm, and my nose on my tee.

Jonas and Brainiac run over to us.

"Hey, Jackie," says Jonas in an over-the-top upbeat thirteen-year-old tone of voice. "DJ, Gee, and JT are at your house waiting to play with you. They brought Cheetos and orange soda."

I sniff again. Pinching my nose, I can't help but grin. Jackie loves junk food and soda. Jewel and I don't give it to him, but the kids do.

Tristen and Brainiac slide the kid carrier off my back. I pull myself together for Jewel and Jackie.

I turn, smile at my son, and kiss his tiny lips. Then I run my thumbs over his eyes—his mother's beautiful eyes. "Go with Brainiac, Jonas, and Papa Pick." I give him a sly smile and poke his belly. "Don't you eat too many Cheetos and turn into a cheeseball on me."

Jackie throws back his head, giggling wildly.

I kiss his forehead and breathe him in. A hint of Jewel's daisy perfume is mixed with my light spice cologne and Jackie's unique scent. "Take him. Pick, call Beau. The satellite number is by the landline."

"Wuv you, Daddy!"

I blink several times and force back my tears. "I love you more, Jackie."

Brainiac kisses me. "Love you, uncle." He swings the kid carrier onto his back. "I'll be back when I have Jackie settled." He mounts his horse and follows Jonas. Pick is bringing up the rear.

I stand and head into the forest with Tristen, High, and General. Shoulder-to-shoulder, we comb the woods.

General cups his hands around his mouth, yelling, "Reagan!" He shouts it to the north, south, east, and west.

"She won't answer to Reagan," I murmur, my eyes on the ground. "It reminds her of all the bad shit."

"She might if she has a head injury, brother," whispers High. He squeezes my shoulder. "We need to try everything."

A half hour into the search, I get the call I was dreading—Beau.

I clear my throat. "Beau." It comes out as a croak.

"Joker, did you find her?" At least his voice sounds strong.

"Nope," and my fucking voice cracks.

"I'm headed home. I just need to get these people to a safe place. Keep looking, and call if you find anything."

"Yup," I croak and blink rapidly. My goddamn eyes are filling with tears.

"Joker, I love you. We'll find her. Keep it tight until I get home. Later."

I slide my phone back into my pocket. "Daddy Beau."

General chuckles. "Are you going to start calling him that, too?"

"Nope. He's my brother, my woman's adopted father, and my son's grandfather." I grin and return to looking.

~

Hours of searching has turned up nothing. I rub my forehead and stare up into the sky. The sun is starting to set in the west. Tremors of fear run through me; my heart picks up speed. We won't be able to search without the sun. The forest will become a dark, dangerous place for my woman—wolves, grizzlies, and mountain cats. Jewel will be terrified. She doesn't know anything about surviving in the goddamn woods. She's never even been camping. I won't leave these fucking trees without her.

POW! POW! POW!

"Three rounds from a high-powered rifle." General looks at me. "Sounded like they came from the south."

All our phones buzz with a text:

Butch: *Becca found boot prints, one silver and white running shoe, and blood. We're on the south side, just inside the tree line. Need a tracker.*
Flame: *Stay where you are, Butch. Wolfe, Hawk, Tank, and I are on our way.*

I start running, mindless of the branches whipping my face or the thorns ripping at my calves. Butch found Jewel's running shoe. There was blood and boot prints. *Briggs...Briggs...Briggs* thunders in my head.

"Joker, goddamnit!" High bear-hugs me and takes me off my feet. "Think, dammit! We need to look for clues!"

"Dad! Over here!" shouts Tristen.

I run my hand over my mouth. High's right; there are clues in these woods. I look over at Tristen. He's by a boulder, examining something on the ground.

I walk over and look down. Furrowing my brow, I stare at the four-foot gold-and-brown diamondback. "A prairie rattler with its head severed."

General nods and searches the ground.

"Jewel couldn't have cut off its head. She doesn't carry a knife. And she's terrified of snakes," I say, more to myself than the others.

"The snake hasn't been dead for that long. A free meal doesn't last in these woods," says General. He picks up a piece of cloth—a camo pant leg.

"I think the bastard got bit. Judging from the length of the pant leg, he probably got it in the calf. The fucker will be sick, if not dead." General points to the gap beneath the boulder. "The stupid bastard didn't know snakes rest under boulders, where it's cool."

"Let's move," I demand. "We're not that far from the tree line."

We walk another hundred yards, and I hold up my hand to stop. The ground is softer here. There are four boot impressions. General and Tristen drop to the ground. High and I follow them down.

"Tristen, what do you see?" asks General.

Tristen runs his finger lightly over the impressions. "Two sets of footprints. The assholes were walking side by side. Definitely, one is male. Size eleven boot. Non-military tread. The other may be a small male or a female. Size…" He hums and stares at the print.

I take over. "Probably a woman's ten. Jewel wears an eight; it looks a couple sizes larger than hers." I examine the prints. "The guy was bit in the left leg. The right impression is deeper. His left imprint is flat. He's also carrying something. His right heel strike is deep, and he's pushing off with his toe. The other asshole is a woman; she's used to wearing heels. Her heel strikes are light. She is carrying her weight on the balls of her feet."

General smirks. "The Army Rangers taught you well, Joker."

"Flame taught me," I snort. "The Army Rangers didn't teach me shit about tracking."

High runs his finger around the male's print. "How much weight are you thinking the asshole is carrying?"

"The fucker is carrying my woman," I growl. "Let's move."

137

We get to the tree line. Becca, Annie, and Liam are looking at the sneaker, footprints, and blood spatter.

"Liam," shouts General. "Find anything new?"

Liam nods. "A few strands of Jewel's hair on a branch. The men are dredging the marsh." He tips his chin toward a small swampy area.

I sprint to it. Flame is in the water with the Sinners, Native Americans, and cowboys. They're pushing back the weeds, searching the bottom. I grab a stick and head in.

Fuck, please don't let us find her here. Please, God, please not here.

My feet sink into the mud up to my ankles. Cool water fills my sneaks. I push back the weeds and keep my eyes locked onto the muddy bottom.

Jewel's smiling face enters my mind. She's making the L sound for Jackie. *"We la-la-la-love Daddy!"* And then the S sound: *"Daddy's our s-s-s-Superman!"*

I choke. My eyes fill with tears. My woman's violet eyes shine up at me. *"I love you, Cowboy."*

"You're not going to fucking come unglued," High growls as he pushes the weeds out of the way. "And you're not giving up hope. She's fucking alive."

I wipe my nose on my palm and continue to search. The sun is setting, making it more challenging to see. Brothers whip out their phones and shine their lights down into the murky water while others push the weeds aside.

"Uncle Joker," yells Brainiac from two hundred yards away. "Scottie and I found footprints and tire tracks over here."

Mafia Man runs to the area. He bellows, "Flame, Joker!" His shadowy form is crouched beside his sons. "You need to see this. I'm not an expert. There are boot prints at what I think are the passenger door, back door, and driver's side door."

I rush out of the swamp and stumble.

Liam catches my arm, preventing me from doing a face-plant. "Calm, brother. Losing your head won't find her."

I walk over and drop to my knees, examining the prints. The sun is just about gone. With a shaky hand, I yank out my cell and hit the flashlight icon.

Flame is beside me, shining his flashlight onto the ground. "The tracks are fresh. The earth hasn't had a chance to dry. Tank!" he yells. "Come here and look at the tracks."

Tank comes over and squats by my side. He jabs his flashlight icon and scratches his head. "Best guess, it was a Jeep with a short wheel-base—Wrangler." He points out the four six-inch-long deeper indentations of the tracks. "The earth sunk a bit when it was parked. Standard issue—off-the-assembly-line, fifteen-inch, all-terrain tires. The fuckers have a balance issue. The tires are scalloped."

"Any thoughts, Flame?" asks Pick. He bends over and rubs Flame's neck.

Pick is the Sinners' vice president and Flame's father-in-law. But, in reality, he is just as much Flame's father as he is Princess's. Flame's mother is Pick's woman. They all live together with Flame and Princess's five kids.

Flame stands and pinches the bridge of his nose. "I think the asshole loaded Jewel into the back seat. The male got into the passenger seat. The woman was driving."

"Why?" asks Brainiac. "Are they fucking creepers?"

"No, I don't think so," says Guard Dog. "If the assholes wanted Jewel dead, they would have killed her in the woods." He sucks in a breath and blows it out slowly. "I think they know who she is—Reagan Sawyer. Best guess, someone will get a ransom call—Joker, Devilan, High, or Beau. They control her money. We need to examine every-thing that happened yesterday at the opening."

Geronimo steps out of the shadows. Christ, I thought he and Mitzi would have been gone by now.

He pulls a pack of Marbs from his tee and flicks a lighter, lighting one. The tip glows red as he takes a long drag. "You think the assholes were at the boutique's opening?" he asks in his gravelly voice.

"Yeah," nods Guard Dog. "The kidnapping was planned. The fuckers knew Jewel's routine. They couldn't have done surveillance up here. Beau, Joker, Mika, High, and more than half the brothers would have noticed them. Someone is always coming and going from Joker and Jewel's house. The best place to gain intel and stay under the radar was at the opening. Maybe Jewel talked about jogging on the trail to one of the girls, and the fuckers overheard her. Or maybe one of the girls was talking about Jewel jogging. They're concerned about her hip."

Geronimo furrows his brow. "What's wrong with Jewel's hip?"

"She has a titanium left hip," says General. "I'll give you the intel on the way back."

"Let's head back to your house and pull up the video footage of the boutique," says Guard Dog, sounding tired as hell. "We'll talk to the girls and see if we can jolt their memories. We won't notify the state police. They're pains in the asses and would get in our way. The county marshal is useless. He usually comes to us for help."

I push the heels of my palms into my eye sockets with *Briggs... Briggs...Briggs* still thundering through my mind.

CHAPTER 22

TAKEN – JEWEL

Ice cold water splashes over my body, drenching me. I jolt upright; my right hand flies up to my head, my left down to my hip. I moan—daggers of pain slice through my brain. Sharp, jabbing pain radiates from my left hip down to my thigh.

A plastic pail bounces onto the wood floor next to me.

"Bitch, wake up!"

I want to tell whoever is screaming at me to shut the hell up. Nausea and dizziness assail me. I hold my head and squeeze my eyes shut, breathing deeply.

The person gives my left hip a hard kick. I scream or try to—all that comes out is a raspy cry. Black spots dance behind my eyelids. *Slow your breathing: in...one, two, three. Out...one, two, three...*

"What do you know about snakebites?" shouts the woman.

Snakebites? What the hell is she talking about? I'm not a doctor.

"Nothing," I moan and continue to hold my head.

"Nothin'?" barks the woman incredulously. "You live out in the middle of fuckin' nowhere. You run in the goddamn woods, and you don't know *anythin'* about snakebites?!"

"No," I groan, wishing she'd shut up.

"Fuckin' perfect! This is just my luck!" she yells; her shadow passes by me continuously. Like a lunatic, she rants, "'It'll be easy,' he said. 'We'll just grab her on the trail.'" She snorts. "'All you need to do is tell the rich bitch you're lost. I'll do the rest,' he said. 'We'll call whoever's in charge. Ask them for ten mil. They'll pay. Argentina, here we come! Livin' the good life, suckin' down mojitos, and watchin' the waves roll in, baby.'" Her shadowy form stops in front of me. "Now look at him. He's fuckin' unconscious, sweatin' all over the place, with his goddamn leg ten times the size it oughta be."

I crack my eyes open. The light makes my head pound in agony. I squint and look at the bed. A thirty-something man is lying on it. His leg, or what should be his leg, is blue. Like the witch said, it's ten times its normal size. The guy is pale and waxy; he looks dead.

I close my eyes; it's too much effort to keep them open.

"Hey, bitch, wake up. Open your eyes. I need to talk to you!"

I force my eyes open, not wanting the witch to kick me or throw cold water on me again. I try to lick my lips; I have no saliva. My mouth is a desert—my tongue is sandpaper.

"Water," I croak and try to swallow.

"Water. The golden goose would like bottled water," she says with airy sarcasm. Her light breeze whizzes by me. "Now I'm a fuckin' servant."

The way she said it, airily, niggles at my foggy brain. I've heard her voice before. *Think! Where?*

"There you go, madam." The woman drops the bottled water in my lap. "Sorry it isn't the fancy water you like—Perrier."

My hands shake. They rattle a chain. *No-no-no!* I look down at my right wrist and moan—yes, I'm handcuffed. I turn my head gingerly and follow the chain. It's padlocked to an iron potbelly stove. I swallow and try to remove the bottle's cap. It's no use; my hands are too weak.

I hold the bottle out; the thing feels like it weighs fifty pounds. "Will you remove the cap, please?"

The woman snatches the bottle from me and bitches about needing to unscrew the cap. "Here," she barks.

I take the water between my shaky hands and drink greedily. Its coolness soothes my throat and tongue. I glance at the label—Moose Mountain.

Why do I know that name? Think! A memory comes to me: Dad and Beau are in the game room. Beau was telling Dad about the city people he took fly-fishing. "I set them up in Moose Mountain cabins. Moose River doesn't run too fast, and it's not deep enough for them to drown. The cabins are set back into the woods. It gives the city boys a camping experience without roughing it." Dad and Beau laughed about the city guys driving thirty minutes to get to Butte. "The men were tired of the outdoor life; they wanted to eat at a five-star steak house."

Beau and Running Deer are guides for ten city slickers. *Are they here? On Moose Mountain?* It wouldn't matter if they were—there's no way for me to alert them. I'm chained to an iron stove. Even if I screamed my head off, no one would hear me.

My left hip feels as if it's leaning against shards of glass. I hiss and try to get into a more comfortable position on the hardwood floor. We're in a single-room cabin. The smell of pine tells me we're in the woods.

"Who is in charge of your money?" demands the woman.

"Money." She wants money. My cottony brain drifts to Joker and me sitting at the kitchen table. I had Princess add his name to everything: bank accounts, stock portfolios, life insurance policies, and real estate deeds. I also had Princess rescind the custody agreement. He's Jackie's father and my man for eternity.

"Jewel, I don't want your fucking money," said Joker. I replied, "Sorry, Cowboy. I'm sort of old fashioned: a couple shares everything. You'll handle the money, house repairs, and yardwork. I'll handle the cooking, cleaning, and laundry." Then I giggled. "You can complain about me running up the credit cards; I'll complain about you not taking out the garbage." At that, he threw back his head and laughed. The next day he came home with legal documents: I had been added to his bank accounts, stock portfolio, and life insurance policy. He wanted

Beau to fly us to Vegas to be married. I said I wanted to be married at the club. "Daddy Beau needs to give me away." Beau growled and grinned at me. "Never."

I close my eyes and rub my forehead. "Cowboy."

"Cowboy?" she snaps. "The hunky Brad Pitt look-alike at the boutique?" She says, wistfully, "*A River Runs Through It* and *Fight Club* are two of my favorite movies. *Benjamin Button* was too weird —creepy."

I groan. I remember her now. She was the woman hanging all over General: *The candelabras, do they come with the candles?* I bet she paid with a stolen credit card.

CHAPTER 23

BRIGGS'S SISTER – JOKER

I set Jackie's toybox in the game room. He's been clinging to me; he knows something isn't right. He was upset when he woke up this morning and didn't find his mother at home. All the girls and kids tried to help, but Jackie wouldn't even let Beau feed him his breakfast. He only wanted me.

Raven and Mitzi come into the game room carrying trays of coffee, fruit, yogurt, and protein bars.

Mitzi walks over to Geronimo. He's lounging in one of the recliners; his attention is on the morning news. "The girls and I will start cooking in a bit, baby." She whispers, "I think they're health nuts. Their fridge is filled with organic fruit, yogurt, and veggies. They have a fuckin' five-pound tub of organic protein powder on the counter."

Geronimo chuckles and pats her ass. He takes a mug of coffee. "This is good, baby."

"Here." She hands him a protein bar. "I tasted them. They're peanut butter with dark chocolate mini chips. They could use another cup of sugar, but they're edible."

"Jewel doesn't put sugar in them. She uses honey," I grumble with my eyes pinned to Jackie.

"They're delicious, sweets. It's good to eat healthy." I catch the eye roll she gives to Geronimo.

I snort and do my own eye roll. I can't be pissed at Mitzi. She was the one who informed us Debra Briggs was Richard Briggs's sister. It was a total fluke. We made it back to the house just as Beau was riding up to it. Beau has Herculean strength—he locked down his rage and kept me from coming unglued multiple times. It was late, after 10:00 p.m. Somehow, Cookie managed to put Jackie to bed. I wanted all the brothers to take their families home. That wasn't happening—no one went home or back to the club. Beau and I gave them the upstairs. It wasn't as if we were going to sleep.

Mafia Man, the computer whiz, downloaded the video footage of the boutique's opening. Then he connected Jewel's laptop to the flat screen in the game room. When the video started rolling, Mitzi got closer to the TV.

"Stop it for a sec, will you, hon?" She turned to Geronimo. "I think that's the woman who was arrested for squatting in..." She snapped her fingers, trying to think. "Baby, you remember...the young, good-looking fucker from Britain that Dakota has a crush on." She wrinkled her nose, humming. "Come on, baby, you fuckin' know his name."

Geronimo snorted. "How the fuck would I know his name, Mitzi? You're the one who watches that shit with Dakota."

"Come on, baby. You fuckin' know it. He played that superhero in Jewel's father's movie—*Revenge*. He was fighting the evil bastard while hanging off the gondola."

"Josh Crawford," laughed Brainiac. "Brie has a huge crush on him, too."

"It was six years ago. E! reported that Crawford's Malibu beach house was broken into and squatters lived there for over six months." Mitzi squeezed her eyes shut, snapping her fingers again. "Bridges... no...shit. Braggs...no, that wasn't it. Briggs!" she shouted. "Debra Briggs."

The whole room went silent; no one moved. My glass of seltzer water hit the floor and shattered into a million pieces.

Mitzi glanced at Geronimo. "What the fuck is going on?" she whispered with just her lips moving.

After the shock, motherfucking rage infused me. "That didn't come out in the fucking trial."

Mafia Man grabbed the computer and worked his magic on the dark web. It turned out, Debra and Richard Briggs were born in Oakland, California. Their mother split when they were young. She left them with their alcoholic father. Ten years later, Briggs senior was stabbed to death in his sleep by his girlfriend—a known prostitute with an arrest record a mile long.

Debra Briggs has a record: stolen credit cards, petty larceny, and passing bad checks. She did three months in the county jail for breaking and entering into Crawford's home. It got even better when Mafia Man found a picture of her boyfriend, Alton Judd. He had been chatting Cutter up on how to become a Sinners' brother. He boasted about how badass he was in the Army. Cutter shut him down. He thought the guy was just an asshole talking smack. It turned out he was Richard Briggs's best friend throughout grade school. Judd was never in the Army: he was a clerk at the Army Navy store for a couple of weeks, until he got caught with his hand in the cookie jar.

Mafia Man broke into the DMV records and found nothing on Debra or Judd, other than they did have driver's licenses. Richard Briggs, however, owned a 2006 Jeep Wrangler that was no longer registered or insured. It probably has stolen plates.

Patriot, Guard Dog, and Rocky flew out this morning with ten of the brothers. They're going to Oakland to get intel on Debra Briggs and Alton Judd. Princess, Flame, and Pick are in the office. They're trying to get permission from the warden to interrogate Richard Briggs.

The Sinners and the Red Devils are scouring every motel, hotel, hospital, clinic, urgent care, and veterinary clinic. Judd was bitten by a venomous snake. If he's alive, he'll need medical care.

"Hey," murmurs Raven. She kisses my forehead. "You haven't slept a wink in over twenty-four hours. How about lying down on the couch to rest your eyes. Sean will watch your phone. If there's a text or a call, he'll wake you."

I shake my head no. "I'll just take a coffee. Thanks."

"Yeah, I knew you'd say that." Raven sighs. "Can I get you to eat a protein bar? They're healthy," she giggles.

"No," I laugh and take a gulp of the coffee.

I look over at my son; he's taking toys out of his toybox. He pulls out a cell and puts it to his ear. "Hewoo, Mommy. When you come home?"

Beau looks at me. "Did you give him a burner phone to play with?"

"No." I get up, walk over to Jackie, and drop down on the floor next to him.

"Mommy, Daddy turn. Wuv you." Jackie holds the phone up. "Your turn, Daddy."

"Thanks, baby boy." I kiss his forehead. Then I examine the Trac-Fone. It's cheap, the kind you can pick up at a gas station. I jab the power button. Nothing happens—drained battery.

"Jackie," I say softly. Christ, I don't want to scare him. "Can you tell Daddy where you got the phone?"

He nods exaggeratedly. "Work."

"Mommy's work? The boutique?"

He nods again and reaches for the phone. "My turn."

It could be anyone's cell. There were hundreds of people in and out of the boutique during the grand opening.

I pick up his play phone and try to hand it to him.

"No, Daddy. I found. Unk Cut. Ground. Mine."

"You found the phone on the ground by Uncle Cutter?"

He nods again. "Mine."

JT runs over to us and plops down on his butt. "Hey, Jackie. Want to trade a bag of Cheetos for your phone?" JT swings the bag in front of Jackie.

I look over my shoulder; Liam is smiling.

My son looks at JT. "Orange."

"You want Cheetos *and* an orange soda?" asks JT, disbelievingly. "For *one* phone?"

Jackie nods and holds up four fingers and his thumb. "One."

I chuckle. I can't believe my fourteen-month-old knows how to negotiate. I push down three of Jackie's fingers and his thumb. "One." I kiss his tiny pointer finger.

"I don't know, Jackie, that cuts into my stash," says JT in his six-year-old badass way.

"JT!" growls Liam. "Make the deal."

"Okay, Jackie. It's a deal." JT holds out his hand. "Shake on it." My son takes his hand, throws back his head, and giggles.

Mafia Man brings over a sippy cup and hands it to me. I give him the TracFone.

"My son is eating Cheetos and drinking soda at nine in the morning," I bitch.

"Yup," nods Mafia Man, chuckling. "I'll hit the internet to see where we can buy a cord for this."

Jesus! I open the bag of Cheetos and hand Jackie one.

CHAPTER 24

RICHARD BRIGGS'S INTEL – JOKER

Princess comes running into the game room. "Hurry, Schnooks. Hook the computer up to the big screen. I want to see the asshole. Mom!" she shouts.

"Corinne, you're screaming the house down," scolds Hialeah. "What do you need, daughter?"

"Take Jackie, Mom. I don't want Briggs to see him. He's a freakin' psychopath."

Hialeah stares at Princess. "Briggs, the monster that just about killed Jewel twice? The devil that took our baby from us? You think he had something to do with Jewel's kidnapping?"

"I don't know!" Princess gives her big eyes. She's clearly agitated. "Take Jackie. Go, go, go!"

I hand Jackie to Hialeah. "Go with Grandma Hi. I'll come and get you after we're done on the phone."

"Daddy, done, Daddy, run, Mommy, wunch time?" He nods and points out the window.

Beau steps between us. "We'll talk about it later, Jackie." He kisses my son's tiny head. "Go with Grandma Hi." He tilts his chin to the kitchen. "Take him, Hialeah."

"I don't know how the three of you did it." I run my hand over my face. "Jackie asks for Jewel all the time."

Pick, Mac, and Godfather lost their wives when their kids were young. Pick's wife was murdered in Manhattan by a stalker. Mac and Godfather's wives died from cancer.

"Corinne did, too," says Pick, putting a supportive arm around me.

Godfather bumps temples with me. "We had our family to help us. You have us; we're family. We'll find Jewel and bring her home."

Mac squeezes my shoulder. "No worries, lad. We'll get Jewel back. Now let's get this done."

Flame kisses his wife. "It's go-time, Corrie. Work your magic, baby."

Princess shimmies her shoulders and shakes her arms out. Then she sits ramrod straight in front of the camera and blows out a breath. "Break the bastard," she whispers to herself.

"Ms. Hunter, we're sending the feed into Richard Briggs's cell. You have ten minutes."

"Understood, thank you, Warden Scholtz," says Princess in her lawyer tone of voice.

"Corinne," drawls Briggs. "Did you Zoom conference me because you wanted to take my case?"

"I did hear you're having some legal challenges: ten dead girls found in a mass grave at Laguna Beach, all with your DNA under their fingernails. I also heard the DA is going after the death penalty. Tough break, your cellmate flipping on you like that. You should choose your prison friends more wisely."

Briggs's top lip curls up; his face reddens. "What the fuck do you want, Corinne?"

"Information about your sister," says Princess airily, obviously happy to have gotten under Briggs's skin.

"Debra? Why would you give a shit about my sister?" sneers Briggs.

"Come on, Richard, let's not beat around the bush. We found her

TracFone. We also know you have a burner phone you've been using to communicate with her. I'll give you a freebie, get rid of it. Your cell will be tossed after our meeting."

Briggs glares into the camera, running his middle finger across his chin.

"It doesn't take a genius to figure out Debra came to Pony with Alton Judd to kidnap Reagan. Tell me where your sister is, and I might be able to convince the DA to take the death penalty off the table."

I grin. Princess just lied, straight-faced and appearing sincere. We have no idea what is on the TracFone, or if Briggs has a burner phone. And there's no way Princess would ever talk to the DA on Briggs's behalf. She wants Briggs dead just as much as the rest of us.

Briggs smiles. "So this little chat is about Reagan. You don't need to worry about my woman. Reagan has Alexandria's Genesis: purple eyes." Briggs gets out of his chair and comes closer to the bars. "I'll let you in on a little secret," he whispers and looks up into the camera. "Women with purple eyes stop aging around fifty. They live to be over one hundred and fifty years old. Reagan doesn't bleed as other women do, but she'll be fertile for her entire life. She's revered for her beauty, sexuality, and fertility. Reagan is immortal, Corinne. I think I've proven that—twice."

I snort. Jewel ended her period a week ago. I should know: I rode the red river for three days. This guy is fucking batshit crazy.

"Richard, you already tried the insanity plea. And you're talking to me. Try again," demands Princess.

"I love your domineering side, Corinne," grins Briggs. He returns to his chair. "You'll get the death penalty taken off the table?"

"I'll talk to the DA on your behalf," lies Princess.

Briggs nods, exhaling. "I don't know where Debra is. Last week she told me she had someone on the hook. She was gonna get me the money for my defense attorney. I spoke to her again last night. Debra asked me what to do for a snakebite. The way she described Alton's leg, he's probably already dead. They have to be somewhere close to Pony." He sighs. "I love Reagan."

"Richard, when a man loves a woman, he doesn't beat her half to death *and* kill her baby." Princess sneers, "You broke just about every bone in her body."

"I was justified!" yells Briggs. "Reagan's a whore: she likes to fuck around with other men. I let that baby die because I didn't want him to suffer as I did. Like my father was, *his* father is a waste product—a drunk with a fetish for whores! The baby is better off dead!"

Rage rips through me, filling every cell of my body. My nerves fire. I growl, ready to let loose my disdain for the asswipe.

Beau puts a hand on my shoulder. "Calm, he's going to get the needle."

"Times up, Ms. Hunter. The guards will search Briggs's cell ASAP. I hope you got what you needed," says Warden Scholtz.

"Thank you, warden . It was enlightening. Goodbye." Princess closes the clamshell, puts her face into her hands, and cries hysterically. Flame and Pick run to comfort her.

I pick up the closest thing to me—a full bottle of Jameson. I roar and whip it at the TV. The bottle shatters; shards of glass fly through the air. The game room fills with the sweet scent of alcohol. Amber liquid runs down the wall and pools on the floor. I don't stop; like a madman, I hurl bottle after bottle at the spiderwebbed screen.

It takes Beau, Godfather, Geronimo, Liam, and General to pin me down. Breathing like a bull, I rage against the pain Briggs has inflicted on Jewel, me, and our family. Tears stream down my temples as I scream my fury for Briggs murdering my son. I bellow my wrath for Briggs hurting my woman. I release the hatred I have for myself for not protecting them.

Beau growls in my ear, "You need to stop, Joker. This isn't helping Jackie or Jewel. Lock it down, so we don't need to lock you down."

My cell vibrates with a text. General slithers his hand into my front pocket and yanks out my phone. He looks at it with a furrowed brow. Then he holds it up to my face and appears amazed it opened.

I roll my eyes, knowing he still uses a password.

Beau helps me into a sitting position.

General blows out a breath and looks at the screen. "It's from a non-traceable burner phone."

If you want Reagan back, it will cost you ten million in small, unmarked bills. You have twenty-four hours. We'll contact you with the drop-off location.

"Jesus Christ," sneers Godfather. "They're dumb shites."

"Ten mil in small bills," snickers Geronimo. He pats my knee. "The fuckers have been watching too much TV."

Brainiac and Scottie come running into the game room.

"I know where Aunt Jewel is being held!" Brainiac holds up the TracFone. There's a cord dangling from it. "Scottie remembered Aunt Jewel has a Tupperware container of old cords." He grins. "We found one that fit."

Mafia Man walks over and takes the phone. "Moose Mountain."

Beau furrows his brow. "Moose Mountain?"

"That's the last number that was called on the phone," nods Brainiac. "Scottie and I think the bastards are holding Aunt Jewel in one of the cabins."

"Christ, I just came from there," growls Beau. He yanks out his phone, jabs a number, and puts it on speaker.

"Moose Mountain," says a female voice.

"Hey, Leslie, it's Beau."

"Hey, Beau. I wanted to thank ya for bookin' the party of ten." She giggles. "Floyd is in the back, removin' a fishhook from a greenhorn's thumb."

Beau runs a hand behind his neck. "Sorry about that."

"No worries, Beau. You and Runnin' Deer had an emergency. Floyd and Junior have them covered. No one has been eaten by a grizzly yet," she laughs.

"Les, I'm going to text you a couple of pictures. Will you let me know if you rented a cabin to anyone in them?"

"Ya don't have their names?" asks Leslie. "I could look 'em up in our database."

"Debra Briggs and Alton Judd," says Beau. He texts her the images we captured from the video footage.

"No one by those names." Leslie pauses for a beat. "I got the pictures, Beau. That isn't the woman's name, though. The gal is Susan Parker. She had ID and paid with a credit card. Beau, what's goin' on? Does this have somethin' to do with your emergency?"

Yes! Thank god. I leap up and run for the gun cabinet. The assholes won't live to see the next sunrise. I grab my cut from the barstool and start stuffing the pockets with mags and clips. Then I grab my Glock and slide it into the waistband of my jeans. I toss my M4A1 rifle over my shoulder.

I whirl my finger in front of Beau, trying to get him to speed up the conversation. *Get to the goddamn cabin number.*

"Yeah, Les," affirms Beau. "They kidnapped my daughter, Joker's woman. Do you have a cabin number for the assholes?"

"Shit," drawls out Leslie. "You need to take a left at the fork and go in through the woods. Come up on the fuckers from the back. I'll send Floyd and Junior now to make sure the cunts don't leave. My boys will show the assholes a little western hospitality; they'll shoot their motherfuckin' asses. Cabin 125, Beau."

Bam! there it is. I sprint for the door.

CHAPTER 25

REAL LIFE IS CRAZIER THAN ANY FICTIONAL STORY –
JEWEL

The sun's rays are beaming through the cabin's windows directly onto me—an ant frying beneath a magnifying glass. Unfortunately, I'm the ant.

The small space is sweltering—my stomach rolls from the intense stench of feces, urine, and body odor. Perspiration is running from my forehead to my temples, down my jaw, and dripping off my chin.

I snort and rest my forehead against my right knee. Now I wish the witch would douse me with a bucket of icy water. Slowly, I raise my head and glance over at the bed. I've only seen two dead people in my life. They looked more alive than him—he's dead.

I peek over at the woman. She's sitting in her bra and panties, fanning herself. I don't know if she realizes we have a corpse in the room with us. Given her mental state, I'm not going to be the one who informs her. I put my forehead back down onto my knee.

"Your man had better fuckin' come through," warns the witch. "Hey, are you listenin' to me?!"

I raise my head again and wipe the perspiration off my chin. I swallow. My mouth is dry as dust—a Maggie expression. I lick my cracked lips. My quirky friend, Maggie. What I would give to be at the club listening to her hipster idioms. She'd say, "The biatch is a fuddrucking evil-weevil who needs to be put to ground." Then her man—Biker Boy to her, Mafia Man to the Sinners, Devilan to everyone else—would do it, because he loves her more than all the stars in the galaxy.

Princess would only need to say, "Jamie" to her husband, Flame, and the woman would be dead. Jillian would toss her hand out to Tank: "Johnathan, clean up this mess." And *poof!* the woman would be gone. Cookie just needs to give High her "look," and then it's lights out for the monster. I don't have a "look" or a "gesture" or a "saying" to convey I want Joker to kill for me. I never needed one…until now. What would it be? The good ones are taken: the look, the gesture, and the word. Maybe a hand signal, like running my finger across my throat. *Lord, that's lame.*

I shift and try to relieve the numbness in my butt. At least my left hip is just throbbing. I can move it without feeling as if I'll pass out.

"Hey, bitch, where would a good drop-off point be for the money? Don't say the woods. I hate these fuckin' woods."

I snort. The witch is asking me—her captive—where she should have my money dropped off to her? Unbelievable! Mom always said real life is crazier than any fictional story. *Keep her appeased until Joker figures out where you are. He'll come for you, and she'll be just a bad memory.*

"I don't know. Why don't you ask your boyfriend?"

Okay, that wasn't my best move. Bringing the witch's attention to the dead guy might send her over the edge.

"Can't you see he's sleepin'?" she huffs out. "Anton needs his rest to heal. It's up to me to make the deal."

The woman is delusional, and she may kill me accidentally. My dad told me people are the most dangerous animals to inhabit our planet. They're right up there with the wolves, grizzlies, and moose. I was surprised about moose: they're not afraid of people, and they don't back down.

"Bitch, I'm waitin'," barks the woman.

I rub my eyes, exhaling. "In the movies, the drop-off is always in a park, an airport, or a shopping mall."

"You're right," she nods. The witch walks over to the kitchenette, turns on the tap, and rewets her cloth. Then she lifts her long blonde hair and places it against the back of her neck. "Do you know where the closest shoppin' mall is? I could kill two birds with one stone. I need a few new outfits for Argentina."

I roll my eyes. No one can be this unintelligent. It's just not possible.

"Do you know where the shoppin' mall is?" she asks again impatiently.

"Ah, no. I have no idea where we are?"

I'm not going to tell her I know we're thirty minutes outside of Butte.

"Hm," she hums. "I don't have any internet service. Do you know where Moose Mountain is?"

"No, I've never heard of it," I lie.

"I guess I can call the front desk and ask the lady. She'll know where the closest shoppin' mall is."

Knock knock knock. "Housekeeping," comes a male voice from the other side of the door.

I grin. I know that voice: *Cowboy is here.*

CHAPTER 26

BULL MOOSE – JOKER

Moose Mountain is one massive outdoor recreational area for the enthusiasts who want some of the comforts of home: a roof over their heads, bathroom facilities, and a kitchenette.

I stop at the fork in the dirt road. Two hundred yards ahead of me, I get a glimpse of a cow moose with her calf. The cow is nothing to play around with; she'll charge a human without provocation.

Beau slides off his bike. "The woods are swarming with moose. The people have been leaving out food."

"Fucking fantastic," barks General. He dismounts from his bike. "Give the moose lots of room. Don't fucking challenge them. They won't back down. If they charge, shoot to kill."

"No problem," grins Geronimo. "I love a good moose steak."

I look over at High. "We'll need to hike in. I don't want the assholes knowing we're coming."

He nods and surveys the area.

High and I have been here hundreds of times over the years. The cabins provide a safe place to party after a day of hunting or fishing—no worries about getting eaten by the wildlife.

Brainiac heads into the woods. "Uncle, the asswipe has fucking flatlined by now. We only have the Triscuit to worry about."

Mafia Man, Liam, Mac, and General snicker as they head into the woods after him.

Geronimo laughs and follows them. "The kid is fucking funny."

Beau, High, and I head into the woods behind them. The birds start squawking, and the squirrels are chattering. They're letting all the animals know humans have invaded their space.

"Give me your plan," demands High.

"I'm going to walk up to the door and knock. I'll tell the bitch it's housekeeping." I step over a giant steaming pile of dung. "With luck, she will open the door. If not, you'll be at the back and take her out through the window."

A mile into the woods, Floyd and Junior step out from behind a tree.

Beau shakes Floyd's hand. "Thanks for keeping watch."

I take Floyd's held out hand, giving it a quick shake. "Thanks for the assist, Floyd."

"Anytime, Joker. We ain't seen any movement other than the woman." He smirks. "The bitch is runnin' around in there with only her skivvies on."

"Floyd, ya there?" comes a female voice over a walkie-talkie.

Floyd brings the walkie-talkie up to his mouth and presses a button. "Yeah, Les. What's up?"

"The bitch just called lookin' for the closest shoppin' mall. Keep your eyes peeled."

"She ain't goin' anywhere. The moose and bear trashed her vehicle, tore the top right off the motherfuckin' thing. The Sinners are here. I'll call ya when it's done." Floyd shakes his head and spits out a brown stream of tobacco juice. "We tell these greenhorns not to leave food in their vehicles. They never listen." He holds out a Sig Sauer. "Found her gun on the passenger floorboard." He tucks it into the front waistband of his jeans. "Finders, keepers."

I tilt my head to the gun. "File off the serial number. There might be bodies on that pistol."

"Planned to," grins Floyd.

The Sinners move in and surround the cabin.

I walk up to the door and bang my fist against the wood. "House-keeping."

The bitch cracks the door open, and I ram it with my shoulder. It flies back. Briggs's eyes become round as saucers. She runs out of the cabin screaming, "Rape!"

Brainiac is clapping his hands. "Come on, you motherfucker! Come and get me!"

My eyes dart to what he's yelling at: it's a bull moose. He's licking his lips. His ears are pinned back with his haunches raised, ready to charge Liam. The moose is too close for Liam or Brainiac to shoot.

Brainiac whips a rock at him. The bull changes course and charges Brainiac, who sprints the few feet and leaps into the Jeep. Debra screams as the bull tramples her. Using his antlers, he tosses her limp body into the air. It crashes down on top of the Jeep's hood. Quick as a rattler's strike, I jerk up my rifle. *Rad-da-tat-tat-tat! Rad-da-tat-tat-tat!* The moose falls with a ground-shaking thud.

"Jewel!" I shout and turn back to the cabin. "Babe, talk to me!"

"Here…I'm chained to the stove," she cries, shaking the chain. "I can't get loose."

I cough at the stench in the cabin and drop down next to her. "Babe, you're hurt."

"My head." She puts a shaky hand to the back of her head. "And my left hip."

I yell over my shoulder, "Get her some water, and find the goddamn key to the cuffs!" I look at Jewel's head. She has a large goose egg. The skin is split, but it's not deep. Then I pull down her yoga pants to examine her left hip. I hiss. "Christ!" Her hip is as purple as an eggplant, and the bruise is as large as one, too. It makes me want to kill the bastards all over again. "Babe, I'm going to slide beneath you."

She giggles. Tears are running down her cheeks. "You're not much softer than the floor, Cowboy." Then she whispers, "The man on the bed is dead."

"Yeah, so is the bitch on the hood of the Jeep," I murmur back and kiss her lips. "Love you, babe." I lift her and shimmy my body beneath hers.

My woman sighs and relaxes into me. "Love you more, Cowboy."

CHAPTER 27

DEFINITION OF TRUE LOVE – JEWEL

The brothers tore the room apart searching for the key to the cuffs. After ten minutes, I was ready to tell Joker to just gnaw off my wrist.

Mafia Man finally found the outline of a key in Debra's bra. He refused to remove it. Touching another woman's boob was out of the question. Not his wife, not her boob—not happening.

Mafia Man's rationale caused High not to want to go there either. After all, he loves his wife, too. It was sweet but irritating at the same time. I mean, the woman was dead. Joker and I were in a sweltering cabin that smelled worse than roadkill left out in the sun for a week *with* a dead body lying on the bed. We needed to wait until the brothers finished their banter—laughing and poking fun at Mafia Man and High. In the end, Liam retrieved the key. *Bikers!*

Joker carried me out and made me drink two sixteen-ounce bottled waters. Then, of course, I needed to pee. There was no way I was going back into that cabin. Joker laughed and carried me behind a tree. He helped me pull down my yoga pants and panties. Then my man started in on the pee jokes: "Babe, I've got a good one for you," he said. "Pissing yourself in public is like being in love."

It was surreal: Cowboy was crouched behind me, watching me pee, and waiting for me to say, *Why?* I decided it was the definition of true love: a badass biker helping his woman pee while reciting jokes to relax her. I gave in and giggled, "Why?"

My man guffawed. "Everyone can see it, but only you can feel the warmth." Then he kissed my lips and wiped me with some leaves. I prayed they weren't poison ivy. An itchy rash down there—good god, no.

Joker sat on the ground with me in his lap. He told me everything that went down after I was taken. I could not believe the witch was Ricky's sister. I didn't even know he had a sister. I was amazed Princess called the jerk in prison. I was astonished that my fourteen-month-old son saved me by finding a cell phone in the parking lot. Joker and I laughed over him negotiating with JT. We laughed harder over JT not wanting to give up his stash.

"Babe, honest to god, I don't know what was worse: finding you in the boutique with our baby between your legs or finding your cell and a clump of dirt soaked with your blood on the trail. Then we had to search the marsh—" My badass biker chokes up.

"Hey, Cowboy. You found me. I wasn't scared because I knew you would. It's all good." I give him a lip touch. Then I sigh. "I would like something unique to let you know I want you to kill someone for me."

"What?" he sniffs and laughs.

"Well, Maggie has this cool hipster way of telling Mafia Man to kill someone. Princess has the one-word thing. And Cookie has a look." I glance up at Joker. "They took all the good ones."

Joker throws back his head, laughing.

"It's not funny," I chide and smile. "I need to think of something. We're a one percent bikers club. I need a word or signal or something. It needs to be cool and unique."

Joker kisses my lips and chuckles. "I'm sure you'll think of something."

I look over at Brainiac, General, Beau, and Geronimo. They're removing the guts of the moose. "Ew, that's disgusting."

"Uncle Joker," calls Brainiac. "Do you want the head and the hide?

Uncle Geronimo is going to split the heart, kidneys, liver, and balls with Papa Bear."

I clear my throat. Scrunching up my face, I look at Joker. "Balls? As in testicles?"

People don't really eat male reproductive organs, do they?

Joker snickers, nodding. "The head and hide are yours, nephew."

"Thanks! Jonas, Abel, Scottie, Conan, and Conor are going to flip the fuck out."

"Yeah, thanks, Joke. We need another dead animal's head on our family room wall," bitches Mafia Man. He holds open a fifty-gallon garbage bag for Brainiac. *Splat.* The mammoth testicles get deposited into the bag. Mafia Man says sarcastically, "Like the twenty we already have aren't fucking enough."

I grin and run my hands up and down the sides of Joker's thighs. "You love to hunt and fish, Cowboy."

"Yup, I do," he whispers and kisses my lips. "Now that my woman is an expert at pissing in the woods, we'll go camping."

"Sounds great," I say airily and roll my eyes. Then I stupidly ask, "Cowboy, what do you do when you need to go—"

He hugs me close. "Need to go, what?" He grins. "Take a dump?"

"Hm," I hum, nodding.

"You dig a hole and cop a squat." He laughs and kisses my lips again. "No worries, I'll help you."

Oh god, lord, no!

Tires crunching grabs our attention. Joker and I glance down the dirt road.

"Here comes Doc. He needs to check you out, babe."

I squint at his vehicle. "Is he driving the refrigerated truck?"

Joker chuckles again. "Brainiac is worried about his moose meat going bad in the heat."

I giggle. Oh, the country life: hunting, fishing, camping, eating wild game, and pooping in the woods. My dad loved it. Joker and Beau adore it. Heck no, I won't be eating any animals' testicles, hearts, livers, or kidneys. I will try a moose steak. Who knows, it might be delicious.

Doc checked me out, and my man's diagnosis was correct; I have a goose egg on the back of my head. It's tender but doesn't need stitches. My left hip is bruised, but Doc doesn't think I did any damage to the titanium cup and ball. When we get to Sinners Urgent Care, I'll have an x-ray just to make sure. *Great.* It's a wonder I don't glow in the dark from all the radiation I've been exposed to.

I watch the ten men use every muscle they have to lift the thousand-pound moose into the truck. My man has the largest bulging muscles. My girly parts do a little dance just seeing them—my nipples join the party. Ugh, I'm wearing a sports bra.

"Babe," drawls Joker, chuckling. "Do we need to hit the woods?"

I laugh. Cowboy and I becoming one with nature—hm, now that might be fun. My eyes go to the dead moose and then to Debra's broken body lying in a heap at the side of the cabin. I love Cowboy. Lord knows his body makes my lady parts sing. But being trampled by a moose in the middle of an orgasmic haze…*oh lord, no.*

CHAPTER 28

THE JOKE THIEF AND PILL SNATCHER – JOKER

Beau and I are riding two abreast up our road. I have Jewel riding sidesaddle on my thighs: my woman loves the bike. She equates it to riding the waves: the sun kissing your skin, the wind in your hair, total freedom. I get it, but her hip wasn't going to allow her to ride bitch. She's my woman; I made it happen.

I slow when we get to the beginning of the trail that leads to High's house. "Beau," I shout and squeeze the brake.

He stops beside me and dismounts. Pick is jogging with Jackie on his back. He looks as if he's been at it for a while. Pick is in great shape, but still: the brother is in his early seventies. I don't want him getting sunstroke.

"Shit," barks Beau and runs down the trail. "Pick, what the hell is going on?"

Pick stops jogging and starts walking. "We're good," he says, slightly winded. "Jackie just wanted to go for a run."

I dismount with Jewel in my arms and set her on the saddle. That's bullshit; I know Jackie was more than likely crying for his mother. Pick wouldn't tell him no: he has a soft spot for all his grandbabies.

"Grab a bottled water out of my saddlebag," yells Beau. He takes Jackie off Pick's back.

I run down the trail with the water. "Are you all right, brother? You look fucking flush and sweaty."

"I'm good," assures Pick.

Christ, he sweating like a racehorse. I yank off my tee and wipe him down. Then I hand him the bottled water.

"Thanks. I didn't realize how goddamn hot it is." He uncaps the bottle and gets ready to take a drink.

"Papa, me," demands Jackie. He sticks his tongue out, panting like a dog.

My son would probably get the Academy Award for best actor. He's learned to be dramatic. *Thank you, Brie, Willow, and Blossom.*

"Jackie, Papa's going to take a drink first. Then you."

Pick puts the bottle to Jackie's mouth. "Tip," he orders.

I roll my eyes. I should have saved my breath. Pick would keel over before he took his drink first. I swipe my hand over Jackie's chin. "Now Papa's turn."

"Cowboy, are they okay?"

I look up the trail; Jewel is hobbling toward us. "Jewel, Jesus Christ! Doc told you not to walk on your hip for twenty-four hours!"

"Mommy, where was you! Papa run." He puts his little hands to his mouth, yelling, "Wunch time." He raises his arms, palms up. "No Mommy!"

Beau chuckles.

Pick laughs. "Our grandson is his father's kid. Bossy, badass, and demanding."

Beau agrees, nodding.

Jewel gets to us. She lifts Jackie out of his carrier and kisses him. "I was checking out a few hunting and fishing spots for Papa and Daddy."

Jackie scrunches up his tiny nose and pinches it closed. "Phew. Fuck stink." He reaches for me with his other arm.

Beau and Pick burst out laughing.

Jewel scowls. "Cowboy, I told you he'd repeat that."

I chuckle and take Jackie. "You do fucking stink, babe." I purse my lips. "We wuv you."

She turns in a huff and hobbles back up the path.

"Hey, babe, I've got a stink joke for you." I hand Jackie to Beau.

"Save your stupid jokes. They're not going to work. You just told your biker babe she stinks."

Pick and Beau are laughing, which makes my son giggle wildly.

I'm not a joke-teller by nature. My father was a rigid naval officer. Jack Frazier commanded his house as he did his men: with an authoritative tone and a firm hand. Dad wasn't physically abusive. It was his house, his rules—no discussion. He had no tolerance for anyone who deviated from societal norms: piercings and long hair were for females. Sex was something married couples did in private. "The Talk" centered around abstaining until you're wed. PDA was strictly forbidden. Tatts were marks of deviance, and surfing was a mindless activity. I rebelled against all his rules. Dad took things away. His money paid for my motorcycle, food, and surfboard; therefore, my stuff was his. I would kid around and mock him to my sister and my friends. They nicknamed me Joker. It followed me into the service and then into the club.

I jog over to Jewel and sweep her up in my arms. "This one is a good one."

Jewel looks at me and sighs. "Hit me."

"If your girlfriend smells like tilapia, don't let her on top-of-ya."

"Shit, that was bad," laughs Beau.

I chuckle over my shoulder. "Made you laugh."

"I was laughing at *you*, not the joke, dumbass," snickers Beau.

I roll my eyes and grin at Jewel. "He's just jealous."

Jewel smirks, and then she breaks out guffawing. "Cowboy, I don't think he's jealous of your jokes."

"Okay, let me try again. I've got another one, babe. Love is like a fart." I give her big eyes and wait.

She giggles. "Why, Cowboy?"

"If you have to force it, it's probably crap." I grin and kiss her lips.

"You know your jokes are bad, right?" she whispers onto my lips.

"They're not really mine, babe," I whisper back. "I stole them from the kids."

"Hm, the joke thief and pill snatcher." She smiles, gazing into my blues. "Do you want to marry me in two weeks, Cowboy?"

I stop and stare down at her, assessing her. I've asked Jewel to marry me more than once. She always had a bullshit excuse for waiting: *this is Beau's busiest time,* or *Jackie's adjusting to Pony,* or *the boutique is just getting off the ground,* or *let's wait until we get pregnant.*

I knew it was her way of slowing us down. Jewel is comfortable in her own skin. She's on cloud nine being the mother of my children. She doesn't want to upset the applecart. Jewel would be happy for the rest of her life as my significant other, my biker babe. The title, *Mrs. Jackson Frazier,* wasn't worth the risk of me feeling trapped and going off the rails.

I inhale deeply and fill my nose with the scent of pine, wildflowers, and the odorous stench of my woman. Yeah, she reeks with the smell of dried blood, caked-on dirt, and old sweat. To me, nothing smells sweeter. She got there—she trusts me to love her forever.

"I want to marry you." A slow grin forms on my face. "Two weeks. You're sure you don't want the big wedding with the white dress and the corny ass music?"

"Nope, I'm a biker babe...an old lady. We don't do boring." She giggles. "I want it outside at the club with everyone there, including Maria and your biological family."

My biological family. No, that's not happening. I haven't spoken to my father in ten years. I used to talk to my mom, my sister, her husband, and their kids once a month. Just small talk about their lives; I kept mine private. I stopped taking their calls after Finlan died. Lisa's husband, Zack, texts me once a month. Zack was my best friend all through school. He asks me to send him an emoji to make sure I'm still breathing. I do, so that he and my sister won't come looking for me. I haven't told Jewel much about "my family," other than their names and where I grew up. Now isn't the time to get into it.

Jewel continues, "A few of those big tents and some chairs. A big bonfire, booze, and food. High at your side, Cookie at mine. No traditional vows; they're inconsequential. We'll say some meaningful words"—she smiles up at me—"that express our feelings for each other. We're good."

My lips to hers, I murmur, "Yeah, we are good."

Jewel reaches up and threads her fingers through my hair. Our lips move, our tongues duel. She moans. I answer with a groan and deepen our kiss.

"Mommy, no kizz! Wunch time!"

I chuckle onto Jewel's lips. "It's dinner time, Jackie. Let's take Mommy home."

CHAPTER 29

*MY CLOUDY DAY BECAME A TORRENTIAL DOWNPOUR –
JEWEL*

"Sister, we need to know where your head is at," says Cookie. She takes another sip of her wine. "I know the kidnapping, the creep's trial, and Joker's refusal to invite his biological family to the wedding are screwing with you."

I turn away, gulp my cab, and stare at all my Sinners' nieces and nephews playing with Jackie in the pool. Joker opened the walls for me this morning; he let the outside in. It started out as a gorgeous day: eighty-five degrees, sunny, with a light breeze. My Sinners' sisters had come over to help me plan the wedding.

Before they arrived, I'd asked Joker to text his family and invite them to our celebration. If they agreed, Beau would fly to Hawaii to pick them up. But Joker gave me an emphatic no, without an explanation. Then he walked out the door. My gorgeous day had turned cloudy.

An hour later, I received a text from the Los Angeles District Attorney's office, Ricky's trial has begun. Richard Briggs, private eye, killed the ten women he was hired to investigate. All the women were accused of adultery by their husbands. The attorneys are in the process of picking a jury. I don't know if it's the norm for the District Attorney's secretary to notify past victims, or if the woman thinks she should keep me in the loop because I'm Reagan Sawyer. I could do without knowing anything more about Richard Briggs. I'm sure the newspapers and gossip columnists will have a field day dredging up Reagan Sawyer throughout Ricky's trial. My cloudy day became a torrential downpour.

"Jewel," calls Raine. She squeezes my hand. "Are you getting cold feet about marrying Joker? It's okay to take a minute."

"It's more than okay," says Princess. She pours more cab into my glass. "Putting off the wedding doesn't mean you don't love Joker. It just means you have a lot going on. There is no harm in stepping back to breathe."

"Yeah," agrees Jillian. She practically inhales the rest of her wine and holds out her glass for a refill. "We've all needed to take a minute."

I don't want to "take a minute"—I'm being forced to. Honestly, I don't know how or when my life became an open book. That's not true: my life became something people could thumb through at their leisure when Richard Briggs was on trial for the assault and battery of me and the murder of my son. Reagan Sawyer had no right to privacy: every piece of my life was made public.

Tears slide down my cheeks. The press will probably home in on Jackie and Joker. Joker's life will be exposed. Given his adamant no to his family coming to our wedding, that isn't something he'd appreciate. Malibu isn't a safe haven for me, but it'll keep the Sinners and Joker out of the limelight.

"Jewel," murmurs Maggie. She wipes my tears away. "This has nothing to do with you getting cold feet. It's about the evil-weevil's trial. You can talk to us."

I clear my throat and nod. Then I blow out a breath. "I'm thinking about going back to Malibu for a while. Just Jackie and I...until Ricky's trial is over and things die down."

"Jewel, no." Cookie shakes her head. "Do Joker and Beau know about this?"

I inhale deeply, filling my lungs with Diva Mountain air. "No, I'll tell them tonight." I reach over and squeeze Cookie's hand. "Let's enjoy the day. Me and my sisters…our kids…and delicious cab."

"Okay, Jewel." Then she says under her breath, "But Malibu isn't happening, sister."

I smile. Cookie is my true best friend. She'd put everything on the line for me, and I would for her. That's why leaving is my only option.

CHAPTER 30

MEDIA CIRCUS – JOKER

Flame's phone buzzes with a text. He pulls it from his pocket and hits the icon. "Shit," he murmurs and throws down his wrench. "I need to cut out early."

I glance over at him. "Everything all right?"

He walks over to the sink and tosses Tank his phone, then washes his hands. "I need to help Corrie with something."

I chuckle and go back to the engine I've been working on for the last hour. Helping his woman usually means a little late afternoon fuck-fest.

"I need to cut and run, too," says Tank. I look over at him. He's handing Tristen Flame's cell.

"Shit," breathes out Tristen. "Look at the time. I need to help Enisi at the Res."

"Is everything all right with Running Bear?"

"Yeah, Joker. It's just a leaky pipe under his bathroom sink," says Tristen, as if it's no big deal.

I smirk. I told Tristen this morning I fixed his grandfather's leaky pipe. Flame, Tristen, and Tank are up to something—a bit of bachelor party planning.

High comes strolling in. "Hey, brother." He fist bumps Tristen, Tank, and Flame as they head out the door. High leans his hip against the counter. "I came to see if I could talk you into bolting early and having a beer with me at Callaghan's."

I set down the wrench, walk over to the sink, and scrub the grease off my hands. High isn't easy to read, but I know him. He's nervous or upset about something. If he just wanted to have a beer, he'd flop down in the chair and give me the lowdown on the boutique. He'd joke about the women trying to squeeze themselves into Jewel's clothing line. He's standing and staring at me, waiting.

I grab the towel and dry my hands. "Do you want to tell me what has your goddamn feathers ruffled?"

He struts over to the door. "I need a fucking beer."

I lock up and follow him across the dirt parking lot. Christ, maybe Jewel told Cookie about me refusing to invite my family to our wedding. That's probably it. Cookie tells High everything.

High holds open the door to Callaghan's. I clock Beau sitting at a table. He has his eyes closed; his fingers are rubbing his forehead. General is sitting next to him, talking softly. My nerves instantly go into overdrive.

Shit! I move quickly and drop onto the seat next to Beau.

General yells over to Rex. "Bring us another round of Jameson."

I haven't touched any kind of whiskey since Jewel came back to Pony. I'll have a beer with dinner or as a nightcap. The taste of whiskey elicits too many unwanted memories.

"I'll have a Fat Tire, Rex."

He nods and pours the whiskeys.

"Well, get to it. Jewel told Cookie I didn't want my family at the wedding. Cookie told High. Now we're here," I say and take my beer from Rex.

Beau harrumphs and rubs his eyes.

High stares at me. "Do you even know your woman?" he asks sarcastically.

"Yes, I know my woman," I answer just as sarcastically.

"No, you don't," barks Beau. "If you knew Jewel, you'd know she doesn't give two shits whether your 'family' is at the wedding or not. She only wanted them invited for you." He gives me a sideways glance. "Did you know the DA's office texted Jewel about Briggs's trial? About the jury selection starting today?"

I furrow my brow and stare back at him. "No. Why would the DA's office text Jewel?"

Beau slams his fist down on the table, sending the drinks flying. "Because it's going to be a fucking media circus, and she'll be right in the goddamn middle of it."

I look at High, not comprehending what the hell is happening. "Why would the media give a shit about my woman? She has nothing to do with Briggs's trial."

General takes Beau's phone and holds it out to me. I take it and glance at the image: a picture of multiple news crews outside the Malibu house's gate.

Maria: *Beau, we need security.*
Beau: *Guard Dog is on it. Three men are on their way from the LA office.*

"Brother, Jewel is Reagan Sawyer." High pinches his bottom lip. "The media is going to dredge up her trial and a hell of a lot more. Jewel plans on going back to Malibu in the morning."

"What? She can't. We're getting married next week."

High clears his throat. "Joke, she's putting that on hold. She doesn't want the Sinners, Beau, or you to be exposed to the media circus."

"Jesus Christ, Joker, you told her you didn't want your fucking 'family' at the wedding. You didn't give her a reason. We're Sinners; she thinks you're hiding skeletons."

"I don't have any fucking skeletons. My father is a goddamn rigid, judgmental asshole."

"It might have been helpful if you'd communicated that to Jewel," mumbles General. He holds his glass up to Rex for a refill.

High exhales. "It probably wouldn't have mattered. Beau is going to try and talk her into letting him take her to Manhattan. I tried to convince her it was the wrong move. Jewel said if she goes back to Malibu solo, the media will focus on her and leave everyone else alone." He stares into my eyes. "Joker, she's taking Jackie."

This is bullshit. High spoke to Jewel before coming to me. It's even more irritating he thinks I'd allow her to go.

"Corinne, Flame, and Pick are on the phone, putting pressure on the judge to close the courtroom. They're working on getting the judge to issue a gag order on all participants, something that should have been done from the start," barks General.

Beau pushes back his chair. "I need to beat feet. Jackie is at the club."

"Why is my son at the club?" Jackie won't go with anyone except Jewel, Beau, High, or me. "Is Jewel at the club?"

"No, she's at home, probably smoking weed and drinking wine." Beau snorts. "She doesn't know that I know she smokes that shit when she's upset." He chuckles. "As if keeping a window open or smoking outside will cover up the smell." Then he sighs. "I confronted Maria. She didn't like the doctors giving Jewel antianxiety medication. She gets the weed from a farmer and gives it to Jewel. She claims it's holistic medication."

I shake my head and laugh.

"None of this is funny, Joker," growls High.

"It's all hilarious, brother. Jewel isn't going anywhere. It doesn't matter if the asshole judge doesn't close the courtroom; no one will get close to Jewel or Jackie. We were brought up in the first trial, and Princess shut that shit down. My mother and father are squeaky clean. My goddamn father was a Navy admiral. He's retired. My mother's a housewife. My sister is a nurse, and my brother-in-law is co-owner of his father's pineapple farm. They have two kids. Their girl, Nirvana, is sixteen, and their boy, Metallica, is fourteen."

High chuckles. "They named their kids after rock bands."

I roll my eyes. "It was Lisa's fuck-you to our old man. My father didn't get it. He thought Nirvana meant paradise and that Metallica was a native island name."

I push back my chair and send a quick text to Buck asking him to pick up the tables, tents, and chairs I purchased online from Home Depot.

Buck: *On it, brother.*

"Have the girls continue with Jewel's vision for our wedding. I need to go home and smoke weed with my woman. Then I'll fuck some sense into her."

Beau chuckles. "Jackie and I will wait for your text. We don't need to see any of that shit."

CHAPTER 31

I'M HER SAFETY NET – JOKER

I swing my leg over the saddle and start my bike. Exhaling, I tie my bandana around my forehead and slide on my shades. Then I pop the clutch and head for home.

Twisting the throttle, I bring my bike up to 140 mph and lean into the curves. The trees become a kaleidoscope of colors as I race up Diva Mountain Road. The warm wind pelting my face does nothing to cool my raging temper.

Honest to god, I thought Jewel and I had gotten to a place where she would come to me with her fears. What pisses me off more is the brothers thinking I'd allow her to leave without me. It's goddamn pure ridiculousness.

I pass Sinners' entrance to the club and make the right onto our road. I hope like hell Jewel's alone. I chuckle. She's smoking pot; she's alone.

Over the years, I've smelled weed when Jewel was on the club's back deck. I figured it was a brother toking up. Many of my Sinners' brothers enjoy a blunt...hell, I like one on occasion to relax. Not in a million years would I have guessed it was Jewel. I don't understand why she kept it a secret. Weed is legal, and even if it weren't, the Sinners wouldn't give a shit. We're against hard, addictive drugs: heroin, molly, meth, and coke. Marijuana doesn't make the list.

I pull my bike around and park beside the porch. Then I turn off the engine and stare at our house, needing a few minutes to calm my temper.

Many Sinners redden their women's asses out of love. It reminds them we live a dangerous life, and they need to toe the line. I snort. My woman doesn't need reminding. She's been on the reciprocating end of what happens when evil comes knocking. The pain of multiple broken bones and the death of our son are reminders enough for her.

I sigh and dismount. Then I run up our porch steps and put my eye to the retinal scanner—the deadbolt slides back. Bruno Major, "Just the Same," is blaring throughout our home. I check the kitchen, the living room, and the game room—no Jewel.

The glass walls of the four-seasons room are still pushed back. I grin. "Let the outside in, Cowboy." The walls are heavy, making them difficult for Jewel to open. The four-seasons room is Jewel's favorite spot—I found her.

I walk over to the pool. "Fuck," I breathe out and crouch at the edge. At the bottom is every book Jenna Sawyer had written. All the awards Jenna, Jackson, and Reagan had received over the years. All the animal heads Jewel could get off the walls, her mother's favorite cuddle chair, a wineglass, and a bottle of costly cab. Floating on top of the water are all of Jackson's movie DVDs and family photos. I stare at the centerfolds, magazine covers, and newspaper clippings about Reagan Sawyer, the young urban fashionista. Her financial reports, checkbook, and credit cards drift by me.

I inhale and blow out a slow breath, amazed at what my woman has done. At least she didn't sink the guns.

The scent of weed brings my mind back to the present. Jewel's in her white string bikini with her mirrored shades on. She's lying on a chaise lounge—wineglass in one hand, pipe in the other. Jewel has her head turned; she's staring at her mother, father, and our son's gravestones. My woman puts the pipe to her mouth and draws on it slowly. I walk to the back of the chaise. Taking her by surprise, I lean over her and smile. I put my mouth to hers and suck in the smoke. Tilting my head away, I blow it out slowly.

Tears are running down her cheeks. "Cowboy," she drawls on a sigh.

The way she says my name, I know I'm her safety net.

"I'm here," I murmur and go in for a kiss. Our lips meld, our tongues tangle in a slow dance of love. Jewel tastes of wine mixed with weed and her own unique sweetness.

I break our kiss and walk around the chaise. Jewel sets the wineglass and the pipe onto the side table. I lift her into my arms, drop down on the lounge, and cuddle her to my body. No words are needed; my woman will talk when she's ready.

She snuggles into me, her nose to my neck. She breathes me in. We lie together, listening to the birds chirping, the squirrels chattering, and the leaves rustling in the warm breeze. In the distance, a moose mewls. I rest my chin on Jewel's crown and watch two eagles with their eaglets soaring, diving, then accelerating up toward Heaven—teaching their babies how to survive.

"I was lying here becoming angrier and angrier at my mother and father." Jewel sniffs. "I thought they loved me." She breaks from my arms and pushes up. Snatching her wineglass, she takes a guzzle. "The Kincaids have JT and Kyle's spirits. They're always with them, protecting them from all the bad crap." She holds out the glass to me. "Please hold this for me."

I take the glass, place it to my lips, and take a huge guzzle. It's oaky. Its tannins are mild—not bad for wine.

Jewel puts the pipe to her mouth, flicks the lighter, and draws on the mouthpiece. She holds the smoke in for a few beats and then blows it out slowly. "I never was into pot. I tried it a few times when I lived in New York. It stunted my creativity." She draws on the pipe again, this time blowing the smoke out more quickly. "After I got out of LA General, I was all screwed up. Every noise would cause me to jump, and shadows made me scream. The doctors gave me antianxiety medication. Maria didn't like it, because the drugs made me loopy. She knows a farmer who grows marijuana." Jewel shrugs. "It's holistic, and it works."

I hand her the wineglass and take the pipe. Then I take a hit and blow out the smoke. "Babe, I think we need to talk about your mom, dad, and the pool."

She sniffs and grasps the bottle of wine with a shaky hand.

"Give it here, baby." I take the bottle and pour more cab into her glass.

Jewel takes a drink. "Maggie has JT's spirit, and he always protects her." She smiles. "Keeley has her biological daddy's spirit. I'm so thankful for that." She pauses and gazes at the gravestones. Then she puts her fingers to her forehead, slowly rubbing from side to side. She sighs. "I guess it doesn't matter. What's done is done, Cowboy."

I take her wineglass and take a swallow. "Babe, I've had time to think about the afterlife. I think Maggie, Mafia Man, JT, and Keeley are connected because they grew up believing so strongly in the spiritual world. They've learned how to connect on a deeper level."

Jewel takes the glass and relaxes onto my chest.

I make featherlight circles around her belly button. "We need to look at what happened to you differently." I kiss the side of her head. "I think your mom and dad are with you. You just don't have the skills to perceive them."

Jewel rolls her eyes and takes a drink of her wine.

I take back the glass and take another guzzle. "Briggs killed ten women in the time he was with you. But he didn't kill you, Jewel. I don't believe it was because he suddenly grew a conscience. I think some force stopped him. Then there's the 911 call. You don't remember making it. I saw the pictures; I don't think you could have made the call. Babe, Briggs didn't make that goddamn call." I hold the glass up to her lips. "Sip."

She takes her sip and tilts her head up to look at me. "You think, somehow, my mother or father's spirit made the call."

"Yeah. It sounds crazy, but I think their spirits did." I light the bowl of weed and inhale. Then I hold it to her lips.

Jewel takes a drag. "They didn't save Finlan."

"No, but they did save you." I take another toke on the pipe. "There was this weird thing that happened to me. When the fuckers kidnapped you, I couldn't get Briggs out of my head. Someone up there was trying to tell me who took you. And, babe, the odds of us making Jackie were slim to none. Jewel, your body was depleted. Christ, babe, there was nothing left of you. Our minds were totally fucked up, yet my seed took root." I give her a drink of wine. "I thank God every day it did. Jackie saved us both, babe."

Tears run down her cheeks. "I don't want to call off our wedding and go back to Malibu."

I set the wineglass and pipe onto the side table. I chuckle. "Babe, you're not calling off our wedding or going back to Malibu." I pull the strings of her bikini top; it falls into her lap. I cup her tits, kneading them. "We have a more important thing to do. Like"—I grin—"making my baby."

"The media," she murmurs and pushes her chest into my touch.

"Who gives a fuck about the media?" I growl and grab hold of the two strings holding her bikini bottoms together. I slowly pull; the bows come undone. I toss them onto the patio floor. "Slide off," I order and yank my tee over my head. I unbutton my jeans and quickly shed my clothes. Reclining the lounge, I lie back down and grin up at Jewel. Then I run my finger between her tiny petals—so warm and slick. "I want to eat my wife's pretty pink pussy."

CHAPTER 32

MESMERIZED BY MY COWBOY – JEWEL

My man's grinning his panty-dropping grin up at me, telling me he wants to eat my pussy, while his magical finger slowly works me. All I can say is, *yes, please.*

But I can't make my feet take a step: I'm mesmerized by my cowboy. Joker is breathtakingly gorgeous. He's like one of the archangels, lying on the lounger with the rays of sun illuminating his blond hair.

My eyes scan slowly down his body; his corded neck; his tanned, tatted, muscled shoulders, arms, pecs; his ripped eight-pack...*lord, I love his abs.* My eyes fall onto his man V and then to his beautiful, long, thick, perfectly shaped cock. His bulbous head is peeking out of its sheath with a pearl of precum at the tip. I run my tongue along my lower lip. His fluid is my drug—one taste, and I became addicted.

"God made you perfect," I whisper, unable to take my eyes off him.

Joker chuckles low and spreads his legs, gripping his stiff shaft. "My woman likes what she sees." He strokes the length of his cock slowly, giving me a show. His finger is plunging in and out of me with the same slow rhythm. Then he shoves his finger deeper inside me and cups my pussy. He pulls me forward gently. "Mount my face, babe," he commands in a roughened tone of voice.

I swing my leg over his torso. Joker takes control. Lifting me as if I'm as light as a feather, he positions my pussy over his mouth. He gets down to business: spreading my cheeks, he licks me from ass to clit.

I shudder and lean back, needing to feel his cock. I plant one hand firmly on his thigh. My other hand blindly finds his long, thick shaft. I give it a hard squeeze and then firmly stroke him from root to tip.

Joker makes a guttural growl and pulls me down, driving his tongue deep into my core. He grips my hips, rocking me against his hungry mouth. He slurps, plunders, nips, and plunges his tongue back into my pussy.

I keen, "Cowboy," and speed up my hand, stroking the length of him. His cock lengthens, thickens, and drips precum. My legs shake, my toes curl—every nerve ending is sensitive to his touch, his sounds, his smell.

Joker groans. He slowly circles my rosette with his nose. Then he runs it between my pussy lips and presses it into my clit. He blows his warm breath over my hole. Then he flicks his tongue and inserts only the tip.

I mewl, "Cowboy," gripping his cock more firmly.

He plunges deep and smothers his face into my pussy, covering himself with my cream.

I screech my man's name and grind down onto his mouth.

Joker roars. He rips his face from between my legs and lifts me, positioning my pussy above his raging erection. In one quick upward thrust, he penetrates me to his root. I scream. My hips gyrate, wanting him to stay deep. He grits his teeth and plants his feet flat on the lounger. He tilts his pelvis up; his blues are locked onto our connection. He rocks my hips fast. My walls flutter, and I moan at the exquisite sensations rocketing through me.

He pulls out, and, quick as lightning, he flips me to the bottom. I have no idea how he accomplished it without toppling us both off the chaise. He pushes my knees up to my chest, spreading me wide. "Love you, babe." My man glides his tongue between my lips and gives me hot, open-mouthed kisses. He sits back on his heels with his heated blues pinned to my pussy. In my hazy, over-sensitized state, I smile. My body has just become my man's playground. Yup, I'm totally down with his playing. I reach above my head and grip the top of the lounger. Looking at my man through half-lidded, lustful eyes, I'm ready for our triathlon event.

Joker grins at me and runs a finger down my cheek. "My woman wants me to get dirty."

I always want him to get dirty…only him.

Humming, Joker smothers his face between my breasts. He snuffles and roots for my nipple. "Babe, I can't wait for your tits to be filled with milk." He pinches my nipples as he blows warm breaths over them. "Nourishing my baby." He suckles and then spreads hot, wet kisses over every inch of my chest.

Joker's words ramp up my need for him. My pussy clenches: I tingle from head to toe.

He places kisses down my body and nuzzles his cheek against my belly. "Here, I'll watch you grow round with my baby." He sits up, his blues pinned to my tummy, his large hands spanning my belly. "I'll feel the life we created."

"Cowboy," I murmur, overwhelmed with my need for him. My man never gave me tender words during sex. His way of expressing himself was with grunts, growls, and groans.

He glides two fingers down my body and circles my clit. He gives me several firm pinches, interspersed with twists.

I moan. My pussy lips swell. My wetness flows down my crack—my body is strung tight. *Lord, I need him inside of me.* "Cowboy," I whimper.

He ignores my plea and runs his thick fingers between my lips. He circles my hole and plunges his magical finger inside me, cupping my mound with his large palm. He forces me to stay still. "Here, I will plant my seed, deep."

"Oh, god!" I writhe. Just one little glide will make me come. *Just curl your fingers; that's all I need to explode into a million pieces.*

He pulls out. *No, no, no, don't leave.* My legs shake as he slides his fingers down my crack to my rosette. Circling, he pushes inside of me. I scream, "Cowboy!" at his sudden intrusion. The intense, glorious burn causes me to spasm around him.

Joker growls and fists his cock. My cowboy is done with words: he snaps his steel shaft against my clit, then runs it between my lips. Sliding his cock a few inches into my pussy, he wets his tip. Then glides it to my rosette and pushes past my sphincter.

"Deeper, Cowboy," I mewl, knowing I won't get my way. My badass biker will keep us both riding the razor's edge until he's ready to topple us over.

He grunts, growls, and groans out his pleasure. Our bodies are covered in a sheen of sweat. I keen with my back bowed, begging for release. Joker has his large hands on my knees, keeping them high and spread wide. In total control, he glides into my pussy, and then into my ass, repeatedly.

"Don't fucking come, babe," he orders, concentrating on our connection. "Not until I tell you to." He hisses in a breath. "You need to suck me off, so my seed will take root."

Is he crazy? I thrash my head, "Cowboy, I can't wait!"

He yanks his cock from my ass and enters my pussy in a quick, smooth thrust. "Go," he yells and crashes his mouth down onto mine.

My toes curl. Every muscle in my body becomes rigid. My nerves zing like an electrical current is zapping them. I cry out into his mouth, my walls sucking on his steel cock. He grunts and covers me, holding me tight. "Ah, goddamnit," he growls into my neck. Humping deep within me, his cock lengthens, thickens, and jerks. It sends me spiraling into a continuous, glorious orgasm.

"That's it, babe," he grunts and gives me short, deep, mind-blowing strokes. "Milk me. Take every drop."

My head is floating in a euphoric haze. Joker slows his thrusts and kisses my lips. "Love you more than life, babe." He does that little thing he always does after we climax. He gently humps and circles his hips, tapping against the mouth of my womb. "Keep sucking on me, babe," he encourages while massaging my ass cheek.

If I had any energy left, I'd laugh. For some reason, Joker is convinced I can control the walls of my vag and suck his sperm up into the vicinity of my egg.

He reaches down and pulls the bottom of the lounger up, putting us into a weird position. I open one eye. Joker has his phone; he's setting a timer for thirty minutes. Then he positions my legs around his waist, his cock planted firmly inside me. "Babe, you need to quit the pot and wine." He grins onto my lips. "We just made Rider."

"Rider." I smile at the name he has picked for our next son.

The last time Joker and I made love, he announced, "We have a Finlan and a Jackson. Rad names, babe. But our next boy will be Rider." I asked, "Why?" I thought he would tell me it's a badass biker kid's name. No, that isn't what he said. He grinned the biggest grin. "Babe, we just rode the open road to goddamn ecstasy. He'll be Rider." I giggled. Our son is going to be named after our amazing sexual experience. We won't be telling him that.

Joker nestles his face into my neck and gets comfy for his self-imposed thirty-minute wait. I need to bite my lower lip to keep from laughing. According to my man, we need to do this in silence: my "egg" and his "seed" need time to "fuck" in a serene environment.

I grin and kiss the crown of his head. There are much worse ways to spend thirty minutes. I enjoy Joker's weight on me, wrapped around me, like a snuggly weighted blanket.

Yeah, it's over the top and a little crazy. But I get Joker: my man is a tad anxious because we didn't get pregnant right after I came off the pill. "Babe, I don't understand. We made Finlan and Jackie in one go." I tried to explain to him that it didn't really happen like that: I was on the lower-dose pill for two months before I got pregnant with Finlan. I'd been off all birth control for three months when I got pregnant with Jackie. That wasn't a good enough explanation for Joker. He hit the internet and implemented everything he read: the thirty-minute serene environment being one of them.

My biker and I want another baby. Cowboy is going to make sure it happens. I giggle and wonder what he'll name our child if she's a baby girl.

CHAPTER 33

YOU CAN'T BELIEVE EVERYTHING IN THE NEWS – JOKER

After the timer on my phone went off, I carried Jewel upstairs to our shower. Under the spray, Jewel expressed her worry for my family in Hawaii. I held Jewel and told her everything about them.

She hummed, nodding. "Your dad is a mainstream conservative thinker. Just as he can't change you, you can't change him." She kissed my lips. "Call your parents and sister. Tell them the media might come knocking on their door." She looked up at me, tears brimming her violets. "Apologize for me."

I ran my thumbs over the apple of her cheeks. "You have nothing to apologize for," I murmured, and then made love to her.

After, we washed each other and dressed. Jewel took off to her studio, recharged and ready to design. I took off to the four-seasons room. I needed to make several calls—my first was to the DA's office. Although it was late, I took a chance someone would still be there. Amazingly, I got through and spoke to the secretary who'd texted Jewel. I informed her I was Reagan's husband—a tiny white lie that will be rectified next week. I went on to explain that any information concerning Briggs upsets my wife. I requested all phone calls and texts come to me.

"I entirely understand, Mr. Frazier. Ms. Sawyer has been through a horrendous ordeal. The DA wanted to alert her to the possibility that the press may target her again. Five minutes ago, the judge ordered a closed courtroom and placed a gag order on all persons involved," said the older woman. "Thank you for calling us, Mr. Frazier. Your number is on file. Have a good night."

Next, I texted Beau a picture of the pool.

Me: *Come home and bring a few brothers to help me clean out the pool.*
Beau: *We're on our way.*

I grin. That's Beau; he doesn't waste time texting questions. The picture told him everything he needed to know.

I exhale a breath and jab the number for my sister. I haven't spoken to her in three years. Jewel is correct; it wouldn't be fair to let the paparazzi pounce on them.

"Hey, Uncle Joke. Long time, no hear," says Metallica in his cool-dude, fourteen-year-old way.

"Is your mom or dad around?"

"Yeah, they're in the living room with Vana, Gramps, and Gram, watching the news. Some smokin' hot designer chick with big knockers and a fine ass was stalked by a lunatic. The bastard beat her up and killed her baby. Gram's all worked up because the designer's mother was her favorite author. Gramps said her father was a big-time movie producer. Vana is crying like she knows the woman. She doesn't *know* her; she only *read* about her in *Top Teen* magazine. Vana's friggin' cray-cray. Now the cops found ten dead bodies buried in the sand at Laguna Beach. The same guy freakin' raped the women and beat them to death with a tire iron."

"Jesus," I breathe out and drag a hand down my face. Christ, I need to speak to my father. The one person I thought I'd never talk to again.

My sister won't be able to handle me telling her it was my son who was murdered. "Listen, bud, I need to talk to your grandfather."

"Sure, but why? You haven't spoken to Gramps in, like, forever."

"Met, just hand him the phone and tell him it needs to be private," I order, with a slight tremor in my hand. I stare into the pool and wait for my father to come on the line. I have no clue how I'm going to tell him about Finlan.

Heavy footsteps come through the phone, and then a door closes. "Jackson," my father says in his deep baritone voice.

"Hello, Dad." I blow out a breath and take a much-needed minute.

"Jackson, is everything all right? Son, I know we've had our differences, but if you need help, I'm here. Your sister tells me you haven't spoken to her in three years. Your mother is beyond worried." He exhales a long breath. "I'm worried about you, son."

I clear my throat. "Dad, everything is fine. I've had a fucked-up three years. The designer on the news is my woman. The baby Briggs killed was my son."

"What?" Metal grates against cement, and then a thud comes from the other end of the line. His heavy breathing comes through the phone. It sounds like he can't catch his breath. Fuck, he's probably having a goddamn heart attack or something.

"Dad, are you all right? Stay right there; I'll call Zack—"

"No," he says in a shaky voice. He swallows audibly. "Reagan Sawyer…Jesus, my god, that poor woman. We were just watching the news…Jackson, you should have let us help you." He pauses for a few beats. "My grandson was murdered by that bastard. I can't wrap my head around that." He blows out a breath. "Reagan Sawyer has another son. The news reporter said the boy's father wasn't in the picture."

I chuckle, grinning. "You can't believe everything in the news, Dad. I'm very much in the picture. Reagan and I are getting married next week."

"Her son?"

I laugh. "Jackie is mine. Look, Dad, I promised Reagan I'd call you. She's worried about the media attacking you. If they come around, the best thing would be to tell the truth: we've been estranged for years, and you know nothing about my life. I need to make tracks, Dad. I have shit to get done."

"Wait!" He exhales again. "I'm sorry. I didn't mean to yell. Your wedding…are you and Reagan having guests?"

I roll my eyes. "Dad, it isn't the sort of wedding you'd want to attend."

Dad chuckles. "I've seen pictures of Reagan, son. The lady is a bit eccentric." Then he surprises me. "Your mother wants to know how she gets her hair to do the peacock's tail thing. Lisa is wondering if she wears contact lenses." He says under his breath, "I'm not going to tell you what Zack wants to know."

I burst out laughing. "Christ, tell Zack they're God-given."

Dad chuckles, which is weird. I expected a reprimand. He was all closemouthed about anything to do with sex when I was growing up.

Jackie comes running into the four-seasons room. "Daaadeee, poow! Zwean now! Zwim!"

"Daddy," says my father, humor in his voice. "I never thought I would hear anyone call you that." Then he chuckles. "Little man is having difficulty with his L's and S's. You did, too. Your mother had us walking around the house making the L and S sound. You caught on in your own time."

Beau, High, General, Tristen, and Mika come into the room; they're staring at the pool.

I lift Jackie into my arms. "Dad, I need to beat feet. My father-in-law just came in with some of my brothers."

"Father-in-law?" asks Dad, confused. "I thought Jackson Sawyer and his wife died in a plane crash over eight years ago."

"Beau is Reagan's adopted father. He stepped up when shit became bad for my woman."

My father sighs. "Jackson, I'm human. I've made a lot of mistakes. My father was a hard-ass on me, and I followed his example. It's not an excuse, son. I didn't know how to help you when you returned from the war—"

"Dad," I cut in. "I found my place as a Sinners' brother. Reagan and I are good. Our son's death is always going to be painful. Briggs's trial keeps it fresh, and the media fucks with Reagan's head."

Splashing comes from the pool. "Twiz, me, zwim," screeches Jackie, waving his arms. "Down, Daddy."

I set Jackie onto his feet. Tristen and Mika are in the pool, diving underwater, retrieving the awards.

"Come here," orders Beau. "I'll put your floats on you."

"Dad, hold on. Beau, Jackie needs Splashers on under his trunks so he doesn't piss in the pool. Jewel put them in the cabinet next to the towels."

My father chuckles. "I didn't need to worry about that in the ocean. Who is Jewel? Jackie's nanny?"

"No, my son doesn't have a nanny. Reagan's nickname is Jewel." I don't give him any more intel. My father doesn't need to know Jewel's history as a sweet butt. Or my three-year fuckups.

"It's a female biker name? I read she has affiliations with the Sinners."

"Something like that," I affirm and watch Beau lower Jackie into the water. High is using the skimmer to scoop up the pictures. "High, I want to lay the pictures out on the table to dry."

He shakes his head no. "Jewel has them on her computer. I'll print new ones."

"Dad, I really need to go. The pool is full of shit, and I need to get it cleaned out."

"Okay, Jackson. I'm not asking you, son. I'm telling you: your mother and I will be in Pony as soon as I can arrange our flight."

"Jesus Christ, fuck no, Dad," I bark. Christ, that's all I need is for him to show up with his judgmental attitude in play.

"Papa!" shrills Jackie. He's trying to paddle with one hand and hold a picture in the other.

"Jackson, I've accepted your need to lead an unconventional life-style. If you can't forgive me, it'll hurt, but in time, I'll accept that, too. You won't need to see me or talk to me unless you want to. All I'm asking is for you to allow your mother to see you and allow us to meet our grandson."

I exhale and rub my forehead. "My wife loves the Sinners and me. We're her family. You can't come and be judgmental."

"Jackson, I won't judge anyone." He snorts and then chuckles. "Did you know Lisa and Zack named the kids after rock bands? I didn't judge that shit."

I laugh. "I'll have one of our pilots fly over to pick you and mom up. I'll text you with the details. Later, Dad." I hit the end call button.

General looks at me with concerned eyes. "I'll have Rocky and Brainiac pick them up."

Jewel comes into the four-seasons room with a large box. "Pick who up?"

I walk over to her and take the box, setting it down by the bookcase. It's filled with her mother's books and her father's DVDs. *I chuckle to myself. I guess my woman had multiple sets.* I pick up one of the books and look inside. It's scripted:

> *Jackson's and my most significant accomplishment was making our precious daughter. She's our sun, our moon, our stars, our universe. We love you, Reagan. XXXOOO Mommy and Daddy.*

Jewel looks into the pool and scrunches up her nose. "I'm sorry you need to clean up my mess."

Tristen snickers. "The heads needed soaking. I'll take them to Enisi—"

Jewel shakes her head no. "Toss them into the dumpster. My father's favorite heads are still on the walls. Everything can go but the awards."

"Your mom's chair?" I ask and run my hand up and down her back. "That's your favorite chair, babe." Christ, she sits in it every night and watches Jackie and me swim.

"It was old, with a saggy seat. Mika and I will design a few new pieces for in here." Jewel looks up at me. "Who is coming to Pony?"

I frown and pull her into me. "My parents want to meet Jackie."

She smiles up at me. "Cowboy, it won't be bad. You have me to run interference for you. If your father gets judgy, the girls and I will nip it in the bud. We'll just introduce him to Honeypot. She'll offer him a free condition and gab his ear off with the gossip around town. Hey, did you know Butch and Annie do the dirty in the storage room?" She nods slowly. "Old Mrs. Fitzpatrick heard them from the dining room. It was scandalously hot. According to Mrs. Fitzpatrick, Butch has a big sausage, and he sandwiches it in Annie's bun." She breaks out into a fit of giggles. "Mrs. Fitzpatrick shouldn't be talking. We know Alroy has been giving her his sausage for years."

I throw back my head, laughing. "I love you, babe."

CHAPTER 34

JUJU BABYMAKING JUICE – JEWEL

I smooth the burnt orange and sunny yellow tie-dyed comforter over the trundle bed and push it under the daybed. Then I place my gift basket filled with nuts, assorted candy bars, and chips with four cans of Coke on the bedside table. Blowing out a breath, I scan my mom's old office, now my design room. It's good. Nirvana and Metallica should be comfortable enough. I make my way to the guest room with my other welcome basket—two bottles of Perrier, Godiva chocolates, Jennie's cheese from Scotland with her homemade crackers, and a bottle of Turnbull cabernet sauvignon with two glasses. I set it on the dresser and check the bathroom. It's all set for Joker's parents.

I walk quickly down the hall and knock lightly on Jackie's door. "Maria, do you have everything you need?"

She opens the door and cups my cheek. "Rea, you, Beau, and Joker need to stop hoverboarding me."

Hoverboarding. I laugh to myself. She picked that up from the kids.

"I have a beautiful room with a comfortable bed." Maria smiles.

"Joker gave me wonderful lavender-scented lotions and soaps. My Jackie and I make great roommates." She giggles. "He doesn't snore."

"Hm," I hum skeptically, knowing Jackie talked Maria into letting him sleep with her last night.

I would have purchased a sofa bed for my father's old office. Now it's Joker's, and he loves it. He spent a week organizing the room, mixing Dad's style with his own—biker meets producer, super cool. That's where my man designs his Harleys on paper—he is mad talented. Limited access would be a buzzkill for him. So I decided we'd sleep with Jackie, and Maria could have our room. Maria wouldn't hear of it.

"Let us know if Jackie's keeping you up at night. Joker and I will trade rooms."

"Stop worrying, Rea. I'll be right down to start the enchiladas."

I kiss her cheek and run down the two flights of stairs to the workout room. Joker moved the equipment to the back wall. The room gets light from the four full-sized windows, so it doesn't have a basement feel. He set up the king-sized four-poster bed, nightstands, and dresser we bought from Montana Furniture. I purchased a white quilted comforter with cream satin sheets. Then I added candles and colorful satin curtains around the room. I wanted to give Zack and Lisa privacy to make love in a romantic environment. I giggle. My man bitched that *we* needed privacy—I put his parents three doors down from us. "I don't give a shit if they hear us, Jewel. We're trying to make Rider. I'm not going to be quiet about it."

Unfortunately, I got my period two days after our love session on the lounger. Joker and I were devastated. My man held me tight as I cried on and off the entire day. "No worries, he'll come, babe. I'll make it happen for us." My man upped his game. He's determined, and I love it.

Joker's parents were supposed to be here a month ago, but Lisa, Zack, and the kids wanted to come with them. Their arrival was delayed because Lisa needed to wait to be granted her two-week vacation.

The delay infuriated Joker: "We're not putting off our goddamn wedding because of them, babe!" I was disappointed, but we were getting married at the club. All our family lives here except for Crank and his family, the Whitefish Sinners' brothers, and the Red Devils. They're just a few hours away, so I figured we'd reschedule.

I run my finger over the solid gold skull on my left ring finger. It's identical to Joker's ring. The eyes are rubies...the teeth are diamonds. Joker surprised me with a wedding two days after we found out about Joker's family's delay.

We were married in Father Darling's nineteenth-century tiny stone church with High, Cookie, and Beau at our sides. Joker had the church filled with wildflowers and candles. Beau walked me down the aisle to Cookie and High singing Firehouse, "When I Look into Your Eyes." I was married in white short-shorts, a silky pink midriff top with a Harley button nipple-line closure, and open-toed high-heeled biker boots—the perfect biker babe wedding outfit. Our nuptials were simple —all about us. Then we grabbed Jackie, and Beau flew us to Malibu.

We spent three weeks surfing, swimming, deep-sea fishing, and eating in little family-owned restaurants. Maria fell in love with Joker and he with her. Part of Maria's love was wanting to feed Joker continuously. Joker's love was dragging her out of the kitchen to enjoy life with us.

On the second to last day, a truck pulled up to the gate. Maria and I thought they had the wrong house. Come to find out, Joker had met a young wine broker on one of his morning runs. "I needed to help the kid out, babe. He's new in the business." I'd laughed when my husband told me he'd brokered a deal for cases of the finest wines the valley had to offer on our beach. "Babe, you emptied our wine cellar at home." He was correct. Over the years, I had given all my parents' wine to the girls. Joker had yelled for Beau. "We'll be back, babe." Beau and Joker leaped into the guy's truck. Off they went to unload the cases into the jet.

We've been back in Pony for a week. Maria came home with us at Joker, Jackie, and Beau's insistence. She couldn't say no to my three men.

We've spoken to Joker's parents every night—tidbits about the club, Joker, Jackie, Beau, and me. Given my man's history with them, I wanted us to break the ice before they hit Pony. Charlotte and Jackson needed to know what to expect. Good lord, I didn't want a family feud on my hands. Joker's parents agreed to keep an open mind and their judgments to themselves. I told my husband that's all we can ask of them.

Today, Joker and I are hosting a family meet/reception party. Rocky and Brainiac are supposed to touch down at 4:00 p.m. with Joker's family. I have a small window of time to make sure everything is perfect.

I run over to the bathroom to make sure Joker put the soaps and lotions in the appropriate places. That's hilarious, because my man is much more organized than me—our walk-in closet and my makeup vanity are proof. If I leave a basket of folded laundry in our room, it's gone within minutes. And he bought three robot vacuums—one for each floor. Like clockwork, Joker starts them as soon as his feet hit the floor in the morning: "Alexa, start the sharks." I laugh at Joker and Jackie; they buzz around the house to clean their filters.

"Babe," yells Joker down the stairs. "Where do you want me to set up the kegs?"

"In the four-seasons room, by the new bar, and make sure to bring up the wine from the cellar," I yell back. "Cowboy, check the potatoes on your way through."

Joker grumbles, "How do I know when these spuds are done?"

"Poke them with a fork," orders Beau. "If they're soft but firm, they're done."

Maria's giggles float down the stairs. "Joker, Beau, get your heads out of the pot and go. I have the kitchen."

I run back up the stairs through the kitchen and living room to the four-seasons room. I come to a skidding stop and take in the room. It turned out gorgeous. Mika and I turned overstuffed couches and cuddle chairs into beautiful Biker Babe pieces of art. At the far end of the room is my wedding gift to Joker: a bar with a 1938 Harley-Davidson EL Knucklehead in mint condition. Mika encased it in a Plexiglas frame and used it as the base. Joker loves it, but he's searching for another Harley to take its place. "Babe, the Knucklehead is my new ride." Mika laughed. "I knew that was coming. The back of the bar is a Plexiglas hinged door. You can slide the bike out, brother."

I glance at the water lanterns with tealight candles. They'll be lit at dusk, and we'll float them in the pool. It's our way of including Finlan. Cookie offered to sing a song of our choice. Joker and I picked Train, "Calling All Angels." Cookie smiled. "Amour will need to help me out with that one." CJ told his father he needed to sing on key. Joker and I burst out laughing. The kid is always busting his father's chops about being pitchy.

General, Godfather, Horse, Rene, Mac, and Pick are in the back-yard, setting up the large tents. I wanted to dine alfresco. The sun is casting a brilliant orangey-yellow halo over Diva mountain. It's illumi-nating the pine and maple trees, painting a majestic picture. I smile over at Jackie. He's standing with one of the centerpieces in his little hands—a vase we made out of mason jars. He'll fill them with Rocky Mountain wildflowers. Two boxes are sitting next to him: one with the rest of the vases and bundled flowers, the other with white tablecloths, chair covers, and twinkle lights. Jackie announced to Joker and me that he was in charge of "staging" the tents and tables. I wanted to pump my fists in the air: Jackie has his L's and S's down pat. Joker gave me "the look." The one that says, *Cool your ass, babe.* He doesn't want Jackie to feel self-conscious and stop talking. As if that would ever happen—Jackie's badass bossy, like his father.

"Papas, tables next," orders Jackie. His violets are pinned to his grandfathers' every move.

Deep chuckling comes from each of his papas.

"Jackie, go get me a cold one," orders Horse as he slams the sledgehammer down on a stake.

I laugh. Heineken is the breakfast of champions.

Jackie sets his centerpiece carefully on the ground. "Okay, Papa. Be right back." He's off, running for the house, and screaming he needs a beer.

I look over to the back of our yard. High, Tristen, Beau, and Joker are rotating the hog over the fire. My man is bare-chested in low slung boardshorts. His skin glistens: my girly parts do a dance. *Good lord, not now, I have work to do.*

Joker looks over at me. "Babe," he drawls, chuckling.

I laugh, not caring who sees my pointy nipples. Joker's my man, and he's yummy.

Beau glances at me, grinning. "Do you need your man to take care of business?" He's aware Joker and I are trying to get pregnant. He also knows we are devastated every time I get my period.

I shake my head, giggling. "Cowboy took care of 'business' this morning."

High throws an arm around my man's shoulders. "You came deep and hung out for a while?"

Joker's smirk is all the answer he needs.

I roll my eyes. The Sinners' brothers are all in, even when it has to do with their brother making a baby.

I walk back inside and over to the wall. Jackie zooms by me with a plastic bag. Bottles rattle—beers for his papas. I hit the button on the stereo and poke "all rooms": the music will play throughout the house and the outdoors. *This one is for you, Mom*—"Tennessee Whiskey" comes through the speakers. My mother loved George Jones's version, but I prefer Chris Stapleton's. I turn it up and head to the kitchen. Maria is chopping veggies at the counter. I take the knife from her. "Dance with me."

Maria laughs, nodding. She takes two glasses off the counter and hands me one. She holds hers up. "To your mommy and your daddy."

I grin and clink glasses with Maria. "To Mom and Dad." I take a big sip of my mom's favorite morning cocktail: a Whiskey Sour Sunrise, double the whiskey. My dad would laugh when Mom explained her cocktail was healthy: it's made with lemon juice, cherry syrup, and fruit. Mom, Dad, Maria, and I would dance a slow, hypnotic dance while sipping on our delicious adult beverages.

I close my eyes and get lost in the past. Rolling my hips in time with the music, I hear my father singing in my mind. I bow my back and spin in a slow circle, seeing him dancing with my mother. Sadness washes over me. *I wish you and Finlan were here with me.* I gulp half my cocktail down. The whiskey relaxes me. I raise my arms, sway my body hypnotically to the beat, and sing the words.

"Go to her," whispers Maria.

Joker takes my drink and wraps his muscled arm around my waist.

"Cowboy," I whisper and snuggle my face into his neck.

"I'm here," he murmurs, nuzzling my hair.

Just like that, cocooned in my husband, my sadness is gone.

Joker sways us, downs the rest of my drink, and sets the glass onto the counter. We roll our hips in time with the music. He dips me; with our pelvises snuggled tight, he turns us slowly. "Love you, babe." He gives me a soft, lingering kiss.

"Love you back, Cowboy." I moan. Deepening our kiss, I taste the Whiskey Sour Sunrise and my man's unique sweetness on my tongue. His erection is long, thick, and rock hard. I tilt my hips and nestle his cock against my lower abs. Then, I slide my hand down to his firm buttock and hold him tightly against me. I have no shame; I love every inch of my husband.

The song ends. I open my eyes to all my biker babe sisters with their men. Yup, they're staring at us. I didn't hear them come in—my thoughts were on my handsome husband's gorgeous bod.

Cookie clears her throat. "I think I just had a mini O from watching the two of you."

High chuckles and stares down at his wife.

"Whoo!" Princess fans herself. "It was like *Dirty Dancing* on steroids." She looks up at Flame and wrinkles her nose. "I just sounded like Mama Cass."

He smirks down at her, chuckling.

White Dove makes a quick sign of the cross. "God rest her soul."

Raine gazes up at Buck. "If they do that in the kitchen, can you imagine what goes on in their bedroom?"

"Don't imagine," he growls and smacks her ass.

Maggie giggles and looks up at Mafia Man. Her blues are all glittery—googly-eyed for her husband. Then she strolls over to the counter and grabs two Whiskey Sour Sunrises. She hands one to Mafia Man. "Drink up, Biker Boy. It's juju babymaking juice."

"Oh, no, no, no," growls Scottie and removes the glass from his mother's hand. "We have enough babies. Aunt Polly said you shouldn't have any more." He cringes and holds the Whiskey Sour Sunrise between two fingers at arm's length. He isn't taking any chances—one drop of the "juju babymaking juice" might magically turn him into a dad. Scottie reminds his father: "Gee did not want to come out."

Mafia Man rolls his eyes. "Your brother came out just fine." He gives Maggie's flat belly a rub. "He didn't want to leave Mommy's snuggly cocoon." Mafia Man kisses Maggie and then grins. "I needed to coax him out."

Joker and I burst out laughing.

"Give your mother back her drink, nephew," orders Joker. "If it were juju babymaking juice, I'd make your Aunt Jewel drink the whole goddamn gallon."

Scottie hands his mother back the drink. "If Mom gets pregnant again, it's your fault, Uncle Joke." He spins on the balls of his feet and walks away.

The whole room erupts in laughter.

"Babe, I came in for the plates and shit. Jackie wants to 'stage' the tables," chuckles Joker.

I look at the wall clock—noon. Good god, four hours to get everything done!

Maria waves her hand. "Go, Rea, we have the kitchen."

CHAPTER 35

I HAVE NO WILLPOWER – JEWEL

Lord, I'm late. I run down the stairs in my short white silk halter-top dress. It's sexy, showing off my navel ring—Joker, Finlan, and Jackie's birthstones. I studded each side of my dress with the same color of stones and paired my eyeshadow to make my violet eyes pop. My shoes are three-inch wedge-heeled Cleopatra sandals—jeweled cobras are winding around my calves all the way to my knees. My hair is sleek and simple: I plaited four braids to my skull on each side and pulled it back into a ponytail. If I say so myself—I'm hot.

Joker is in the kitchen, standing by Maria. As soon as he sees me, his eyes grow dark, wanting me. He walks over to me and pulls me into his arms. Then Cowboy backs me into the game room. "Lift the dress," he growls into my ear. His erection is pressing into my belly.

I run my hands up and down his back and tilt my neck to give him access. "Your family will be here soon. I can't smell like sex," I breathe out. "Besides, I need to do the final prep. Go take a quick shower and get ready," I order in an unconvincing tone of voice.

Who am I kidding? I have no willpower when it comes to my man. A few more thrusts of his hips, and I'll lift my dress. Joker knows it.

"Aunt Jewel," yells Keeley. She comes running into the game room. "Where are those little galvanized buckets you bought for the wine?"

Joker whines, "No, no, no. Five fucking minutes, that's all we need."

I giggle. "Tonight, Cowboy." Then I kiss him and slip out of his arms. "Come on, Keeley. Uncle Joker needs a minute."

CHAPTER 36

BLOOD DOESN'T MEAN SHIT – JOKER

Thanks to Keeley, the little cockblocker, I needed to take a ten-minute cold shower. I jog down the stairs. All the women are buzzing around the kitchen to the tunes of Hozier. The kids are lined up in front of Jewel, waiting their turn for a platter to take outside.

Jackie is holding up his arms. "I can do it, Mommy." He looks over his shoulder and grins his baby-tooth grin at DJ.

DJ grins back. "You got this, Jackie."

Jackie nods and turns back to his mother.

"All right, Jackie," sighs Jewel. She holds out the shrimp and lobster ceramic platter. A bowl of dipping sauce is in its center. I snicker. She didn't remove the plastic wrap. "Keep it level and *go slow.* The seafood platter needs to be put on top of the bar, in the iced tray. Ask one of your papas or uncles to help you." She places the platter into Jackie's arms and curls his tiny fingers around the edge. I chuckle, knowing she's praying he makes it.

I jump into line ahead of DJ. Kissing Jewel's lips, I whisper, "No worries," and grab the other seafood platter. "Let's go, baby boy."

Every two seconds, I need to straighten Jackie's platter to keep it from dumping onto the floor.

"Here, Papa Beau," shouts Jackie from ten feet away. "Bar. Ice tray."

Beau chuckles. Jackie's seafood has shifted all to one side in a massive clump.

DJ zooms past us with a tray of guacamole, salsa, and chips. "Great job, Jackie."

Brie runs past us with bacon-wrapped scallops. She smiles. "Mega-fantabulous, Jackie."

Anna stops and nods. "Good job, Jackie." Then she's off with her veggie and cheese platter.

Abel glances at Jackie's platter and giggles as he zooms by us with steaming puff pastries filled with chicken pesto and cheese. He yells over his shoulder, "Awesome, you made it, Jackie!"

The triplets come out carrying bowls of chips. JJ is trying to keep Cass, Joey, and Meadow from spilling them as he juggles the dips.

"Papa," shrills Jackie, speeding up his baby steps.

Beau chuckles again and takes his tray. "Cool it. There's plenty for you to do."

Jackie takes off, doing double time back into the kitchen.

I grin, remove the plastic wrap, and straighten out the seafood. The Sinners' kids aren't slackers. They're taught that family takes care of family. The kids came together and helped Jackie with his S's, L's, and sentence structure. Now they're teaching him to pull his weight.

Out of the corner of my eye, I catch Jackie carrying a watermelon the size of him. Conor has a knife between his teeth; his arms are wrapped around a gigantic fruit salad bowl. He's hopping on one foot and keeping a knee under Jackie's melon.

"Christ," I bellow and run for Jackie and Conor.

"Heavy, Daddy," grunts Jackie.

I take the watermelon and the knife. "No hopping around with a knife in your mouth, Con," I growl.

"Okay, Uncle Joke." He puckers his lips for a kiss. I give him a peck, and then he's off to the backyard.

Zoom! Jackie's running back to the kitchen.

I stroll out into our yard. The place looks like a magazine picture: billowy sheer white curtains cover the tentpoles. The tables and chairs are covered in white linen. Multicolored plates, sparkling silverware, and wine goblets line the tables. I grin at Jackie's centerpieces—mason jars stuffed with wildflowers and twinkly white lights.

High, Mafia Man, Tank, Lee, and Flame are helping the kids arrange the food tent. Jewel wanted to serve family style. I talked her into serving buffet style—too many people and too much food to be passing. No one would get to eat.

At the far end of the yard, the older brothers are drinking beer and manning the hog and barbeque grills. All the Sinners have an open-door policy. Jewel, Beau, and I adhere to it—our home is their home.

Hozier, "Take Me to Church," starts playing. CJ starts belting out the song. Even though he just turned four, like his mother, he has a great voice. JT joins him, and, like JT's blood relatives, his voice is off the charts, incredible. The kids join in and sing the hook. I chuckle and hand High the watermelon. Then I head back into the four-seasons room.

A tidal wave of Sinners, Native Americans, security specialists, and Red Devils roll in. Their kids fly past us, yelling for the Sinners' kids. Beau and I are greeting them with bro hugs, fist bumps, and chin lifts. "Nice crib, brother." "Fucking awesome spread." Many of them hover around the room and check out my 1938 Harley-Davidson EL Knuck-lehead bar and the furniture.

Jackie's coming back into the room with a platter of mini meat-balls, toothpicks sticking out of each one.

Conan is beside him with flutes filled with Whiskey Sour Sunrises. "Straighten the tray, Jackie," he orders. His eyes go wide as Jackie's tray slowly drifts downward. "The meatballs are going to roll onto the floor!"

"Fucking fufu drinks," chuckles one of the Red Devils. He straightens Jackie's tray and then takes several meatballs and a flute from Conan. "Thanks." The brother takes a guzzle of the Whiskey Sour Sunrise and pops a meatball into his mouth. "These are the shit."

Geronimo bends down and takes Jackie's platter. Geronimo, Mitzi, and the Red Devils have stayed close since the kidnapping. It's not unusual to get a text from Geronimo asking how we're doing mentally with the bullshit surrounding Briggs's trial. It's appreciated.

"Kiss and hit the backyard," chuckles Geronimo. "Your work is done. Playtime." Jackie gives him a smack and waits for Conan. Geronimo takes Conan's tray; he smirks at the drinks. "Kiss." Conan gives him a smooch on the cheek, and then they're off to find the kids. He looks over at me. "What's left to do, brother?"

I laugh. Geronimo's two trays come up empty in one point four seconds.

He looks down, bitching, "The fuckers didn't save me any. I'll be back." He struts off to the kitchen in a huff.

"Grab the two pitchers of Whiskey Sour Sunrises and bring them out to the bar," I shout over the tunes. I join Beau in manning the kegs and mixing drinks for the brothers and their women.

Jackie and JT come running into the four-seasons room. They climb up on a chair near the stereo's control panel. They're scrolling through the albums on the touchscreen. "Hit the dragon, Jackie," commands JT.

Mitzi and Dakota step up. Mitzi grins. "Cute little fuckers."

I laugh and kiss Mitzi's cheek. "What's your pleasure, Mitzi? We have Screaming Eagle cab." I pull a Coke from the bar's fridge and pop the top, then I hand it to Dakota.

"Your old lady is a fancy bitch," she chortles. "Give me a glass of that, sweets." She grabs a small light blue ceramic plate off the pile next to the seafood platters. "We're gonna be doin' dishes into fuckin' next year." She piles the plate high with seafood. "Paper and plastic are the way to go. Eat, toss, done."

Dakota gives her mother an eye roll. "Mom, Aunt Jewel is the new generation. She's a classy biker babe," she explains in her fourteen-year-old, know-it-all way.

I snicker. It must be the age; Brie is just like her—she-devil attitude.

Mitzi tells her daughter she'll be doing the dishes and moves away.

Jackie and JT are standing on the chair. Beau and I laugh at Jackie, trying to sing "Demons" with JT. Every other word, he emphasizes with an exaggerated head bob.

Brainiac walks in, holding up his beer and belting out the hook. I do a slow blink; he has his arm slung over a blond-headed teen. The kid is grinning up at Brainiac as if he is a god.

"Aunt Jewel, your favorite eldest nephew has returned," bellows Brainiac. "Bring me some love."

I laugh. Fuck Uncle Joker. All the kids are about Aunt Jewel.

"Timmeee, get me," shouts Jackie, waving his arms.

Brainiac chuckles and walks over to Jackie and JT. That's when I get a glimpse of the couple behind him. My father appears older. He still stands tall, with his shoulders back, sporting the same crew cut. Dad's wearing a white polo shirt, light khaki pants, and brown loafers, a bottle of Fat Tire in hand. My mom is beside him. She looks the same: her hair is short and gray. She's wearing her usual attire: a flowered sundress with sensible flat sandals. The Whiskey Sour Sunrise in her hand is surprising; she wasn't much of a drinker. They have their blue eyes pinned on the kids.

Brainiac hands JT his beer and swings Jackie onto his shoulders by one arm. My father flinches, ready to catch him if he falls. Jackie giggles wildly and latches onto Brainiac's blond man-bun.

JT leaps and wraps himself around Brainiac like a monkey. He hands Brainiac back his beer.

Brainiac turns to my parents, grinning. He taps his bottle against Jackie's leg. "This little dude is my cuz, Jackie. The blond dude is one of my baby brothers, JT." He tilts his head toward Jewel. "That's my Aunt Jewel."

"Fuck," I murmur and move through the crowded room to get to Jewel.

"Charlotte, Jackson," smiles Jewel. She's trying to move quickly through the crowded four-seasons room with a tray of mini bean taquitos. Every two steps, she stops to receive respectful pecks on the cheek from the brothers.

My father, mother, and nephew's mouths are hanging open.

"Mommeee," shrills Jackie, waving her over. "They're hungry." He opens his mouth and points to it. "She'll come with food," he assures, staring down at my parents.

I bow my head, chuckling. Nope, that's not the reason Mom, Dad, and Met have their mouths hanging open—my wife is more of a goddess in person than in any picture.

Brainiac grins and takes a swig of his beer.

"Jackson, Charlotte, Metallica, welcome to our home." Jewel purses her glossy plum-colored lips. "Kiss." Brainiac gives her a smack on the lips. "The flight went well?"

"Hm," hums Brainiac. "The winds were with us. The jet needs to be restocked with chips and soda."

"Uncle Joker will take care of it," assures Jewel. She turns her attention to my parents and holds out the tray for them. "Bean taquitos."

I smirk. JT's sticking his foot out to keep my mother's drink from spilling.

"Oh my goodness, I'm sorry," says Mom and quickly adjusts her glass. Flustered, my mom takes a napkin and one of the bean taquitos. She smiles. "Your home is gorgeous." Mom elbows my father in the ribs. "Isn't it, Jack?"

My father clears his throat, nodding. He takes a napkin and a taquito. "Yes, beautiful."

I walk up beside Jewel and thread my arm around her waist, taking the tray. I hand it off to one of the brothers passing by. "Mom, Dad, how was your flight?" I don't make any move to kiss or hug them. I doubt it would be welcome.

"It was excellent, son," says my father. He holds out his hand. I take it for a brief shake. "Timmy allowed me to sit in the copilot's seat. Sean is an excellent pilot."

"Where are Zack, Lisa, and Nirvana?"

"Tommy, Doc, and Aunt Polly are at the house, putting the horses in their stalls. Uncle Sean stopped to help. They opted to stay and watch," says Brainiac, then he takes a swig of his beer.

"They were hoping to see the inside of the mansion," murmurs Metallica under his breath.

"Metallica," chastises my mother.

Brainiac laughs. "I'm sure my mother will invite you all over for dinner."

Beau comes over. He kisses Jewel on her temple.

"Beau, this is Jackson and Charlotte." Jewel runs her hand up and down Beau's back. "This is my adopted dad, Beau."

"Papa, time to eat?" asks Jackie. He points his tiny finger at my parents. "They're hungry."

"No, we're great, honey," says my mother nervously. "Look," she pops a taquito into my father's mouth. He just about chokes on it. "See? We're eating." She takes a bite. "Mmm, so delicious. Right, Jack?"

He gives her a what-the-fuck look and swallows. "Right, Char."

Beau chuckles. He shakes my father's hand and then my mother's. "Nice to meet you. Sweetheart, the girls want to know if they should bring out the food. I need to change out the kegs."

"JT, Jackie, grab the trays for the meat. The papas need to start carving," shouts Brie into the four-seasons room. She holds out the platter of hors d'oeuvres to several of the brothers. "Timmy, Papa wants you to fill the tub with ice and add more sodas. Grandma Fitz needs another Sunrise. FYI, she's half blitzed; water it down."

"Go, babe," I chuckle and give her a kiss and then an ass pat. "I've got my parents." I lift Jackie off Brainiac's shoulders. I give him a kiss and set him on his feet. JT purses his tiny lips. I give him a smooch. "Take Jackie and get it done."

"Me," puckers Brainiac. I give him a kiss. "Get to it, and take Metallica," I chuckle. "Make sure you water down Grandma Fitz's drink. I don't want her to fall out of her wheelchair."

"The children are very affectionate," says my mother. She's watching the kids dash off. "They work well together." Mom runs a hand down her dress in a self-conscious manner. "The women are so beautiful." She's watching the biker babes run from the kitchen to the

213

backyard. The brothers are taking the bowls and platters from them. "The men are attentive."

I drag in a breath and slowly exhale to maintain my cool. The way my mother is talking makes me feel like we're an exhibit on display. Pete totters over to me with his little arms raised. I lift him and cradle him to my chest. "Naptime, little man," I whisper and kiss his crown. "Snuggle in." I look at my parents. "Let's freshen our drinks and head outside. We'll walk and talk."

Beau hands my mom a glass of wine and my father a fresh beer. "Do you want me to take Pete?"

I take my brew from Beau. "No, he's good." We walk out into the backyard. I give my parents time to watch, hoping they will understand. If they don't, it's their loss.

The smell of roasted pork, chicken, and steak fills the air. The men are in their cuts, and the women are decked out in biker babe attire. Some of the kids are on the jungle gym, others are jumping on the trampoline. Their giggles rise above the music and voices. Brie, Willow, and Blossom are running around beside their fathers, doing whatever needs to be done. It's their party. They want everyone to eat, drink, and have a good time.

"Your backyard looks like it came straight out of *Beautiful Homes* magazine," breathes out Mom.

Jackie comes out. He's grunting over the weight of the tray. Christ, it's as tall as he is. "Keep going, Jackie," encourages JT, who is struggling with his own two. "Don't drag it."

Dad crouches down, smiling. "Can I help you two men with your trays?"

Jackie looks at JT. JT tilts his head to my father and nods.

Jackie nods and gives my father his tray. He pushes JT's toward Dad. Dad chuckles and takes the metal trays. Jackie points to the hog pit. "My papas need them."

My father looks over to the men standing by the hog and then back to Jackie and JT. "Do you think it would be all right if I were one of your papas, too?"

Jackie and JT look up at me. I give them a slow nod.

"All right," confirms JT. "We'll call you Papa Jack." JT grabs Jackie's hand. They take off, running and giggling.

Jonas, Scout, and Runner come out of the house with buckets of ice filled with beers. Jonas tilts his head, grinning. "For the guys."

I follow his eyes to "the guys." Brainiac, Scottie, Mouse, Rabbit, Tristen, Cole, Mika, Robbie, Lye, Istu, Running Deer, and Eagle are sitting on the ground, shooting the shit. They're the new generation of Sinners—all young, badass, and with our values. "Take the trays to your papas. Tell the guys: no one rides wasted."

Scout smirks. "Aunt Jewel beat you to it. We're sleeping in the game room tonight."

I chuckle and hand them the trays. They sprint off, buckets bouncing.

My father runs his hand down his face. "Jackie doesn't know I'm his real papa," murmurs my father, with a hint of sadness in his voice.

"Dad, the younger kids don't know the difference between blood and chosen. The older kids don't give a shit. "Those men"—I point to the hog pit—"Pick, Godfather, Kelley, General, Horse, Mac, Aaron, Running Bear, Herb, Burt, Alroy, and Rene, are all their grandfathers. They love their grandchildren; they'd give their lives for them."

I hate that I need to explain our way of life to my parents. It's none of their goddamn business. But I do it for Jackie and Jewel. "We're not a cult; we're a subculture. We don't live by mainstream norms. We teach our kids family comes first." I rub Pete's back. "This little guy is Rene Pierre Fontaine; we call him Pete. His father is my best friend, High. His mother is Jewel's best friend, Cookie. He's a Sinners' kid."

"He came to you for love and comfort when he was tired," murmurs my mother. "I've read Jenna Sawyer's book—*American Subcultures*. It disabused many of the stereotypes. Enlightening."

I refrain from rolling my eyes. I'm not surprised my mother read Jenna's book. She was always an avid reader. I'm questioning her "enlightenment."

I run my hand around Pete's tiny back. "I'm Pete's uncle. Most of these people are his aunts and uncles. All of us would give our lives for him."

Cookie whizzes by us on her three-inch heels; she's carrying a humongous bowl of potato salad. "Pete might need his diaper changed, Joker."

I chuckle and tap his butt. "He's good for a few, sweetheart."

Dad laughs. "Part of an uncle's duty is changing diapers?"

"Yeah, Dad. Uncle, father, grandfather, or brother—titles don't matter. We all change shitty diapers, kiss skinned knees, feed, bathe, clothe, and discipline our kids. We love them unconditionally."

Dad puts his hand on my neck. "That's good, Jackson. The kids are loved. I love you, son. When you were a boy, I just showed it differently—"

"Dad, it doesn't matter how you treated me when I was a kid. I'm a man. If you want to be a grandfather to Jackie, it's unconditional love without judgment, or it's nothing."

"Joker," a woman shrills from behind me.

Pete startles. I pat his back gently. "Shh, settle."

Lisa is running toward us. "Sorry," she squeaks out and gives me a kiss. She puts a light hand on Pete's back. "Let me see him."

"That one isn't Jackson's," chuckles my father. He points to Jackie. "He's the one being held by General. General's the president of Jackson's motorcycle club."

"You met Jackie, Dad?"

"Hm," hums my father. "He's beautiful. Jackie's all Jackson, but he looks like his mother."

"He got Jackson's grin," smiles Mom. "His mother is like a young Elizabeth Taylor, only more beautiful." She giggles. "Who would have thought that could be possible?"

I laugh and rub circles over Pete's tiny back. "Where are Nirvana and Zack?"

"Vana is pinned to your wife's side. I'm sure she's trying to weasel an outfit out of her. She already convinced Tommy to take her on a trail ride tomorrow. The man is a doctor: the only surgeon at Sinners Urgent Care. He gets, like, one day off a week." She snorts. "As if he wants to spend it teaching Vana how to ride."

I chuckle. "No worries, Patriot will probably have one of the kids teach her."

"Zack is at the bar. He's having alpha hot male time with the hunky men. I think he's begging Beau to take him fly-fishing." Lisa scowls. "They have no shame, Joker."

I chuckle again.

Bang bang bang! I turn toward the noise. Jewel is standing with Jackie on her hip. His head has flopped against his mother's shoulder—droopy-eyed—his hand is gripping her ponytail possessively. Jewel has her arm around Vana; she's talking to her. Probably explaining who is who. The biker babes are standing around in a semicircle. Beau and Zack are on Jewel's other side. Christ, Honeypot was the one banging on the pan.

"Thanks, Honeypot." Princess rolls her eyes. "I have an announce-ment. Our sister, Jewel, is making this day a celebration of family. At dusk, we'll be lighting the lanterns in the four-seasons room for our Finlan." Princess's eyes well up with tears. She clears her throat. "We want to make sure Finlan knows he isn't forgotten. Finlan is loved."

There are hollers from the Sinners: "Finlan is with us, Jewel!" "He's a Sinner, never forgotten, sweetheart!" "Finlan is riding free, cradled in his Papa Coin's arms." The brothers are tapping two fingers against their chests, kissing them, and pointing to the sky.

"Thank you," says Jewel. She wipes her tears onto her free shoul-der. "You all own my heart."

I blow out a breath. Tears sting the backs of my eyes. *Christ, I can't lose it now.*

Dad puts his hand on the back of my neck. "I get it. These people gave you what I didn't: the freedom to be you. Give me a chance; I'll make it right."

"Come." I walk over to Jewel and give her a kiss with a bit of tongue. "You shouldn't be holding our son on your left hip, babe," I murmur onto her lips.

Vana smiles. "I can hold Jackie for you, Aunt Jewel."

Jackie shakes his head and reaches for me.

I run my lips across Jackie's forehead. He's warm, salty, and exhausted from running around with the kids. "He's tired, Vana." I shift Pete to the right side of my chest. Jackie wraps around my left side and lays his head on my shoulder. He fists my hair and snuggles in.

Dad places his large hand on Jackie's back. Rubbing gentle circles, he speaks to him in a soft tone of voice. I want to tell him to take his goddamn hand off my son's back. My father's hand is identical to mine. His voice is the same as mine. I fought hard not to be my father, yet when Jewel was pregnant with Finlan, I became him: cold, distant, angry, and punitive. I lost everything and needed to battle my way back. Then I needed to fight for my son's love, trust, and affection. There aren't any free passes—blood doesn't mean shit. A person needs to earn their place.

Jackie shakes his head and yawns. "Love Daddy."

"I love you more, Jackie," I whisper onto his forehead.

Zack comes over to us. He hugs my head. "Missed you," he whispers and bumps my temple with his. Then he glances at my father. "What did you do to the old man? He's showing PDA."

"Zack, mind your own goddamn business," growls my father. "Can't you see my grandson is whipped? He needs some comfort."

Lisa snickers. "I think Hell just froze over."

Jewel giggles and looks at my dad. Hope is in her violets. "You're up, Cowboy."

"Hey, brothers and family," I chuckle. "These are my blood relations, Char, Jack, Lisa, Zack, Vana, and Met. Chow's on. Let's party."

High steps up to me; he grins at his baby boy, asleep on my shoulder. "Come to Daddy. Uncle Joke has shit going on." He takes Pete and hugs him to his chest.

My father extends his hand. "Hello, High. I'm Jack."

High takes his hand for a brief shake. "So I've been told," says High without warmth in his voice.

High and I have had conversations about our parents—we differed in that he missed his. Rene was judgmental over High quitting college for a devious bitch. High's head was fucked-up. It's a long, ugly story with a happy ending. His parents, Rene and Dana Fontaine, conformed quickly to the Sinners' way of life: they sold their home in Butte and turned over their commodities business to the Sinners. The couple moved into High and Cookie's home. They're all about High, Cookie, their grandkids, and the Sinners.

My father was judgmental of everything I did. I never missed my parents: I was happy to get away from them.

High won't give my parents a pass. They'll need to earn the right to be part of our lives. Unlike High, I don't want my parents living in Pony. Short visits, I might be able to tolerate.

Honeypot comes dancing over. "High, Cookie needs your help." She smiles up at my father and links her arm with his. She leans into him. "I'm Amelia, or Honey, whichever you're comfortable with. I'm the cosmetologist at Sinners Beauty Salon." She leads him to the food tent. "Come by, I'll give you a free hot oil treatment for your scalp. Some people are unaware that their skin is the first line of defense against disease." She hugs him closer. "It's super-important."

My dad looks over his shoulder; fear is in his eyes. "Charlotte!"

"I'll take a little bit of everything, darling," replies my mother without looking his way.

Darling. That's new. I've never heard my mother call my father an endearment. "Jack"—that was it. I look over at my mother. She's sipping on a glass of wine, talking to Raven, Bess, Hialeah, Dana, White Dove, Aveline, and Mable. They're telling her about their "wine club," which is them getting shit-faced on the club's back deck.

"You should join us," invites Raven. "We meet every Saturday night at the club. On Fridays, Cookie sings at Callaghan's. It's the kids' 'date night.' We're usually babysitting for one or more of our grand-children."

Bess takes a gulp of her wine. "Jewel, Princess, Maggie, Raine, and Cookie hook us up with different wines to taste. They're mainly from California: all top-shelf. The girls never scrimp on us."

Aveline nods her agreement. "Never."

"The girls love us. They don't want us to drink cheap wines, with all those chemicals and preservatives," explains White Dove. "Our girls give us a wine experience." She titters and takes a sip.

Mable holds up her glass. "This particular vintage is Screaming Eagle from Napa Valley. It's probably a bit pricey. But I think it's worth the money."

My mother nods and takes a drink. "It's delicious."

I grin. My mother is half in the bag.

"The girls and Merrill, he's the club's chef"—Dana points to Merrill in the food tent—"have a cooking club. They meet every Saturday and prepare us something that pairs well with the wines." She sips her cab. "Their food is fabulous. Better than any five-star restaurant."

General steps up beside me, chuckling. "How much green did the wine set you back?"

I smirk and roll my eyes.

"Devilan told me you're covering all the expenses on the three properties. It costs you a fucking bundle."

I snort. "Do you think I'm going to allow my wife to support us? The money Jenna and Jackson left her is for our kids." I smile over at Jewel. "My wife's been through hell. It makes her happy to throw parties and give our women their 'wine experience.' The green doesn't matter."

"Starting next month, the club is covering all the expenses on the Malibu property. I'm paying for half the party." He chuckles. "My wife and her 'wine club' are sucking down the cab as if it's two bucks a bottle. I'll get the number from Devilan."

"You don't need to do that. I'm staying in the black."

"I'm going to keep you there," growls General. Then he walks away, heading toward the hog pit.

I look back at my father. Jewel has saved him from Honeypot. She has a plate, and Dad has three in his hands. Keeley, JT, Anna, and JJ are pointing to their choices.

"Daddy, I want barbie and corn," says Jackie lazily against my neck.

"How about Mommy's potato salad?" I murmur onto his head.

"That, too, with orange."

The older kids fly by us with their towels flapping and their plates piled a mile high. Swimming always makes them hungry.

Jackie whips his head up and looks into the food tent. Kids are choosing their food with the brothers and their women.

"Jackie, we'll save you a seat," yells Jonny as he zooms by us.

"The corn's going quick, Jackie. I got you an ear," shouts Jacob. He's running behind his brother.

"Jackie, grab extra potato salad. I missed it," yells Jonas as he zips by.

"Daddy, go," he orders. He's pointing to the tent as if I'm the one holding him up.

I chuckle and walk inside. We arranged the tables in a horseshoe shape, so people could access both sides. The two lines are long but moving quickly.

Guard Dog, Liam, and Rocky take the plates from my father. "Thanks, we'll get them set up in their seats."

Jackie stares at the platter of barbecue. "Papa Jack, barbie!" he screeches from ten feet away.

Dad turns and looks at him; his brow furrows. "Which one is barbie?"

Jackie points. "*Barbieeee!*"

Pick, Horse, Mac, and Godfather come into the tent loaded down with trays of barbecued pork, chicken, steak, and corn.

Godfather laughs. "Jackie wants you to save him some barbecued pork. It's his favorite."

"If you stick around, you'll find out Jackie and Joker are father and son." Pick guffaws. "They both are protective of their food."

Dad chuckles. "That's because Jackson's older sister used to eat everything in sight."

"God, Dad!" barks Lisa, filling her plate.

"She still does," mumbles Met.

"Metallica!" shouts Lisa.

"Mom, you did eat the last bag of chips on the plane," reminds Vana. "Then you complained about your butt spreading east to west."

The brothers chortle low.

"There's nothing wrong with fat-bottomed girls. Queen has a song called just that," grins Sly. "If your husband doesn't give a shit, who fucking cares?"

Zack smacks Lisa's ass and grasps a handful. "I like a lot of junk in your trunk," he chuckles.

"Zack!" shrills Lisa.

Patriot and Brainiac hold up their beers, singing "Fat Bottomed Girls." That gets the kids singing along.

Dad is bent over laughing.

"Do you see this, Joker?" asks Lisa. She's throwing out her hand toward our father. "The man who made us is laughing over his daughter's butt."

"Yeah, Lis, I'm seeing him," I chuckle.

It's weird but fantastic all the same: Dad never laughed much when we were teenagers. He was promoted to admiral, and his sense of humor left him. Lisa thought it was because Dad's title and responsibilities stressed him out. I thought it was because he was a dictatorial, judgmental asshole. Watching him laugh now, I wonder which one of us was right.

CHAPTER 37

THE LANTERNS – JEWEL

I thought lighting the lanterns was going to be a piece of cake. After all, I wanted Finlan to be a part of the family celebration. Lord Jesus, now that everyone is in the four-seasons room waiting to light the damn things, it feels more like we're mourning him. I take a deep breath and blow it out slowly. Blinking back my tears, I look at all our family and friends. "Joker and I want to thank you all for helping us include Finlan. He would be three years old—a year younger than CJ." I force a smile and grip the only thing I have of my eldest son: the cylinder charm encasing Finlan's hair that hangs around my neck. This shouldn't be painful, but it is: the lanterns were a bad idea.

"Babe," murmurs Joker, rubbing my lower back. He leans down and gives me a soft kiss. "Finlan is with us. Always. We will see him when it's our time." Joker wipes my tears with his thumbs. "Cookie," he commands in his forceful way.

"Joker and Jewel chose the song 'Calling All Angels.' If you know it, sing with High and me as you light your lantern and float it in the pool."

"Sing on key, Daddy," reminds CJ, looking up at his father.

I sniff and giggle at CJ's reminder. High has an excellent voice. He does sound a bit like Pat Monahan with more rasp. He's not a natural singer; more importantly, he doesn't like to sing. Cookie's forever dragging him onto Callaghan's stage with her and her band, the Heartbreakers. She loves him and wants to share her man's "gift." In truth, it wouldn't matter if High sounded like a cat on a hot tin roof. The people love him. He's a gorgeous hunk—American Frenchman—eye candy the women love to drool over. Secondly, he loves Cookie; it shines when they sing together.

The Jameson bottle comes around. High tips it back and takes one…two…three big swallows. "Christ," he breathes out and passes the bottle on to Patriot.

The Heartbreakers couldn't be here tonight: Cal and Woody's wives just had babies. Lex and Max are helping them out. If the band were here, they'd save High.

Patriot tips the bottle back and takes a long swig. "I've got your back, brother. Let loose, I'll follow."

Cookie starts the intro on her portable keys. She smiles up at her husband and gives him a nod.

High spread-eagles his arms and tilts his head back, holding his face up to Heaven. "*I need a sign to let me know you're here…*" The room fills with voices singing the words: mostly women. Very few badass bikers sing unless they're four sheets to the wind.

I look over at High and start laughing. People must think I'm crazy, but I don't care. The look of relief on High's face is hysterical.

He smirks at me and gives me a two-finger kiss. The bottle of Jameson comes around to us. Beau takes a guzzle and then passes it to Joker.

Joker puts it to my lips. "Little sip."

I grin and take a big sip—liquid courage. Joker takes two guzzles and passes the bottle to Mafia Man. The Native Americans have a pipe. Bikers have a bottle.

I'm relieved Joker got over his aversion to whiskey. Then I laugh at myself. *You like that your husband likes whiskey.* No, it isn't that I like the fact my husband likes whiskey. It's that Joker has returned to his biker badassness: whiskey, beer, bikes, rock, and hot monkey sex with only me.

Joker, Beau, and I light our lanterns. "Daddy, Mommy, and Papa love you, Fin," whispers Joker as we float them into the water.

The kids are at the edge of the pool with Jackie. They're helping him light his lantern. Joker and I smile at each other. They're good kids, and they love their little cousin.

Scottie holds Jackie just above the water. He whispers into Jackie's ear.

"Love you, big brother," repeats Jackie and lets go of his lantern. Then he looks back at Scottie and gives him a big baby-tooth grin.

Jackie doesn't know the meaning of the lanterns. He can't grasp the concept of Finlan. He's a concrete thinker: what he sees, he knows.

I take in the room and wish I had a glass of wine. Like magic, Princess materializes by my side, holding out a glass. "Fortification, sister," she grins and sips on her own drink. She clinks with me. Then she sways back into the waiting arms of her husband.

I take a big gulp and savor the rich, smooth fruitiness with a hint of oakiness rolling over my tongue. My nerves settle, and my mind drifts to my sisters.

Biker women can be as mean as junkyard dogs: mess with their family, and they'll mess with you tenfold. The women have an iron-clad sisterhood that I'm proud to be a part of. We don't have the motto *Ride free, die free, in brotherhood*, but, like the brothers, no matter what happens, we take each other's backs.

Mitzi is one of the toughest biker women I've ever met: she's ridden many rocky roads with her man. Her exterior is as hard as nails. Internally, she is as soft as cotton for the sisters, brothers, and our kids. Mitzi dabs her eyes, murmuring, "The needle is too good for that motherfucker. One of those assholes on the inside should cut him up for what he's done." Geronimo pulls her into him and holds her tight. The sisterhood agrees with nods and nose wipes.

God knows, I love these girls—they're mine.

There are bikers in the California State Penitentiary. Princess told me they're not alliances of the Sinners or the Red Devils. She doubts they know about us. "It doesn't matter, Jewel. If I can get the warden to put the bastard into gen pop, they'll torture him. Bikers don't have a tolerance for baby killers or pedophiles. The asshole wouldn't last a day."

Princess and I were overjoyed when the warden agreed. Then we were crushed: Ricky's attorney got a court order to keep him in solitary.

I know Ricky would have been murdered. The Sinners and the Red Devils are hard as steel—unyielding when someone screws with our family, turf, or beliefs. Our men will kill without remorse. In contrast, they're also the most loving men on the planet.

I sigh and lean into Joker and Beau, sipping my wine. We watch the brothers light their lanterns and listen to Cookie, High, and Patriot sing. Some of the bikers pound their fists over their hearts. Others kiss two fingers and hold them up to Heaven. Some whisper their own form of a prayer. All of them come over to give their respect to Joker and Beau. Our loss is their loss. Then, as bikers do, they amble out to the backyard, ready to party.

Joker's biological family is standing across the room. They look like fish out of water. Charlotte and Lisa are hugging the kids. Zack has his arm around his father-in-law. Jack is emotional. I'm guessing that doesn't happen often.

I know about mainstream people, having lived among them during my fashionista days. They're complex. Often, society's rules are contradictory: if a person shows emotion, they are considered weak. In contrast, if a person doesn't show emotion, they are considered cold and unfeeling. I've heard mainstream parents scold their boys for crying: *Stop crying like a little girl. Get up and brush it off. It doesn't hurt that bad.*

Disciplining children is a tight rope for civilians: spankings are a no-no; it's child abuse. Taking away your kids' possessions is cruel. Yet not disciplining the children is unacceptable. Giving the kids material things is considered overindulgent. Not giving them something is selfish. I noticed threats without follow-through were common. Promises often went unfulfilled among fashionista parents. I wonder how mainstream parents are supposed to parent with so many contradictions.

You're lucky, Jewel. You'll never need to know. Our men don't follow norms. They love our kids openly. I grin. The boys probably get more hugs and kisses than the girls, given they get hurt more often. Sinners clearly lay out expectations for their children. If the kids do something unacceptable, there is a *long, long* conversation before punishment is doled out. Spankings are rare: several of our kids were physically abused by their biological parents before they were adopted by the Sinners family. Spanking them is strictly prohibited. Also, the brothers believe corporal punishment is easily forgotten—cleaning horse stalls for a month without help makes more of an impact. Taking the kids' possessions away doesn't work. Our kids are resourceful; they find other things to do. Timeouts work the best on the younger kids. I snort. Making them sit down for ten minutes to think about what they had done is torture on everyone.

I suspect Jack didn't give Joker clear expectations when he was a child. There probably wasn't a long conversation before he punished his son. As with many mainstream parents, more than likely, their relationship was based upon "just do as I say."

Mom always said, "Children are molded by their parents."

Many of the Sinners weren't raised with societal norms. The ones who were managed to break the mold. Jack is making an effort to heal the breach with Joker. It's my job as Joker's wife to support my husband. Joker is conflicted. He doesn't trust his father—contradictions breed mistrust. I exhale. I need to throw Jack a lifeline, me.

I walk over to Jack and hold out my hand. I smile and wipe his tears. "Papa Jack needs to light a lantern for his grandson." I slide my arm around his waist and lead him over to the pool.

Jack stares at the lantern in his hand. He swallows and sniffs. "I don't know the protocol, Jewel."

Joker kneels beside him and flicks his lighter to life. "There is no protocol, Dad. Say what you feel or say nothing at all. No one will judge you here."

Jack nods and takes the lighter. He lights the candle and sends the lantern afloat. Then Jack does something unexpected. He grabs Joker and hugs him, breathing in his scent.

I kiss Joker's crown and stand. "Take a minute with your dad. I'll be outside with Beau." I walk over to Beau and feel so grateful I had a wonderful father, and now, I have a spectacular dad. I walk out into the backyard with Beau. Wrapping my arms around his waist, I ask, "Did I ever tell you how much I love you, Daddy Beau?"

He chuckles low. "Over the years, more than a billion times." He hugs me tight and kisses my crown. "I love you, too, daughter."

CHAPTER 38

THE DEATH PENALTY – JOKER

It's been twelve days, fourteen hours, and thirty-five minutes. I know, I've been counting down the time until Lisa, Zack, Nirvana, and Metallica go back to Honolulu. We have twenty-four more hours to endure. I wanted to ship them back a week ago. If I hear, "Aunt Jewel, will you get me—" or "Aunt Jewel, can I have—" one more time, I'll blow a fucking gasket. My wife has been waiting on them hand and foot: cooking their meals, picking up their wet towels, getting them their snacks, making their beds, and washing their clothes.

Beau flew Maria back to Malibu three days ago. I suspect she had enough of Lisa and Zack's kids, too. The Sinners' kids treat Maria with respect. They don't call her grandma, but to them, she is one of their grandparents. Nirvana and Metallica treated Maria like she was the hired help—no "please," and no "thank you," just "get me" and "bring me."

I lost my shit over it. Lisa gave me an eye roll: "God, Joker, calm down. The kids will say please and thank you. They'll pick up their wet towels." Zack said nothing. It became apparent that my sister and her husband have become the mainstream parents they vowed they'd never be.

Surprisingly, my father had my back: "His house, his rules." As a kid, I hated it when Dad said that. It isn't about "my house, my rules." It's about having respect and courtesy for my wife and Maria. Even so, I appreciated my father speaking up.

Brainiac and Scottie took Vana riding two days after she got here. The girl is still bitching that her ass and legs are sore. She rode for a whopping fifteen minutes.

Beau, High, and I took Zack and Metallica fly-fishing. I spent all my time untangling lines. We came home after I cut the fish hook out of Metallica's thumb.

Jewel and I took the "family" to the Native American Village. Lisa bitched about the heat and the long walk. For Christ's sake, she's a nurse. At Sinners Urgent Care, the nurses run their asses off for twelve hours a day. My mother informed me: "Lisa is a telehealth nurse. They monitor the 'clients' using a computer."

The family outing was enough for my parents: now Mom and Dad borrow my truck and disappear. Every morning they grab their coffees and muffins from the diner. Then they head over to the library to read the newspaper as if it's a goddamn Starbucks. After that, my parents drive to the club for lunch, where they socialize with Merrill and "the boys." They travel out to the Tucker-Adams ranch for midday drinks and to watch the cowboys train the horses. Or they head over to the Reservation to do god knows what. Then my parents hit Pony Diner for the early bird special with the older crowd. I haven't a clue who the hell the "older crowd" is—the Sinners' older couples are home with their families. After that, my parents beat feet to Callaghan's Bar for after-dinner drinks.

The frosting on the cake was on Saturday. "Dad and I are heading over to the club early." Mom said it as if she were going to a country club—Sinners is a one percent biker compound. "We're participating in the cooking club with Merrill and the girls. Shrimp étouffée, paired with a white chardonnay. Scrumptious." My mother actually rolled her eyes like she couldn't wait to experience a three-course meal in a five-star restaurant. "It's Cookie's turn to provide the wine. I'm sure it's going to be delicious." I was sure the wine would be "delicious," too. It was coming from my wine cellar.

Last Thursday, during church, I told the brothers not to purchase wine for the girls' wine club from the Butte distributor. I had that deal with my young wine broker in Malibu. I was getting a thirty percent discount; he was getting a five percent commission. The brothers were down with that. Mafia Man is going to connect with him. He wants to make a deal for Callaghan's Bar, the club, and the brothers' homes. "We'll help the kid out and see if we can get a deeper discount. The markup on wine averages in the neighborhood of two hundred percent," explained Mafia Man.

The club officially took over the expenses on the Malibu property. "We can finagle it as a business expense and write it off on our corporate taxes," said Mafia Man. I wasn't sure how he was going to do that, but it was fine with me.

The NYC apartment will be leased to a corporate executive from Netflix. Pick and Princess are working on the terms. "We're asking for forty-five grand per month. That will include utilities, the association fee, and parking for two vehicles. The deal is good for the exec, given the location, the square footage of the apartment, and it's furnished. For you, it will cover all costs and put a decent amount of bank back into your pocket." I agreed. Jewel and I have no desire to go to NYC any time soon. Even if we did, Mrs. Fitzpatrick, Godfather, and Mac's homes, along with Mafia Man's brownstone, are available to us. I walked out of church a happy man: I wouldn't need to worry about how I would keep paying for three properties.

On Saturday, Mom also informed me: "We're staying overnight at the club, Jackson. Dad is playing poker with the guys, and I'm joining the wine club with the girls."

That served to piss me off. Jewel and I had opted out of Saturday night because the "family" was "exhausted" from all their activities. My wife loves her wine and cooking club, Jackie loves to play with his cousins, and I like to kick back and relax with my brothers. Jewel said, "Cowboy, it's no big deal. It's just one Saturday." She planned a movie marathon and pizza night. It turned into an argument: Lisa and Nirvana wanted a chick flick, Metallica wanted a horror movie, and Zack wanted an action film. Jewel and I gave up and took Jackie to our bedroom. Jackie and I watched motocross. Jewel worked on the designs for the clothing line.

My parents' voices at the top of the landing get my attention.

Mom and Dad come down the stairs, hand in hand. It's weird seeing them all goddamn touchy-feely. Dad walks over to Jewel and kisses her on the cheek. "We need to make tracks to the library. The Dish internet guy will be there by nine o'clock."

I furrow my brow. *Dish internet? Who in the hell ordered that?* I look over at Beau. He shrugs and wipes Jackie's face.

Jewel smiles up at my dad and then walks over to the drawer. She pulls out several pieces of yellow paper and hands them to him. "I paid the invoices for Dish, Montana Furniture, Apple, the newspaper distributor, the diner, and Amazon. Are you going to be available to oversee the deliveries?"

What the fuck are they up to?

Mom nods. "We'll be at the library all day."

Dad takes the invoices and reviews them. "I don't know, honey-bunch, I think we should have gotten better rates than these. It's a library."

Honeybunch. I chuckle. *Who is he, and what happened to my dad?* I walk over to my father. "What the hell is going on?"

He hands me the invoices.

Jewel explains quickly, "The librarian, Gola, called me. Well, technically, she's not a librarian, but she's worked at the library since Mom opened it. Anyway, she told me we've had a significant influx of people since your mom and dad have started eating breakfast there."

"Hm," I hum and look over the invoices. *Shit, all of this should have gone through the nonprofit's account.*

"The library hasn't been updated in years. And since people are going there, I decided it was time for a makeover: computers, comfy furniture, new books, and a breakfast nook. Everyone was busy, so I just made a few online transactions."

"A few," I snort and carefully examine the invoices. Three computers, two printers, inventory library software, two new sectional couches, six cuddle chairs, eight knotty pine side tables, all the books on the *New York Times* bestseller list, one hundred children's books, and a commercial breakfast cart. Thirty newspapers per morning—ten each of *The Wall Street Journal*, *Montana Standard*, and *Los Angeles Times*. I blow out a breath and pinch my bottom lip.

I look over the agreement with the diner: Twenty-five each: muffins, pastries, bagels, fruit cups, and yogurt parfaits. Two thirty-two-ounce thermal carafes of regular coffee, one thirty-two-ounce thermal carafe of decaf coffee, teas, juices, plastic utensils, and paper products. No charge for packets of sugar, sugar substitute, butter, cream cheese, jellies, nondairy and half-and-half creamers, or hot water. I choke and suppress my cough when I see the price Butch is charging: five hundred dollars per day. "You're purchasing the food from Butch and Annie at full price?"

Jewel nods. She looks at the invoice with me. "We didn't want to undercut Butch and Annie's business. We're purchasing the modified continental breakfast from the diner. We're asking people who can afford it to make a donation. Many of the people who join your mom and dad are older. They're on a fixed income." Jewel giggles, her violets glittering with delight. "Are you going to yell at me for running up our American Express card?"

Beau laughs. "Let her have it. It'll make her day."

I chuckle and kiss her lips. "Nope, I'm going to yell at you for not involving me. Babe, all this should have been done through the library's nonprofit account."

I'm going to tear Butch a new asshole for taking advantage of my wife. He knows we could get the food for free from the Native Americans. They're our family; they'd accept the donations. There's no goddamn way we're paying one hundred and eighty grand per year for breakfast.

Dad furrows his brow and looks at the invoices in my hand. "Christ, I knew we should have consulted you." He shakes his finger at the diner's invoice. "That one didn't seem reasonable. Can it be fixed?"

"Yeah, Dad. Mafia Man, Beau, and I will take care of it." I glance at him. "Our finances are complicated. My wife knows she can buy anything she wants. The money needs to come out of the correct account." I hold up the diner's invoice. "I won't allow Jewel to get ripped off. Butch is a friend. He's also a businessman. Friend or not, it doesn't matter to him. If he can make a buck, he will."

My mother grabs her purse. "Jack, we can't be late." She grins up at me, humor in her blues. "Your father needs to figure out how to set up the computers and install the software. I can take it from there. I volunteered at our public library at home. Jewel bought me the same software." She practically dances out of the kitchen in excitement.

The front door bangs open. "Joker!" shouts Princess. She comes rushing in, almost mowing my father down. "Oh, sorry, Jack." She runs over to me with her phone held out. "I need to show you the text I received from the LA DA's office."

Mom comes back into the kitchen. Dad wraps his arms around her. Anytime the DA gets mentioned, it sends everyone's heart racing. We've been waiting to hear news on Briggs's trial. I've decided: if the justice system doesn't take him down, I'll pay someone on the inside to do it.

I hug Jewel to my side and read aloud: "Corinne, I'm happy to inform you we won the conviction. It was unanimous—ten counts of premeditated first-degree murder. Richard Briggs received the death penalty. I have not contacted the Fraziers due to the date of execution. The twentieth of May, next year."

Jewel takes a sharp inhale, clutching my tee.

"Fuck," I breathe out and reread the date.

"I know," says Princess tearfully. "The day the bastard killed Finlan. I think the judge picked the date hoping it would resonate in Briggs's psychotic brain. But, Joker, the average length of time a prisoner stays on death row is six years—"

I jerk my head up. "The fucker dies on May twentieth, Princess. He is not goddamn living for six more years."

She nods. "You know Daddy and I will do everything in our power to make it happen, Joker." She reads the last portion of the text: "I hope this news gives the Frazier family some comfort in that justice has prevailed. It's customary for two family members to be invited to witness an execution. If you would be so kind as to submit the names to me. I'd like to get the persons vetted ASAP. Again, my condolences for your family's loss."

I hand Princess her phone and blow out another breath. Finally, the fucking bastard is going to be wiped off the face of the earth. Hell is too good for the asshole.

Jewel sniffs and tosses her head back, smiling up at me. "We got the conviction. I can't go to the execution. I don't ever want to see Richard Briggs again. Besides, it will be a media circus." Her violets move to Beau. "Daddy Beau, will you take my place?"

Beau scissors his fingers through his hair. "Yeah, daughter, I'll be happy to watch the fucker die. My only regret is I'm not the one putting the bastard to ground."

My father looks at me and pinches his forehead. "Son, if you can't handle it, I'll go with Beau."

I glance at my father; my eyes burn with indignation. I'm a one percent biker. I've sent many evil bastards to hell. The one who counted—the fucker who killed my son—was untouchable. No one is taking my place at Briggs's execution. "I have lived the last four goddamn years of my life trying to find a way to murder the mother-fucker. I'll be at his execution for my wife, my sons, my family, and for me."

My mother's lips firm; she nods. "Jackson got his gumption from me. An eye for an eye."

Dad and I look at each other. Both of us grin and fight back our laughter. If a tiny lizard found its way into our house, Mom would scream her head off for Dad or me to get it out unharmed.

Princess's phone starts playing "Wild Horses." Her golden eyes light up. "Schnooks," she breathes out and reads his text. She dashes for the door, shouting over her shoulder, "I need to go. Something is happening at the library. Schnooks needs me. We'll talk later."

My father and mother's eyes widen, watching her run in three-inch high-heeled red pumps.

Zoom! She's gone.

I grab Jackie's helmet, his shades, and the harness. "Babe, let's go take care of the library."

"Oh my goodness, Jack, we're late!"

My dad chuckles and pulls my truck fob from his pocket. "I think Schnooks has it covered, unless his wife breaks her ankle before she gets to him." He scowls at Mom. "I've never seen you knee-to-chest like that for me."

"Jack"—Mom rolls her eyes—"have you seen Princess's husband?" She leaves it at that, humming "Wild Horses" out the door.

Dad mocks low, "Have you seen Princess?" and follows her through the door.

Jewel and I burst out laughing. I scoop up Jackie, and we head for the bike.

CHAPTER 39

JOKER IS OUR HERCULES – JEWEL

Montana winter is coming upon us quickly. The first of November has arrived. It's the benchmark for Sinners and Native Americans to close Diva Mountain Native American Village for the season. I awoke with a mild case of melancholy thrumming through me. Unlike many of the Sinners and Native Americans, I've come to like the energy that the tourists bring to Pony. Vacationers bustle around our tiny town, excited to enjoy our little piece of Heaven. Come winter, like the bears, Pony as a vacation destination will hibernate until spring.

At six this morning, a faint orangey-yellow glow barely kissed the mountaintops: dawn was breaking. The air was crisp, with a hint of moisture—snow is on its way. Joker swung Jackie up into his arms. He grabbed the thermal travel mugs—coffee for him, hot chocolate for Jackie—and then he zipped out the door.

Joker's parents, Beau, and I trudged silently behind him. Jack and Char slid into Beau's Ford, and I climbed into Joker's truck.

My man chuckled at me. "Tired, babe?"

I said nothing. My morning routine has changed. I no longer leap out of bed at the crack of dawn—I'm loved awake by Cowboy. My husband nuzzles my neck and hums his deep, throaty hum into my ear while massaging my breasts tenderly. Then he glides his massive erection inside me, loving me awake slowly.

This morning I awoke to the blare of Godsmack, "Rocky Mountain Way." To make it more irritating, I didn't even get a cuddle: Joker was already in the shower.

Slightly surly, I sipped my coffee and stared out the passenger side window as we followed Beau. There is no denying it: Diva Mountain is beautiful in the fall. The greens, yellows, oranges, and reds against the Rockies are breathtaking. Still, it would have been more enjoyable with my typical morning wake-up call..

Once at the Native American Village, we were divided into teams. The work was immense: the unsold merchandise, food, and paper products needed to be packed into boxes and taken down the mountain to the Reservation. Two hundred picnic tables needed to be scrubbed and stacked. Hides had to be removed from their teepee stands and then cleaned, rolled, and stored—hundreds of lights had to be taken down. The septic tanks were pumped out, the water was drained from the pipes, and the electricity turned off.

The replica of the Native American school and the restaurant got a thorough cleaning. Sheets were placed over the furniture and appliances. Then the windows and doors were boarded up.

Just taking care of the twenty Painted Ponies was a daunting task. Bales of hay and alfalfa were transported to the Reservation, along with the horses. The barn was scrubbed from floor to ceiling and then boarded up so that no wild animals could get inside.

The paddocks, arenas, and grounds needed to be groomed. It's maddening—there can be a trash can less than a foot away, and people will still litter.

At three o'clock, Jackie was done—droopy-eyed and staggering to stay on his tiny feet. Joker wrapped Jackie in a rabbit fur blanket, put him into his kid carrier, and swung him onto his back. I don't know how my man did it. He kept working as Jackie slept. I took pictures so I can remember it when we're old and gray. Joker is our Hercules.

By 6:00 p.m., it was pitch-black outside. The temperature had plummeted to a whopping thirty degrees, and there was light, wet snow falling from the starless sky. I was grateful our work was done. The Native American Village was winterized. Lord knows, if I'd needed to work another hour, I would have passed out.

Entirely exhausted, we all went to the club for dinner. Merrill had made three different kinds of hearty soups, beef stew, chili, and a variety of subs. It was a good thing, because I doubt any of us women had the energy to cook. We barely had the strength to chew. Our men appeared as if they could go for another twelve hours. How? I haven't a clue.

Once home, Joker needed to help his parents up the stairs. They were wobbly on their feet. I smiled when I heard my man ask, "Dad, can you undress Mom, or should I—"

He didn't need to finish. His father chuckled his deep chuckle. I've come to love hearing it, because it's Joker's amused chuckle. Jack told Joker to go; he had his mother.

Beau carried Jackie up and tucked him into his toddler bed. I poured Joker a whiskey and me a wine. Then I carried them up to our bathroom, set them on the white tiled ledge of the tub, and lit the candles—lavender for muscle fatigue. I drew Joker and me a hot, steamy bath.

Now I'm relaxing against my man's chest and sipping my wine as the jets of the whirlpool work their magic on my sore muscles. The soothing music of Adele is playing low. *Lord, this is heavenly. I'm never getting out of this tub.*

My mind drifts to Char and Jackson. I say lazily, "We need to make a decision regarding your parents, Cowboy."

"Hm," he hums and runs his hand up and down my torso. "What decision?"

I take a sip of my wine, enjoying the feel of my man's roaming hand. "Lisa called me crying. She and the kids miss your mom and dad. They were supposed to go back to Honolulu on October first."

To Gola's relief, Jack and Char made the decision to oversee the library. She was overwhelmed with the increased volume of books and the new computers.

Gola is an older Native American. She's in her eighties and has lived on the Reservation her entire life. She is a valuable friend and employee—an asset to the library.

To my knowledge, Gola has always come to work in her beautiful beaded buckskin dress, moccasins, and feathered headdress. She hasn't missed a day since the library opened its doors.

Over the years, Gola has added old and new pictures of the Native Americans and Sinners to the walls. Sinners were and still are an integral part of the Cherokee's survival in Pony.

Gola's also added to the artifacts. The Native Americans have given her items to display: an old baby rattle made out of a snake's skin, clay bowls, and woven baskets handed down through the generations. There's a little baby buckskin dress and a tiny pair of moccasins so old and delicate, General encased them in Plexiglas.

My mom chose Gola and paid her better than any librarian in the US: Gola is our historian for the Trail of Tears and how their small tribe came to Pony. It isn't the Cherokees' homeland—most settled in and around Oklahoma after the Trail of Tears. Visitors adore listening to her stories.

I'm not sure what we'll do when Jack and Char decide to leave Pony. I know one thing: Gola's not going anywhere. Joker will work it out, just as he's fixed all my blunders.

My man severed our tie with the diner. No hard feelings; it's just business. Now Raine and her staff from the Reservation provide the modified continental breakfast. What surprised us: the donations were more than four times the cost of the food.

My shrewd husband got the newspapers donated to the library for free. And he found a book distributor that automatically sends us the new bestsellers and children's books at a discount.

As with all our businesses, the Sinners pay close attention to the library and its finances. All of us figured that by October the traffic would die down—the tourist season ended. To our amazement, it didn't. In fact, traffic has picked up. We failed to recognize that the low-income families surrounding Pony need the resources the library offers. Word of mouth spread quickly: Pony Library has internet and computers to use for free.

The early morning crowd continues to be older people coming in to enjoy their breakfast and newspapers. Midmornings, parents continue to bring their preschool children in to pick out a new book. The kids look to see if Gola added a new picture or artifact, and they love to listen to her stories. In the afternoon, people come to use the computers. They search through the help wanted ads or apply for a position online or post an employment ad on our free website.

Some people need to pay their utility bills online so they don't get cut off. It became tricky; several of the low-income families don't have a debit or credit card. I was surprised that many of them don't even have a bank account. I said something to Joker about it. Lord almighty, we live in the twenty-first century! It's the height of online banking and shopping. "Babe, they work off the books for less than minimum wage and get paid in cash. Hand-to-mouth, babe; there is nothing left to deposit into a bank account."

People would ask Jack if they could give him the money and use his credit card. Jack called Joker and asked him what he should do. Joker would leave work multiple times a day, call the utility companies, and use one of our credit cards. He needed to ensure our number didn't remain on the person's account. It wasn't practical: it took Joker away from Sinners Bike Shop. It was also a bit unsettling to give our credit card number to various utility companies multiple times a day.

I asked Joker what the people did previously. "Babe, the families went without until they could get somewhere to pay the bill." I found out many low-income families lived in trailers: no oil, no heat—no propane, no stove—no electricity, no lights, and no fridge. Forget about the washer, dryer, and TV; those were luxuries. Unacceptable—the dilemma needed to be solved ASAP.

The library doesn't handle money, except for the donations the Native Americans receive for the food they provide. Pony Grocery

Store and Pony Pharmacy don't offer prepaid credit cards or Western Union: there isn't enough demand. The Sinners decided the easiest way to handle the problem was for Callaghan's Bar to provide prepaid Visa cards. The Sinners absorb the transaction fee. For a poor family, five dollars is the cost of dinner. Problem solved. But it seemed as if we'd just get one issue solved before another would instantly pop up to take its place.

The weekends created another difficulty—low-income kids flooded the library to use the three computers. And, no, it wasn't to post on social media. The public-school teachers would assign research projects. They didn't take into consideration that some kids didn't have access to a computer at home. In truth, neither did I. We live in a technological age, where kids walk around with cell phones, iPads, and laptops. The school computers were available to them for short periods during the school day and after school. Most children couldn't stay after school: they needed to work, or, if they missed the bus, there was no way to get home. And public schools aren't open on the weekends. Again, I asked Joker what the kids did previously. "Little to nothing, babe." That wasn't acceptable: kids need a solid education, or the cycle of poverty will never be broken.

It was a three-part dilemma that needed to be solved. The first part was easy; we purchased more computers, printers, and paper.

The second part was a little more complicated: we didn't have a degreed librarian who could help the kids. Once again, the Sinners and Native Americans came together. Raven and Aaron Donnelly stepped up and offered to work at the library on Saturday and Sunday afternoons. They're teachers on the Reservation. They could help the kids complete their projects. Understandably, General wasn't happy his wife was now working seven days a week.

Those of us with computer experience divided up every Saturday and Sunday afternoon to help out.

Raven came to our rescue. She told Joker about two young Native American women who were graduating from college in December. Raven had been their teacher from kindergarten through twelfth grade. She knew they would be an excellent fit. Joker called them and asked if they would like the job. Luckily, the girls were thrilled. They will be hired as full-time librarians. I wanted the girls and Gola to have a benefit package: paid vacation, sick time, health insurance, and a retirement account. Joker told me, "The library doesn't make any money, babe. It bleeds fucking green. We need to move cash around to pay the girls and give them benefits. We're working on it."

The third part of the dilemma is our biggest obstacle: we've run out of space. The library is sandwiched between the fork in the road and the US post office. The land behind us is woods and boulders. Removing them would cause a drainage problem and interfere with the library and post office's foundations. The Sinners decided that would cost too much money. Besides, it would ruin Pony's landscape. Wolfe said the only thing we can do is go up or find another spot for the library.

Joker and Beau voted against moving the library: it was my mom's gift to Pony. The Sinners voted to live with the small, overcrowded space until spring. Then the roof will be removed, and another two stories will be added, with an elevator—the computer room and the children's room. William Bull is working on the blueprints.

"Babe, you disappeared on me," whispers Joker. He kisses my temple. "You said we needed to make a decision about my parents."

I grin. "I was thinking about the library and everything you, your parents, the Sinners, and the Native Americans have given to the surrounding communities. Free, without any expectations in return." Tears prickle my eyes. "My mom would be in awe and so, so, happy."

"Hm," hums Joker. He sighs. "The truth is we missed the boat. None of the brothers realized how much poverty was in our surrounding communities until the people started showing up at the library. General, Raven, and Running Bear were livid over it. Our goddamn government doesn't give a shit." He takes a sip of his whiskey. "It would drain us all dry trying to fix the problem. We can give the people the library and a free meal." He pauses for a few seconds. "Becca is going to stock the library with premade sandwiches, salads, chips, and drinks."

I turn to look at Joker. "Something is going on with Becca. General assigned her to his team this morning. Becca told him she and Annie would prefer to work on their own. Then Liam invited Becca and Annie back to the club for dinner. Becca refused and said they needed to get home."

Joker nods. "Yeah." He sighs. "General was off-the-chain pissed when I told the brothers Butch was going to charge one hundred and eighty grand per year for the library's breakfast."

"Joker, I told you that was my fault."

"Yeah, I should have kept my mouth shut."

Joker goes on to tell me that General confronted Butch in front of Becca. General reminded Butch he bought the land, built the restaurant, and fronted Butch the money for the appliances, tables, and chairs. General didn't take a dime of rent until Butch started making a decent profit.

Butch is a handsome, brown-haired, brown-eyed, tall, muscled ex-rodeo bronc rider—an older Hugh Jackman comes to mind. His smile is a killer. I don't know Butch well, but I know his type—like my father was, Butch is a proud, independent man. Reminding him how he got his start wasn't a smooth move.

I wrinkle my nose. "Oh god. What did Butch say to that?"

Joker takes a gulp of his whiskey. "Christ, baby, Liam said it was fucking bad."

I look up at Joker. "Liam was there?"

"Yeah." Joker kisses my temple. "Butch said he appreciated what General did for him and reminded General he had paid him back in full, with interest. Then he walked away."

I groan. "Butch, Annie, and Becca helped search for me, Joker. They must hate me."

"No, they don't hate you. The Sinners, probably." Joker blows out a breath. "It got worse, babe. Becca said it would have been nice if someone had informed her father that the library planned on giving the food away for free. She reminded General that her father was born and raised ten minutes from Pony. He would have gladly donated the food to his people."

I moan. "Ouch. I didn't make my intentions clear when I spoke to

Butch."

Joker gives me a squeeze. "It's not your fault, babe. General and I handled it all wrong. Anyway, Becca thanked 'Mr. Kincaid' and 'Mr. Callaghan' for stopping by the diner and letting them know where she and her father stood in the Sinners and Native American community. She wrote General a check for the next six months of rent."

I furrow my brow and glance up at Joker. "A check…Butch usually pays in cash. Becca has dropped it off at the boutique."

"It was Becca's kiss-off to the Sinners, babe. She told General and Liam that she and her father would provide the lunches, and the library could keep the donations." Joker snorts. "What she meant was we could stick the money up our asses." He blows out a breath. "Liam tried to smooth things over. It was a no-go. Becca held the door open for them to leave."

"Oh my god," I drawl.

"We won't be going to the diner any time soon for the seafood tower or the coconut cream pie. Becca would probably poison us."

I roll my eyes. "Butch, Annie, and Becca are good people, Joker. Annie and Becca showed up at the Native American Village today, and they worked their butts off."

"Yeah, they did." Joker sighs. "Raven, General, and Tristen are fucked up over Becca not wanting to work by their sides. They've known her all her life. They're worried about her for some reason. Liam's feathers were ruffled—Becca refused to speak to him. Doc told Liam to leave her be. She had enough on her plate to deal with."

I twist my upper body and look up at Joker again. "What does that mean? Is Becca sick?"

"I don't know. Maybe." Joker takes a drink of his whiskey. "The Sinners are the last people she'd confide in, babe."

I turn back around, slump against Joker's chest, and take a drink of my wine. I need to send Butch, Annie, and Becca an apology for the misunderstanding. Maybe I'll ask them to dinner.

"Honeypot didn't come to the Native American Village," I say more to myself than Joker.

The one person in this world Honeypot loves and respects is

General. She'd follow him into hell if he asked her to. General saved her, put her through beauty school, and started her baby—the salon. Honeypot not showing to help with the Native American Village is worrisome.

"Nope." Joker exhales. "Something is going on with her. Sly said she hasn't been back to the club since our party."

Sly is the Sinners' brother who would notice: he's the gatekeeper of the surveillance monitor.

"Where is she living? In the motel?"

After Honeypot discovered Marshmallow's deceit, she did a one-eighty. The ditzy, carefree girl has been replaced by a quirky, intelligent, hard-working woman. The psychedelic dresses and platform sandals have been replaced by semi-sexy conservative clothing. Cookie told me she saw Honeypot leave our party after she floated her lantern for Finlan—no goodbye, just gone.

I take a drink of cab and try to remember if Honeypot had mentioned any friends she might be staying with. I know she doesn't have any family except for her grandmother, who lives in a nursing home.

"Horse would have said something if she was living in the motel, babe. There has been some talk around the bar; she's thinking of moving on."

I furrow my brow. That doesn't make sense; Honeypot is collecting food and clothing donations at the salon. She's giving everyone who donates a free deep condition.

Honeypot's deep conditioning treatment is to apply conditioner to the client's hair, and then she plastic-wraps the person's head. She pops the client under a dryer for fifteen minutes. It probably costs the salon twenty cents, but Honeypot charges twenty dollars per treatment. She doesn't get that money. The Sinners pay her a weekly salary and bonus her out at the end of the year. She keeps all her tips.

Even after everything that's happened, I'm happy Honeypot found her niche in life. She built the salon into a thriving business. She works six days a week, twelve hours a day.

Honeypot has clients who come all the way from Helena just to get their hair done. Part of it is her appeal—she's bubbly and makes her clients feel special. Honeypot offers them coffee, tea, wine, or soda as soon as their feet cross the threshold. She makes it a point to chat up her clients: she's excellent at feigning interest in what is happening in their lives—husbands, kids, grandkids, and pets can be a thirty-minute discussion. Gossip is a big part of the salon's environment, but she has one rule: the Sinners and Native Americans are strictly off-limits, but everyone else is fair game.

Honeypot is continuously looking for new things to entice clients, like the electric massage chairs—fifteen dollars gets the client fifteen minutes. I've heard more than one person say they're fantastic.

Joker runs his hand over my boobs. "Babe, you disappeared again."

"I was thinking about Honeypot and the salon. She's come a long way from being a sweet butt. She's grown as a person, and she has a natural intuitiveness about business." I take a gulp of my wine. "If she decides to move on, it won't be good for the Sinners or the salon. Her clientele will go with her. The people love her, Joker."

Joker huffs out, "There are more hairdressers in the world, babe."

Yeah, there are, but they aren't Honeypot. She promotes all Sinners' and Native Americans' businesses through word of mouth. She's the trumpet when our community is in need. The new cosmetologist would be devoted to themself, not General, the Sinners, the Native Americans, or our community.

Joker's semi-erection floats between my thighs. Unthinkingly, I reach down and stroke him lightly. "That brings us back to your mom and dad."

Joker chuckles. "Babe, you're playing with my cock while talking about my parents."

I giggle and move my hand.

"Nope," he says and returns my hand to his cock. "Keep doing what you were doing and talk. I'll deal."

I grin and stroke my man a bit more firmly. *What can I say? I love Cowboy's cock.*

"I think your parents are staying in Pony because of the library."

"Nope, they're leaving in the morning. Conversation over, give me your mouth," he demands, leaning forward.

The change in position makes his hard cock rub up against my sensitive clit. My body tingles, my pussy blooms, and my toes curl. "More, please," I murmur just before his mouth takes mine.

CHAPTER 40

SHE'S IN HEAT – JOKER

"*More, please.* So polite, babe," I murmur and kiss her deeply. Tangling our tongues, I taste the oakiness of the wine mixed with all her unique sweetness.

Blindly, I take my wife's wineglass and set it on the ledge. Our mouths melt together. Jewel's breaths quicken. Her demanding hand on my cock squeezes and strokes a bit more urgently. Moaning, I palm her enormous tits and pinch her gorgeous nipples into tiny, firm buds.

My wife's frame is small; my hands are large. I spread my fingers wide, gliding my hands slowly down her warm, silky skin, covering every inch. At her belly, I linger in the hope that my hands will be a conduit for our love. That's lame, but I'm becoming desperate. I need a little divine intervention to convince my wife's egg to accept my seed. I'm unwilling to believe the price we need to pay for my mistakes is infertility. In the eyes of God or the universe or whoever is in charge, I may deserve that, but my wife doesn't.

Jewel arches into my hands; her neck cranes. Her mouth demands more of my mouth, her body begging for more of my touches.

The old me would have complied: round one would have been me lifting her onto my hard, throbbing cock. Jewel would have taken me reverse cowgirl—a quick coupling to take the edge off. Few words would have been shared between us. After completion, it would have been on to the next position—a triathlon event. It's fun fucking, but the new *us* needs more. I need my wife's words, and she needs mine whether we make love fast and hard or slow and soft.

"You need my cock," I murmur onto her lips. I slip two fingers into her pussy and slowly slide them in and out.

She whimpers against my lips. Her sounds, her touches are making a beeline to my cock. It twitches and thickens, ready to fuck.

"Love you, Cowboy," she breathes out and pushes down my fore-skin with her thumb. She massages tiny circles just beneath my mush-room while running my shaft between her pussy lips.

"Christ, babe," I moan, burying my face into her neck.

I know she's riding the edge: she's holding me in place, her hips speeding up.

Goddamnit. I grit my teeth to keep from plunging deep into her pussy and fucking like a bull. *No can do—get up, get out, and make love in the bed. To make a kid, you need to stay deep and hang out for a while.*

"Love you, babe." I nip and then kiss her lips. "We can't make love here."

I stand with Jewel cradled to my chest. Rivulets of water run off the sides of her beautiful breasts. The purple strands of her hair shimmer in the light. Her violet eyes are heavily lidded; her pupils are dilated with want for me. I put my mouth to hers and give her hot, tongue-tangling kisses. Then I carry her out of the bathroom and over to our bed. I don't give a shit about the trail of water I'm leaving in my wake. I don't care that our bed will be damp all night. My only thought is to be inside my woman and give her what she needs: me.

I lay her on the bed. "My Jewel," I murmur and lean over her.

She smiles. "My cowboy." She bends her knees, spreading them wide. A blatant invitation to come inside.

I grin the grin I know heats her blood, running a finger between her pussy lips. "So wet for me."

"Always and forever," she whispers. Her eyes are pinned to my engorged cock.

I slide on top of her and forego all our usual foreplay. I have the urge to just be inside my wife, loving her soft and slow. I chuckle low, the way I do every morning to wake her. My Jewel was surly this morning over not getting her usual wake-up call.

"What's so funny, Cowboy?"

I grin. "You woke up with an attitude this morning. You missed me nuzzling your neck, massaging your tits, and gliding into your pussy."

She rolls her eyes. "I awoke to Godsmack blaring in my ear. You weren't"—she pauses for a second—"in our bed to give me a cuddle or kiss me good morning."

I position my cock and glide in slow. Jewel closes her eyes and purrs like a kitten.

"I brought you coffee in the shower," I murmur onto her lips and slowly pump my hips.

"That isn't this, Cowboy. So sublime," she breathes out and wraps her legs around my lower back.

No. It isn't our morning position: I start out by taking my wife in the spoon position. Ultimately, we end in what I refer to as the semi-doggy position.

Jewel runs her hands down my back to my ass. She digs her nails in and gives me a jiggle. She's urging me to move and stay deep.

I grin and look into her eyes. This isn't my wife's way: she takes what I give her when I give it to her. *Except*...I stare at Jewel and search for any other signs of the night we made Finlan and Jackie. I didn't realize what was happening with her. She wanted me to hurry, stay deep, and end my thrusts with a punch. *Fuck me, she's in heat. Hallelujah, finally!* This changes everything. I pull out.

"Cowboy, what the hell?!"

I bite my lip to keep from laughing aloud. Quickly, I grab the spare pillows and command, "Lift your ass, babe." I tuck the two pillows beneath her and spread her knees as wide as they will go. Then I do something totally messed up: I slide my finger into her pussy and gather up her cream. Rubbing it between two fingers, I check to see if it's thicker than usual. I've been reading a lot lately about how to tell if a woman is ovulating. *Lord, ovulating, what the hell? I sound like High.*

Jewel leans up on an elbow, her brow furrowed. She snaps, "Is something wrong with me?"

I don't answer her. Like a moron, I bring my fingers to my nose. S*niff...sniff...sniff.* Then I slide them into my mouth. *Fuck yeah, her pussy cream tastes sweeter.* I'm not sure if that's scientific, but I read it on a website.

Jewel rips the pillows from beneath her and throws them off the bed.

"What the fuck, Jewel?" I scramble off the mattress to retrieve them. "We need these!" I toss them back onto the bed.

"Ah, no, we don't," she says sarcastically.

I grin like a fool. That's another sign; my woman is frustrated, short-tempered, and easily irritated.

Jewel huffs and flips onto her side, punching her pillow.

I furrow my brow and stare at her incredulously. No, we're not doing it in the spoon position. It needs to be in the missionary position, with her ass up in the air. Stay to the root, come deep, ass up, and hang out in...the...missionary...position. That's what the website said.

"Babe, we can't make love like that tonight. It needs to be in the missionary position," I announce and slide back onto the bed.

Jewel harumphs and moves further away from me.

What the fuck? Then it dawns on me. She has no idea what the hell is going on with her.

I nuzzle my face into her neck. "Babe, you're in heat."

"Heat!" She's trying to move away from me. "I'm not a freakin' dog, Joker."

"Nope," I murmur and cuddle her. *For Christ's sake, I'm not telling anyone I needed to give my wife an educational tutorial before we made Rider.* "I did some research on the internet. Women have cycles and do go into heat. It's different than animals…the signs are less noticeable." I grin onto her neck. "Babe, you're primed to make Rider."

She turns over and stares at me. Hope dances in her violets. "Are you sure?"

Last month, we were both devastated when Jewel got her period. She cried on and off for the entire day. Beau took Jackie to the club, and I stayed home and snuggled with her on the couch.

I tip her chin up and look her in the eyes. "Yeah, I'm sure. We have a three-day window." I kiss her lips. "We'll give it our babymaking best."

I send up a prayer to everyone we've lost: Jackson and Jenna, Jewel's parents; Finlan, our son; JT Senior, JT's dad; Kyle, Keeley's dad; Coin, Flame's dad; Skeeter, our Sinners' brother from Whitefish; and Mama Cass, our house mama. I'd pray to the fucking man in the moon if I thought it would help. *Please, give us our baby.* I add a quick, *Mommy and Daddy love you, Finlan*, just in case he's listening.

A very light breeze blows over my face. I grin. I've heard of JT's ghostly breeze; with luck, it's his. *Thanks, brother.*

Jewel is in a frenzy, almost giddy. She's piling the pillows. Then she leaps upon them and angles her knees, spreading them wide. She shimmies her shoulders and blows out a breath. "I'm ready."

"Ready," I chuckle onto her lips.

She squinches up her nose. "It's too much pressure…to perform. It's too clinical." A tear leaks from the corner of her eye. "You needed to educate me on my own body." Her eyes move to my semi-erect cock. There's a sadness in them.

I brush her tear away and slide between her knees. My cock instantly goes solid from the feel of her warm, wet pussy nestled against my shaft. I move my hips in a slow, rhythmic motion.

"There is never pressure to perform. Wrap your legs around me," I demand and knead her firm globes. I move my mouth to hers and run my tongue over her plump lips, nipping them. I grin, slowly gliding my hard cock inside her. Fucking heaven.

Jewel inhales my breath and runs her hand down to my ass. "Love you, Cowboy," she says on a hitched breath.

"Love you, babe."

I speed up my strokes and give her a punch at the end. My wife's entire body stiffens, and she snarls out my name. Her teeth sink into the bite mark tatt on my shoulder. Her nails dig into my ass, and then her pussy walls flutter.

"Wait for me," I growl into her ear.

I stay deep, rutting and humping. The tingling is in my lower back. Like lightning, it hits my balls; my sack draws up.

"Fuck!" I roar through clenched teeth. "Love you, babe. Suck me off."

Jewel's arms and legs wrap me up tightly. She holds her pussy up. I cover all of her and hold her, giving her my weight. My hips are on autopilot—powerful, rapid, short thrusts. Her pussy walls clamp down on my steel shaft. I'm grunting words of love into her ear, encouraging her to keep coming.

She mewls her words of love back to me as my cock elongates, thickens, jerking out my seed in intense bursts.

"Ah, goddamnit. Yes, babe. Fucking yes," I bellow against her temple.

My nerve endings are tingling, my head buzzing. Black spots are dancing behind my eyelids. *Slow down your goddamn breathing.* I breathe rhythmically to my languid, short humps until my mind clears.

Every inch of Jewel is covered in a sheen of sweat. She's trembling within my arms. I hold her tighter to me, knowing she's in her cloud of euphoria. Her climax slowly recedes; her body relaxes as she comes back to me.

"Cowboy," she barely breathes out. She takes a long inhale and snuggles her pelvis into mine. "Did you set the timer?"

I chuckle and look into her tired violets. Without a doubt, in her post-orgasmic state, she is the most beautiful thing I've ever seen. Her face is flush, her pouty lips are swollen from our kisses, and her hair is wild. I sweep it away from her face and give her a soft, heated kiss.

"Love you more than life, babe." Then I reach for my phone and set the timer. I don't need to; I know we made Rider.

Jewel gives me a lazy smile. "Love you more, Cowboy. Always and forever." She snuggles into me, her arms around my neck, her legs around my hips.

I kiss Jewel's temple. "Always and forever, babe."

CHAPTER 41

MY HAPPY BUBBLE – JEWEL

It's been two weeks since Jackson and Char left for Honolulu. Things have been out-of-control busy with Sinners Biker Babe Boutique and the library. Black Friday is creeping up on us quickly. The boutique has experienced an explosion of new online orders.

With the weather changing from mildly cold to frigid, more and more people have been coming into the library. The Sinners now have two prospects working with Gola until Robin and Hummingbird graduate. The first of the year can't come soon enough for them.

Word spread throughout the surrounding communities: people are in need; drop off anything you can spare at the library. The food and clothing pantry has expanded. It's pushed our limits from overcrowded to "suck in your gut" status.

Good Samaritans are dropping off frozen meats, poultry, veggies, and fruits—all from their farms. Handmade coats, mittens, and hats are coming in by the dozens. The library looked like a *Hoarders* episode: hand-me-down clothes were stored in bins under every table and chair. Multiple one-hundred-and-fifty-quart coolers were stacked in every empty space, even the bathroom. Draining the water and adding new ice to the coolers took the prospects hours. We had a significant problem—no room and no freezers.

Buck moved one of the Native American Trucking Company's trailers into Sinners' parking lot to use as refrigerated storage. The Native Americans couldn't afford to lose one of their trailers: they're in use twenty-four seven. They did it anyway.

Joker went to the postmaster and asked if we could rent their top floor. He received a call five days ago with a proposal. The government wanted to sell the property to us for twenty-five grand. The building is old; it needs a new furnace and will need a new roof. The US Postal Service has been unprofitable for years. If we don't buy the property, the government will close our post office and sell it to someone else. Not having a post office would be inconvenient for our businesses. The community at large would suffer: people on Diva and Rock Head Mountain don't have mailboxes. The Sinners made the deal and agreed to lease the bottom floor to the post office for ten thousand dollars per year. It covers the cost of insurance and taxes. Princess and Pick finagled the quickest closing known to man—three days, and the property was ours.

Yesterday was an unforgettable whirlwind of activity: we moved the food and clothing pantry to the post office's top floor. Wolfe and his men spent the entire day building shelves. High and Joker purchased four humongous chest freezers from a big-box store. I held my breath watching the two of them manhandle the freezers up the steep, narrow staircase. High was at the top, Joker at the bottom. My man was carrying most of the load. If High had slipped, I thought for sure Joker would be crushed. I was at the bottom, over to the side. Each time High swore, I squeaked out a prayer.

Beau laughed at me. "Sweetheart, we were behind him. Your man wouldn't have been crushed." That was true, Beau and Mafia Man were right behind my man, but still, it was scary.

After it was over, Joker held me in his strong, sweaty arms. He grinned his panty-dropping grin and kissed my fears away. Then he rubbed my belly. "No lifting, babe." He's convinced we're pregnant and didn't want to chance a miscarriage.

It took the girls and me all day to sort through the clothes, coats, shoes, sneakers, and boots. We put them on the shelves according to size. The hats, mittens, gloves, and scarves, we kept in open bins. Our men filled the freezers and stocked the shelves with canned and dried goods. When it was done, General realized we hadn't assigned anyone to oversee the pantry. The Sinners were out of men. Running Bear came to our rescue with two older Native American women, basket weavers who worked for Diva Mountain Native American Village. According to them, they can work anywhere, provided they have good light, a bucket of water, and a comfortable chair.

Joker and High went to our house and took two recliners from our game room. Their new home: the top floor of the post office. I insisted the ladies get the same salary and benefits as Gola, Robin, and Hummingbird. Joker chuckled and made a quip about us going broke from my generosity. I shrugged, giggling, "Rich or poor, we'll be together and happy." He replied, "True that, babe," and kissed me.

Joker, Beau, and the Sinners keep a close eye on our finances; we won't ever go broke. My husband jokes about it because it makes me laugh.

Becca and Annie are kicking off a toy drive for Christmas. Becca refused my invitation for dinner—she gave Joker a BS excuse. She was polite, but it's clear she's keeping her distance.

The biker babes decided: whatever we buy for our kids, we'll double it and give the other item to Annie and Becca for the toy drive. I snicker to myself. I'm sure Joker will say, "The credit card is smoking, babe." Or "Has the plastic fucking melted yet?" Or "How's your finger, babe? Has it blistered yet?" For some insane reason, that always gets my lady parts dancing for my husband. I bust out laughing. I have a husband fetish revolving around my credit card usage. *That's too weird, even for you, Jewel.*

A low chuckle comes from behind me. "Hey, babe, what are you laughing about?"

I turn. Joker is leaning against the guest bedroom's jamb, holding a paper bag. He's grinning his panty-dropping grin at me. His blue eyes are twinkling with excitement. For what, I'm not sure.

I choose to ignore his question. Telling my husband I have a fetish would cause him to whip out the credit cards and make a jest in front of the brothers. *Nope, not happening.*

Tilting my head, I smile at him and ask my own question: "Why aren't you at work?"

"We have important business to take care of, babe." He holds up the bag and jiggles it.

Knowing my husband the way I do, anything could be in the bag: a trinket for his bike or a sex toy he wants us to try out. I won't lie: I'm hoping for the toy.

I giggle. "What's in the bag, Cowboy?"

He grins, his eyes going to the bag. "Pregnancy tests."

My face falls. I stare at the bag like it's my enemy. *God, no. I'm not ready to take a pregnancy test.* If it's negative, it will be worse than the last time. There wasn't a baby, but it felt as if there was—a hopeless black hole forms in my heart.

I shake my head and return to my dusting. "I'm not ready to take the test just yet," I say, trying to make my voice sound light. "I think we should wait another week."

"Babe, we were due for our period a week ago." He wraps his strong arms around my waist and murmurs into my neck. "We're pregnant. We just need to confirm it and see Polly."

I look at him via the mirror. "I don't want to," I whisper and hug my arms to his. "I want to stay in my happy bubble, even if it's a lie." My eyes brim with tears. "I just need a little more time."

He stares at me intently. "Jewel, I love you. If we never make another kid, that won't change." He picks me up and runs through the door and down the hall. "But we did, and you're pissing on all three sticks." He bolts through our bedroom and into our bathroom. "Strip, babe. I need to read the directions."

He's so excited, I can't say no. *Jesus, Lord up in Heaven, please give my man two pink lines.*

I inhale deeply and blow out a breath. I lower my yoga pants and panties to my ankles.

Joker makes a flicking motion with his hand. "All the way off, babe. I need to get in there."

"In where?" I squeak out, "You're going to hold the sticks?" I kick my pants and panties halfway across the room.

He looks down at me like I've lost my mind. I don't know; maybe I have. I'm sitting on the toilet, naked from the waist down, shaking.

He bites his lower lip, reading the directions. "You need to piss on the sticks for seven seconds. Then we cap them, lay them horizontally on the vanity, and wait for five minutes."

I relax a bit and refrain from giggling. My husband is so sexy when he takes charge.

Joker drops to his knees between my legs and uncaps the tests. Good god, I can't help it; I'm laughing. He's staring at my privates, in a ready position.

He looks up at me, furrowing his brow.

"I can't pee with you staring at me."

"Babe," he drawls, grinning. "I've helped you piss, wiped your pussy, and eaten you more times than we can count. Just shut your eyes, relax, and piss."

I shut my eyes. *Think of warm, running water. The four freakin' glasses you needed to drink before your sonogram.* To my relief, I start to pee.

"Great, babe, keep pissing," encourages Joker. He starts counting the seven seconds aloud.

I giggle and squeeze my eyes shut, trying to do as he commands.

"Good, babe. We got all three." He leaps up and goes over to the vanity.

I don't move. I can't; I'm too nervous. I bend, leaning my forehead onto my thighs, praying again.

"Babe," murmurs Joker onto my crown. "No worries." He swipes my panties off the floor and slides them up my legs. Then he grabs the wipes and cleanses me. "Lift," he orders and pulls my panties into place. He picks me up and bangs the toilet cover down, dropping down onto it with me on his thighs. "While we wait, we need to talk about something."

My head feels like a million bees are buzzing around my brain. I can't talk.

"Concentrate on me, babe."

I clear my throat and shake my head, trying to concentrate on him.

"Old man Peterson grabbed me while I was in Pony Market. He's financially busted."

I blink, furrowing my brow. "Busted, as in bankrupt?"

Joker sighs. "Yup. He took out mortgages on the market, the pharmacy, and the land the Chinese takeout place sits on. He needed to pay his wife's hospital bills and home care. The goddamn properties are mortgaged up the ass. The balloon notes are coming due at the end of the month, and he doesn't have the cash to pay them."

"Does he want us to loan him the money?"

Joker rubs my belly. "Nope, he wants us to buy him out so he can go live with his son in Arizona."

I nod. "That makes sense. Mr. Peterson's wife has Alzheimer's. He brings her into the salon every Tuesday to get her hair done. She loves Honeypot."

"I'm glad someone does," he murmurs under his breath. "I looked at his books—it's bad. Peterson is in the hole for over a mil. If we don't purchase the properties, a chain might. I don't want large corporations coming into Pony."

"Me either. Once big organizations get here, they'll change our town. Mr. Peterson owns enough property to put in a few stores. We'd end up with a Dunkin' Donuts or a Dollar General. Just buy him out, Cowboy," I order, my jaw set firm. "I want him to walk away with enough money to take care of his wife and himself. He's worked all his life." I furrow my brow again and look up at my husband. "How much money does Mr. Peterson need to take care of his wife?"

"I don't know, babe. The old man has a number in mind: three mil. That will take care of his bank and distributor debts. He'll walk away with a little over a mil."

I nod. "That's good." I giggle. "I'm not sure what the Sinners will do with a grocery store and a pharmacy. At least the Chinese takeout place won't need to be managed. One of the guys can just collect the rent."

Joker chuckles. "Babe, fucking taxes, upkeep, and insurance? It isn't just collecting the rent. The Sinners have money, but shelling out that much green would be risky."

I shrug my shoulders. "They're not shelling out the money: we are. We're family. We'll put the money in the pot, and they'll buy the property. You need to call Princess and Pick to make the deal ASAP."

Joker laughs as the timer goes off.

My entire body trembles. I shake my head. "I can't look."

Joker stands, with me cradled to his chest. He walks over to the vanity. Then my man lets out the loudest whoop. "Babe!" He laughs. "Look down."

I crack one eye open. Two pink lines are on each test. "Oh my god!" I wail, crying. "We're pregnant!"

"Babe, let's celebrate," drawls Joker. He's carrying me into our bedroom. We get down to business and celebrate the badass biker way —with my husband loving every inch of me. *I love...adore...freakin' breathe for my cowboy!*

CHAPTER 42

MUNCH – JOKER

I open the French doors and let the outside into our Malibu bedroom—Jewel loves the ocean breeze. The rhythmic swish of the whitecaps rolling to shore is hypnotic to my ears. The scent of brininess with a slight hint of fishiness tingles my nose.

At the ungodly hour of 6:00 a.m., the sun's orangey-yellow rays light up the horizon. A single strip is glimmering in the center of the ocean, as if it's a path to our home. I like to believe it's my eldest son giving his old man a "good morning." I smile. "Mornin', Fin. Daddy loves you."

Jewel comes out onto the balcony with Rider cradled in her arms. I toss the pillow onto the lounger and help my wife to settle between my legs. She lies back against my chest, getting comfy. I free her tit and give her nipple a few light pinches, then run it across my son's tiny lips: my munch monster snorts and latches on, sucking with vigor.

"Ooo," hisses Jewel and stiffens. Her violets are pinned to our little bundle of joy.

I kiss my wife's temple. "Relax, babe." Jewel's nipples are tender from nursing our son every two hours around the clock. Polly assures me it's normal. Her nipples are healthy; the tenderness will pass in time.

Rider Beauregard Frazier was due on August fourth. Despite all my efforts, my son finally decided to leave his mother's cocoon on August fourteenth. Rider got every part of me, including my greedy appetite— my tiny munch monster. Jackie nicknamed him Munch.

I support Jewel's arm and gently press down on her tit, giving my son room to breathe. We birthed Rider at our home in Pony. Jewel and I decided we'd go the way of the Sinners—natural childbirth, coital stimulation with penetration.

Our son's delivery wasn't complicated, but ten hours of labor was no joke. Staying hard on and off for six hours was a challenge. Jewel pushed for a solid two hours; that was way beyond challenging. Christ, we were both exhausted by the time my son slipped into my arms. Rider was born perfect: six pounds, two ounces, and ten inches long with a full head of blond wavy hair. I examined every inch of him—ten tiny fingers and ten tiny toes with itty-bitty nails. His little head was the size of a softball, perfectly shaped.

He looked up at me with his big blue eyes. Then he scrunched up his teeny-tiny face and wailed out his irritation. My baby boy let his old man know he didn't appreciate being pushed out of a small hole. He settled the moment he heard my voice.

Jewel claims her pussy is fine. I know she wants me, and lord knows I want her, but I'm staying steadfast to the unwritten rule: no penetration for four weeks.

Knock knock knock. Our bedroom door swings open. Jackie comes running in, with Beau following close behind. I grin and watch Jackie carefully place the plate of danish onto the table: his mother's favorite, cheese and apple. The aroma of java is heaven to my nose.

It has become our family routine, whether we're in Pony or Malibu: the four of us spend the early mornings bonding as a family.

"Good morning, baby boy," coos Jewel. She purses her lips for a kiss.

Jackie climbs onto the lounger and crawls up my body to get to his brother.

"Gentle," reminds Beau. He drops down into the chair next to us and sets two mugs down on the table: mine a dark roast, black, and Jewel's an herbal decaf tea.

Jackie places a smack on his mother's lips. "Morning, Mommy." Then he puts his tiny lips to Rider's head and gives him a smooch. "Morning, Munch."

I purse my lips, and he gives me a kiss. "Morning, Daddy. Maria's eyes just popped open."

I grin. "Did you give Papa Beau a break and sleep with Maria last night?"

He firms his jaw and shakes his head, pointing to Beau. "Only Papa."

Beau chuckles and takes a sip of his coffee.

For the last two weeks, Jackie has wanted to sleep with us. Jewel thinks it's a slight regression because Rider sleeps in our room. I insisted he start out in his bed. Rider wakes Jackie, and then he's up for hours. I need Jewel to get as much sleep as possible. Like clockwork, Jackie scampers to Beau's room as soon as Beau hits his bed. I'm sure he woke his grandfather's ass as soon as his eyes "popped open."

"Papa said Mommy can't take me surfing today. She needs to heal." Jackie's eyes go to Rider. "Munch can't take me; he's a baby. Maria can't take me; she can't swim. You and Papa Beau can't take me because of work." He folds in half, dropping his forehead onto his knees.

That causes his mother to cry. *Fucking hormones.*

"Calm, babe." I release the suction of Rider's lips with my pinkie. I tilt him up and rub circles onto his back. "When Papa Beau and I get home, you and I will hit the pier for pizza, ice cream, and amusement rides."

"Mommy, Rider, Papa, and Maria, too," he mumbles onto his knees.

"Jackie," I drawl, trying to choose words that will avoid a meltdown. If Jackie has a crying jag in front of his mother, it will send her over the edge. *Two crying jags? No way.*

Jewel runs her hand over Jackie's hair. "We'll all go, Jackie," says

Jewel in an over-the-top-excited tone of voice. "I need new pictures of Daddy, Papa, and you with Rider on the merry-go-round."

"Jewel, goddamnit, there is no damn way you're going to the pier," I growl and fumble to get her other tit out of her tank.

I never fumble—my nerves are fried. I've had little sleep, and today is the goddamn asshole's execution. I saw red when it was delayed for four months. Briggs's attorney had petitioned the California Supreme Court to review his case. It was denied. I don't know how Princess did it. Corporal punishment cases are usually carried out in San Francisco. Since all the victims were from the Los Angeles area, Princess petitioned the court to hold the execution at California State Penitentiary, Los Angeles County. After many exchanges and thousands of signatures, she got it done.

Beau tilts his head toward Jewel. "Do you need me to—"

"No," I breathe out.

Christ, get your shit tight. I give Jewel's nipple a few pinches and then help Rider to latch on.

Jewel doesn't hiss. She's too agitated over Jackie. "Cowboy, I have two sons. Rider and I will be fine. We're going. That's the end of it."

Jackie leaps off my legs and rolls his hips, pumping his fists in the air—the "happy dance" he learned from his cousins. "Yes!" He runs from the room, screaming, "Maria, we're going to the pier!"

I try to reason with my wife. "Jewel, the pier is fucking filthy. Our son is two weeks old." Before we had Rider, she wouldn't say word one about my decisions. Now her hormones are all over the goddamn place. Added to that is her need to ensure Jackie doesn't feel left out. It would be a hell of a fight getting her to stay home, one I'm not up for.

"Oh, look at the time. You had better jump into the shower, Cowboy. You don't want to be late for death by injection," she says airily.

Beau chuckles. "Sweetheart, there's no clock out here."

"The sun," she giggles and squints her eyes up into it.

I chuckle against her temple. "All right, you win, babe." I look down at my son and smile. He's just hanging out, relaxed and snuggled into his mother.

Beau stands and takes Rider. "I'll get little man changed." He walks into the bedroom, talking to our son: "If your mother ate broccoli again, she's going to get a goddamn timeout. It gives you the shits, grandson."

Jewel looks up at me and snickers.

I grin. "You're bad, babe." I hand Jewel her tea and take a gulp of my coffee.

Jewel reaches over and grabs a danish. Then she holds it up to my mouth and sighs. "I need to call your dad and check on your mom. They might need more pot."

My mind drifts to my mother and father. My parents offered to come back to Pony and help out the Sinners. They had only been gone a few weeks, but we had multiple irons in the fire—the library, Pony Market, and Pony Pharmacy, on top of our other businesses. The Christmas season for Sinners Biker Babe Boutique, Raven's Nest Boutique, and Sinners Bike Shop is an insanely hectic time of year.

I made a deal with High: I'd rent High's old cabin for my parents. He laughed and joked, "You don't want your parents in your backyard, so you're putting them in mine." High didn't want any money, but I insisted—utilities aren't cheap.

My father booked Mom and himself a commercial flight; the guys were too busy to fly over and pick them up. The day before my parents were supposed to leave Hawaii, Mom went to the mall with Lisa and Nirvana. I roll my eyes. I still can't believe she purchased a pair of high-heeled boots, wanting to be "fashionable." Mom slipped and fell on the marble floor. She broke her left ankle in two places. Now she's the owner of two metal plates and a dozen screws.

My mother became depressed when Bess and Mable called her. They told her all the news in Pony, including how busy everyone was trying to juggle the workload—we'd started construction on the library.

We weren't supposed to start construction until spring. Wolfe, William, Liam, and I were at the Pony Diner, having a lunch meeting to review the blueprints. Butch was our waiter; Becca avoided the Sinners whenever possible.

I asked Butch what he thought. "Joker, Pony will be teeming with tourists in the spring. The weather is holding. It'd be better to pop the top now."

"Now? It's the middle of November, Butch." I said it like the man didn't know the month. Then I laughed at myself: it needs to be a whiteout and twenty below before born-and-bred Montanans take notice of the weather.

He sucked air through his teeth and stared out the window for a beat. "We have the manpower—the Native American village is closed for the season. Wolfe's construction company is slow. With everyone working, it'll probably take a couple of weeks to get the walls built and a roof on. If the weather turns, we'll button it up with a tarp."

The decision was made; we started tearing off the roof the next day. It was man versus weather: Wolfe's construction team, the Native Americans, the Sinners, the security specialists, the cowboys, Butch, Annie, Rex, and even Becca swung a hammer.

Becca was a porcupine, ready to shoot her barbed quills at any brother who came within an arm's length of her. Liam is a badass, domineering Sinner; he stepped up to her challenge. Eventually, Liam won the battle, and we were forgiven.

We all worked crazy hours—anyone who had a minute pounded nails. Butch was right; by the time the bad weather hit, we had the walls up and the roof on. It should have taken six months to finish the renovations; we had the library done in three.

Robin and Hummingbird graduated in December and started work immediately. My wife calls them the dream team. The girls are twenty-two, they both have a bachelor's in education, and they're excited to share their knowledge. Robin and Hummingbird named the first floor (Native American Book Emporium), the second floor (Kids Nook), and the third floor (Sinners Illumination Center). They've created all kinds of programs for ages two to ninety-two. Gola still does her thing, only now she gives scheduled tours. The Sinners oversee the money; the girls run the day-to-day.

Mom became more depressed over missing Jackie's birthday. Jewel became anxious when the doctor prescribed an antidepressant. She called my father and told him she was sending him marijuana for my mother to smoke. Surprisingly, my father agreed.

I laughed when Lisa phoned me: "Both our parents are potheads, Joker." I already knew that by the amount of weed I was mailing them. If it helps them, I'm all for it.

My mind flits to the day we started popping the top off of the library. I had General call for church right in the goddamn library's parking lot—no beers and no gavel. All the Sinners were there. Time was ticking, and I needed to give Peterson an answer. I told the brothers about old man Peterson going bust.

The brothers agreed to purchase his businesses and land. "It doesn't matter how much green it's worth. We need to make the deal," said Mafia Man. "We don't need conglomerates or Uncle Sam up our asses."

The brothers voted against taking the money from Jewel and me. "You said that green was for your kids. We're not touching it. We'll drain the goddamn rainy day fund," announced General.

Within a week, Princess and Pick had the closing—cash deals happen fast.

Lye and Istu took on the management of the pharmacy. They set up a smaller satellite pharmacy at Sinners Urgent Care—a convenience that Doc, Polly, Patriot, and Bluebird appreciated.

Raven was ecstatic when a few of the Native Americans applied to pharmacy school. "Lord knows, Joker, we can use them. The two pharmacists we have are older and getting ready to retire."

Mouse and Rabbit took on the day-to-day management of the market. Still, it was bleeding money: food about to expire was given away by the cartload. Maggie, Mafia Man, Liam, and I combed the books: prices were too high for the quality of goods sold. To make the market profitable, we needed a niche that would draw in customers. Maggie thought homegrown was the way to go: "The new generation is all about wholesome. You know, no chemicals and no preservatives. We'll use all the buzzwords: 'homemade,' 'homegrown,' 'all-natural,' and, of course, 'organic.'"

All the big-name products were removed from the shelves, meat cases, and deli. We featured local farmers' beef, pork, poultry, dairy, fruits, and veggies. Canned food was replaced with jars made by the community. Swanson was out; Farmers' wives made frozen, ready-to-heat meals. Wonder Bread and Pepperidge Farm were gone; we have local bakers. Goodbye, Barilla: we have our own pasta makers. See ya, Dial! The hygiene products were replaced with Faith's—they're all-natural.

Our laundry and dishwashing supplies are made by a middle-aged couple living in the backwoods a few miles from Pony. I laughed when Lou told me he refused to put electricity in their cabin. "This is the first time Heidi and I've had money to put under the mattress. Ain't gonna give the goddamn electric company all our profits, Joker. Heidi and I are stickin' with oil and wood. Butch and the Chinese give me their old cookin' oil for free. A little filterin', and it burns like a charm." I said a small prayer they wouldn't die from carbon monoxide poisoning. Then he grinned at me proudly. "Got the kids their boots from over yonder at the food and clothing pantry. I donated five dollars and two pounds of soap. The ladies were happy to get it, too. They said Heidi and my soaps make the best suds."

I held my breath, not for the Sinners—we have investments to keep us above water. Our communities need the market to work.

It was a what-the-fuck moment for all of us when the hybrid grocery store took off. Word of mouth spread; people started showing up with large coolers, some having driven for hours. "Best TV dinners," claimed one shopper. Another shopper claimed, "The sausage, pasta, and sauce are out of this world."

I laughed my ass off when Rabbit called me at the garage: "How much are we charging for ice?" *Come on, we're not Wally World. It's free!*

We still need to purchase some things from Silo. Jewel giggled. "It's just a matter of time until one of the locals figures out how to make paper products, Cowboy."

Three important things happened with the market's success: all the Sinners' businesses picked up, the Native Americans in college had jobs to come home to, and the farmers needed to hire more people.

Everyone was working their asses off, including my pregnant wife. At Horse's insistence, White Dove turned over the management of the motel to him. It became too much for his wife with all the in and out traffic. General hired two Native American teens to clean the rooms.

Our house became daycare central. The kids decided on our home because we had an indoor pool. Dana, Rene, and White Dove were our designated babysitters. It was funny as shit when Rene bought a yellow school bus. He'd go to all the Sinners family's homes and pick up the five and under kids. They'd hit our house at 7:00 a.m. loaded down with breakfast, lunch, and snacks. Merrill became a cooking machine —he provided dinner for the Sinners' families.

Jewel was working from morning 'til night on her clothing line— her sewing machine was smoking. She was also designing for Mika.

Maggie marched into our house, with Gee in tow. "I've been watching you for two weeks, Jewel. It's too much. Joker is going to find a community seamstress for the clothing line."

I had no idea where the hell I was going to find people who could sew. The Native Americans couldn't do it: they were making shit for Raven's Nest Boutique and the Native American Village Gift Shop. I decided word of mouth worked the best. I told Rabbit and Mouse to tell the farmers we were looking for seamstresses.

I was in Sinners Bike Shop, painting a Rocky Mountain scene onto a tank, when five women walked in toting ginormous sacks. "Mister, Heidi sent us. We need to know where your shop's at," said a spindly older woman. Her tanned, wrinkled face was a testament to years of hard labor. "These here are my daughters. We sew."

Flame, Tank, and Tristen gawked at them, grinning. The ladies were the definition of mountain women.

"Guess that's the job interview," chuckled Tristen.

"Where is your shop?" laughed Tank. His eyes were pinned on the ladies.

Not at our house, that was for damn sure. Christ, we'd only put the word out that morning.

"We have the top floor of the pharmacy," said Flame. "It has heat and air conditioning. We'll move the stock to one side of the room."

"Me and my girls will move the stuff. Just bring us the good lady's designs, cloth, leather, baubles, and machines," ordered the old woman. Then she opened up her sack and pulled out awesome, hand-dyed threads; a variety of badass, embroidered biker patches; and bone, stone, and wood-carved buttons. Our eyes widened—we'd just hit a motherfucking gold mine. "Your woman might like to use these on her fancy women's wear." I looked closely at the buttons; they were all biker carvings, Harleys in all vintages, Harley patches, bike parts, and skulls. The woman cackled. "My man started carvin' them three years ago. He had me and the girls do up the embroidered patches, thinkin' he'd sell 'em to the lady. Then she came up missin'." She snapped her bony fingers. "Just like that, gone. But he kept carvin' and we kept embroiderin', thinkin' she'd turn back up sooner or later. My man said no one's gonna put that much money into a buildin' and not use it." The woman's four daughters nodded like bobbleheads. "He'd like to get ten pennies apiece for 'em."

"Ten pennies apiece," repeated Tank, smiling.

All five of the women's heads bobbed.

I chuckled, knowing Jewel and I would be divvying up the buttons and patches. They'd look great on the saddlebags. I also knew we were going to make the old lady's husband a very happy man: the buttons and patches were worth a hell of a lot more than ten cents apiece.

Two days later, we had the ladies set up on the top floor of the pharmacy. Jewel fell in love with the women. "They're amazing artisans. I give them a design, and they embellish it into something extraordinary," she gushed. I couldn't believe it when the love of my life became possessive over buttons and patches. I needed to make friends with the old woman to pilfer the supply.

Jewel smiles up at me, running two fingers down my cheek. "Where did you go on me?"

I chuckle and kiss her lips. "I was thinking about the whirlwind we've been living in for the past year."

Jewel giggles. "The Sinners are a giant cyclone of energy that zaps people into the right place."

I laugh and swing my legs over the side of the lounger. Cradling

Jewel in my arms, I stand. "We need to shower." I look into my wife's violets. "We haven't talked about how you're handling today."

Jewel looks out into the ocean for a few beats. "I'm a biker's wife," she says matter-of-factly. "I can't deny I wanted you to torture the monster so that he would suffer. I've dreamt of him feeling the power of your fists beating his flesh and the edge of your blade cutting through his skin. You know, extracting our kind of justice for Finlan. Now I realize that was selfish of me."

"Selfish," I echo.

"Hm," nods Jewel. "Ricky murdered ten women. Today, those women's families are getting the opportunity to see justice done. It's closure for them, Cowboy." She gives me a soft kiss. "I'm good with what the universe decided."

I carry my wife into our bathroom. Call me selfish: given the opportunity, I'd exact our justice slowly, methodically, and *very, very* painfully.

EPILOGUE

FOREVER MINE – JOKER

Beau and I weave our bikes through the throng of protesters in front of the prison. I wonder how many of these people would feel the same way if Briggs murdered their daughter or son. I'm sure few.

We ride up to the gate and show the guard our IDs. The guy looks at me with sympathetic eyes. "Straight ahead and to the right, Mr. Frazier. Condolences, sir."

"Thanks," I mutter, looking to where he indicated we should park. I do a slow blink. All my Sinners' brothers are standing by their bikes, the ones they keep in our Malibu garage. I have no clue how they managed to get them without me knowing they were there. I glance at Beau. "Who the hell is taking care of the home front?"

Beau grins. "Some things are more important than business, Joker."

My nose tingles, and my eyes tear. I blow out a quick breath, popping the clutch. "Let's get it done," I order, riding slowly over to the Sinners.

Beau and I park our bikes, then we receive bro hugs and fist bumps from the brothers.

General pulls me in for a long hug. "What the hell are you all doing here?" I ask, hugging him back.

"Joker," he drawls, as if that says it all.

He hands me off to High, who hugs me close. "The girls are back at the house with Jewel. We're not allowed inside, but we'll be here when it's done." He pins a patch onto my cut. It's angel wings cradling a baby swaddled in a blue blanket. Curved over the top of the wings: "Sinners Son." Curled beneath: "Finlan Jackson Sawyer Frazier."

All the brothers hold up their left forearms. They all have it inked into their skin.

"Finlan will never be forgotten, brother," affirms Mafia Man. "Sean and I will tatt you and Beau when we get back to Pony."

He whips out his phone and shows me a video. Geronimo, Mitzi, Running Bear, Butch, Annie, Becca, Robin, Hummingbird, and Gola are with all the farmers, cowboys, security specialists, Sinners, Native Americans, their wives, and children. They're holding up a picture of the patch, yelling, "Justice for Finlan!" The soap guy, his wife, and the five seamstresses are in front, shouting the loudest: "We're with you, Joker! We're with you, Good Lady!"

That's the five seamstresses' name for Jewel: Good Lady. I look up to the bright blue sky and blink back my tears. *Over... fucking...whelming.*

My phone dings with a text:

Dad: *The family is here. We're with you, son. Call me if you need to talk. Love you.*
Me: *Thanks. I'm good. The brothers are here.*

I'm not there yet, with the "love you" shit, but Dad's making an effort, and I appreciate it. It's good to know he's thinking about us.

Beau tosses his arm over my shoulder. "Let's make tracks," he says and leads me into the building.

A month ago, we received a packet: California's protocol for capital punishment. It was a ridiculous multi-page document spelling out every step of the execution. Included was a small blurb: "Due to heightened security, all visitation will be suspended on the day of commencement."

Beau and I fall into line behind several somber-faced men and women. It doesn't take a genius to figure out they're here for the execution.

After we go through the metal detector and pat down, we're led down two flights of stairs into the building's basement. The hot, musty air infused with body odor assaults my nose. *Christ, the stench is puke-worthy. They should have provided barf bags.*

The florescent industrial lights are illuminating the dank gray walls and the cement floor. Our footsteps mix with a few of the women's muffled gags. The sounds echo loudly as we are herded like cattle into a large, windowless room. I ignore the priest, who is standing to the left of the door. He's cupping people's hands, offering them words of comfort. His words won't bring me any solace.

The walls are made of cinderblocks painted the same dank gray. Five rows of gray metal folding chairs are lined up in front of a glass partition. Behind the glass is a gurney with leather straps. Next to the gurney is a metal table with IV equipment placed neatly on top. To the left is a large white machine with four feet of IV tubing attached to its front. A computer keyboard is plugged into its side. Deadpan-faced nurses and EMTs are standing to the machine's left, their hands clasped in front of them.

"Mr. Frazier, Mr. Briggs has no family. He requested you be seated in the front row."

I'm about to say *Fuck him* when Beau grips my arm and leads me to a seat directly in front of the gurney. *Front rows seats to the shitshow.*

A middle-aged, balding guy in a white coat comes through the door. He stands in front of us and clears his throat. "Folks, my name is Dr. Howser, and I'm in charge of Mr. Briggs's execution. Before I review what you're about to witness, I want to extend my condolences to each one of you."

I tamp down my irritation at the word "condolences"—a meaning-less word mainstream people use because it's expected.

Dr. Howser informs us that California State Penitentiary has adhered to all protocols. Then he tells us the fucker had surf and turf for dinner, a beer, and enjoyed one of Jewel's father's action flicks with his goddamn priest.

I snort. Rage crawls up my spine. *How in the hell is this justice?* My wife was beaten half to death twice, and my son died on a fucking floor.

Beau puts his arm around my shoulders and pulls me into him. He's about to whisper something into my ear when an irate man bolts out of his seat. "That asshole brutally raped and murdered my daughter, and you people served him steak and lobster! The fucker *enjoyed* a movie!" He points a shaky finger at me. "That bastard beat this man's wife and killed his baby. And you people gave him a beer. Now you're telling us the motherfucker gets to say a few last words? Fuck this!" He grabs the hand of the woman beside him and storms out.

I blow out a breath and drag my hand down my face. The warden steps in front of us and babbles nervously about state requirements for capital punishment. *Christ, I could have saved the state a lot of time and money.*

Seven guards escort Briggs into the room. He looks at me and frowns. I grin, growl, and bare my teeth at the asshole. The fucker didn't want me in the front row; he wanted my wife. I have my eyes pinned on Briggs as the "execution team" prepares him.

Why it takes thirteen people to put one asshole to ground is beyond me.

The priest asks Briggs if he has any final words. The bastard looks directly at me. I hold up my left hand and tap my wedding band. My way of letting the cunt know: he scarred us, but he didn't break us.

Like a rabid dog, Briggs snarls at me.

Bullseye! I hit my mark.

Briggs says to the doctor, his eyes on me, "Lock and load. I've confessed my sins and cleansed my soul. Bring on the white light. I'm ready to meet my maker."

A woman three rows behind me whispers tearfully, "Isn't he going to say he's sorry? Or ask for our forgiveness?"

Briggs's eyes move to her. "Forgiveness? For what? Your daughter was a cheating whore!"

The room breaks out in shouts of rage. "Burn in Hell with the devil, you monster!" yells a woman shaking her Bible at Briggs. Shoes and boots are being hurled at the glass. One sandal bounces off the glass and clocks the priest in the head.

I'm not sure if the warden kept to his protocol, because after that things advanced very quickly. The drugs were administered within sixty seconds—flatline. Briggs is dead. Before the doctor can pronounce him, the families are on their feet, cheering loudly. They have their fists pumping in the air like their team just won the World Series. The priest is so taken aback, he's standing statue still, his mouth hanging open. The warden appears horrified. The media is eating it up. They're snapping pictures of the families so quickly it's a wonder their fingers don't cramp.

Beau and I look at each other and laugh. *There goes the code of conduct.*

"I'm sure California State Penitentiary has seen its first and last execution," grins Beau. "Let's get the hell out of here."

The warden and the guards are too busy trying to control the crowd to pay attention to us. We slip out, haul ass through the corridor, and take the stairs two at a time. We are outside before anyone knows we've left the building.

General looks at us with a furrowed brow. "What the hell is going on in there? We just saw ten guards bolting for the front door."

I chuckle and throw my leg over the saddle of my bike. "The families are getting rowdy. Let's make tracks before the prison goes into lockdown."

~

Two hours later, we hit the pier with our Sinners family. *Shit, it's crawling with people.* I put Jackie's ball cap on his head and slide his shades onto his face. Then I swing him onto my shoulders. His tiny hands grip my hair, holding on. I chuckle. My little baby boy is dressed identically to his big brother, complete with his ball cap and shades. I quickly unstrap Rider and take him out of his car seat. There's no way in hell he's riding in his stroller. People could get to him...touch him... breathe on him.

Beau reads my mind. "We'll surround the four of you."

I nod, cuddle Rider to my chest, and lace Jewel's hand in mine.

All the news stations were blasting out stories of Briggs's capital punishment. The news anchors reported Jewel wasn't at the execution. She was forgotten in favor of more entertaining news: interviews with the dead women's families and the protesters. I shut the TV off.

Briggs's execution didn't bring me closure. My son is dead— nothing will heal that gaping wound. Forgiving myself for what I did and didn't do for Jewel and Finlan will never happen. My wife absolved me, and that's everything to me. Hindsight is always twenty- twenty: three years ago, I was riding the razor's edge between life and death. I don't have one doubt I would have eventually killed myself. But Jewel saved me. I live and breathe for my wife and my sons.

"Mommy, there's the pizza place," yells Jackie. Fisting my hair, he turns. "Papa, your favorite. Pizza and beer straight ahead."

Beau chuckles. He reaches up and takes Jackie from my shoulders.

Rider fusses, emitting tiny cries.

I grin and put my lips to his warm, silky cheek, breathing him in. His scent is a combination of Jewel and me. "You're hungry, too, baby boy. Hold on for Daddy. Five more minutes."

The pizza parlor sits just feet away from the ocean. Its deck is on pillars, allowing the waves to lap beneath it. I don't need to ask, but I do. "Inside or out, babe?"

Jewel smiles up at me. "Out."

The Sinners pull the tables together and make a wall of privacy around Jewel, Jackie, Rider, and me. I give Rider to my wife and settle her onto my lap. We order pizza, wings, salad, and soda for Jackie, and pitchers of beer for the adults.

Jackie stands on his chair and leans over Rider. "Hold on, Munch. We're getting pizza and wings for dinner." He giggles and glances at his grandfather.

"Fuck no," moans Beau. "Jewel, *do not* eat the goddamn wings."

I chuckle and free my wife's tit as she gabs with the girls. Jackie has his tiny arm around my neck. He's smiling down at his baby brother. An overwhelming feeling of peace and love runs through me. Jewel, Jackie, Rider, and I are silhouetted in the orangey-yellow glow of the setting sun. I inhale deeply, knowing Finlan is with us.

Daddy loves you, Fin. Always and forever, you're mine.

ABOUT THE AUTHOR

Susan Liberty grew up in Central New York. She obtained a Bachelor's Degree from Chamberlain College of Nursing with a minor in English. She furthered her education at the New York State University at Albany, focusing on American Literature and Creative Writing.

Susan Liberty has published:
The Promise Series:
Broken Promises: Promise Series – Book 1.
A Vow to Love and Protect: Promise Series – Book 2.
A Pledge for Eternity: Promises Series – Book 3.
Sinners Series:
Hearts that Burn: Sinners Series – Book 1.
Bound by Love: Sinners Series – Book2.
Forever Mine: Sinners Series – Book 3.

THANKS FROM ME TO YOU 🖤

I hope you enjoyed *Forever Mine: Sinners Series – Book 3.*

Reviews are appreciated on Amazon or Goodreads.

Sign up for my Newsletter to get the latest information on my new releases and free offers.

Follow me on Goodreads, Facebook, or Amazon.

Kick back, relax, and enjoy the read!

Gratitude,

Susan

www.ingramcontent.com/pod-product-compliance
Lightning Source LLC
Chambersburg PA
CBHW020734250626
47155CB00003B/750